BLACKER THAN A THOU

P9-CJM-854

DATE DUE

DE 9 '96			
July 9			
AP 24 '02			
AP 2 1 '08			

DEMCO 38-296

ALSO BY SUSAN STRAIGHT

Aquaboogie
I Been in Sorrow's Kitchen and Licked Out All the Pots

BLACKER THAN A THOUSAND MIDNIGHTS

BLACKER THAN A THOUSAND MIDNIGHTS

Susan Straight

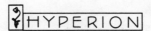

New York

Lyrics from "Move Me No Mountain" by Aaron Schroeder and Jerry Ragovoy. Copyright ©
1974, 1980. Reprinted with permission.

Portions of this book first appeared, in different form, in *The Los Angeles Times Magazine* and
Aquaboogie (Milkweed Editions, 1990).

Copyright © 1994 Susan Straight

Designed by Gloria Adelson/Lulu Graphics

Library of Congress Cataloging-in-Publication Data

Straight, Susan.
    Blacker than a thousand midnights / Susan Straight. — 1st ed.
        p.   cm.
    ISBN 0-7868-6003-0
    1. Afro-American fire fighters—California—Fiction.   2. Afro-
American men—California—Fiction.   I. Title.
PS3569.T6795B57   1994
813'.54—dc20   93-30432
                                                        CIP

FIRST EDITION

10 9 8 7 6 5 4 3 2 1

For Delphine, my smallest queen . . . dreaming peaceful midnights.

Serious thanks to Derrick Sims, Anthony Harper, Brenda Richardson, Paul Embleton, Holly Robinson, Jay Neugeboren (Darnell's first friend), Richard Parks and Pat Mulcahy, Gail and John Watson, Alberta and General R. C. Sims, and Dwayne Sims, who redefines brotha-man-hood every day.

Message to my nieces and nephews: Heads to the sky, eyes to the stars.

Move me no mountain
Turn me no tide
Swim me no ocean
long, deep and wide,
Just say you love me
long, strong and true . . .
Move me no mountain to prove that you do.

—Chaka Khan

BLACKER THAN
A THOUSAND
MIDNIGHTS

TOE UP AND SMOKE DREAMING

DARNELL WAS WHORE of the day. He looked again at the calendar. December 3—Tucker. In the dark pantry he found several jars of Ragú, and then he went outside with the trash. The station was still on high alert, and pine needles scraped the screens; the wind was steady. All day the crew had been out for little boot-stomper fires everywhere. Brush went up from an exhaust spark, a train wheel striking track. Nothing blazes; just weeds near wheels. The air was so dry he felt it deep in his throat even with his mouth closed, felt it rush down his nostrils to steal his spit. Smoke in his crotch, his armpit hair. The creosote bush and manzanita seemed to crackle, waiting, ready.

He looked at the dying flowers beside the wooden sign: CALIFORNIA DEPARTMENT OF FORESTRY—FIRE STATION 42. When the seasonals got laid off, Fricke, the only man on permanent crew at this deep-woods station, would replant the flower bed, rake, paint, and wait for the next fire season.

3

Darnell smelled the soot dark in his collar. Brenda couldn't wait to watch him wash the smoke out of his clothes one last time. He tried to imagine her belly rounder; spoons clinked in the kitchen, coffee steam riding the faint dust.

Fricke. He never lets the ho make coffee. Darnell went for the door, smiling, remembering the first time Fricke had explained whore duties to him. Damn—almost eight months ago? The sound of the words had been jarring to him that first week at the station: *Whore. We're going to the store.* That's *your* job.

"Smell it?" Fricke asked. He whistled softly on the hot coffee. His mustache hid his mouth, and Darnell knew he was smiling only because of the two tiny lines cut deep below each eye. When Fricke kept his face blank, the lines were white grooves in his sunburned face. "You can't tell your lady Brenda what she wants to hear. Smell that chaparral crackling dry? You aren't going home yet."

"Yeah, I watched the sky," Darnell drawled, sitting at the table. "I sniffed the wind like a good rangehand. Your only buffalo soldier." The windows turned purple and lightened. "Why you up?"

Fricke raised his brows. "Why are you?"

Darnell stared at Fricke's eyes, blue like old Levi's. "At least eighty-five degrees yesterday, and the wind's still hella strong." He heard muttering from the hallway. Perez and Corcoran were awake. "Everybody's tired as hell of bein up here."

"It's December," Fricke said. Darnell was silent. "You're not tired."

"Naw, not me. And not you." Darnell stood up and put his coffee cup in the sink. The sun edged out, and the sky was bright as noon, no moisture wavering anywhere. "Scott's toe up again?"

"Does that mean he's playing dead?" Fricke asked, smiling.

"What?"

Fricke raised his foot stiffly, boot flexed. "Toe up, playing dead."

"Damn, man, you guys and your *r*'s. Whore of the day. In my locality, we say *ho*. Tore up. *Toe* up—he's drunk." He went back to the pantry, leaving Fricke laughing at the counter.

But the call came before breakfast. The fire had been going since early morning, about the time he and Fricke had been drinking coffee. On the engine, Fricke said, "It was way deep in the canyon and the lookouts didn't even see it until now. Zero humidity and the fuel's thick as it gets. Up there behind Ortega Highway—where that chaparral hasn't gone up in fifty, sixty years."

"What kinda asshole's building a campfire now?" Scott asked, rubbing the short blond bristles he called hair. Darnell saw them glisten thin as needles when he looked past Scott at the brush along the road.

"Uh-uh," Fricke said. "Target shooter. Crews are coming from Ventura and San Diego."

Darnell glanced back at Corcoran and Perez following in the second engine. "Where we headed?"

"We got the west flank, cause there's a bunch of new houses out there past Seven Canyons," Fricke said. "You know, the rugged ranch life-style for people who drive to their office buildings in LA to play with pencils." Fricke smiled.

"Yeah. Let's save these rugged individuals' new homes, built where the chaparral is supposed to burn itself clear in the natural world. Hope you guys slept good last night."

Darnell bit his lips. Raycraft, the regional guy, was coming up to the station today, and seasonals could get sent down for good. No, baby—not today. Not with this big one. A conflagration. Fricke loved that word. Panic shifted from side to side in Darnell's stomach, swayed with the shoulders beside his, wobbling loosely with the lurches as they went around the curves. Used to the rhythm after the long drives up and down the highway, Darnell tried to breathe to keep the bubble of scary air from jumping into his lungs.

You ain't scared of the fire. You scared this is the last one. Raycraft ain't lookin to call me back for next year unless Fricke pushes. Raycraft don't like my name, my face.

He saw houses behind a beige wall and wrought-iron security gate that said CANYON ESTATES. Up the narrow highway, they dipped over the ridge, and Fricke said, "Your date, gentlemen. She's gonna take you through the night."

They packed the gear, Corcoran sucking his mouth into a lipless line beside Darnell. "One a these fifty-year jobs," Corcoran said. Darnell felt the fire shelter, a foil tent in a packet on his hip, and he gripped his Pulaski, the long-handled ax-hoe. He tramped after Fricke, seeing the smoke quilt-thick over the sky. No billowing, delicate start-up puffs—this bruise already stretched for miles in the wind.

They started cutting the line, leaning into the gusts, and Darnell felt the prickle above his hipbones, stronger even than when Brenda pulled her fingers up his thighs. His shoulders stretched wider, skin melting away. "Goddamn this wind!" Scott shouted.

"Goddamn a target shooter!" Perez yelled back, and smoke flew into their mouths.

Fricke checked the line. The wooden handle was slippery-slick in Darnell's hands, the chamise and creosote flying in chips. He couldn't hear the others now, only the roar he knew was coming this way. The roar pulled in all sound, erased everything but the tremble of flame. He couldn't tell what time it was, but they were facing the sun when the airborne tankers dropped water and Phoscheck. The liquid hung thick in the air before it laced down.

In the early darkness, they could see the south flank of the fire racing up one of the canyons. They went over the ridge and down into the next descent, and Perez fell out on the decomposed granite slope, his bad ankle rebroken. Darnell helped Fricke pull him up the gully, Perez's upper lip high over his gums the only way he showed the pain. My man know he ain't cut out for this, Darnell thought, feeling the crystalline pebbles slide under his boots. His ankle broken twice—he better not try and come back next year.

When he half slid back down to find the others, he saw the fire advancing up the slopes across the valley, jagged blood lines glowing in the black. "Goddamn chain gang," Scott said again and again, and Darnell heard the thud and cracking of Pulaski blades hacking the thin fire line. No dozer gettin in here—these canyons are hella steep, he thought. Corcoran muttered somewhere nearby in the dark. The roar of the fire was like a blanket over them, high above the harsh breathing and cusswords, the skittering of animals against leaves and branches.

The wind lifted the smoke and brought it back around, gusting even harder toward midnight. The metallic taste of what he'd eaten still harsh in his throat, he lay down with the others. "If the wind shifts, it'll be here in fifteen minutes," Fricke said. "Just catnap."

Darnell felt the granite crumbly underneath him, smelled the manzanita leaves. Seven Canyons. Fricke had told him early in the season about the firestorm, the one that swirled through so many years ago, like a bomb, picking up speed and exploding down the chutes to char a crew of seven men. Each of the canyons was named for one of them.

Darnell thought hard, trying to recall the map. Miller—that was one of them. Schmidt. Neuborn. The next gust was so hard it threw pebbles against him. Darnell Tucker Canyon. Raycraft wouldn't like that one. A colored canyon. Named for "the colored kid," like Raycraft called him when he thought Darnell couldn't hear.

The tiny stones hit Fricke's gear, next to him. Darnell stood up. He imagined bears running from the fire toward him, coyotes low, tails streaming. The fire ate at the chaparral in waves, rolling fast as a tumbleweed. He gripped the Pulaski and walked away from the others.

Up the canyon, he looked toward the ridge where the fire would crown. Fricke would see it and yell, "Crowning!" and the others would stagger to their feet, clumsy as bears in all their gear. Darnell moved through the thick brush, felt the branches snatch his legs. If you dug a hole six feet deep, you'd have enough air to breathe when the firestorm raced over, trying to suck the oxygen from your mouth, reaching all the way inside to pull it from your lungs. Because you wouldn't burn up, just like that, like people thought. The fire would be black because your eyes would be closed.

He stopped to touch a tree, and closed his eyes—the roar was closer, stronger. When a deer leapt into the canyon past him he thought about their bellies, tight in the spring when they walked slowly up the napalmed feed trails, their round pale awkwardness the same color as Brenda's belly skin, lighter, thinner, every week.

The wind-smoke swirled around his ears now. Fricke? Was that Fricke calling, "Tucker!" or one of the others cussing in his sleep? He lay next to a white boulder, a dome beside his arm, his coat an envelope where he could breathe inside. He had the fire shelter—a turkey cooker, they called it. But the flames would take your breath fast. Not like bullets—unless you got a slug in your brain or your heart, that shit would pound into your leg or your gut and tear you up. He'd seen a guy shot in the parking lot at school once, screaming, rolling, and humping on the asphalt. Cuco Rojas—pressing the ground like he was praying it would hold in his blood if he pushed flat enough. The fire would race over, the sound would whisper and pop and roar. He saw the veins inside his eyelids, the veins along Brenda's hips, traced and crossing. His boots pointed to the sky. Toe up. Toes up. They were heavy, and he flapped them against the ground, letting them fall to the outside and then pulling them back inward to crack against each other, sole to sole, toe to toe. Toes up— pounding so loud someone would hear, so hard he felt his shins quiver. He had to keep up the pounding until Fricke came.

He lay with his shoulders propped on his pack near their engine at the temporary fire camp. Corcoran's pale feet faced him, the balls round and pink as baby hams. Darnell felt the sweat along his spine and neck cool, with his T-shirt loose, his coat off. His nostrils were thick with soot; his ankles still felt swelled hot in his high boots, from the long walk out from their position. It was cooler today, and once the eastern flank had been knocked down, the strike team called in from up north would be mopping up. Darnell closed his eyes; he didn't want to see Fricke's blue stare.

"So they called in that hotshot crew from San Bernardino, huh?" Perez said. His ankle was fractured slightly, wrapped stiff.

Fricke said, "They just got back from Oregon. Some job up there, where they saved a hotel. They love that danger. Right, Tucker?"

Before Darnell could turn his face, Perez said, "Nineteen guys?"

"Three women," Fricke said.

"That's the kinda woman for me," Corcoran said, fanning his fingers through the curly hair by his ears when he sat up. "She don't mind dirt."

"Just don't try to get a piece of her ass in the shower," Scott said, pointing to the shower truck at the edge of camp.

Darnell looked at all the engines, the shower, and food trucks. "Damn—was that a serious overtime shift or what? I'm tired as hell."

"Yeah?" Fricke said, looking at him.

"When that strike team got here, man, that was it," Corcoran said.

"You see that Sikorsky copter, dude, that sky crane?" Scott said. He loved vehicles. "Picked up two thousand gallons from the lake like it was a swallow."

Darnell stared at the branches and said idly, "When do we torch feed trails?" and Fricke stood up, tossing a stick at his leg.

"Don't you need a goddamn break, Tucker? You want to get back to work right now, huh?" He looked at his watch. "Weren't you whore of the day when we were last home? Get your ass back to the kitchen if you want to work."

"Fricke, baby," Corcoran said, his head cocked. "You that hungry?"

"That was two days ago, man," Darnell said. "Scott's turn now."

Driving with the horizon still rust-tinged behind them, they were silent. Fricke had found Darnell while he lay staring, listening to the firestorm approach. When they were back on the fire line later, Fricke held him by the shoulder and said in his smart-ass drawl, "I don't know why you didn't get over that death-by-fire shit when you were younger; I can't classify that as normal behavior."

Darnell looked at Fricke's eyes, even lighter with the smudges of black underneath from where he'd rubbed his dirty sleeve against his face. "Normal is I'm on the street at home and some brotha step *to* me cause he think I said somethin, so he pop the trunk for his shottie. Normal is like my homey Max, when we were kids and he got too close to a train, right? Normal is I go out cause of somebody *else*. Nothin to do with me."

"I don't know what you're talking about," Fricke said, hard, and Darnell blew the dust from his nose.

"Yeah, you do," he said, and he turned toward the creosote.

Purple evening drifted down from the huge pine trees around the station. Perez and Scott turned the video back on, and Corcoran went for the showers. Fricke headed for the kitchen to make coffee, like he always did after a fire, and Darnell thought: Damn, I know this dude better than I know Brenda sometimes. Hella long season. I've known Brenda since I was a kid, but I've seen Fricke more this year. I know she read the paper and saw the fire. Let me go in there and call. Is the season over yet? That's what she want to know. You ready to come home? He looked at the rims of black around his fingernails, in his knuckles, and clenched his hands.

Corcoran went past him and yelled from the kitchen, "Tucker! You gonna eat this burrito?" Darnell remembered the bag of fast food Scott had brought.

"Damn, Corcoran, don't you never wait for somebody to *offer* you food?" he said. "You gotta scavenge everybody's grub daily?"

"Is it a red burrito?" Corcoran hollered. "I like the green ones better, the ones with jalapeño."

"It's my burrito, okay?" Darnell said. "Don't matter what color it is, I'ma eat it." He went outside to sit on the cement slab and take off his boots. He heard Scott whisper something, and Perez laughed.

Yeah. Lemme guess what you said, Scott, with your predictable ass. It's his, so it's a black burrito.

Scott was always talking smack when Darnell could barely hear him. It was a red burrito, the milder kind. Brenda said the baby craved red burritos. She bought two fifty-nine-cent red burritos every day on her lunch break. Her mother said all that hot sauce meant the baby would have a lot of hair when it was born.

Her pops is on swing shift now, so he's gone to work. Let me call now, he thought, rubbing his forehead. She gotta be worried.

The phone was in the kitchen, and Scott had slammed a pot onto the stove. "Everybody bitches no matter what after Fricke cooks," Scott grumbled. "He makes all that fancy shit—what the hell was that last thing he made?"

Darnell folded his arms. "Black-bean soup," he said, grinning, and Scott frowned. You okay on the fire line, man, but you ain't too sharp, Darnell thought. But he liked Scott when they talked about cars. "Cioppino," he told Scott. "Italian fish stew." He saw Fricke carry his coffee across the driveway. Darnell had waited until everyone was out of the kitchen to ask Fricke how to spell it. The thick stew reminded him of the Louisiana gumbo Brenda's mother made for special occasions.

The phone rang and rang, and he imagined her standing near her mother's lemon-fronted oven, at the sink with the see-through white curtains, where he used to stand outside and poke his face while she washed dishes. No one answered, and he hung up. The tomato sauce in the frying pan was thick at the edges, red-black, and he told Scott, "You don't have to kill tomatoes, man, they're already dead." Scott shrugged. "You don't care what you eat, huh?"

Scott said, "I care about what I drink, dude. That's why I'm so healthy, cause I kill all the bad germs in my stomach every night."

"Yeah. Whiskey medicine," Darnell said. He went outside, heard Fricke's boots crunch the leaves, and the laughs and card clicks behind him from Corcoran's eternal poker game. Fricke and Scott would drink, especially after the long shift they'd done on the big fire, and the thin, gold liquor scent would mix with the pine gum on his boot soles when he came in from the trees. Corcoran would play Rolling Stones while Scott and Perez argued for Megadeth.

At home, his father would be playing Charles Brown in the back room, drinking beer with the men from the neighborhood, slamming down dominoes. "Bad, bad whiskey made me lose my happy home," Charles would sing.

Brenda needed him for a happy home. The last time he'd called, she'd said, "You been on high alert for two months, Darnell. I haven't seen you once." She stopped, then said, "I'm starting to show. I went to the doctor, and he said five months along." Her voice was a cloudy waver on the phone.

The pine needles were leather between his finger and thumb. *I ain't even been home for a couple of years, counting Conservation Corps. Not for more than a month.* He heard Scott laughing behind him. *I go from this room to Pops' house. Sleep on the couch. Never even got my own crib yet. Now I gotta get a baby crib.* He remembered the raspy breaths of his baby sisters floating from their cribs, his mother hovering, his grandmother saying, "They ain't gon die, these two. That the one, that boy there—he were trouble, but he big enough now." And he had slept on the couch ever since. Brenda's belly—his mother big, lying still to keep the babies. *Just me, Brenda, and a baby.* He leaned against the old shingles, remembering his father's favorite Charles Brown song, the deep-blurred voice singing, "You don't need no narcotics, no antibiotics—you got a virus called the blues."

On the way to the tumbleweeds a few days later, he leaned back against the seat and dreamed of napalming feed trails in the spring. The Helitorch set off charges, then dropped Alumagel in liquid fire loops that fell on dense patches of hundred-year-old chaparral, making scar trails in the thick-tangled mats of vegetation, singeing precise lines for the deer and other animals that couldn't force their way through the brush. It wouldn't be till after they got called back from the seasonal layoff. They'd only done it twice last year, right when he was first hired, and he smelled it now, the smoke turning to steam with the scent of recent rain and moist leaves rising over the slopes.

"When do we torch trails?" he asked Fricke.

"Dude, no way," Corcoran said before Fricke could answer. "Rio Seco County's only gotten three inches of rain for the whole damn year. Fricke said you gotta have five inches to torch." He sound so proud of himself, Darnell thought. *Yeah, always talkin about his dad* is a fire captain in Santa Ana, his grandpa was fire chief in New York.

He looked at Fricke, who said, "We're in a big-time drought."

"Shit, we been here since what—April?" Scott said. "Season don't usually even start till May."

Darnell kept looking at Fricke. "You're the engineer, so you decide when we torch, right?"

"Not enough rain's gonna fall while you seasonals are laid off," Fricke said.

"That's the wet months, though, when we're off," Darnell said.

"Not this year, home boy." Fricke smiled.

Darnell said, "Your home ain't my home." He looked outside. "But we torch first thing when we get called back for the new season, if it rains enough, right?"

Fricke laughed. "You better wait and see who gets called back. I heard the funding might get cut; we might have fewer seasonals up here."

"No way," Scott said.

"Yeah, a second ago you were talkin drought and now you say fewer guys—what kinda shit is that? Drought means bigger fires, more guys on the crew," Darnell said.

"I feel a greenhouse effect working," Fricke said. "No bullshit." He raised those bushy eyebrows, and Darnell knew he would play dumb cowboy and change the subject. "Gets hotter and hotter every year, right?" Fricke turned to Perez and said, "Glad about your ankle? All you have to do today is watch."

"Tumbleweeds," Scott said, pinching the skin between his brows. He drank up large last night, Darnell thought, and now he in a world a hurt.

"Dude, season's gotta be over, it's December," Perez said.

"I'm gonna go out every night when we're off," Scott said, smiling big now. "Find me some beach babes, cause first week I'm crashin with Corcoran in Newport Beach."

"Not me, dude," Perez said. "I'm findin sleep, forty-eight straight hours. No chick snoring, nobody snoring. No goddamn night fire." He pushed Darnell's shoulder. "Hey, you don't look thrilled about going home. Or you still hate doing tumbleweeds?"

Darnell didn't answer; he looked at the banks along the steep roadway. Yeah, I'ma tell everybody I want to stay, he thought. I love it up here. Right. Tell em I love not gettin any sleep, hearin Megadeth and cowboy music. Tell the crew a permanent season's cool with me cause next week I won't have no job and my lady's pregnant. I can see inside their brains: Of course she's pregnant—that's a natural condition for black chicks, right? When that volunteer crew buddy of Corcoran's came up here and his wife was out there pregnant, they all joked about Irish Catholic. Brenda's Catholic. But that ain't the same.

Perez pushed him. "You okay, dude? You want the Helitorch so you can fry somebody back in Rio Seco?" Everybody laughed.

Darnell breathed hard. "I need to fire up that nasty shirt Fricke's been wearin two days straight."

"Ah, but nobody smells it except me, until I go down to the flatlands to relax," Fricke said. "Then I catch women with that firefighter-smoke aroma, because I'm not a kept man. Kept on a leash like you. Awhoooh." His lips were a coyote-howling circle under the Marlboro Man mustache.

They loved to jam him up about Brenda's questioning voice, more and more frequent on the phone. Corcoran was the only other one with a girlfriend, and she was a forest ranger up in Eureka, so he got letters. "I'ma see her soon enough, okay?" Darnell said. "I'm a good dog. Bow wow wow." He looked outside again, so they'd stop talking about her.

But Scott said, "That's what you get for single-chick action."

Corcoran said, "Diseases are what you get for *your* action."

Fricke said, "Darnell undoubtedly has higher standards than yours, Scott."

Perez laughed. "Scott'll screw anyone that'll screw him."

Darnell had to laugh, and Fricke shook his head. But Scott said, "So I ain't into Fricke's metaphysical-soulmate shit, or whatever he calls it."

"That was a joke, Scott," Fricke said, and they busted up again. They were off the mountain now, on the freeway, and Darnell let out a long breath.

Fricke always tryin to mess with Scott, talkin about "Was that a joke, or just a cliché?" Scott tried to set me up with that white girl from a bar, talkin about she wanted to try a black guy. "A black guy"—the way he says it busts me up. "Home boy." Home. I'ma be

in easy-touchin range every minute I'm home. She's been waitin for
months.

Early in the season, when he'd come down for the weekend, Brenda
would spend all Sunday at the house, and by afternoon, when all the
guys hung out in his father's yard talking smack and fixing cars, Brenda
kept her hand on his shirt, his belt, her fingers delicate and persistent
as the raccoons' when they came to the station looking for food.

She was going to show big soon—her stomach swelling. The mass
of fear grew hard in his stomach again. Different from fire-scared;
that was like the liquid smoke his father added to barbecue sauce,
warmth that made his muscles slide against bone, his joints swing
with the shovel. Fumes that turned to the hot feel of Yukon Jack, the
stuff he'd swigged off Scott and Perez a few times.

But this panic, that yesterday's fire was the last, that he'd be home
in Rio Seco for good . . . Stepping off the truck, he raised his arms
to smell the ash in his sleeves, to muffle his breathing while everyone
else groaned at the tumbleweeds, huge and humped as Volkswagens
covering the fields.

Orange vests were scattered against the dead brown bushes, and
Corcoran said, "Road-camp guys? I thought they only did fire
roads."

"Don't matter to me," Scott said, smiling. "I don't care who does
these damn weeds, long as I don't."

"You *do*," Fricke said. "They fork em, you guys supervise the burn."

Darnell knelt quickly to retie his boots. His neck felt thick with
warmth, and he didn't want to look at the prisoners yet. Every time
they ran into a crew from the minimum-security facility in Banning,
Darnell saw somebody from the Westside doing time for dinky shit.
These guys never gotta look for faces, he thought, pulling the laces
harder. Their friends are in college. Or wherever. College—Fricke's
up here talkin about fewer seasonals next year, and I'd have to put
in three years seasonal and take Emergency Medical Tech before they
even look at me for permanent crew. Shit. Department of Forestry
wants all college and academy boys.

He stood up, watching the road-camp faces carefully. Can't stare
too hard, even at a brotha, cause he might get pissed. This is the
only time I see a dark face up here. Nothing but brothas, *vatos,* and
even the white dudes look darker when they're on the road camp.

He glanced at the faces over the swinging arms that worked the tumbleweeds. Charlton Williams—Darnell had heard he'd been picked up on a warrant for outstanding tickets. Then Darnell saw Victor Smalls look up at him. Victor raised his chin a half inch, and Darnell lifted his face back.

What was Victor out here for? Darnell looked for Fricke. Don't make Fricke call you, he thought, joining Scott and the others checking the ditch by the highway for flammable debris. Victor—he'd ask Darnell about Melvin, Darnell's older brother, who had left Rio Seco the minute he turned eighteen. Darnell saw their faces the way he had as a child, when Melvin and Victor were five years older than him, always saying, "Get away from here, boy." He remembered the feathery hairs over their mouths when they were sixteen and he was still only ten.

The road-camp guys piled tumbleweeds into the cleared ditch, the stiff thorns crackling hollow. Darnell pushed the breaking stems down farther with his shovel, waiting until Victor and Charlton worked their way toward the field's edge, and he said, "What up?"

"Ain't nothin but a deuce," Charlton said. He'd gotten two months.

"Trey, baby," Victor said.

"Three? On what, man?" Darnell said.

"I didn't feel like givin the government no money, man. I wasn't drinkin my intoxicants in a licensed, public venue," Victor said, leaning on his fork.

"He been hangin out with Brother Lobo again, talkin like that," Charlton said, smiling. "Learnin that political shit."

Victor's forehead was glossy with sweat, and he ran his palm over his braids, looking off at the cars speeding past on the freeway. Darnell saw the moisture sparkle on top of the thick rows. Victor had worn braids long before anyone else; he'd quit high school football, refusing to shave his head like the other players, and he'd kept his cornrows perfect with red, black, and green rubber bands circling the tails at the nape of his neck. The coaches hated him. He and Melvin had gotten suspended for outlining the flies of their jeans with rhinestones, for spelling out "Superfly" and "The Stick" in gold studs down the thighs.

"I ain't seen Melvin in hella long time," Victor said, spitting at the dirt.

Darnell said, "He's still in LA."

"Melvin probably still ain't doin nothin in LA either," Victor said. "He just think LA nothin is better than Rio Seco nothin."

Charlton said, "You just missed Ray-Ray, man. He got out last week. They busted him for child support."

Darnell felt cold travel like fingernails along his scalp. "Say, man, you better get to work," Victor said. "You the shit, man, you gettin *paid* to be out here. Don't be fraternizin with the niggas, now."

Darnell said, "Man, don't even trip like that. I don't play that." He looked down the ditch at Fricke, who watched him. "Later—I'll check, homes."

Homey, doncha know me? That's what brothers said on the Westside if you didn't see someone's wave or you didn't acknowledge him. "Home boy." Scott and Fricke and the others loved to say that word, chop it in two. Darnell felt the sun on his shoulders, heard the wind rattle the tumbleweeds. When they were done, the dust would swirl off this field for days if the Santa Anas kept up. He knew Brenda was at work seeing the palm trees bend with the wind; now that she understood about the wind and dryness, after he'd been working fires for two years, she hated anything like a breeze. He heard the voices and laughing come closer, and saw Victor and Charlton working their way back with the rest of the orange cloth that advanced like slow flames.

They were silent, waiting until the others had passed them, and then Victor said, "Darnell, man, you out here choppin like you think this is cotton and shit."

"My man love his job," Charlton said.

Victor said, "How's Itty Bitta Yella?" Darnell had to laugh. He hadn't heard anybody call Brenda that name in a long time. Victor's sister Sonia had always terrorized Brenda in school, calling her that name.

"She ain't gon be itty-bitta no more," Darnell said without thinking, and before he could close his mouth, Charlton and Victor saw his face and laughed.

"Itty gon have a baby?" Victor said. "You's a fool, man, cause her daddy gon kill you. She takin college classes, got a good job, and you a never-home Westside brotha. Oh, man, you ain't got *no* sense."

Darnell gripped the shovel and slashed at the roots of the weeds near his feet. Why I have to open my big mouth? Damn. He said, "Brenda don't like nobody callin her Itty, man. That was back in school, okay?"

Victor said, "You what, twenty?"

He gon give me the older-brother rap now, Darnell thought. "Twenty-one in April, man."

But Victor didn't laugh and hit him on the back and say what Darnell was waiting for, the stuff about it had to happen and now you ain't gon get no peace nor piece. Victor said, "One more nigga down, couple million to go," and he worked his way back toward the road.

"It ain't that bad, man," Charlton said. "Me and Lesa got two, and I give her some money, I take em out to the park on the weekend. You ain't seen my boys, huh? Lesa stay out in Pomona with her aunt."

Darnell said, "Boys, huh?" But he watched Victor, who didn't even pretend to move the bushes into a pile. Victor walked straight back to the ditch.

Charlton went one way and Darnell the other when they neared the asphalt. Corcoran leaned against the engine, watching the road-camp guys near the prison bus. The smoke rose and wafted over the highway, and cars ripped the black veils into the air. "I heard these guys are doing a lotta stuff now," Corcoran said. "Like tumbleweeds, fire roads, and somebody said they got a prison crew doing the Highway 74 fires. They're gonna start using prisoners up north, too, for big burns."

Darnell stared at Fricke. "So that's how we save money on seasonals, huh? Get all the brothers and *vatos* for free."

Fricke spat in the dirt, and Darnell folded his arms, waiting. "People would ask what the problem is," Fricke said. "The jails are overcrowded, so get guys outside all day and they don't want to fight as much, huh?"

"I know all that fresh-air shit by heart," Darnell said. "I spent last year in the Conservation Corps, remember? 'Low-income youths between eighteen and twenty-three. We promote spirit and instill discipline.' You're talkin free labor. And I got a promoted spirit. Uh-uh, save that shit for somebody else, man." Darnell walked part way up the road, listening to the rattling tumbleweeds and the muffled tremble of flames. Perez laughed.

High alert: for days, the wind would calm to a tremble in the warmth and then pick up again, racing under the station eaves. But they'd been idle since the tumbleweeds, and the men shifted in the garage, in the kitchen, jostling each other. "No campers left up here, man," Perez would say. "Just us. Come on, Raycraft."

Darnell watched Fricke edge away from him in the rooms, and he knew why. Fricke don't want me to ask the question, he thought. Raycraft gon call me back or not? I did a good job. He rubbed his neck, watching the browned pine needles, and went outside to get away from the silent phone.

He lay flat on the piece of cardboard, his face close to the belly of the Spider, and when Scott squatted next to him, he said, "The clutch is messin up again."

"Yeah, *again*," Scott laughed. "FIAT means Fix It Again, Tony."

"Well, the dude fixes mine ain't named Tony," Darnell said. "But he charges serious ducats cause he hates this car."

"I bet it's the clutch disc," Scott said. "Italian cars mess up on the disc."

Darnell slid out from between the tires and sat on his heels. Scott bent his buzz-cut hair to the primer on the door base. He always talked about spending days in the driveway fixing Volkswagen Bugs, and Darnell would nod. If he wasn't with Brenda, he and his father talked around and under trucks.

"I adjusted that bad boy, but I'ma have to test it before I go down the mountain," Darnell said. He looked at the chalky primer. "I got a friend with this color all picked out for my paint job. Rainstorm— like a gray and black and blue all mixed together. Nacho, man, he's serious about colors. He can do pinstripes and everything, too."

"How much?"

"Too much." Darnell wiped his hands. "Cause he only does this on the side. I been saving for a while."

"Yeah, it's bullshit that we gotta pay for board up here. CDF don't pay enough anyway, and then we gotta give some back," Scott said. "Forest Service don't charge for board."

"Because you're only working days, technically, when you work for the Forest Service," Fricke said from the doorway. "If you don't like paying, Scott, you can always sleep under the trees. Like a natural man." He smiled.

"Just let me go home soon, man, call off this wind," Scott said.

Darnell started up the Fiat, and Fricke came over to the window. "Taking a drive?" Fricke said.

"Yeah, I gotta check this clutch again." Darnell looked at the darkening pine trunks.

"You mind driving up the mountain to the store?" Fricke said, touching the end of his mustache. "I need to restock my beverage supply."

"Bring me back some Jack!" Scott yelled from the yard when Darnell pulled around.

Fricke smiled. "As usual, he forgot to pay in advance," he said, and Darnell downshifted to head up the curving road.

Darnell listened to the engine for a long time, Fricke looking out the window, until he said, "So who were those guys?"

Darnell knew who he meant. "A guy I went to school with and one a my brother's friends." The clutch didn't engage until his foot was almost off the pedal, and he concentrated on the sound. They were almost to the tiny, dark-shingled mountain store now.

Fricke went inside and came out with a brown bag. He opened the Jack Daniels when Darnell started up the car, fitting his lips around the glass circle carefully, taking small sips like he did with coffee all day.

"You ain't gon share that with Scott, huh?" Darnell asked.

"Scott's a big boy. He can buy his own." Darnell looked at the flat bottle wedged between Fricke's thighs. Open container, he thought. Yeah, drive around with Victor and Charlton, keep that bad boy in my legs, I'd be swingin on road camp crew, too. But Fricke get stopped, he gon be a off-duty fireman, tired and workin hard. Darnell shook his head.

"You ever been to jail, man?" he asked, and Fricke licked his lips. "Nope."

Darnell waited for the question, but Fricke was silent. After all these months, this long-ass fire season, he knew Fricke liked him. He was always standing near Darnell, saying something quiet. But he only took another sip of liquor, wiped his lips. Then he said. "You're the only one not making feverish plans for the off-season."

Darnell gripped the clutch and listened again. "Just hopin this car makes it through the spring, man. And you probably goin kayakin or mountain climbin, in Montana or somethin, right?"

Fricke smiled. "I'm going to Canada with a woman, a marine biologist. We're going to Baffin Bay. Heard of that?"

"If you're goin, all I need to know is it's way the hell from anywhere else." Darnell smiled, too, and then Fricke clicked his thumbnails against the thick glass of the whiskey bottle. Darnell saw the brothers at Jackson Park, drinking from curved palm-fit flasks around the trash-barrel fire. "Charlton, the skinny dude you saw, he's doin two months on road camp cause he got tickets. Open container."

Fricke only nodded.

"Cause he didn't have the cash, didn't show up to court," Darnell went on. "So he gotta push tumbleweeds." When they came out onto the mountain face and swung around the curve overlooking the valley, Darnell saw the scattered pricks of light below. Hella dark up here, he thought, like always. We could drive all night and never see a cop. Just us and the rangers.

"Saving taxpayer dollars," Fricke said now. He was always quoting imaginary taxpayers from the flatlands, the ones who wanted more firemen for less money, in his imitation Reagan-husky voice. "Delegating other responsibilities."

Why he gotta pick that word? Responsibility. I can't wait to hear my pops shoot that gift. "Fricke," he said, "you ain't gon get married?"

Fricke grinned. "Marriage wrecks any decent relationship."

"You don't want kids?" Darnell stared ahead at the steep granite banks glowing spongy by the road. He heard the hollow hiss of lips on the bottle rim.

Fricke said, "I might change my mind, if the right woman shows up."

Darnell said, "Man, you done had so many, and you can't decide?"

"Decide is kind of a bloodless word, Tucker. Shouldn't it be like a lightning bolt? Or the equivalent clichéd feeling?" The white lines by his eyes disappeared.

Darnell shook his head. "Don't even start that metaphysical shit, okay? It's gotta be some middle ground between you and Scott."

"And that's where you and Brenda sit. On that comfy middle ground," Fricke said, whisking off an imaginary cape from the bottle. Like magic.

Darnell tightened his fingers on the wheel. "Fricke, man, I spent a night in jail."

Fricke kept his face set blank. "Probably a long story, and this is a short drive. We're almost back."

Darnell heard the clutch whine, and he said, "Yeah." Why did he keep thinking about that one night? Ricky Ronrico, an older guy from the Westside, had been in there with him. Sprung dude, been smoking rock cocaine—gray rim around his lips, hair dreading wild. Darnell stared at the total black of the forest slope across the highway. No house light, cigarette glows, headlights.

"Somebody busted my taillights," he said to Fricke. "Went to warrant after I got a ticket."

"And you spent the night in jail until somebody paid." Fricke raised his palms and shrugged.

"My pops."

"He paid for the tickets, you got out, end of story. Familiar story," Fricke said, and Darnell pulled into the yard, saw the blue light from the TV shifting, the yellow porch beam steady. Fricke slid the bottle under his armpit. "The government gets its money in cash or work. End of story. But if Scott assaults me for my beverage here, we're talking felony, right?" He smiled, and Darnell had to grin, at the way Fricke's voice always clanged when he changed the subject. Always tryin to make me laugh, get me to lighten up. Yeah—lighten up. Nobody gon say *that* out loud.

But he sat back after Fricke had slammed the door, his knees under the wheel, neck against the seat. Ricky Ronrico? Five months— Brenda said that's how far along she was. He knew the night now. It wasn't a broken Trojan or Brenda forgetting her diaphragm.

July: Ricky Ronrico had shot two deputies, and the cops had hunted him all over the Westside. Crazy saturation, somebody had called it, and Brenda was caught at his house. "Call your daddy, Brenda," his father said. "You ain't goin off the porch with my son till they find that fool." They'd slept tight-pressed on the couch, his father in a chair by the front door, the helicopter clattering endlessly over the roof. He'd smelled her, felt himself against her miniskirt all night, knowing he'd be back up the mountain for at least a week. On Sunday night, after Ronrico was caught and the streets had grown dark again, without the wide glare of copter search beams and red patrol strobes, he felt her fingers pull him down in the car, away from the windshield, in a parking lot.

That was it. That night. "Don't bring home no babies. You wait for them babies." All the older voices from doorways and porches, above folded arms, watching him and his friends pull away from the curb, had chanted that like absent-minded humming. He breathed the sharp scent of the bay tree near the station and felt thin air at his elbow.

All he made was coffee, and then he went to check the bathroom. Leaving the door open, he crouched in the shower to pick up rogue pieces of soap.

Thrown-away ovals of Dial were cemented to the floor. Perez and Corcoran were slobs, and everybody was in a bad mood today, tossing clothes and dishes around, talking shit to Fricke, because they wanted to go home. When Corcoran said his grandfather was a fire chief in New York, straight from Ireland, Scott yelled, "So fly his old ass out here and he can take my place!" Darnell rubbed the chips like chalk in his palm. This morning, they'd all been waiting for the visit from Raycraft; they thought he'd say the word and they could pack. But he hadn't shown yet.

He heard boots, and the pot lid clanked hollow. Scott said, "I thought Tucker was whore of the day."

"He is," Fricke said.

"Nothin here. Man, I thought he'd make fried chicken or somethin, one a their hot-weather specialties."

Darnell moved toward the door, and Fricke said, "Specialties?"

"Yeah, you know. Fried chicken, watermelon." Scott laughed.

Darnell stood in his face. "Ho, ho, *ho*. When you gon learn to say it right, man? *Ho* of the day. That's how I say it. Speak so I can understand you, boy, cause *yo* attitude is to the *curb*. Shoot that gift on my street and you might get smoked." He pushed Scott against the counter, and Fricke's forearms slid up his sides and pulled.

"Dude, what's your problem?" Scott said, his upper lip rising square, incredulous, the way Darnell hated. Don't show me your gums, man. "It was a joke, bro."

"I'ma kick your ass all the way to the Colonel, home boy," Darnell said. "Buy you some Original Recipe." He jerked his shoulder away

from Fricke. "But then again, I ain't normal, huh, Fricke? So I guess
I can't be a normal nigga either."

Scott was out the door. "What difference does it make?" Fricke
said, his voice even. "It didn't apply to you, anyway. Fried chicken
is a southern dish, and you're a native Californian. Scott's a little
ignorant about regional cooking, but he's handy with clichés."

Darnell shook his head, gripped the sharp metal strip at the
edge of the counter. Fricke always tried so hard; under that Willie
Nelson drawl, there was something whenever he talked to Darnell.
Fricke touched the ends of his mustache again, not twirling the
tips like some guys did to call attention to the hair. He just liked
the feel, Darnell could tell. "You always want me next to you when
we're on the line," Darnell said. "You're always tryin to tell me
somethin."

"You're a demon on the line," Fricke said, "and you're the best at
chopping rattlers. I don't know where you practiced that."

Darnell saw the snakes rushing ahead of the flames, and he thought
of how he loved to slice the Pulaski blade at them, but he knew what
Fricke was trying to do. "We're not talkin about my talent, man. I'm
not gettin called back next season. I know it. If anybody's cut, it'll
be me. Scott ain't about nothin, but I'ma tell you somethin—I hear
Raycraft when he talks about me, I listen. Every time he says my
name, it's a hesitation." He stopped, not knowing how to explain.
Fricke didn't care about cars, so he couldn't tell him—but it was
Raycraft's voice stopping, like a transmission that wasn't working
right, leaving the gears hanging. It was his name—that was what
Raycraft didn't like.

"What are you talking about?" Fricke called, but Darnell was already back in the bathroom. He'd heard Raycraft say, "Darnell, Carell,
Martell. You watch the NBA and half the names are ridiculous. Colored give their kids a burden in them names."

Darnell threw water on his face, looked at his hair in the mirror.
I need a haircut, he thought. Can't get a serious fade—then Raycraft
and the rest of em really trip. His skin was reddish brown, darkened
from all the working outside just like his father's. His nose had an
Indian bump like his father's. He touched the scar on his forehead
from a rock fight when he was a kid—the thin line etched up into
his hairline like the beginning of a razored-in part. Yeah—let me get

a few lightning strikes shaved into the temples here—they'd all love that.

Fricke's voice followed him. "If you don't get called back, and I'm saying *if*," Fricke said, and Darnell sucked his teeth, "it wouldn't have anything to do with your ability. In fact, you know Scott's the other guy on that training grant for low income. It's just a matter of funding, for both of you. *If* it happens."

Darnell turned from the sink. "Save that shit, too. I'm goin down the mountain early."

The wind had cleared out the valley, so when the Spider came out of the last curve and Darnell looked east, he could see the string of cars stretching to the desert. Wind—still high alert, and I shouldn't even be half an hour away from the station. What if Raycraft comes by? Damn, what can he do? Fire me? Name a canyon after me.

But what if I miss the next fire? The last one. He drove faster past the empty field where the tumbleweeds had been. The air smelled peppery with ash. Victor said, One more nigga down. No surprise. It was a surprise to me. Darnell left the highway at the Morongo Indian reservation, where the lights from trailers and houses were. He parked along one of the narrow roads, where he could hear the cattle hum at each other now and then when they stepped over the prickly cactus and stones.

The slopes of the hills above were cut in on each other, a series of V's as soft as the creases under Brenda's breasts, the fold between her thigh and hip. How would she look with a curved belly? She was so small. Itty Bitta Yella—he hadn't heard that in so long. When they were kids, Brenda heard it all the time. And once, in the seat where he rested his boots, she'd whispered, "They heard Mama say it. She used to call me Itty Bit. She'd say, 'I gotta watch you good, cause you a Itty Bit of a child.' "

The sound of the cattle made him remember his father's stories of mules and bulls in Oklahoma, of hunting. "Ain't no game left in the whole damn state," his father and the other men used to joke. "We ate whatever moved."

So I can feed Brenda some rattlers, right? Chop down that deer runnin from the flames. If I see any more flames.

After the hunting stories, sometimes an older man would say,

"Plowin with them damn mules. Hoein the ground. Damn. What they used to say? God put two packages down on the ground and told the white man and the nigga, 'Pick your pick.' Nigga rushed over there and grabbed the big one. He got the hoe and shovel. White man got the small one. He got the pen and paper." Melvin and the younger men would roll their eyes and say, "This brotha don't need neither one."

Damn, Darnell thought, watching the hills turn red with the low sun. I don't mind the Pulaski and the gear. I'll take it. The air's still dry. One more.

"None of your buddies with you? No Jack Daniel's? Not even Yukon Jack?"

Fricke shrugged. "Still high alert. I have to be especially sharp when one of my best guys takes off." He watched Darnell sit down.

"You tell the boss man I left?" Darnell raised both hands. "No—wait. It doesn't apply to me anyway, right? Cause I ain't gettin called back."

Fricke said, "You ever want to toss a match? When you were a kid, waiting for a fire, you ever throw a match just to see?"

Darnell met the pale blue stare. "No." But he'd wanted to; he'd stood in the riverbottom, in the brush, hearing his friends call him.

"I did," Fricke said. "I was thirteen. Got caught, ended up in Juvey. Bakersfield."

Darnell heard the other guys pull into the lot in Scott's VW. "So?" he said, but then he held his lip hard with his teeth. "So now somebody else throws cigarettes. And you're the hero."

They waited for the phone to ring.

Spindly yellow grass and shaking-tall wild oats. That's all there was to catch and crackle. No—this ain't acceptable. This don't even *qualify*, Darnell thought. The fire flew with the breeze and barely touched down, hanging just moments, like orange cobwebs on the stems, never burning hard but skittering across the slope.

Darnell clambered up the hill behind Fricke, watching the thin flames jump across the highway. This roadside went up every year, Fricke had said, and Darnell remembered it from last year. He'd been here with the Conservation Corps, and most of this same stuff had burned off. Now the cars idling impatiently on their morning commute down the mountain highway thrummed in the air; their exhaust shook above the hoods, and Darnell could see faces turned down to newspapers, or looking in rearview mirrors, or glancing at the men and trucks and hoses. It had been so dry for so long that cigarettes started these all the time. Fricke saw him looking at the cars, and said over his shoulder, "Hell of an inconvenience, right, Tucker? Let's get this over for them."

Scott and Corcoran were on the east side, in the smooth-furred flat area near the asphalt where the fire had begun. Darnell followed Fricke with the hose to the scattering, moving flames up the hill.

The blaze disappeared instantly under the water, but little patches of the silence the flame made, the quiet of sucked-up oxygen and reaching heat, landed like rags. Then they were gone.

Disappointment washed hot below Darnell's throat. No—this don't even qualify, hell, no—we're just half-steppin here and this is the last one. Not *hardly* acceptable. He heard the hiss of smoldering ground. Victor was the one always sayin that back in school. Acceptable. But he was talkin about women. Not fires. He'd laugh silly if he heard me.

"Tucker!" Fricke called from down the hose. "Quit sleeping! Don't get that glazed look again, all right?" He laughed and inclined his head toward the ridge of boulders a few yards away. "Go," he said, hard. "This is it."

Not lacy, knee-high flames. In the pocket behind the rocks, where moisture collected to grow the brittlebush in a clump, the fire caught and burned hard. Darnell dragged the hose, and when the gold turned orange and sound clotted for a moment, he dropped onto his knee to feel the heat on his face. He pulled his hand from the glove to stretch out his fingers, and the breeze blew a glowing stem at him; the twig breathed in when it flew and lit hotter, and before he could feel Fricke's boots behind him or lift the water, he turned his palm to the ground. The stem fell on the back of his hand, etched itself into his skin, thin there over his bones, a slanted pain he let burn before the black shrank and cooled.

SPRUNG

WHERE THE HIGHWAY snaked through the pale hills everyone called the Sandlands, Darnell felt the clutch grinding harder, seizing up, felt his own breath puffing cold on the raised burn line across his hand. He tightened his grip on the steering wheel, and the swollen skin throbbed a little.

He'd waited until night. The beige hills, with their sparse tufts of dry winter grass, glowed in the high-desert moonscape. The fog wouldn't work its way here for a few hours yet. The mist had been so heavy in the morning that Raycraft's silvery hair blended into nothing where he stood beside his car, telling Fricke it was over.

Somebody in the Conservation Corps had called these the Hooter Hills—a white guy from Sacramento who'd ridden to Rio Seco with Darnell and some others. Another man who said he was part Indian told them there was a Sleeping Woman Mountain where he was from. Darnell remembered Brenda's chest larger, harder, the last time he'd touched her.

When she'd lived on his street, Picasso Street, when they were kids, he'd watched for her face when he knocked, the small ears above two thick braids at her neck. She'd peer out, but she never opened the door. Her father was strict.

"Mrs. Batiste, Mama say here your pattern," he used to say, and behind Brenda was Mrs. Batiste's cushioned chest, her knees touching the hem of her housecoat, and behind them both was a white-cloth dummy with jutting hips and mesh-stretched breasts.

"You want to take back these bobbins, baby," Mrs. Batiste would say, and while he waited in the kitchen, staring at Brenda's baby brother playing with army men under the table, Mrs. Batiste would call, "Give him some teacakes!"

Brenda would say, "Here," and then stand near the doorway, watching him. Her mother came out with the silver wheels tiny in her palm, saying, "I see you start to get you daddy's color, I see that red under there."

Everyone called Darnell's father Red Man, for the skin and nose he'd gotten from his Creek grandmother and passed on to Darnell. And Darnell watched Brenda's narrow back, her eyes flickering. He'd heard what they called her. But she wasn't yellow; he thought about her when his mother sent him to check the apricots on the tree in the yard. They weren't ripe yet—they stayed a blurry gold. Brenda's color.

Out of the Sandlands, he sped through the few farms that skirted the last mountain range. Flatlanders—that was what Fricke called everyone who lived off the mountain. Darnell had been the last to go. Scott and Perez were both going to Corcoran's house near the beach, and they spun out of the driveway together. Darnell packed up his stuff, took out the trash one last time. Peering over the edge of the dumpster with the bag, he saw a torn picture from *Penthouse*. Scott was into centerfolds, but this photo was just bootie, a round behind tanned except for a long strip of white. "No tigers for me," Darnell said, "I like mine all one color." He closed the lid tight. Brenda's color. She'd probably been sitting up every night, waiting for him to call, cussing him out into a wet pillow so her parents wouldn't hear her cry. "What could I say if I called?" he muttered. "What I'ma say now? Hey, baby, want to get married? I just got laid off, I ain't got my last check, and my clutch about to go out. But I love you, baby. Smooth rap, brothaman."

In the kitchen, he'd asked Fricke, "Why you like so many different women?" He kept his voice low, like the others were still drifting around the room.

"Instead of one?" Fricke folded his fingers around his cup.

"Yeah."

"Because the pursuit is more interesting than the capture. Captivity isn't good for men nor animals."

Darnell had frowned. "You always make it somethin fancy, man, a great quote. I'm just talkin about don't you ever *think* you might just want one?"

"Nope," Fricke said. "But you do. You *think* you do." He stood up and headed outside to the garage, leaving Darnell with his gear. "Let me know how you survive. I hope your burn heals nice. I hope your brain heals quick."

The bare-plowed ground smacked up against the low pass through the Agua Dulce Mountains. Darnell ground the clutch hard to shift down for the gradual descent. Rio Seco spread in a half-circle below what everyone called the Sugar Ridge, the wall of rock and scrub that caught smog and held it in the basin for days.

But the wind-cleaned air still wavered over the sparkles of street-lights tonight, and he could see the fog rolling in from LA and the coast, pulling close like a quilt.

Even the huge boulders beside the freeway were creamy bright. In school, books had only shown triangular mountains, shark-toothed points with pine trees and snow. Darnell had always stared at the Sugar Ridge, an arc of brown humps with boulders and the blinking red lights of the police radio tower at the highest point. The green sign flashed by now: RIO SECO—POP. 324,000.

The tiny dots, laid out in miles of squares, grew larger, and he could see the freeway cutting through the center, passing over the riverbed to head for LA. The police helicopter sent its gray-blue beam slanting over the streets, and Darnell smiled. "Yeah, you can point me home in a minute," he said, leaning into the windshield. "Put the spotlight on for me." The shaft of light swept back and forth over the Westside, found something, and the helicopter began its tight-lassoing circle, the glare pinned down.

But Darnell turned off early, following the exit at the base of the foothills. He stopped at the wide turnout, littered with glass and fast-

food wrappers and condoms, where everyone from Brenda's neighborhood parked to fool around. The first time he'd pulled in here,
she had ducked her head, but he motioned toward the fire. She'd
laughed then, and he said, "Up here you got much better fires than
on the Westside. Too crowded down there. You got plenty of hills,
even though there's not much to burn."

The red taillights had circled the freeway at the pass, and the
brighter-glowing flames moved jagged up the hillside. He was afraid
to explain the fire to her, and her lips were soft on his, her hands
fanned out along his back.

She understood the fires, but she hated his absence. "You have to
live up there, too, even for seasonal?" she'd asked. Darnell ground
the clutch again to leave the glittering lot. Season's over, he thought.
And people been gettin what I missed right here. I haven't touched
her for two months.

He followed the wide avenue to the Ville. The streets were quiet,
bare and open with the city-planted palms that never grew into shady
tunnels like the Westside's pepper and carob trees. His parents had
driven up here with everyone else when these tracts had been built,
when he was in elementary school; his mother liked the ranch-style
shingles and Spanish-style stucco houses, so sprawling compared to
the old wood-frame houses on the Westside. Melvin and Victor had
named it Casperville right away, and now even though the neighborhood wasn't white, like it was when Brenda's father had moved
his family here, people on the Westside still called it the Ville.

He turned on Brenda's street, looking for the black New Yorker in
the driveway. Her father wasn't home yet, but he would be soon.
Darnell slowed at the curb. A square of light showed at her bedroom.
A dim glow—one small lamp. She was getting ready for bed. He cut
the engine, glad he was heading downhill because of the lousy clutch.

Crossing the grass, he stood between the two large bushes on either
side of Brenda's window. Pops comin home in a few, and I ain't hardly
acceptable. Don't even qualify. Just give me a minute to look at her,
he said to the helicopter, waiting for a face like his poking around in
the Ville.

In the crack between curtains, he saw her sitting on the bed's edge,
her hair in a wide, flat braid. The back of her neck was thin and pale,
a narrow hollow down the center. He wanted her to turn around—

how big was her belly? Let me see her mouth—the lips, two narrow front teeth slightly longer than the others, like a pair of piano keys, that made her keep her mouth closed when she smiled, made her look even shyer, more distant, than the other girls in school.

"Miss Thang think she too good to speak," they'd said. She whispered to Darnell how she had to be quiet at home, and then quiet was wrong everywhere else. He heard her voice now, wafting through the glass. Her shoulders bent over a magazine; she sang with Anita Baker on the radio.

He stood frozen, not letting his feet shift and crackle leaves. She only sang when she was alone. Her voice swirled and hummed softly, spiraling past his face like a night moth. She never sang in the school choir, which was dramatic-type white girls and churchgoing Westside girls. She only sang in the car, a few times when he watched a fire and she slumped, waiting, in the front seat, her feet dangling from the open door and no one else around but him, staring at flame loping up the hillside. When he came up behind her, caught her with a dark-trembly voice flying out of her heaving chest, her eyes went wide and her mouth thin.

A car passed on the street, and Darnell pressed closer to the thorny hedge. Brenda's voice murmured smaller, the song fading away, and then she stood up and walked to the door. He couldn't see if her back was thicker inside the nightgown, but when she turned to the closet, her silhouette was wider through the cotton nightgown. His breath caught at his ribs; he heard the door click, and he squatted for a moment to smell the damp-dripping earth near the hose.

Sitting in the pew nearest the Virgin Mary, he breathed candle smoke and polished wood and hot brass. Our Lady of Perpetual Help was a tiny whitewashed chapel, with close walls, where his GranaLene had brought him every day while he stayed at her little house in Gray Hollow. His father took Melvin to school, took Darnell to Granny Zelene's, and dropped his mother at work. But Darnell had never been to mass here; his father always said, "He ain't gon be no Catholic cause he need to know more than that. It's reasons things happen, not just fate and now forgive me, please. No. Uh-uh. You can't confess all that shit away and fix everything with no candle."

He stared at the wavering baby-flames that always swayed the whole

room, swayed his body stronger and dizzier than a real fire. Mountain
flames were sheets of color shifting, racing, while he stood still and
watched the water rush from his wrists and fingers. The eye-pricks
of yellow had lined up to watch him while his GranaLene had lit wick
after wick for her dead children, and when she'd turned to him finally
and said, "So many souls," he'd felt his forehead bulging with heated
cotton. "Marie Eulalie. Marie Anastasia. Marie Dominique. All my
baby girl gone when they just commence to smile. And I name you
mama Mary. No French no more—cause I leave there, that Louisiana.
Mary Therese. And she have Melvin. Then I light a candle for her
one die before you. Antoine. And the twin who leave her while you
till restin inside. He don't have no name. But you here—look at you,
so strong and smart. Five years old. Come on."

When she'd stood, he'd looked back at the five new, tallest flickers.
And she'd pulled at his shoulder. "Come on. Time we go and have
some lunch."

He'd felt the hard wood at his spine. He asked his mother at night
about the twin, and her eyes sheened over with tears. "Why you tell
him all that?" she said to GranaLene, who slitted her own eyes and
cracked pecans in her chair by the fire.

"So he know how much he mean," GranaLene said.

"And he think on things too much," his mother said, going out to
the front yard to call Melvin in from playing football with the older
boys in the street.

GranaLene said, "I seen you drop that egg," as if his mother were
still there, her blouse big with Sophia. "You drop two yolks on the
floor, both red as could be. And you too big."

When his mother came back in with Melvin, his grandmother
pushed a pecan into her mouth and one into Darnell's, and stared at
his face. "Come on read GranaLene a book, baby," she would say,
and Melvin crowed, "While he readin, can I have his piece a cake?"

Darnell stood up, hearing voices behind him. Spanish. Two Mexican women came into the church, shawls over their hair, nodding
to him, and he held on to the smooth wood for a moment before he
faced the door, the gold lights still blinking behind his eyes.

His father was from Oklahoma, and he hated all that Louisiana
Catholic talk, so his grandmother would stop when he came inside.

But when his mother's belly had been swollen with his sisters, GranaLene's curl-fingered hands were always touching the thinned skin.

Darnell sat in his car, looking at the few shacks left in Gray Hollow. The small low-lying area off the Pepper Avenue arroyo used to be housing for citrus-grove workers, and there were pockets of shotgun shacks left near the riverbottom. Blue Hollow, White Hollow. He saw shadows of men walking near Jackson Park, at the far end of the hollow, and the vacant lot where his grandmother's tiny house had been. He smelled candle wax on his fingers and touched the hot line on his hand. "All that death," his father used to grumble at him. "Don't listen to them Louisiana people. Country and Catholic a hella combination."

His mother would say, "No. Not all. Just her."

Brenda's parents were Creoles, from Louisiana. This had been Mrs. Batiste's church, too, when they'd first come here to Rio Seco. He'd seen her lighting candles, too, when he was small. Maybe she lit candles now to bring Darnell home. She'd always liked him, told him to be patient.

He drove away from the park, out the back way up the narrow alley that dipped sharply and then rose up to Pepper Avenue. The striped windows of the few storefronts were dark, but the fast-food signs were still lit. Crossing Sixth into the Westside, he passed the two tallest Victorian houses at the edge, the ones that were in the middle of lemon groves years ago. Now they were apartments. He saw that one small, leaning bungalow had been straightened, the peeling wood covered over with light-blue stucco since he last came home. More Mexicans and Guatemalans, he thought, cause they always use plaster and stucco and wrought iron. Those guys know how to keep a house warm.

He saw Roscoe's yellow house with the small river-rock porch. The big Apache truck was in the long driveway, but the lights were off. Roscoe must have walked over to Pops', Darnell thought. Roscoe Wiley was his father's partner in the tree-trimming business. His wife had died when their son, Louis, was small, and now Roscoe took care of Louis's daughter, Hollie, because Louis was out of the house, running the streets.

Darnell waved at Mrs. Dauphine, who stood in her yard with a trickling hose, and the wind made the water jump and sparkle. He turned down Picasso Street and saw all the trucks gathered in the packed-dirt area between his father's house and Mr. King's.

His father's faded-red Chevy had the plywood gates up, and when Darnell parked, he could smell the crushed eucalyptus branches. Mr. King's two old Fords, the '49 and the '72, were full of scrap concrete chunks and twisted chicken wire. They must have cleared another construction site.

Mrs. King sat on her front porch, still in her white nurse's uniform, and she lifted her face when Darnell got out of his car. "Hey, Mrs. King," he said.

"How you doin, Darnell?" she said. "They all back there—can't you hear em? I don't know how your mama get any rest."

He smiled. "She can sleep through what she wants to." The house that his father painted white every other year was dark at the front, and the boards had gathered dust from the wind. The small porch, just a wood overhang above a cement slab with three steps, was an empty cave lined with his mother's tiny pots of miniature roses. She and his sisters were asleep, he knew, and he heard the deep voices from the back. He walked through the narrow sideyard, past the hulking trucks.

The back used to be a screened-in laundry porch, but over the years his father and Roscoe had built walls with scrap lumber and spare time. Now it was a small, warm wood-brown room, where the men gathered in winter. His father, Roscoe, Floyd King and his son Nacho, his nephew Snooter were probably here. Snooter yelled, "Take yo ass to the boneyard, Roscoe!"

The domino slammed onto the table, and Mr. King said, "He got fitteen out that."

Darnell stepped up to the doorway and called, "It's me, Pops." His father let him in, the big grease-knuckled fingers on the doorknob, and Snooter called out, "Nature Boy! He back from the wilds!"

"Shut up, man," Darnell said. "How you doin, Mr. King? Hey, Nacho."

They all nodded, and Snooter said, "Mountain man! You freezin yo ass off yet?"

"It ain't that much colder up there," Roscoe said.

"Not with that hot Santa Ana wind still blowin," Darnell said. "But now it's fog time." He sat down near the table and looked at the sharp corners of the domino game laid out between Roscoe and Snooter. "I see y'all cut up a eucalyptus."

"Big one," his father said absently, looking out the black-reflecting window at the sideyard. "Them shallow root systems were poppin up from last week's weather."

"Domino!" Snooter shouted, slapping down the ivory piece so hard the paper cups full of liquor trembled. Snooter liked Canadian Club.

"What's wrong with you, Roscoe?" Mr. King asked. "You let this shit-talkin boy beat you—that ain't right."

"I'm tired," Roscoe said. "Nacho can play him."

Nacho stood up, slapping Darnell's shoulder. "You ready for me to do that bad paint job yet? No other color like it . . ."

Darnell took a tiny sip of his father's gin. He shivered and said, "I'm thinkin about it, man."

"Get your underage hands off my drink, boy," his father said. "Don't even think about it."

"I know them mountain men be drinkin serious up there," Snooter said, whirling the dominoes on the table so they clicked and clicked.

Darnell sat back against the wooden slats of an old chair and waited. "Where you get the chair?" he asked his father, who sat in a new black recliner in the corner of the room.

His father shook his head, and Roscoe answered for him. "Melvin came by last weekend with some dude from LA, had two chairs on a truck. Don't ask where this other guy got em. He took one down to the Hunters'."

Darnell's father grumbled. "He didn't spend no time with them boys. They rip and run around like they ain't got no sense."

Darnell looked at his father's boots. Melvin had two sons with Alicia Hunter, who lived at the far end of the street with her parents. Clinton and Lamont—they were wild and smiling, in and out of his mother's kitchen for snacks and whacks.

"They got in trouble last week," Roscoe said. "Throwing rocks and hit Calvin Cook's new Mercedes. Dented the door! You shoulda seen him carrying the boys up here, asking who they belong to. They cried like women on a soap opera."

Snooter laughed. "I'd cry if Calvin Cook came after me—shit, everybody in the NFL cry."

Roscoe was seeing a woman whose sons played football for the LA
Rams. Darnell said, "That where Hollie is now? Over at Marietta
Cook's?"

Roscoe nodded. "She's got her grandson Freeman, and Hollie
wanted to spend the night over there." Darnell looked down at the
scratched wooden table, covered with layers of faint rings from cups.
Hollie—who Louis ain't takin care of. Lamont and Clinton—who
Melvin don't take care of. Damn, I'm real set up here now. Let me
just tell Pops and Roscoe about mine, so I can be just another foolish,
irresponsible nigga—I can hear their favorite words right now. I can
say em for myself. He felt the taste of gin ringing in his stomach.

But he waited until the Kings had left. Roscoe asked, "You get that
other chain saw working?" and his father said, "Yeah, might as well
knock out that trunk before we go to the dump."

"You need some help in the morning?" Darnell asked, stacking
Roscoe's dominoes in their velvet-lined case.

"What you doin down here anyhow?" his father said sharply. "Season ain't over."

"Yeah, it is," Darnell said. "It was this morning."

"Well, you probably be over Brenda's soon as the damn sun come
up, so I don't know why you offerin to cut wood," his father said.

Darnell touched the red velvet and thought he would get it over
with. "I don't know if her daddy gon be waitin with his .38 or not.
Brenda's pregnant." He pushed his finger into the thicker plush at
the corner and waited.

"What! Goddamn if you ain't a fool!" his father shouted.

"Don't holler and wake everybody up," Roscoe said, looking closely
at Darnell. "I thought you were being intelligent. Being careful."

"I was," Darnell said. His father was silent, his long nose even
longer with his lips pulled in grim.

"That doesn't matter now," Roscoe said. "What are you planning
to do?"

"Her pops hates me," Darnell said. "That ain't gon change. He
been toleratin me, waitin for me to get burned up or sent to another
county."

Roscoe said, "Are you? Getting sent to another county? Another
job?" Darnell stared at the stem over his hand bones. He shrugged.

His father shook his head. "You ain't college and you ain't Catholic."

His teeth plucked in skin from his lip. "Batiste a hard man. I knew him when we first got stationed out there at the airbase, and I axed him where he was from. Some other cat told me, 'Don't ax him where, cause he from No More, Louisiana. All he gon say is "Someplace I don't live no more." ' Somebody said his daddy was white, and his mama run away from the plantation where she was born."

Roscoe still watched Darnell. "Batiste isn't going to like you till you get a good job. He's been at Royal for twenty years now. He was there when they worked on the B-52."

Darnell looked at the amber bead of liquid someone had spilled on the table.

"Yeah, well, Royal's layin off now, not hirin," he said. Brenda's father was a supervisor, and he'd kept his job when a lot of the assembly-line people lost theirs last year.

Only the dogs barking in faraway yards and the distant whine of the police helicopter hung in the air, until Roscoe said, "How far along?"

"She said five months."

"Louis didn't even know until two weeks before his baby was born." Roscoe stood up and put his hands in his pockets.

"Yeah, but he wasn't really tight with Geanie," Darnell said, uncomfortable.

"Tight enough," Roscoe said quietly, picking up the domino case.

"You and Brenda was tight enough, too," his father said. "God-damnit. Now what you gon do? You can't stay up there and play at no part-time firefighter gig. You gon have to get you a job."

"You think I ain't been workin hard?" Darnell said. He spread his palms where the dominoes and hands had worn the table smoother, but his father didn't glance at the burn; he went out the door behind Roscoe.

Darnell heard them talking in the sideyard, and he went through the doorway into the hall. He walked carefully past the two bedroom doors. His sisters snored in their room, and his mother breathed quietly in the black space that showed at her half-open door.

Darnell lay down on the couch where he had slept since he was old enough to leave the girls' room. He remembered when they were born, the raspy crib breaths of Paula and Sophia clotting the air, his mother's shadow in and out of the room, murmuring with GranaLene, always watching them to make sure they didn't slip away. His mother sometimes slept curled around one or the other on her bed; he imagined Brenda, lying curved around her belly now. He stretched his legs straight and folded his hands on his chest. When he was small, first sleeping on the couch, he'd fallen off a few times. His mother wanted to put pillows on the floor all around him, but his father had said, "Let him fall hard and he'll learn how to stay up there."

"You sleep like a zombie," his grandmother used to say, whispering it in her slurry voice from her chair by the fireplace. The brass buttons glowed dull in the firelight. His grandmother stayed in the front room while he took his nap. She came every day then, since his mother had the twin babies. She watched him lie down, saying, "So I keep my eye on you. So no spirit sneak in here take you."

Louisiana. When his mother was just a baby, Granny Zelene had taken her to Oklahoma. No one knew why, or how, and she just shrugged when Darnell used to ask her. "Just went," she'd say, never moving from her chair, only her fingers twirling with the silver needle when she sewed.

"Zombie everywhere in Louisiana. Sometime a spirit just come inside a person head, a spirit dead and don't want to leave, and he want company in the spirit world." His grandmother wouldn't even look at him when she said this; her fingers never stopped pulling thread slantwise above her lap, and her eyes might check the embers in the fireplace. Only when she was finished with the skirt hem would she stare at Darnell and say, "Come in the kitchen and get you some hot chocolate."

When Darnell had walked beside Melvin to take Granny Zelene home, he'd watched the smog-shrouded summer sky or the silvery-pale clouds in winter, wondering where the zombies rested while they chose their heads. And when he asked his mother, she frowned and said, "Granny Zelene had a hard life. She talks about things you don't have no concern with. Ain't no zombies—only on Halloween."

Darnell moved his palms now so that they covered his hipbones, stretching his fingers. The fire his mother must have made that night, where she sat with his father before she went to bed and he joined the men in the back, was only a smidgen of sound, of pulsing ash. Lacing his fingers again, he kept his feet still, touching at the big toe, and his elbows close to his chest. "You sleep like a dead person,"

Brenda had teased him, the few times she dozed beside him on the couch or in someone's borrowed bed. Darnell heard the sparkling sigh of the last embers.

Before he could see the trucks in the heavy dawn fog, he heard them from all the way down Picasso Street, pounding, booming the bass lines into his ribs. Gasanova's black Toyota was first, cruising so slow Darnell could read MIDNIGHT painted in curly white script over the door.

"What up, D.?" Gasanova said, and Kreeper smiled from where he rode shotgun.

"You got it chopped sleek, man!" Darnell said. The truck was lowered, doors inches from the asphalt, and its bed was full of speakers covered with black canvas. Behind him was Cartunes, and Darnell squinted at the purple flames along his hood and doors. Then the truck bed raised up on the back hydraulics to slant sharply, and the same song poured out of the cracked-open space even louder.

"Oh, homey—the *dump!*" Darnell shouted, smiling back. "Check out my boy!" He went to the back of the dump truck to see the hydraulics and the tires. "Y'all up early," he said.

"We were out all night, man," Gasanova said. "These two females in San Bernardino, man, we met em at the car show."

Kreeper said, "Gas is in love."

"I ain't playin that. It's only room in here for two," Gasanova said. "But then I could throw your ass out, huh?"

"I didn't know you guys had these finished pretty," Darnell said. Gas was a year younger than Darnell, and his brother Leon a year older. Their mother lived at the end of Picasso.

"You ain't around, homey. I *been* had it done," Gas said. "You were goin into the Conservation Corps when I first bought it, right?"

"Yeah, I been in and out the hood for a couple years," Darnell said, looking at the glossy doors trembling in the fog. The mist that had muffled the voices back at the station had shrouded the pines and beaded on Raycraft's truck when he'd parked to tell them it was over. The fog would surround Brenda when she took the bus or drove to work in her mother's car; she'd read the newspaper, he knew. She'd seen the article about the welcome winter coolness signaling the end of fire season in this sixth year of drought. . . . She knows I'm home.

And I ain't came by yet—I ain't called. I ain't callin until I can say somethin.

"No!" Gasanova shouted, leaning out to look at the sideyard. "The Spider back there with the terminal patients and shit!"

Darnell smiled and shook his head. "Clutch started goin out on me, man, comin down from work."

"Kickstand gon fix you up?" Cartunes asked.

Darnell blinked. "I can't keep puttin all my dinero in the Spider, man."

"You gon let her die in your daddy's graveyard?" Gasanova said, staring at the sideyard, where an El Camino truck and a '63 Cadillac were nestled in tall grass, wild mint, and used tires.

"Hey, the Spider's wheels are still visible, okay?" Darnell said.

"You should get you a truck, come and boom with us," Gas said. He looked down the street. "Here come your pops and them." Darnell folded his arms and let the music hit his knuckles.

"You gotta wake up the whole damn street?" Darnell's father said. He got out of Roscoe's truck holding a paper bag. They'd gone early to the fish market for red snapper, Darnell's mother's favorite.

Roscoe looked at Cartunes's dump truck. "You from Treetown?" he asked. "You gon waste a perfectly good vehicle like this?"

"It ain't wasted," Cartunes said. "It's boomin."

Darnell watched his father walk around Gasanova's truck. Every time he and Roscoe heard the fuzzed electronic drums shake the back room, they rolled their eyes. "See, that's a truck," his father said, pointing to Roscoe's. "Nineteen forty-seven Apache with a dump bed. Yours ain't no damn truck. You can't haul nothin in it, so the word don't even apply now."

"What you gon call it then?" Gasanova asked, smiling. He loved to bother them.

"A goddamn nuisance!" Darnell's father shouted.

Roscoe and Marietta Cook stood on the curb. Darnell never knew what to call Roscoe's lady friend; she was almost six feet tall, always serious in the set of her face. "How you doin this morning?" he said, and she nodded.

"Look like nothin more than a house shoe," she said softly.

Roscoe smiled, his eyes slanting off to the air like they did when he thought poetry. "What a metaphor—a truck as little and low as a slipper," he murmured. But he blinked his eyes clear again, focusing on the tires. "Just like your brother Leon's four-wheel-drive vehicle— useless for what it's intended. All he carries around is fools." Darnell knew he was thinking of his son Louis. "This desire for loud music instead of space can't be normal," Roscoe said hard. "Driving around pounding your brains into submission until you shoot each other. I heard gunfire last night up on Sixth Avenue."

Gasanova folded his arms impatiently. "That ain't me," he said, lifting his chin. "I ain't Leon. See, you look at the hooptie and think you *know*. I ain't into bangin, I'm into *boomin*."

"Speak English, boy," Darnell's father said.

"It ain't a gang, Pops," Darnell said, but he could tell that Roscoe was still picturing Louis in the back of another vehicle, staring at Gasanova and seeing Leon instead of his brother. Roscoe took Marietta's arm and steered her toward the big cab.

"His son Louis still gettin in trouble with Leon?" Darnell's father asked.

Gasanova shrugged. "I guess they tight. I see them in the street, but that ain't my business. Darnell, man, you want a ride over to see Kickstand?"

Darnell said, "Yeah, Pops, I'ma go see about this clutch. I'll be back." His father frowned hard, like he had at dawn when Darnell's mother asked why he wasn't calling Brenda.

"Don't come back deaf," his father said, turning to go into the house.

Darnell's shoulders mashed against Gas and Kreeper when he squeezed in, and Gas said, "See? I ain't got no room for ladies unless y'all walk."

Darnell leaned back, feeling the music and the engine and their breath close. This desire for music can't be normal, he thought. According to Roscoe. I can't really classify your behavior as normal— that's what Fricke said. No room for ladies here. No room for babies in the Spider. Damn.

"You sleep, D.?" Gas said.

Darnell shook his head. "You still workin at the Holiday Inn?" Gas had been a cook in the coffee shop since they graduated. His uncle had taught him to short-order.

"Yeah. Eggs over easy every day. But this fine new waitress named

Tamiko just moved here from Oakland. She don't know nobody yet."

"Your favorite kinda woman." Darnell laughed. "She don't know you ain't about nothin."

"Brenda still your favorite kinda woman?" Gas asked.

Darnell looked at the clinging fog when they passed Gray Hollow and the arroyo. "Yeah. She's still my lady."

"What up with the firefighter thang?" Kreeper said.

"Season's over, man. I'ma get unemployment, but I don't find out if I get called back to the station till March." He touched the line on his hand; it had faded to a black, tight-pulled mark. "I need some serious ducats fast."

"Ain't nothin at the Inn," Gasanova said.

"Ain't nothin nowhere," Kreeper said. "You want some quick dinero, talk to Leon." Darnell twitched, startled, and Gas spat out the window. Kreeper laughed. "Leon flashin much ducats. Got him a new Bronco, huh, Gas? Sweet black with some *fat* rims."

"Leon slingin cane?" Darnell asked. "That what Roscoe talkin about?"

Gas sucked his teeth. He was slightly darker than Leon, but both brothers had the same wide mouth, small teeth, and square hairline cut deep over their temples. He said, "He's crazy. Yeah, he gettin paid, but them guys from LA cruise out here to the country and smoke you if you get in the wrong territory. I don't even see Leon— he pass by the crib now and then to say hi to Moms and give her some money."

Darnell saw the gray-green olive groves and the dry gullies of Treetown. "Man, remember when we used to ride bikes all over here?" Gas went on, lifting his chin at the dirt paths winding through the trees. "You wasn't around then, Kreeper. Darnell, me, Leon, Louis—"

"That the tall dude they call Birdman?" Kreeper interrupted.

"Yeah," Darnell said.

"He was a good ballplayer," Kreeper said. "They call him that cause he could jump hella high, right?"

Nobody answered. Darnell wondered if Gas remembered how Louis had first gotten the nickname, when they were riding under branches here and Louis was mesmerized by the birds flocking near the riverbottom. "Donnie Harris used to ride with us, too," he said, glancing at the dried-hard wrinkles in the ditches. No water in a long time. Donnie was always lookin for water back then, and Louis was always watchin for hawks and seagulls, tellin us all the names. And me—I was checkin for smoke.

"Yeah, Donnie's back, too," Gas said. "Him and Birdman both quit playin ball and came back from school." Gas shook his head. "Birdman's pops lookin ballistic—I heard he ain't spoke to Birdman since."

"Dude look crazy sittin in Leon's Bronco," Kreeper said. "So tall he all bent over."

Darnell thought of Roscoe's face and said, "So Louis slingin, too?"

Gas said, "I don't know what he doin. He hangs with Leon, but he never says nothin, he don't carry no cash. He trippin hard." He spat out the window. "And your pops think I'm off into that. Shit."

Darnell saw the stone barn and old house, Arrow Towing and Repair, and Demetrius Thompson in the barn doorway. "Remember the Thompsons, G., they used to kick everybody's ass. Always boxin."

"They old now," Gasanova said. "Got big old kids to be nubbin with. Not no babies. Gray hairs."

Darnell ran his tongue around his teeth, thinking, Yeah, I'ma be old, too. "Thanks, homey," he said, pushing Kreeper out the passenger door.

"I'ma go check this stereo," Gasanova called. "I'll look for you."

Darnell said, "How you doin?" to the men in the barn. Kickstand was lying all the way inside the open hood of a Cadillac, his shoes dangling off the ground. Darnell waited, uncomfortable. Kickstand was in a permanent bad mood, and you had to wait for him to speak first.

"What you want me to do to your piece-a-shit Italian car now, boy?" Kickstand asked, sliding himself off the engine. "If it was a horse and we was in Texas, I'd shoot it."

"Lucky we in Treetown," Darnell said. "My clutch disc is gone, man."

Kickstand frowned hard and said, "Man, I gotta get the transmission jack up in there and part the tranny to even *get* to your little clutch disc. Shit. Two hundred, minimum. And you know your brakes is shot, too, boy."

Darnell leaned against the sawhorse, feeling the bones around his eyes ache. "I might have to look for somethin else, man, before I spend that. Somethin bigger, cause I need some more room." Kickstand raised his eyebrows, and Darnell thought, Might as well get used to it, if I'ma do this. "My girlfriend's havin a baby, and I gotta think about a backseat."

"Look like you already spent some time in the backseat, nigga." Demetrius laughed.

Darnell sucked his teeth and said, "Give me a break, man."

Kickstand said, "I got four kids. I ain't changed my drivin habits for they mama." He pointed at the Cadillac. "Get you one a these, you got plenty a seats, but you better be ready to pay near bout a grand for a new tranny." Then he gestured out to the back of the huge lot, where cars lay in a dusty patchwork over the dirt to the riverbottom. "But come on back here with six, seven hundred, and I can drop a engine in somethin you find out there." He smiled at Darnell. "Or bring that much and I'll let you throw it away in Italian."

"Let me think about it," Darnell said, turning to the street. "I'll check."

"Check your wallet," Kickstand called after him, "before you come."

Darnell started the walk back to the Westside, watching the last of the fog blend in with the gray-shimmery olive trees to make a ghost forest. He touched the trunk of a pepper tree growing spindly by the asphalt. Seven hundred for a new engine, more seats, wheels to look for work. And an apartment. He had four hundred he'd been saving for the Spider's clutch and paint job. Every month, his paltry Forestry paycheck had gone for board, fast food if Scott or Perez cooked, and weekends with Brenda. He liked to take her to dinner, to movies, and he'd bought her ruby earrings for her birthday.

Christmas comin up and I ain't got no present. He looked at the winter-silver sun, late morning high now. Call her? What I'ma say? Hey, baby, you workin hard? I'm back from the station. No shit, Sherlock—she knows the weather, too, by now.

He heard Gas's speakers thumping, and waited for the truck. He only nodded and said, "Damn," and they were silent. Crossing over the five sets of railroad tracks at the edge of Gray Hollow, where the asphalt-and-dirt was pitted deep, Gas drove slow for his frame, and they passed the tiny store built of round stones that sold mostly snacks and beer now. In the alley where ghost men lit the glass pipes and slept on discarded couches and mattresses, where the last two boarded-up shacks always had girls called strawberries haunting the porch railings looking for customers who could pay cash or cane, someone was wrapped in a blanket near a cement foundation, but Darnell couldn't see whether it was a man or a woman.

The pile of scrap wood and crates marked the edge of Jackson Park. At the far end of the yellowed lawn was the playground and Our Lady, its round-arched door open, but this end of the park belonged to the men around the domino table. Darnell saw the morning crowd, not the heavy drinkers who gathered by early afternoon and lingered until after midnight. Morning guys had spent the night in their cars parked around the fire in the blackened trash barrel, the guys waiting for someone who wanted day labor, and a few who wanted to play a quick game of dominoes before the card table and folding chairs were surrounded by men three deep and drunk, hollering at the players.

Gas slowed when he saw Ronnie Hudson, with an army-surplus jacket and knit cap, and Darnell leaned out to nod. "What up, brotha-man? I ain't seen you in hella long," Ronnie said.

"I know," Darnell said. "I saw your runnin buddy Victor on road camp."

"Yeah," Ronnie said, sipping his coffee from a foam cup. "Homey pulled three."

Two men came from the warehouses toward the tracks, carrying paper bags, and Ronnie said, "Here come somebody's breakfast."

"I love dealin with sprung niggas, man, they so desperate," another man said, pushing his hand into his pocket.

"Who need some Seagram's?" one of the men said, holding up a bottle, glancing toward Darnell. He shook his head. Sprung dudes— they smoked rock, and they looked jumpy, jerky, wound up too tight, their eyes poking out in their long-boned faces. The pipe gave them pipe-stem legs, pipe-cleaner arms, he thought. Hair clump-grayed, arms ashy-grayed, palms bloodless when they held out their hands for dollars.

"I don't know how they steal that shit," Gas said, starting the truck. "I wouldn't even let nobody look like that in the damn *do*."

Do, Darnell thought. Man, don't let em in the *sto*. Ho of the day. He saw Fricke's mustache for a moment, looked at Gasanova's soft-fringed lip and his fingers stroking down, down. Yeah, they'd be comedy together, but Fricke's with some marine biologist. And I'm toe up.

"Look like Dawn of the Dead out here," Kreeper said. "Serious sprung."

He stayed on his back under the Spider for a while, so he wouldn't have to talk to his mother, or to his father and Roscoe when they rumbled up in the big truck. Then the sound of the chain saw, while they cut more eucalyptus and Darnell stacked the wood, let him be silent.

After school, Lamont and Clinton came racing down the street from their mother's yard. Lamont blew out his nine candles fast and reached for the two boxes on the table. He opened Darnell's present, a Magic Johnson T-shirt, and the other box, which held five pairs of new socks.

Darnell's mother saw his face. "What's wrong with you, Lamont?" she said, folding her arms. "You lookin for more?"

Clinton said quickly, "He wanted some Air Jordans." Lamont hit him in the back with a sock package.

"Well, he need a better air supply to his brain, then, cause he a fool," Darnell's father said, going toward the back room. "Them Air Jordans cost damn near a hundred dollars."

Darnell's mother sat down to cut the cake. "What your mama get you?" she asked Lamont offhandedly, and Darnell folded his arms. His parents hated Melvin's ex-girlfriend, never spoke to her unless one of the boys was sick. When they wanted the boys to come over, they sent someone to Alicia's mother, who owned the house. "I ain't got no quarrel with the mama," Darnell's father always said. "She didn't have no raw material to work with, cause Alicia came *out* a fool."

Alicia had dated Melvin in high school, had the boys during their junior and senior years, and then, when he didn't spend enough time with her, she reversed her car to slam the front end of his old Monte Carlo. She told the police he had rear-ended her maliciously, and he lost his driver's license. He left Rio Seco a few months later, to stay with a friend in Compton, and he'd never come back for more than a few days.

"Mama got me a jacket," Lamont said through the cake crumbs. "She put it on layaway."

"Uh-huh," Darnell's mother murmured, taking the frosting-coated knife.

Sophia and Paula came in late, breathless, and grabbed cake. "Darnell, you still here?" Sophia said. "Did Melvin come yet?"

Lamont said, "My daddy be here."

Paula said, "He got us some bad gold chains." They had turned fourteen in October. Darnell sat on the couch to watch TV.

Melvin cruised in just after dark, a package under his arm, and Lamont ran to tear it open. The Air Jordans were nestled inside, and Lamont hollered after he put them on; he jumped off the porch and all over the dark lawn.

"I'm *so* good," Melvin said, stretching his arms over his head. "I got a friend to get me discount."

"Shut up, man," Darnell said. "If you gotta tell people, you ain't good." He watched Melvin eat the cake his mother had set aside for him. Melvin's hair was short, pressed waves at the back and gleaming longer waves brushed from his forehead; his lips were square under his little mustache, and his cheeks were rich curry, the color of a sauce Fricke had made once. Victor used to call Melvin "Low Yella" when they were friends. "You ain't high yella, man, you lowdown yella. And the ladies love it."

Darnell heard Melvin talking to the boys on the front lawn for a minute, and then his brother's voice floated down the sideyard and into the back room. Melvin never stayed long to talk to his father; if more than fifteen minutes passed, they'd be shouting. Darnell waited. Melvin came through the hallway, hugged his mother from behind, while she was gathering up the plates, and then he pulled Darnell out to the curb.

"What up, baby bruh?" Melvin said softly. "You permanent back at the pad? This ain't a weekend."

"No, it ain't," Darnell said. He looked at the boys running down the sidewalk. "Brenda's pregnant."

"Oh, man," Melvin said. "You gon do the ring thing?"

"I guess so," Darnell said, stopping. Why was he telling Melvin? Melvin would bust up laughing, say Darnell was a fool. But Melvin just smiled.

"Lemme tell you somethin, baby bruh," he said softly. "Sex with a pregnant woman is the best there is, better than any other time."

"What the hell you talkin about?" Darnell said.

"No, man, listen. Gettin some with a pregnant woman—they ready, they ain't scared, and they tighter." Melvin walked away, calling to his boys, "Get over here, Lamont. I'm fixin to hat up, now, come and say later to your daddy before I can't see your little black asses in the dark. Hey," he said to them both, leaning close, and Darnell couldn't hear what he whispered, his arms around their narrow backs.

"He never forgets their birthdays," Mama said in the back room, where Darnell's father and Roscoe sat, looking over the checks they'd gotten that week.

Darnell's father said, "That and Christmas don't make him a father."

Darnell sat in the chair opposite his father, reading the newspaper. "You talkin to me?" he said, resting his elbows on the edge of the table. "You see me runnin?"

"I ain't even studyin you, boy," his father said, turning over a check.

Roscoe took a sip of the gin in a jelly jar by his arm. "I wish Louis had been shorter," he said suddenly, and Darnell was surprised. He rarely heard Roscoe speak his son's name since Louis quit college. "I wish he'd had his mother's head—not a dreamer's head like mine." Roscoe put down the jar and went outside.

Darnell thought of Brenda in bed right now, touching her stomach in the dark, waiting for him to call. The baby—a boy?—curled?—his head against her skin, her heart. Whose head? Not mine, he thought. Not the one I got right now.

One more day. Ain't no need to call her yet. I'ma do it all tomorrow, and then I'll just go get her. When I have somethin to say.

"Did the week come out good?" he asked his father.

"Why? You need some money?" his father said, looking up.

"Yeah," Darnell said, drumming his fingers. "Cause they gon want first and last for an apartment, and I only have four-fifty."

His father paused. "You find out first, and come tell me how much. You can owe me. You owe me your ass anyway." He didn't smile; he just looked at a pink bill, the kind Darnell recognized from the fabric store where his mother bought her material, and he rubbed the thin chain-saw scar on his forearm absently, like he always did.

She liked downtown, the old buildings with long windows and courtyards. They used to walk around during her lunch hour and look at these places. He was taking city college courses then, right after graduation, waiting for the Corps, and she already had the clerk-typist job for the county. All those English, typing, and computer classes in school—she had this job on a special World of Work program when they were seniors.

He checked out the buildings within walking distance of the county plaza. No hooptie yet—she could walk a short way to work until he got a car. A running car.

The tiny Vietnamese woman who answered the fifth door he tried that said MANAGER told him, "Five hundred, okay? First and last require to rent."

It was a tiny one-bedroom, three blocks from Brenda's building, but the big front window looked out on a courtyard with an old fountain planted with ivy. "I'll be back," he told the woman, who closed the door.

"I don't know if I can do this, Pops," he said in his father's truck. "Fifteen hundred. I'm comin to her with no job and a place rented for two months." His head burned above his ears.

His father looked straight ahead through the windshield. "How you think I feel if some boy got a baby on Sophia or Paula?" He started the truck and drove home, silent.

Darnell sat stiff against the hard seat, staring out the window. The girls in the neighborhood always said, "Yeah, she had a baby for Tiny," and "Girl, she done had three girls for David and he gone to North Carolina." For him—he remembered Fricke and Scott and Perez talking one night about women, Fricke saying, "Having a baby with a woman doesn't guarantee anything except the fact that you can make sperm." With. For. Get a baby on her.

Darnell sat in the back room, facing his father and Roscoe. Roscoe said, "Hollie's only five. She doesn't gulp down much money yet. You can take this five hundred from me. Pay me back on your own terms."

Darnell looked at the fresh hundred-dollar bills. His father said, "I didn't ask the man to do that—he's crazy enough to offer you his money. I think you should get a job first, but I don't want Etienne Batiste to come down here and talk to me about how I raised this son." His father counted out three hundred more, and pushed the thin stack across the scarred table.

Darnell swallowed and ran his tongue inside his lip. "You know three of them managers' offices tried to charge me a big security deposit because I'm black."

"You black?" Darnell's father frowned. "Well, hell, give me my damn money back. Don't you know black folks is a high lending risk?"

"Not as high as son folks," Roscoe muttered.

The office never changed. The fake-wood desks, with phony striations and grain under his elbow where he waited, leaning on the shelf near the door. The fake plants, too green with impossible turquoise blooms, still sat near the coffeepot and paper cups. The piles of folders everywhere, the stiff-haired woman at the receptionist's desk who still glanced up fearfully at first, not remembering that he stopped by sometimes for Brenda.

Lunch was in three minutes. They would all come out this way, the women from Personnel, Accounting, and Benefits. All the women who worked in the huge county building would stream out into the elevators and courtyard. The men, the bosses, either left early or went out later, because there were no crowds of them, just two or three at a time, with their suits and white shirts. Gold-rimmed glasses, gold rings, gold pens.

She came out with an Oriental girl. Brenda stopped and looked at Darnell, and the other girl stared, her face lifted. Darnell smiled, glanced down at Brenda's belly, hidden by her loose blazer.

"Can I buy you a couple of burritos?" Darnell said. "If you aren't too busy?"

Brenda whispered something to the girl, who looked hard at Darnell and kept walking. Brenda was silent until they were out the glass doors, and then she turned to him. "You the one who's so busy."

"I'm sorry," he started, but she cut him off.

"Two weeks since you called, Darnell. Two weeks, and I'm reading about this big fire in some canyon, I know you were there. And now you're home for what—two days? Three days?" She kept walking, heading toward a bench at the far end of the pedestrian mall. "I thought you were dead. So you might as well be."

"Brenda," Darnell said, standing while she sat and pushed her hand deep in her purse, looking for something. Her eyes were smaller, swelling pink with tears, and she wouldn't raise her face to him. "I didn't know what to say."

"You know what you wanted to say," she whispered. "You wanted to say, 'I'ma keep playin with fire. I'ma stay up here forever.'"

"I didn't stay," he said, sitting down.

"You didn't have a choice yet, Darnell," she whispered, lower. "And I don't have a choice about this." Her shoulders were curved over her thighs.

"I'm choosin, Brenda," he said, leaning in close. "Come on."

Her lips fit into his mouth. They were small, too, and her top lip was plump, delicate, above his tongue. He touched the dip at the center with his finger when she pulled away from him.

He could see the small belly now, round like a mixing bowl, in the gap of her jacket, but when he touched it, afraid, all he could feel was a ridge of zipper at her skirt. "I had to buy bigger pants last week," she said. "Pretty soon I have to make maternity clothes."

"I couldn't even see anything last time," he said, looking at her face. "You weren't even sure." Her hair was pulled back into a knot; her eyes were dark gold, liquid-clear as whiskey, and he put his arms around her for a moment. Then he felt the mound press against him, at his own belly. He could feel it better than see it.

Her eyebrows lifted. "You haven't been around recently, so how could you see anything? The season lasted forever."

He took her to Zamora's. Mr. Zamora and Darnell's father had been friends since the Air Force. Brenda touched the red peppers planted along the parking strip near the adobe building, and Darnell said, "You need some real burritos, not fast food."

They sat at a tiny table near the jukebox, which played only Mexican music. The fast-rolling guitars and trumpets swirled with the ceiling fans, and Mr. Zamora said, "Take these to your dad.'" He held a long stack of tortillas in a plastic bag. "He cut down that tree tearing up my parking lot, that sucker tree." Brenda was looking at photos of Mr. Zamora's grandchildren, lined over the cash register. "Numero sixteen," he said proudly, pointing to a baby in a white gown.

Over the fat burritos, Brenda said, "Mama's thirty-nine. A grandma at thirty-nine." She stared out the window at the traffic. "She's happy. But my dad—when we drive anywhere and he sees somebody pregnant, and they look young, he starts talking about welfare mamas and babies having babies."

"You ain't a baby," Darnell said, rubbing floury powder on his thumb. "I ain't a baby."

"I look young," she said, half dreamy. "The ladies at work always tell me how young I look. I'm the youngest one in Benefits." She bit her lips. "I see how people notice me downtown now. In my dresses. Everybody thinks they know what they see when I go in the county building. And they don't think I'm going to work."

Darnell folded his arms. "You can't worry about *everybody*. You don't even know *everybody*." But she'd always been like that in school. She watched faces, remembered gossip and frowns. And he didn't know what to tell her about her father. All he could think of was what the men had always said about Batiste: "Always got two jobs, and come home drinkin hard. But he gon make his money. Make no mistake."

"So you home," she said nervously, and he touched her wrist, where it lay on the gold-specked table, and bent his face up under to see her eyes. He knew he was supposed to say it. Ask her the big question. Tell her, "This is what we gon do—I got a plan." But he didn't even have a key yet. Mr. Zamora set down another plate of rice, and Brenda's face was wreathed in steam.

Darnell watched her tiny fingers, her shoulders held straight, and he kept his face to the table. When the heavy oval plates were cold and Brenda was silent, her eyes blurred, he said, "What's wrong?"

"I'm tired," she whispered, and he felt a jolt of fear hit him again.

After he drove to his mother's house, Brenda lay on the couch, wrists curled close to her nose, and was asleep in minutes.

"You always fall out like that," his mother whispered, watching her. "You can't help it, when you expectin." She looked at Darnell, then went back to her table. The sewing machine hummed hard; she had an order for curtains.

Darnell sat on the arm of the couch, seeing the glisten at the corner of Brenda's lips, her stomach slanted high against her elbows. She looked bigger lying down, and he said to his mother, "How you know if it's twins?" His breath felt hot under his nose.

She looked up, startled. "Huh? What you talkin bout twins?"

"GranaLene said I was a twin, remember?" He walked over to her, and her finger went behind her ear, the red polish sparkling.

"Granny always want to talk about the sad things," she said, finally. "You know that."

"She said twins run in our blood," Darnell kept on.

"Brenda ain't hardly big enough for no twins," his mother said, bending over the fabric. "Don't start rememberin all that again. You better hush, you gon wake her."

Darnell stood near the couch again. Brenda always joked that no noise could wake her once she was asleep; he always opened his eyes at any small sound when he lay on this hard-cushioned boat of a couch. He watched her between the shimmery noise of needle and breathing. "She gotta go back to work soon." The words hurt his chest. "And I gotta stand in line at unemployment, just down the way." He headed for the door. "You wake her up, Mama. I'm in the car."

Darnell got Honoré to make the cake. Honoré made cakes and pies in his tiny apartment and sold them to people for parties, weddings, reunions. "You want all the flower and garland and leaf?" Honoré said in his accent, soft Louisiana like Brenda's mother.

"Yeah," Darnell said. "Those purple ones." He looked at the cake Honoré had on display at the long shelf near the back wall. Violets and tiny pointed leaves and flourishes of pink everywhere. "Make it pretty."

Honoré shook his head impatiently. "How else you see me make em?"

At George White's apartment, Darnell waited in line behind two other men for a haircut. Here's the plan, he thought. Brenda's daddy gotta see a clean head, if he don't bust it open straight off. And then I can say I'ma get unemployment, and it ain't shit, but I might get called back in March. Only three months. And I'll have another job in the meantime.

He sat in the chair, looking into the mirror over George's low metal shelf lined with bottles and hairdress cans, and he watched George's hands with the clippers. George didn't talk unless you did. Usually, the other men on the couch kept the living room loud. But the place was empty for long minutes, and Darnell stared at his own face, half sleepy. His ears flat, his forehead square, the reddish tone under his cheeks and neck that Brenda's mother had teased him about when he was a boy. Not pretty like Melvin or Snooter—not tall like Donnie

or Louis. Just a everyday brotha, with a everyday face. Need a every-
day job right now.

George said, "You want cuts?" He held the razor over Darnell's
head, and Darnell hesitated. White people didn't like the parts etched
into scalps, the slanting lines or lightning strikes, especially not letters
or numbers. He'd heard Scott and the others make fun of college
ballplayers with them. I have to look serious square. L-7 suburban,
like Gas says. "Not this time, man," he said.

George was brushing the tiny hairs from his neck when Leon,
Mortrice, and Louis came in. "Darnell, man, heard you was in town,"
Leon said, touching Darnell's palm. "Baby bruh told me."

Louis nodded. "Long time," he said, hands in his pockets to hunch
his wide shoulders. He was so tall the mirror reflected his chest
instead of his face.

Mortrice said, "Two years, right? You was in the hills and shit?"

"Yeah," Darnell said. "But wasn't nobody up there to cut my naps,
so George *been* seen me." They all laughed, and George pointed
Darnell off the chair.

Darnell watched Leon sit down. Before George got older and began
staying in his apartment all the time, he drove a van that said MOBILE
STYLE on the side, and all the fathers on Picasso would push their
sons inside, where they would twitch while George shaved their heads
for summer. He was a former military man, and he wouldn't let them
keep their big naturals.

"Just trim me up, man," Leon said, closing his eyes. George started
happily on the fade at his temples. He loved the short styles everyone
had now.

"Darnell, man, how's Brenda?" Louis asked in that soft voice. Darnell dipped his head, shrugged.

"I guess we gettin married, man," he said, feeling the word hum
on his lips. "She's havin my baby—what can I say?"

"So you a daddy?" Leon said, handing George a bill when he got
up. "Ain't no serious hardship, except your dick belong to somebody
else if you gettin married *too*."

Darnell turned for the door. "Yeah, well, lemme take my dick and
the rest of me where I gotta go."

"You stridin, brotha?" Leon said. "I didn't see the Spider."

"You might not see it again," Darnell said.

"Come on and ride, man," Leon said, and Mortrice pushed open the door for him.

In the Bronco, a head swung around to see who approached. Leon said, "This is Vernon." Louis got behind the wheel, saying, "So you puttin a ring on your thang, huh?"

Leon laughed before Darnell could speak. "Shit, this nigga never was into much hoochie. Just Brenda. But, Darnell, you did Marlene once. Tell me you ain't gon miss that."

Darnell looked out the window. He and Donnie had been with Marlene behind the snack bar at the stadium. Her hands on his elbows, pulling hard; her breasts low and wide, pressing his chest in the wrong place. He'd smelled not Brenda's heated baby powder, the scent he'd always dipped his head near, but a jagged salty smell rising from Marlene's chest. And when he closed his eyes and pulled her hips harder, he saw Brenda's high, round breasts, the tiny nipples. Keep a cherry pit in your mouth, that'll stop your thirst, his father always said, and that was what he felt on the center of his tongue with Brenda, a slippery-hard cherry pit to keep.

But mostly it was Marlene's voice. "Do this," she said. "Do that now." And she kept talking, getting mad when he stopped. "You ain't like your brother," she'd said. "You ain't about nothin. He could teach you somethin."

And somebody's cousin from LA, in Melvin's friend's apartment. Melvin's girlfriend of the minute had brought her for the party. Darnell only remembered the red velvet spread, the wet heat between their legs, the drops of sweat falling from his forehead onto her hair, and her hand brushing them away. Her name was Lonna; she had smoked a lot of weed.

Melvin and Victor, Leon and Marlene, all the older kids from the neighborhood, played hide-and-go-get-it, behind fences and hedges and sheds, and you had to do the nasty with whoever you found. Darnell had lain on top of a few girls, moving his jeans against their shorts, but he was only ten, and he didn't know what to do. And he'd found Brenda behind the bush at Mrs. Dauphine's, crying because she was afraid to kiss whoever would push his way through the pyracantha branches. She was scratched by the thorns, the blood dark on her pale arm, and he thought about apricots. "Don't be scared," he'd told her. "I ain't gon mess with you." But she'd kept shaking, head buried in her arms, until he told her a story about how he and Louis had gone to the city lake to fish and Louis fell into the dirty water trying to touch a goose. Her head hadn't lifted, but she'd turned it sideways to face him, one cheek still resting on her arms and the other shiny with wet.

"He can't say nothin, see, cause he *know* his dick ain't gon stay married." Leon laughed, throwing his head back. "Dicks don't get married. Fingers do."

Darnell shook his head, and Louis spoke from the front seat. "Brenda's not no hoochie, man. Leon don't know." His eyes were half lidded, faraway, and Darnell remembered all the smoke and birds he and Louis had searched for in the riverbottom. Maybe he is trippin, Darnell thought. He's one a Leon's boys, but he don't act the part right.

When they passed the Thunderbird Lodge, a man tried frantically to flag down the Bronco, and Leon raised his chin. "Man, I hate sprung niggas. Wantin pharmaceuticals for free. He ain't got no cash, and he always want me to front him some."

"Strawberries are sprung," the guy named Vernon said. "I love strawberries if they still look good."

"Man, you better be careful," Darnell said. "Strawberries might kill you one day." He remembered glimpsing the lips shrouded gray on the porches, like the smoking rocks in their pipes had pulled blood ember-like from their bodies.

"Darnell don't want to talk about fruit," Leon said. "Cause he only gon get one kinda taste now. Whatever Brenda want to give him."

Darnell smiled. "Man, I ain't cryin. Do you see me cryin?"

"Not yet," Leon said, leaning in the Bronco, the bass booming from the windows, his lips pursed in a big fake kiss.

The women swerved around him again, their smells of perfume and hairspray and waxy lipstick wafting past. She bit her lip when he took her arm.

"Can you walk a ways?" he asked.

"How you think I catch the bus?" she said, staring straight ahead.

Three blocks to the small side street and the apartment building. Before the courtyard was a strip of dirt at the foundation, and Darnell bent quickly to look at the tiny notch-edged leaves of a few weeds.

"Damn," he said. "Filaree, comin up already. Somebody must throw out wash water or somethin, cause we ain't had no rain yet."

She paused, her face blank, and he led her up the stairs. He wanted to hold her hand, but she kept her fingers on the purse strap, and when she stood in the small living room, looking out the window over the courtyard and street, she said nothing.

"You could sing in the shower," he said behind her, putting his hands on her shoulders. "Every day. Cause we can get married." He felt the cold finger trails of fear again, felt them travel up through his fresh-cut hair. The words, coming off his teeth. Her father would have to hear them.

And she turned around and laughed at him. He was seeing her father's face, and she put her hands on her hips. He saw her belly better when she did that, the curve by each knuckle.

"You so sure I want to marry you, just waiting to hear you ask,"she said. "And you think I'ma be happy to be with you for a couple months, and then you take yourself back up to some mountain and wait for fire." Her chest swelled with one long breath and she walked past him into the kitchen.

Darnell heard her heels click on the linoleum. "So what you want to do then?" he said, angry.

"It ain't about what *I* want to do," she whispered. "I already told you that."

"Well, damn, you kinda took me by surprise, you know, when I got that call up at the station and you told me," he said.

"Like I did it on purpose," she said. "All alone."

"No, I ain't . . ."

She said, "I had already paid for fall semester at city college, okay?"

He knew what she meant. "Brenda, we were talkin about movin in together anyway. We been thinkin about it for a while. I been in love with you a long while." He thought she would smile; he stood in the kitchen, close to her, and she didn't move. Her eyes reflected in the sunlight and he could see the flecks of gold inside, floating. Then they wavered with a film of tears, and she pushed past him.

"Nature Boy. Remember everybody called you that? Darnell, I been up to the mountains with you a lot of times, and I'm not a nature girl, okay? You know I'm not into poison oak and bears and all that.

But those fires you used to take me to, and I would sit there and watch you . . ."

The racing edges on a slope, Brenda's legs glowing, dangling from the hood . . . "The wind could shift them," she said, and stopped. "You always told me about backfires and digging breaks, about the animals and the trees. And all I see is fire. You want to leave me. I got enough ways to lose you daily when you here in Rio Seco. Gang-bangers, police. You want to add fire. You want to go back up there and leave me, so I can wait for a phone call."

"Brenda," he said, holding out his hands. "I asked you to marry me. I didn't say it just to scare the shit out of myself."

But she frowned harder. "See?" she said, and his wrists swelled when he tightened his fists. "That's what you want. You love to scare yourself. You can't wait to run off to the next one, hoping it's big like the one I saw in the paper. But I don't have time to be scared extra, baby. I have to go eat lunch now. I have somebody else to feed." She went out the open front door and down the outside stairs slanting below the window.

He lay on the bare mattress on the floor in the front room. He'd bought it from Roscoe, an extra bed. Least Roscoe didn't say, "Thanks for my own money, boy," Darnell thought. He stared at the burn mark on his hand. The scar hadn't been serious enough to swell and rise; it was a flat black line, like Magic Marker drawn across his hidden bones.

Fricke had a serious scar on his shoulder, a rosetted welt of thick tissue. Darnell had never gotten the nerve to ask him where it came from. He felt the callus ridges on his palms with his thumbs, watched the striped shadows of the wrought-iron railing move across the bare window and onto the floor where he lay after the streetlights came on.

At ten he walked back through downtown and up Sixth Avenue to the Westside. His father sat alone in the front room, watching TV. "Where you been?" he said to Darnell. "You eat?"

"Yeah. I left the Spider at the apartment. Clutch won't hardly move." He hadn't told his father about Brenda, just said that he'd gotten the place and the key. "Can I borrow the truck?"

"You goin to see her now?" his father asked. "I thought Batiste worked swing. He's comin home now."

"I gotta see him sometime," Darnell said. Yeah, his girl don't even want me, he can't stand my ass, and I'ma head on up there right now.

His father's truck rumbled hard. He left Pepper Avenue, where the Westside was set off by the few remaining orange groves, passed the fast-food windows and Thunderbird Motel on the edge, and drove through the business buildings in no-man's land. Then a few fortress-like apartments with thick wooden balconies and swirled-rough plaster. Cost eight hundred a month, he thought. The salmon-stuccoed corner mall, and then the wide-set streets of the Ville.

He parked to wait for the black New Yorker. Mr. Batiste's car purred up the driveway, and Darnell knew the man sat there, wondering what the hell Darnell wanted so late. Darnell got out and stood near the arch over the front steps. He leaned against the white stucco.

"It's late," Mr. Batiste said, coming up the stairs. "What you think you lookin for this time a night?"

"I came to see Brenda," Darnell said, and he was tired of her father's thin face always thrown back, the eyes sparkling slits in the yellow porch light. "Who else?"

"See her at a decent hour," her father said. "Tomorrow." His pale face floated near the doorway, and he pulled out his key.

"She has to go to work," Darnell said. "I need to see her tonight."

"This ain't a weekend, speakin a work," Mr. Batiste said. "You lose your job?"

Darnell smiled. "Yeah. I did." He stood close to her father's shirt, smelled the oil and chemicals. "I came to ask her the big question."

But her father's eyebrows didn't even move. His hand on the door-knob, he puffed air through his nose and said, "Huh! Some question." He looked at Darnell. "She says you don't drink or smoke. I can see you ain't got no racin car. So what's your poison?"

"What?" Darnell folded his arms.

"Every nigga got his own poison. Brenda know what yours is, and she still want to marry you, she ain't got the sense God give a goose. And I ain't got a damn thang more to say about it." He left the door open behind him.

Heat rose around Darnell's temples, and he stepped inside the dark front room. Brenda's mother sat in the bright dining room, sewing at the table, like always, and her father took off his watch, slapping it on the counter.

"Miz Batiste," Darnell said.

"Darnell, let me get you some coffee," she said, taking the pins from her mouth. She poured him a cup, like she did every time he came to the house. He sat down, looking at the dark wood table, and said, "She tell you?"

Mr. Batiste went into the hallway. Brenda's mother said, "She ain't tell me nothin today." He took a sip of the coffee. It was so much stronger here than anywhere else—Louisiana coffee, tasting of chocolate and wood and mud, that his GranaLene used to let him smell. Mrs. Batiste rolled a pin in her fingers and said, "You ain't so young, Darnell," in her soft accent, her smooth forehead filling with lines. "People have children early where I come from, have baby fifteen, sixteen. But it only matter if you grown in the *mind*, eh?"

How you tell if your mind is grown? Darnell thought. He sipped the coffee so he wouldn't have to look up or speak. Man, you out your *mind?* guys always said. Out your mind—if a zombie pulled you away. He heard his grandmother's voice in the dark room. The thick sewing needle thrummed harshly, and when he looked up, startled, Mrs. Batiste only said, "Tell you mama I'm workin on the baby things. Go see Brenda."

He knocked and said her name before he pushed open the door. He could hear her brother's radio through the walls. Brenda sat up in bed, holding the sheet in front of her.

He sat on the bed, his back near her legs. "You look different now," he said. Her face was fuller, her jaw wider.

"Yeah," she said. "Dark circles. I'm tired, and I got a lot on my mind." She stared at her window, and he could see her face in the reflection.

"Brenda, I was trippin hard when I was in the Canyons fire. I can't lie. But now I'm done. If you worried about that, I'm done. When I was up there, I was thinkin about you."

"What an original rap," she said, smiling a little. "I was thinkin bout you, baby." She poked out her lips like a guy working hard.

"See, you can't talk smack like that to anyone else but me," he said, laughing. "Come on. You need to marry me."

She put her face near his neck. "No fires?"

He felt her breath. "I don't know—I might get a job in town, right?"

"No," she said, not moving. "You taught me that much. You'd need to get in the fire academy, take the EMT training, all that."

"Yeah," he said. "I know."

"Just say you won't leave," she whispered. "That's the woman's nonoriginal rap. It's what we all say."

"Come on," he whispered. "Just bring your clothes for tomorrow."

On the way to the front door, Brenda held his arm hard, and her mother only smiled, no teeth, not a big smile, just her lips curving tight to carve deep dimples near the corners. He moved his hand to Brenda's back and went toward the doorknob.

He kept hearing Melvin's voice in his head, saying, "Oh, man, it's the best there is. The best." It had been weeks since he'd lain on her with arms along her face, his lips at her neck, and now, in their apartment with nobody to burst in on them, no cold leather bucket seat or borrowed bed, on their own mattress, her belly was a slippery, shifting hill. Not hard, not soft, and he imagined the baby, his son, curling away from him, toward her backbone. But she laced her fingers across his back and pulled him down harder.

HARD WORK

"**Y**OU DON'T LIKE THIS? Go get you a nine-to-five then."

All his life he'd heard that. His father and Roscoe used to say it every time a big job came up, years ago. If a vicious Santa Ana had ripped up a whole stand of eucalyptus, Melvin and Darnell and Louis would have to ride the flatbed for days after school, all weekend. Chopping, carrying the wood, throwing it on the trucks, dodging sawdust at 6 A.M. on a summer Saturday. Melvin, tired from partying the night before, would sit on the curb and bitch.

"Boy, you can't handle this then take your ass somewhere and find you a nine-to-five. When you *grown* and somebody else feedin you. Now get up and move them branches."

Fricke always said it when Scott or Perez complained on the fire line or dressed slow for a night call. "You can always go down to the flatlands and get a nice nine-to-five."

What the hell were you supposed to wear? A white shirt and gray corduroys. Brenda said loafers, reddish brown. She brought them home from the mall. She'd touched his hand this morning when she left. Her fingers were hot. She said being pregnant made the blood circulate faster, and at night when he lay touching her leg and hip, he felt how heated her skin was, imagined the blood racing furiously.

The interview wasn't until ten. He opened the freezer door. Brenda had asked him to make more orange juice. She said the baby needed vitamin C.

The wedge of cake, wrapped in plastic, sat in the center of the almost-empty compartment. Darnell could see the purple flowers. The women had told him to put a piece in the freezer—he and Brenda were supposed to eat it on their first anniversary.

"You suppose to put the whole top layer in there," Brenda's mother had said softly, standing in the kitchen. "When you have one a them big four-layer cakes, you put by that bitty top one, with the people, for a year." She ran her hand along the counter, her face turned away.

Honoré's cake had been one circle. His mother and Brenda's had brought dishes and forks. His mother made fried chicken with lemon pepper, and Brenda's mother made gumbo and rice. When school let out, Darnell's father and Roscoe picked up Sophia, Paula, and Brenda's brother James from high school. No one mentioned Mr. Batiste. The little party stood in the courthouse room, at a table, and a woman did the ceremony. Brenda's mother had stayed up all night to make her a simple silky dress, with tiny pink flowers against the white.

He took out the juice. Honoré's cake. Honoré had always made cakes, as long as Darnell could remember, for birthdays, weddings, just plain hungry weekends. People said, "I feel like a Honoré cake. Go by there and see what he got."

George did haircuts. His mother and Brenda's sewed curtains, dresses—especially wedding and bridesmaid outfits. He licked the frozen juice from his finger. It had hurt Brenda's mother not to sew bridesmaid dresses for a big wedding, not to see the cake and kiss people on the cheeks and clear from long tables the matchbooks printed with "Darnell and Brenda Tucker" and little bells below the date. When it got dark in the apartment, she'd said, "No dollar dance. Y'all didn't get a dance at all."

He and Brenda should have danced the first long, slow song while the wedding guests took their turns, the men handing Brenda fan-folded dollars or fives, the women tucking bills into Darnell's tux pocket. But he'd worn this jacket, the one he had on now.

The mirrored windows of the tall county and city buildings glared, silver sheets in the morning sun. Clerks like Brenda, secretaries and typists and receptionists and cashiers, all women, filing and talking on phones and staring at computer screens and nodding and laughing and looking behind them to see what he put on their desks. The stale air, smoky-sealed windows, the silk plants and wormlike letters crawling on computer screens—too green and fluorescent.

For weeks, he'd watched his hand write on the application papers: Graduated from Fairmount High, one semester Rio Seco City College, one year California Conservation Corps, one year seasonal firefighter for the California Department of Forestry. Didn't take long.

He had flipped through the rolls on the job book, stared at the postings on the walls at the city building, the county, the university, and the city college. Custodian, maintenance, landscape maintenance, warehouse. The personnel rooms were always crowded with other guys: young, old, dressed every which way. He'd lay the paper on the woman's desk, and she'd turn: The application process consists of two parts. . . .

Behind her and the other women were doors that led to the men he hadn't even been called to see, until today. Soft stomach. Glasses and ring and pen. He talked on the phone, too, sent out papers, handed files and instructions to the women, who handed them to Brenda.

He sat in the waiting area, hearing the electronic beeps of the computer letters under the hands of the woman who typed. Brenda would come home to tell him about how long she sat while she input people's information, how the computer lost things. "Nothing yet?" she'd say, her belly rising when she sat deep down in the couch. "Yeah. I input the stuff for two new guys today. Seventy-eight thousand a year, consulting to the county on transportation. Eighty-two a year, executive administrator for county housing. They give out loans to low-income people. They get full benefits. Vision and dental, too."

If she didn't have the benefits, she wouldn't be seeing the doctor once a month. Registering at the hospital. He tried not to shake his leg in the chair. Ain't no need for me to be around. Not unless I'm bringin in some dinero.

He sat in another chair, across from two men. One had the suit and glasses, and the other had the green Park and Recreation uniform. Like a ranger, Darnell thought, and the man spoke.

"We're looking for a landscape maintenance guy for Park and Rec, taking care of property, doing a variety of things. So I see you've been firefighting. You didn't like it?"

"I liked it," Darnell said, folding his hands. Shit. I loved it. "But it's seasonal. I need a permanent job."

"Uh-huh," the suit man said. "Do you have any landscape experience?"

"My father is a tree trimmer," Darnell said. "I've worked with him for a long time. And I've done gardening work, too."

"What's the first step you take to fix a broken sprinkler?" the ranger man asked.

Darnell swallowed. "You have to dig all around the area to get to the pipes." Was that right? Their faces didn't change.

The suit man said, "If you saw a fight on city property, what would you do?"

"Excuse me?" Darnell said.

"What actions would you take?"

"Try to break it up, I guess."

The suit man only smiled. "How would a young man like yourself feel about going to work in, say, a city park in Terracina? Young men in Terracina often don't get along with young men from the Westside. I see by your address that you live on the Westside."

Shit, Darnell thought. I put down Pops' address out of habit. What was the man asking? Gangbanger stuff? "Fine with me," he said, looking straight ahead.

Ranger man's turn. "What are the first steps you have to take to clear a field for fire season, with a city-owned tractor?"

Darnell smiled. "I used bulldozers in the mountains. I guess with a tractor I'd check the field for rocks and gullies that might break the machine."

Ranger man grinned back and nodded slightly. "Okay," he said.

Darnell walked off the elevator. Fifteen minutes, he thought. He headed off the plaza, feeling the loafers tight on his feet.

Strip malls were always the same. The small square spaces like garage doors, the shiny plastic signs. He bought a doughnut from an Oriental woman, who smiled, handing him his change silently. He stood in the tiny parking lot. Always a doughnut shop, always an Oriental man holding trays of glazed. A nail salon—Oriental women, small and pretty with carefully painted eyes and nails, sitting at low

tables holding women's fingers delicately, barely touching. Always a
fast-food place—pizza or subs or hamburgers or Chinese. Men with
skin darker than Fricke's but lighter than Darnell's behind the counter
and grill. Greek, or maybe Middle Eastern. They looked at him
impassively when he bought a soda. Tiny movable letters on the lit-
up menu high on the wall spelled out, at the bottom, "Ibrahim,
Suleymon, Mina—Allah bless and protect us."

And always a liquor store. He knew these men were Korean because
of the squared letters on their posters and newspapers. Korean writing
looked almost exactly like gang graffiti, he thought, buying a candy
bar on his way to the Westside. I'ma borrow a car from somebody
and go out to the cement plant past Terracina.

"If it's a boy, do we have to name it Darnell?"

Her voice pressed deep into his chest, and he had to throw his
head against the pillow and laugh. "Darnell? No, baby, I wouldn't do
that to nobody else," He rubbed his fingers up into her damp hair.
"You think it's a boy?"

Brenda shifted onto her side of the bed. "Women just come up to
me like they been known me all my life, touching me, talking about,
'You carryin that so high, have to be a boy. Look how he's ridin.' All
kinda women, in the store, at lunch, everywhere."

"You didn't say what you think," Darnell said. He was still afraid
to press his palms against her skin, like she kept making him do to
feel the tiny lump kicks. Every time she said, "Hurry up, right here,"
the foot or whatever it was receded back inside her, like it didn't
want any part of him.

"I dream about a boy." Turning to put her face in the pillow, she
whispered, "I dream he has all his teeth and I can't feed him cause
he bites."

Darnell lay still, knowing he was hard against her thigh, trying not
to see her tightened nipples in the light, the way he used to, trying
not to taste them. When they lay on their sides, so the baby wouldn't
press against her heart and lungs, he could barely fit himself inside
her, and if he dipped his head to her breasts, she pushed at his
forehead, saying, "They're too sore."

He was silent for a long time, not wanting to move toward her or
away, and when he thought she was asleep, he put his arms behind

his head. "We could name it Darnella if it's a girl," she said suddenly.

"What? You crazy," he said. "You still thinkin about that?"

"Yeah. Darnella. There's a lady at work named Waltrina. After her father. And another lady named Johnetta."

"Just because their daddies had big heads don't mean I'm a fool." He had to laugh. "Waltrina?"

"One of the supervisors in Benefits, an older white lady from Kansas. She has pictures of her grandkids on her desk." She stared up at the ceiling, and then looked at him. "My dad didn't name James after him because he said Etienne was too French. He said it would sound wrong in California."

Darnell said, "I always thought your dad's name was sharp. It's different." He slid one arm under her pillow and pulled her closer. "You like your dad's name? Maybe he won't be permanently pissed at me if we name the baby for him." A soon as he said it, he knew it was a mistake. Her eyes shone brighter and she didn't make a sound, but her shoulders shook until he held her still.

"I don't miss him," she said. "I miss my mom. Sometimes when she's sewing stuff for the baby, she calls me and says we have to get a good crib, not a cheap one. Her voice gets funny and we hang up." Darnell felt the wet on his chest, felt sweat where her belly touched his ribs.

"Everybody else seen them ads, too," his father said. "Come on."

It had rained hard for two days, and Darnell spent the time playing dominoes with Roscoe and looking through the classifieds. His father was driving him to San Bernardino, where a new Smith's Food King was opening in a month. The ad said "All positions."

The sun was hot and hard already, the clouds gone, and the mud had quickly settled in the few puddles, leaving clear water. Crows gathered in the vacant lots to drink, and broken glass glittered, washed clean. Darnell smelled the watery vapor drying fast. Five inches of rain before you torch trails. Fricke was laughing at him. "That was just a trace, home boy. Drought piss."

"Look at that," his father said, cutting through the valley to San Bernardino. "Snow level's down to about three thousand feet." The mountain range was a ridge of dark purple with bleach-pure snow in a perfectly iced line.

"I'ma have to get a good vehicle if I get a slave out here," Darnell said.

"Don't get too happy," his father said. The crowd was already gathered at the industrial park. Shit, Darnell thought, seeing the mass of heads in the parking lot, the long line straight up the sidewalk. Brothers in dark knit caps, white guys with baseball hats, Chicano guys with black hair shiny as helmets.

"Just go on and I'll catch a ride with somebody," he told his father, but his father shook his head.

"Too wet to work today," he said. "I'll get some coffee and wait."

Darnell stood in the line, listening to the short sentences of people just meeting, hearing the long mumbles of friends who'd come to apply together. He stared at the palm trees, skinny and new, just planted in this fresh business park. Two guys behind him were meat cutters. He heard people talking about cashier experience, box boy, bakery, deli counter. When he got to the women inside, he filled out his application quickly, checking every box under Position Desired.

In the truck, he had to say something to break the quiet. "Dudes behind me were meat cutters. Drive all over LA, wherever they get sent."

"Then they ain't union," his father said. "Nobody's union no more. But butchers still make fourteen, fifteen an hour." He gripped the wheel. "Kaiser Steel used to pay that. And Goodyear." Darnell remembered the big smokestacks at Kaiser when they used to puff white clouds. He'd thought they were fire smoke a few times when he was small. "Brenda's daddy makes them kinda wages at Royal," his father went on. "One a the last places. And they layin off nonunion, too."

"I can't get in no union," Darnell muttered, and his father raised his chin to frown at him.

"You feelin sorry for yourself already? Been lookin two months?" Darnell tried to say something, but his father cut him off. "You see Floyd King layin cement, boy?"

"No," Darnell said.

"And when we came from Oklahoma, he was a cement-layin fool. Made benches, sidewalks, everything. He tried to get in the union back in the sixties. They let colored work, all right, but then they lay you off just before you get your hours required. Every time."

"Yeah, Pops. I know the story." Darnell looked at the freeway. His father had turned off an early exit and was heading up a canyon road into the foothills. "You lost?"

"Don't get smart, boy." The truck headed slow up past the already-bristling shoots of grass after the rain. "You know, I ain't seen the snow on a clear day like this for a long time. I hardly ever come out this way. Look up there—Cajon Pass, all the way to the desert."

Darnell saw the mountains, the strip of freeway cutting through. "Cold up there today," he said.

His father was still watching the hills. "Me and your mother came down that way, when we drove out here from Oklahoma. We could see the whole valley laid out, all the way to Rio Seco. Orange groves, lemon, grapefruit." He leaned out the window to spit, and his voice was lost for a minute. "And jobs all over. Shoot, we bought that house on Picasso, half the men on the block worked at Goodyear. The other half was in the Air Force."

"Memory lane ain't gon help me," Darnell said, folding his arms hard. "Hey, I'm not tryin to disrespect you, Pops. I'm just tellin you."

His father's lips pulled tight over his teeth. "You better listen. I came out here, and your mother was pregnant with Melvin."

"You didn't stay at Goodyear. Mama said you quit cause you didn't like it." Darnell couldn't meet his father's eyes.

"I wanted to be outside," his father said, though, his voice softer. "Man, I used to hunt in Oklahoma. Came out here, went up in the mountains, wasn't no game I could get. All government land."

Darnell remembered the rabbits and snakes fleeing the fires, and he said, "I know that. I worked that land, remember?"

His father's jaw worked, pulsed, near his ear. "You better work for yourself. Ain't no good jobs now. Memory lane done closed down, okay? You got a baby comin." When Darnell opened his mouth, his father raised a hand. "You first told me about this firefighter thing in high school, about the college classes and the academy you'd have to get in, and I thought it might work. But you done made your choice now, and you got people to feed. I was thinkin, maybe when you get a vehicle, we can go in on a mower and edger and you try to get some yards."

"Like Snooter and Nacho, huh?" Darnell smiled. "I don't want to be out there cuttin grass all summer in the smog."

"Better than starvin all summer," his father said, starting the engine. "Does Brenda get time off with the baby?"

Darnell breathed hard. "Six weeks, I think."

"Let me tell you somethin from experience. You was a baby, hard as it is to remember." His father paused. "You don't want to be a man at home all the time with a mother and her new baby. You'll be in the way. You'll be about as useful as a third tit."

Darnell laughed. "Great. I feel useless now."

His father looked down the steep road. "When you got kids, only thing useful is money."

"How'd you get so good at this?" Brenda said. "I thought guys didn't know how to do this. Your father sure doesn't."

Darnell gave her more of the spaghetti and garlic bread. "The mountains, remember? We had to cook for ourselves." He stared at his plate. Yeah, seem like ten years ago, he thought. Ho of the day. Fricke makin curry and Chinese. Scott puttin a whole jar of jalapeños in the Sloppy Joes, till even Perez was cryin. He wondered if they had jobs. Fricke's gotta call me back in April. Baby's due in April.

He washed the dishes, too, and sat next to her on the couch. "I didn't get the call," he said. "I got the letter."

He showed her the paper. "We have reviewed your application. . . ." Brenda laid it on the coffee table. "I knew," she said. "Cause after you told me about the questions, I asked Waltrina Stovall. Her cousin works in Park and Rec. She said that one question, about the fight, was cause the city's liable." She bit her lip. "They're liable if anything happens."

Darnell nodded, staring at the TV. "I ain't liable to find out, right?"

"We just have to be patient, Darnell," she said. "I'm not in a hurry. I mean, we're living."

"We're livin small," he said, remembering Leon.

After a while, she fell asleep on the couch, with her head in his lap.

Demetrius Thompson was silent when they went up and down the rows. Most of the cars out by the riverbottom were ancient, and Darnell used to poke around here when his father was getting a truck fixed. When he was small, he'd touched the heavy chrome on the '57 Chevy too smashed for even a lowrider to love; he'd run his finger over the rust patterns on the ugly Pintos and Pacers. If a car made it to this lot, none of the men who hung around had spoken for it, no one had asked the Thompsons to keep an eye out for it, and it would probably never move again.

Darnell said, "You ain't got much new."

Walking back to the barn, Demetrius said, "No shit. The cops don't bring their tows here no more; they take em to Abella's."

In the shade near the sawhorses, Darnell said, "You gon find a cheap two-door for me, man, somethin with a straight-six, just for transportation? Like a Nova."

"Dude brought in a nice deuce-and-a-quarter last week," Kickstand said.

"I ain't got the cash for no Buick like that," Darnell said.

"You done fightin fires? Why you ain't working with your pops?" Demetrius asked.

Darnell squatted near the stone wall. "My pops and Roscoe usually get just enough jobs to make it themselves, unless they get some big removal calls. I guess I'ma do one with Pops next week."

"You don't want a truck?" Demetrius went on. "You can't do no pickup jobs or nothin in a Nova."

"Yeah, but I need some room for a car seat." He raised his chin. But nobody made fun of him this time. "Don't your dad still have that old El Camino, the one he used to bring in here?" Kickstand said. He rested his foot on an old battery, and his bandanna was tight around his forehead.

"Yeah, but he blew the head and cracked the block big time," Darnell said. "You know that was a long time ago."

"Shit, that got enough room for your woman. Bring it in here, and I'll drop a new engine for you. Six hundred."

Darnell rubbed his knees. He and Sophia and Paula used to fit on the bench seat of the El Camino when they were small; his father kept chain saws and axes in the back, and they would slide back and forth, scratchy metal on metal. His father and Roscoe had first started the tree-trimming business back then, and soon they needed a bigger truck to haul all the branches and wood.

On the walk back through the olive groves, he touched the trunk of one wild tobacco tree sprouting from a ditchbank. Trimming trees with his father. He wondered how his father would divide the jobs if business was slow. Uh-uh, I can't see it. Man, I wouldn't be able to do anything right anyway. Pops used to holler at me steady ballistic, just outta habit, and Roscoe was the same with Louis. He thought of Louis, rolling with Leon. Roscoe had wanted Louis to play ball, even when Louis hated every free throw he took in the long driveway. What does Pops want me to do?

At Jackson Park, a big crowd surrounded the smoking trash barrel, and he saw Ronnie Hudson. Then Victor Smalls turned around, lifted his chin. "What it is? You a daddy yet, brothaman?"

"Not yet," Darnell answered. "Almost."

Victor laughed. "Ain't no such thing as almost. You feedin the kid now."

"No, I ain't," Darnell said, smearing a line of broken glass from the sidewalk with his shoe. "Brenda is."

Ronnie said, "You lookin, too? I was fittin to ax *you* if your pops had any big jobs comin up. He don't need no help?"

Victor said, "Floyd King had a big construction haul goin."

"I ain't heard," Darnell said. A car with a loud muffler pulled up, and two men got out. One was thin, walking slow and careful up to the curb; his eyes lifted blankly toward Darnell, and his small goatee pointed stiff from his chin.

"Brother Lobo!" Darnell called. "You still here."

"Darnell Tucker. The boy who so loved fire he was willing to risk his only begotten butt every time he saw one." Brother Lobo sat at the domino table.

He had been their Black History teacher back in junior high, and his classroom was where Darnell, Nacho, Louis, and the others had gathered to draw on the blackboard and insult each other while Mr. Green, as he was known to everyone else, told them stories and read passages from his huge book collection. But he was legally blind, almost sightless in one eye, and one of the newer, louder teachers. He was laid off when the school district decided that in the eighties a separate Black History class wasn't really necessary.

Brother Lobo squinted at the dominoes and prepared for his performance. Darnell held his smile tight when each of the seven bones almost touched the eyelashes, and then Lobo slammed down the double six. The man who had driven him there, Mr. Talbert, slammed down the six-three and yelled, "Fitteen! You got it over with."

"Darnell," Brother Lobo said, shifting the bones in his palms. He took his time, looking up for a second in the circle of shouted conversation. "How is your fire? Has it been contained, partially or fully? Those are the right terms?"

Darnell said, "Fire's out. I'm home."

Brother Lobo slapped down his domino. "The shy Brenda?"

"Still workin downtown at the county," Darnell said. He stopped, but Victor was silent.

"I don't know how you drink that weird shit," Mr. Talbert said, looking at the red can on the sidewalk by Lobo's foot.

"Dr Pepper isn't weird," Lobo said. "People all over the South drink it religiously."

"You from the South?" Victor said.

"No. I have been to the South," Brother Lobo said. He slammed a domino so hard the table shook, and said, "Twenty! Please!"

"Where you from?" Victor pressed.

"A place where I am not now," Lobo said, turning to squint at them. Then he drew his face back down to the table and the snaking line of dominoes.

Darnell leaned against one of the abandoned couches near the pepper tree, feeling wispy branches brush his neck. No More, Louisiana—where Brenda's daddy was from. "Place so little you never find it," was what his GranaLene always answered.

A place where I am not now. Darnell listened to the shouting, heard more car doors slam. The sun was bright on his eyelids. Whenever someone asked his brother, Melvin, "Where you stay now, man?" he would always smile small and answer, "Not here."

She was vacuuming, not singing but muttering along with the radio, not hearing him, and when the door slammed, she shook.

"Only me," he said to her startled face. "Why you look like that?"

"Yeah, I'm both," she said angrily. "So?"

He'd meant her twisted-tight forehead and her frown. "Huh?"

"Barefoot. Pregnant. Mama always told me to vacuum barefoot so I can feel the dirt I missed. The dirt you can't even see." She looked down at the linoleum near the counter.

"So your mama ain't comin over," he said.

"She taught me to clean like that cause my father hates dirt. He found a piece of rice in a corner one time, and when he still saw it the next day, he cussed her out."

Darnell put his arms around her, coming from the side because she hated him to feel how big she was now. She kept saying she was huge, and his mother kept saying it was because she had started out so skinny and the baby knew what it needed. "I ain't worried about no dirt," he said.

"And I ain't worried about you," Brenda snapped. "I been vac-uuming this way since I was six, okay?" She turned the machine back on and he got out of her way. He sat on the couch to wait.

When she was finished, she stood in front of him. "When you came to walk me home, you didn't see that woman ahead of us, huh?" she said. "Blonde, about forty. She looks like Vanna White. She's a su-pervisor in Accounting, and she decided she wanted a baby. She went to a sperm bank in San Diego, and she's due before me. I hear the other ladies talking to her, and she says it's, like, some life-style choice or something like that. Me? Yesterday these two old ladies saw me come out of the county building, I had to run something over to Health, and one of em said, 'What a shame.' Like I'm deaf. See, I'ma be a welfare mama no matter what I do, what I look like." She stopped, walked to the window. "Remember when we were in school, if I wore nice clothes, people from the Westside talked about me. And if I didn't, my daddy got mad."

"You ain't livin with your daddy" was all Darnell could think to say. He pulled her toward the couch gently. "Didn't you tell them old ladies your wedding ring didn't come from no gumball machine? You mean I paid money for it and you think nobody sees it? Damn." He touched her chin, grinning.

Brenda bit her lips and blinked, and then she said, "Okay. I quit."

Darnell said, "We're out of milk again, so I'm fixin to go to the store. Now don't you want me to bring back some, what, pickles and pistachios or somethin?"

She shook her head. "Just bring back a clock that goes fast-forward."

"What?"

"Five more weeks," she said. "So it'll be over." She leaned back on the couch finally, her feet up, the huge round belly all the way up under her breasts; he'd seen her pushing baby powder inside the deep creases.

He couldn't stand to sit there every night, no talk about what somebody said at work or that damn phone again, nothing like that coming out of his mouth, so he tried to have something to buy all the time, little treats for her. He walked the few blocks to the store downtown. Honeycomb. So far, that cereal was the only thing she really craved. He'd tried a couple, dry, the way she snacked on them, and he stared at the holes in the flower-edged shape. It burst into chalky-sweet powder between his teeth, and he looked at the back of the box. How did they make these? Flour, sugar, all that—but what kind of machine made the shape, the holes?

When he was alone, it was all he could think of now. A job. He saw the shopping carts abandoned on the sidewalk beside him, at awkward angles to each other like grazing cows under the streetlights. He pushed two of them together, felt the metal heavy and cold. Who made shopping carts, what kind of machine, in what factory? He passed a mailbox, the old cast-iron kind downtown, and he went back to see. BRIDGEPORT CASTING COMPANY—BRIDGEPORT, CONN. said the raised letters. The pitted iron was thick as his mother's frying pan. Did they pour the metal into molds?

A few men were pushing cans and forty-ounce bottles into the recycling machines, but since he was walking, they only glanced at him. They figured he didn't have spare change. He thought of something he'd heard: No such thing as *spare* change, brothaman. I *needs* my change. Get you a spare job.

He wandered the aisles, staring at packages, picking them up to look at the backs. Glasses, spatulas, cereal boxes, egg whisks. Pampers. Toilet paper. Green Giant peas. Popsicles from Mexico. In the back of the store, the meat was red, flecked with fat, cases stocked full this time of night. He knew who cut that up. Produce section— a guy sprayed the broccoli, lettuce, carrots. Farmers owned the farms, the older white men with caps and big belts he'd always seen when his father took him out to roadside stands. Mexicans weeded and picked, moving up and down the rows with bandannas trailing curtainlike over their shoulders, held in place by hats. His father brought cases of strawberries back for several of the women on Picasso Street.

The cashier pulled the milk carton over the glass square, then the

Honeycomb box. Her hair was brown, blown into a high wall of bangs. Darnell paid her, felt the cold milk through the bag. Yeah, Smith's never called, he thought, going out the door. Surprise, surprise. He looked at the blank, raw outlines on the wall by the recycling machines. The phones were gone. Drug dealers had been camped out, making calls, and the company had taken down the booths. Ring-ring, Darnell thought.

He left her buried in the blankets when the sky turned gray. Bending to her neck, he said, "I'm goin to work."

With his father, he waited for Roscoe in the driveway. Darnell saw the men leaving Picasso as the sun edged out: Floyd King with Nacho and Snooter, in their trucks; The Bug Doctor (ALL MY PATIENTS DIE) from down the street; Mr. Albert in his roofing truck with his hot-tar trailer. "Wake up, boy," his father said, and Roscoe's Apache roared around the corner.

All the way past the new tracts, the few orange groves left between the walled-in acres of houses, Darnell could see the gradual slope and then the steep hills of Grayglen. They wound into the older, narrow streets of old-money Grayglen then, and the thick, ancient eucalyptus and tall cypress cast instant dark over the asphalt. The houses were tucked way back on their land, surrounded by trees, and Darnell said, "Plenty of game up here, Pops. Cats, dogs, gerbils."

His father didn't smile. "Yeah. One rich lady up here has llamas."

This house was on a slope, and the two massive carob trees had raised the lawn, buckled the sidewalk over and over, Darnell could tell. The new cement, which the city couldn't have poured more than two years ago, was already warped. His father watched Roscoe's truck labor up the narrow street, and he said, "These trees committed the cardinal sin—they messed up the plumbing."

Carob roots were notorious all over Rio Seco for wrecking sewer lines and sprinkler systems. Darnell's father always said carob trees kept him from going hungry—the branches, full of heavy brown pods, needed trimming, and eventually people got tired of the whole tree.

They took chain saws to the thick branches, the dust flying, and then while Darnell cut and loaded wood on the truck, his father and Roscoe started on the trunks. Showers of chips and splinters and shavings almost hid them, and then the trees fell the right way, on the lawn. The already-cut branches had left a scarred, short trunk, and Darnell went to work on the logs.

They rested in the shade of the huge hedge at the edge of the property. "Them stumps gon be hell," his father said.

"After all this drought," Roscoe said, rubbing his chin, staring at the massive circles of wood. "We should start soaking the ground now."

Darnell went toward the house to look for the hose. It was one of those wood-and-glass contemporary types, with huge windows everywhere. He saw a figure move from the picture window right in front, and the woman opened the door quickly to step out. "Did you need something?" she asked.

"Just the hose," Darnell said, standing still. They didn't like for you to move around once they were right there. His father had taught him that long ago, when he was ten and just starting to come along on jobs.

"I'll get it," she said, going behind a bush near the house where the hose was coiled neatly. He wondered where her husband worked. She was pretty young, maybe in her thirties, with long brown hair pulled back into one of those ruffly circles.

"I couldn't believe just the three of you could do all that," she said, shading her eyes with her hand. Darnell looked at the trees. She was one of the kind who stood at the windows and watched every move you made; if you looked right at her, she'd step back and pretend to be doing something else. "Do you need a drink?" she said, looking at the hose in Darnell's hand.

"No, we have to soak the ground to pull out the stumps," he said, and she frowned slightly.

"You don't have one of those machines, the ones that chew everything up? I've seen the city use them."

Yeah, stumpers, Darnell thought. Cost much ducats—more than two trucks. "No, ma'am," he said. "We'll pull the whole stump out and fill in the hole."

She saw Roscoe pulling chains out of the Apache, and she brought her hand to her mouth. "Oh, God, I hope the truck doesn't tear up the yard. But I guess the other machine leaves wood chips all over. What a mess." She was almost whispering. "Last year my husband hired two Samoans to trim those, and they brought their families, I mean, the women sat right on the lawn to watch, the kids played in the branches. It was terrifying."

Darnell stood awkwardly. Let me get in a plug or Pops will be hot. "Well, we can do all the trees for you next time," he said, pulling at the hose.

Soaking, digging for another day, chopping at roots and mud, and then they fit the chains around the stumps. The Apache shuddered, a huge dinosaur with flat nose and metal teeth, the wheels digging hard into the dirt to rip out the thick stumps, their roots grabbing clumps of earth in desperation and then heaving out to stiffen in the sun.

"Oh, my God," the woman said, holding her checkbook away from her body like a dripping cloth. "My husband was supposed to leave me new checks." Her cheeks swelled up toward her eyes.

Roscoe said, "That's no problem, ma'am, we'll pick up the check tomorrow."

In the truck, Darnell's father said, "What does she do all day? He gotta order new checks?"

Darnell cracked the covers of mud on his knuckles, tapped his mud-rounded boot soles on the floorboard. "Damn! I need this hoop-tie!" He stared at the thick trees. "Brenda can't keep walkin to work."

Her feet were swollen so her ankles lined up straight with her narrow calves. She winced when the baby kicked. He'd walk into the bedroom, her back to him, and stare at her body quilted with fat. She kept herself covered all the time now, and he saw the bulges at her sides, where her back used to narrow and curve to her behind; the round pillows erased her whole silhouette, even from the rear.

She whirled around and said, "Don't stare. Okay?"

"Brenda," he said, "I just look at you cause I miss you." He sat on the bed, but he couldn't say it: Cause it ain't no need for me to be here, takin up space, hangin around. And I can't even make love.

"I feel bad enough that we can't do it anymore," she said, starting to cry, and he let her wet his neck, his shirt. Her breasts were wide, hard-pressing his chest, and he couldn't even touch them. Yeah, he thought, my love life ain't what I thought it would be. Got this big bed, all this room, and can't even get close to her. The guys at the fire station used to talk all that yang. Scott always said, "Who gives a shit about her brain? Show me her tits." Fricke would shake his head. And they'd check me out. "Yeah, black guys are studly; they get it all the time," Scott said. Neither of us fittin the form right now, huh, baby? he wanted to say to Brenda, but he was silent. Wait, I'm fittin one form. The brotha with no job.

Gasanova gave him a ride. "You got time to cruise to Grayglen?" Darnell asked when Gas stopped on Picasso.

"Yeah, homey, I don't have to be at the Inn till lunch crowd." Gasanova drove up the commuter road everyone used to come out of the hills and down to Rio Seco. He bobbed his back against the seat with the bass line, cruising slow. "That's right, I'm *boomin*," he said, smiling into the rearview mirror at the line of cars forming behind him. "Got my Alpines blastin, and I *love* to drive the speed limit in front of you."

Darnell laughed. The cars on this street, the men in Beemers and Broncos rushing to work, rushing home, always roared past as soon as they could. He saw the flash of a face turned toward them.

"Oh, that's right, I'm wearin a hat," Gas said. "And I'm boomin— wait, did you see *Colors* and did you read about Crips and Bloods? What color was that hat—red or blue? Oh, see, I'm wearin the *Angels* hat, red and blue. What is this? He's not bangin or slangin? Just a Westside nigga, plain boomin?"

Darnell said, "You love to run your mouth."

"Man, I can ID you guys, too," Gas went on. "There go a Grayglen mommy—minivan, blonde, she just dropped off the kids and now she goin to aerobics. Lunch. Don't be late!" he called to the van.

His speakers pounded even louder in the silence of the yard, with the two wet-raw holes in the grass. The woman said, "I'm so sorry," peering over his shoulder at the truck.

"Thanks," Darnell said, and in the truck, he waved the check. "This brotha's goin mobile, man! I'ma get me the El Camino tomorrow!"

Gas shook his head. "Boring vehicle, man. But you a boring brotha now."

Darnell laced his hands behind his head. "Long as Brenda don't think so, I'm set," he said.

He spent a few hours cleaning the cab, taking a toothbrush to the grimy seats and dashboard, and he brought home the car seat Brenda had picked out at Kmart. She was still at work; he stared at the car seat beside him, like a tiny recliner for an old man, leaning cool and padded.

He was hosing down the ridged metal bed when Louis came into the apartment courtyard. Louis's face was blank and careful, his eyes fixed on the spray of water and the channels sliding off the dropped gate, but Darnell saw the flat drops of sweat nearly joined at Louis's hairline.

"You look thirsty, brothaman," Darnell said casually. "You stridin?"

Louis nodded, raising his eyes for a moment. "Got a hooptie now, huh?" he said softly. "I heard the Spider got retired." He passed behind Darnell to sit on the pebbled bottom stair, his long fingers gripping the rail. Darnell checked the street for Leon, but Louis said, "Just me, man."

"You need a soda?" Darnell said, turning off the hose.

"Yeah," Louis said. "But I need a ride."

Darnell brought two cans downstairs with him, and when Louis stood, his face was level with the balcony. He looked up at the door Darnell had closed. "Brenda still at work?" he asked.

"I gotta pick her up in a couple hours," Darnell said, getting into the El Camino. He smelled the hot Armor-All on the dashboard. Louis was silent when he started the engine, and Darnell thought, What I'm supposed to ask him? I ain't seen him in all this time—ask him how's business with Leon?

"Where you goin?" he asked at the corner.

"The riverbottom," Louis said, looking straight at Darnell then. "By the pecans."

Darnell felt the warmth rise in his throat, the hard yellow shine on the polished windshield against his eyelids. The pecan grove was Louis's secret place, where the riverbottom met the trees and hundreds of birds sheltered in the branches. Louis had always wandered there, and even when the other boys laughed, he told Darnell about the herons stalking irrigation ditches, the crows and hawks and owls in the groves. Darnell turned toward Pepper Avenue, and Louis said, "I can't walk now—cause dudes seen me with Leon and they wanna act hard."

"I heard you ridin with him," Darnell said. He stopped.

Louis leaned back and lifted his knees slightly. "I hang out. I crash on his couch sometimes, eat over there."

"What happened with school?"

"I didn't feel like playin ball. So they said, 'Then you don't feel like goin to school.'" Louis kept his eyes on the glass. "You ain't in the hills."

"I felt like workin. But they felt like cuttin the funds." Darnell drove toward Treetown, listening to the engine, and when he saw the olive groves, he said, "Why you didn't get a ride with Leon?"

Louis breathed in hard; his nostrils widened, and the long fingers flexed on his leg. "His boy gets on my nerves. Vernon. He from LA, and always talkin yang about Rio Seco fulla country niggas, nothin to do." He paused. "He always sayin 'Birdman.' Always sayin it, like he think it's funny."

Darnell drove slowly past the orange trees heavy with fruit, then down the long, unmarked sandy road. "Leon the one started callin you that, way back when," he said, when he reached the dead end. Across the field of fading wild oats was the pecan grove.

He walked beside Louis along the faint-marked trail; no one had been through here for a while. The pecans came ripe in fall. Louis was silent, and Darnell could hear their knees shake the seedheads on the oats. "Leon and them the ones started callin you Nature Boy," Louis said suddenly, from behind him, and then they came out into the clearing.

"Mountain Man," Darnell said. "Leon always talked smack."

"Leon don't want to see no nature," Louis said, moving fast over the soft crushed leaves and pecan shells. "Leon want green long as it got dead presidents on it." He didn't smile, but Darnell nudged his elbow when he passed him to enter the grove.

"But Leon could talk his way outta anything," Darnell said, grinning. "And you couldn't." He stood, looking up into the curve-leafed branches, seeing the burst brown stars left behind by the pecans. They'd only ridden here once or twice, all of them together, because Donnie and Leon liked to stay closer to Treetown or the Westside. They would holler and argue, and Louis had to come here on his own. Darnell had had to find the sources of rising smoke alone, too. "Don't nobody care about no damn fire," Leon would say, astride his bike, and Donnie would yell, "And don't nobody want to ride down there and look at birds. Both y'all stupid."

The branches were silent. No crows. Darnell watched Louis pace around in the far end of the grove, then work his way closer. It was four o'clock, and the sky was still gold through the tree trunks. Darnell knew that when the air turned silver with early evening the flock of crows would start to pass over Rio Seco, over the Westside, on their way to sleep in the riverbottom, usually here in the grove. Louis had told him a hundred times, while they were clearing the last of the trimmings their fathers had left in someone's yard, while the chain saws snarled off the final branches, where the crows went.

"You still watchin them?" he asked Louis now. Louis had slid his back down a pecan trunk, and his legs were bent, his long feet flat over the bent grass. He nodded, and in the tree's shadow, his light skin looked almost gray. "Big as you are and them birds don't see you?" Darnell said, without thinking.

Louis drew one side of his mouth up hard and said, "Shit. All anybody see is big. Tall." He breathed hard, stilled his face again. "Like a tree, okay? If you don't move. Hummingbird pecked on my ring one time." Darnell stared at the fingers splayed on Louis's knees, at the red-stoned class ring Roscoe had bought. "Khaki," Louis murmured. "You see my khakis? Birdwatchers wear khakis, jackets and all that shit. Bangers wear khakis, right? My boxers ain't showin." He looked up at Darnell. "You still chasin fires?"

Darnell buried his thumbnails in his palms; the smell of the warm grass and drying stems rose around him. "I ain't a free man like you, okay? I can't cruise around all day. I didn't quit—" He stopped. "Neither of us doin what we—"

"What we supposed to be doin?" Louis said. His face was grayer, darker now, in the shade. "Ain't no supposed-to for you, man. You ain't six-seven. You ain't 'refusin to fulfill your talent' every time some asshole seen your picture in the paper stop you on the street." Louis stopped, breathing hard. "It's about that time, homey. You didn't never like all that noise."

Darnell knew he was talking about the flapping and hoarse cries that filled the branches when the flock descended on the grove. When people came to pick pecans, the crows shouted and dipped.

"I didn't like fire, neither," Louis said. "Scared the shit out of me, man, that one time you showed me." He looked away, toward the riverbottom where the water was hidden by the wide bank covered with brush and cane and cottonwoods. "I heard you was in a helicopter, up in the mountains," he said. "Nacho told me."

Darnell tried to remember the Helitorch, to explain the only time he'd been in it. He'd been entranced by the liquid Alumagel, the fire loops, and the flight was lost to him—just the smell of damp air and chemicals and Fricke's voice. He said, "I don't think it was like a bird."

Louis only nodded, and Darnell turned to go back along the trail through the field.

Brenda came slowly up the stairs after him, holding the rail hard, and Darnell turned at the top to watch her. Louis used to have a serious crush on her, he remembered. Brenda never talked yang to him about the birds; she always listened to him with her eyes steady, and her smile was wide, all her teeth showing, when she watched him play ball. Darnell would sit in the gym, pressed against her shoulder, jealous for a few minutes, but after the games, Brenda would watch Roscoe talking to Louis, and she'd say, "Nobody pays attention to him. Just basketball. I feel sorry for him."

Darnell didn't tell her about the pecan grove, about where Louis slept at Leon's. He only said, "I gave Louis a ride today. He's doin okay."

She sat heavily on the couch and took off her shoes. "I'm glad he didn't see me this big. I don't like anybody seeing me like this. When I used to watch women on the street, and they walked all swayback, I'd be thinking, No, uh-uh, I'm never gonna look like *that*."

He said, "I'm seein you that big." He leaned against the counter, watching her press fingers into her ankles.

"You the reason I'm this big," she said. "And this hungry."

After dinner, Brenda's mother came with baby clothes, just appeared at the door with her arms around two bags, and then they sat in the living room like they'd seen each other only yesterday. Darnell knew her father was at work, but all Mrs. Batiste said was, "I ain't studyin him," and she folded T-shirts small as Kleenex squares.

Darnell went to the bathroom to splash water on his face. Eighty degrees already on March 3rd—fire season gotta be hella early again this year, he thought, looking at the tiny opaque window above the shower. That's how I'm still cuttin up the year. Hot and bone dry— no Helitorch this year. He remembered the paler grass today in the clearing. Fricke know who's gettin called back by now. I got the hooptie—I could ride up there and see.

He dried his face. No news is good news, right. Maybe. I ain't goin up the mountain until I got a steady-freddy. I'm not goin up there and say I'm still lookin.

The steady murmur of their voices came through the door. Brenda ain't said much for days, but she got a lot to say to her mama. I don't— No, Miz Batiste, I still don't have a job. I drive around and look at buildings and lettuce and cans, just trip out.

In the living room, he said, "I'll be right back."

The buildings downtown glared with the low sun. The phone booth was hot and full of cigarette butts. Fricke answered. "Forty-two." Darnell heard the cowboy guitars playing. "Hello? Yeah?" Fricke hung up.

Brenda settled back in the car seat on Saturday afternoon. "You want to go to the lake? It's so nice out. Maybe we could go to the movies."

"I have to bleed the brakes first, okay?" Darnell said.

She smiled. "What, this car is diseased, too?"

"Why you always talkin smack about my hoopties?" He loved to see her front teeth when she let her whole face open up and laugh.

"You were always bleeding the brakes on the Spider," she said. "Just hurry up and give this one a whole transfusion." Then she was quiet until they pulled into his father's driveway. "Everybody on the Westside is nosy, and when they see my stomach, I'ma have to hear about what I need to be eating, and why ain't I bigger than this, and what you fittin to name that boy you carryin?"

Darnell put his lips under her ear and smelled the baby powder below her neck. "Come on, don't try to be evil, cause you ain't good at it. I'll only take an hour, and Mama's in there cookin. Let her get excited, huh? She ain't gon say nothin." Brenda opened her eyes a little wider and pushed him out his door.

Sophia and Paula were eating fish and cornbread, and they looked up happily at Brenda. Before Darnell could say anything, Sophia crowed, "My friend Detrice is in love with your brother."

Brenda smiled. "Yeah, James is a junior now, and all you little freshman girls think he somethin, huh?"

Darnell reached over Paula's shoulder for cornbread. "I feel sorry for the brothas at Fairmount with both y'all there now. Double-barrel mouth, and I know how rough it is."

His mother came out of the kitchen, a plate of fried snapper in her hands. "Brenda," she said, smiling. "Come on get you some lunch."

She didn't say anything about eating for two. Darnell put his arm around her shoulders, so soft after Brenda's small bones, and said, "Miz Batiste told me she sewin baby stuff. Now you have to call her up and argue about what *you* gon make."

His mother put a clean plate in front of Brenda and leaned against the wall. Her housecoat was dark blue velveteen, the kind she'd sewed for herself since Darnell was small, first tracing the nap and hearing that word: velveteen. Her skin was coppery against the Chinese collar; her earrings, which she put on first thing in the morning, swayed gold against her neck. "Can't have too many baby clothes," she said, and Darnell saw her blink and look out the window.

You gotta take good care of her. That was what his mother had said that first morning he was off the mountain, when she'd seen his feet on the couch. She flicked his soles and laughed, but when he told her about the baby, she'd pressed her mouth tight, leaving a red lipstick ridge on her lips. "She probably scared, and she so small. You take care of her. Don't let that baby go."

Brenda's head was bent over her plate. Darnell saw his mother put her forefinger into the hollow behind her ear, rubbing slow, staring at his sisters. Their braids swung gently when they laughed. Don't let that baby go. His mother saw the headstone: Antoine. The boy she'd lost before Darnell was born, the boy between his name. Darnell Antoine Tucker.

He heard his father's shouts from the yard. "Y'all bring that thing back Monday." Darnell touched Brenda's back and went outside.

Nacho and Snooter were wheeling out the battery recharger. "You the ones let somebody steal my best dolly last month. Left it in the yard—*gave* it away."

Roscoe said, "They're stealing hoses, trash cans. Anything for a smoke of poison."

Darnell crouched beside the El Camino. Choose your poison. He dragged the cardboard he'd lie on, staring at the rusty circlets of dried blood on the edge, where his father had cut himself months ago. The baby was riding in a cushion of blood. All that secret stuff with his mother and sisters, with Brenda every month—the baby clung to red soft lining. His grandmother made his mother stay in bed when she was big with his sisters, when Darnell was seven. "I seen a spot a blood—you ain't takin no chance," she'd said. "You ain't forget what happen with him?"

"Hush," his mother had said, and Darnell slid from the bedroom's doorway.

Snooter shouted, "You bleedin them brakes again?" and Darnell blinked before he nodded, flexing his knees. "Hey, girl, you got your Nature Boy back, huh?"

Darnell saw Brenda watching from the wrought-iron screen door. "You ain't even started yet?" she said, her arms crossed high. Darnell slid under the car; he could tell she was gone when Nacho said, "What's wrong with her?"

"Bellyache," Darnell's father said. "And it ain't hardly gon get better." Folding chairs scraped across the driveway and forks clinked on the plates they got from inside.

He was still under the car when he smelled the burning, acrid and far away. Pulling himself out, he walked into the street to look at the sky. From the way the smoke rose and roiled, hung there while the afternoon turned plum-dark as sunset, he knew the fire was in the riverbottom again. Sometimes homeless people living down there started cooking and didn't know the wind. This was thick cane and bamboo, black smoke, flames blazing fifty, sixty feet down into the cane stand, where water and retardant couldn't reach. West of the city, he thought, the sun soon so completely gone that Esther, two doors down, came out looking sleepy, like she'd napped with her new baby, and called to her kids. "How it get dark so fast?" she asked Darnell.

"It's not evening yet," Roscoe said. "Fire." They squinted at the ashes falling like snow, the flakes rocking back and forth until they settled on car hoods.

"Look at that," Roscoe said, his head thrown back. Streams of crows flapped over, quiet, not jostling each other. "They got fooled, heading to the riverbottom because they think it's time to bed down for the night."

Yeah, Louis the one taught us all where the crows sleep, Darnell thought, and then Esther called out past him, "Girl! Look at you!" Darnell turned to see Brenda behind him. "You can't hide from me!" Esther laughed. "I had six!"

Brenda bumped him from behind, tickled his sides. He lifted his head again to the sky. "What y'all starin at?" she said into his back. "Helicopter chasin somebody?" Damn, he thought, watching the red-tinged sidewalks, the palm fronds lifting like hair in the wind.

"Bring that belly over here," Esther said. "We lookin at the smoke."

"Not another one," Brenda said, swinging around to face Darnell.

"You better hold that baby," he said, taking Esther's girl gently. "You need the practice." He cradled the heavy head in his arm for a moment, made himself stare at the tiny lips, shiny-wet. And her breath smelled clear and citrus, like 7 Up. He leaned closer, startled, and Esther laughed.

"Smell good?" she said. "That's why baby's breath is a pretty little puff of flowers." He couldn't look at Brenda; he'd only wanted to distract her. The baby turned in his elbow, and he passed her to Brenda.

"I'ma go finish up," he said.

Half an hour later, the sun lowered itself from the smoke, hanging in the band of sky between the pall and the line of hills. No progress for the crew, he could tell by watching the smoke, rising just as dark and no white puffs to signal success. The way the whole day had changed, the darkness, called to him like always, like when he was ten and riding his bike for miles to find the fire in the orange-packing house, in the fields near a freeway, on the Sugar Ridge Mountains. He kept his face away from the west, waiting for Brenda to come back from Esther's.

But when she padded across the street, Esther behind her, he said, "You want to go for a test drive, see if the brakes are okay?" And she knew that excitement in his face.

"Nigga—please," she said, her voice even. "Why would I want to sit somewhere right now and look at a fire? Cause that's where we'll end up. Every summer, that's all we did. Drove around to get as close as you could."

His chest filled with panic, and he made his voice angry, not scared. "Hey, wasn't a whole lot to do for a poor brotha," he said. "Couldn't go shoppin with my gold card, couldn't play golf with your daddy."

"No. Uh-uh. Don't try and shift that over on me or nobody else," she said. "You in a trance again, and after all these months, that whole

season of me worrying about you getting hurt, you want me to look
at a fire now?"

"That's just the baby talkin," Esther said. "Y'all ain't gotta holler
and argue."

"If that's how the baby talks now, I'm in serious shit when it gets
here," Darnell said, getting into the El Camino. He was glad the
men were all in the back room now. "Come on, Brenda, let's go
home." He knew better.

"No, we ain't gon go home and do nothing like every day," she
said. "We need to go somewhere nice." Her feet angled outward,
like she was off balance, and Darnell wanted to step out and put his
hand behind her back, to straighten it and help her to the car. But
he couldn't. His shoulders, heavy as sandbags, held him against the
seat. The last one. This is the last one. I promise. "Get in," he said,
softly, starting up the car, and he didn't watch Esther's eyebrows.

"Okay," she said when they neared the blank drape-backed window
of their apartment. Darnell nodded to the black-railed balcony so she
could get out before he parked in the stall under their floor. But she
stayed. "Go. Get as cozy as you can to it."

The sun slid away in the smoky sky, while he drove silently, trying
to remember which of the small dirt roads led to that part of the
riverbottom. Red glowed near the Jacaranda Avenue bridge; he could
see the flames slant forward with the wind and then climb the cane
and sky again. Around a swath of cleared land, he found the end of
the sandy trail and the taillights he knew would be gathered there.

When the engine stopped, Brenda said, "See? You never need me
for company. You got all your fellow pyros." She leaned her head
back and closed her eyes.

"Pyros set fires, Brenda," he said. "You know that."

"Yeah, you're right." He got out and walked to the barbed-wire
fence sagging in the sand. The older white guys in baseball caps and
binoculars, the ones he'd always imagined were ex-firemen, and the
kids on bikes behind him, voices threading high through the gathering
dark, all stared when a lone palm tree caught in the canopy of vines
and cane below; the top burned wildly, a sparkler held to the sky.
He'd parked far from the others. The fire popped and dry tree trunks
cracked loud as gunshots. The flames were maybe seventy-five feet

high, but far away, wavering in the bamboo, the giant arundo cane. He wasn't close enough. The shaking silence only came when you were nearly inside, and he paced back to the car, snapping twigs under his feet. Brenda sat in the open doorway of the car, like always, and her knees were round and pale as tiny faces watching him. The panic fisted inside him again.

"I know you're not a pyro," she said, resting her elbows on her knees so that he had to sit on the sandy ground to hear her. "You want to be a hero."

"No," he said, "that ain't it," but she went on.

"Remember when you first started talking to me in school? We used to see each other at the cemetery, on All Saints' Day, and you never said anything. Then when I moved away, that's the only place I saw you. And at Fairmount, when you started telling me about the fires, I thought you wanted to be a hero, saving people from burning houses and all that." She raised her head and pointed to the glow. "In the street today, I knew where the fire was when I saw the big ashes. See, I always listen to you."

"I wasn't lecturin."

"You were just talking, always telling me about the different colors of smoke. Like today with the big pieces of ash—you said that's vegetation. But I remember once we were driving around and I saw smoke, and you just said, 'That's a house,' and you didn't even try to find it."

He remembered. The black, roiling smoke, carrying the ash of couches and chemicals and clothes and . . . He'd never tried to go close to a house fire, not since the fire on Pablo that killed three children in his kindergarten class. He'd run from the screams and gray rivers of water pouring down the gutter from the firemen's hoses.

"You aren't into saving people," she said. "You just love the fire. You told me about fire lines, and then I started getting scared, that you'd be real close, like you told me, and you'd get hurt. Or die." She stopped, breathed, and said, "Can't you be a hero just staying here?"

Darnell placed his palms down in the sand to support himself where he was squatting. He looked at the thin stem-mark on his hand, remembered the boulder where he'd rested his cheek while he waited. Then he looked up at her face, so much rounder, her eyes slashed underneath with darkness, her knees wide. "That doesn't scare me," he said, twisting his head toward the fire. "That ain't scary."

"You think I'm not scared?" she whispered, eyes fixed on him. "I am. Every day I'm so afraid. Every night."

She kept her face turned away while he drove home. The ashes were powdery on the stairway railing.

In the dark bedroom, with the passing headlights circling the walls now and then, he knew she wasn't asleep. She half sat, propped on pillows so she could breathe, and he was afraid to get up and sit in the living room, afraid to leave the breathing he knew wasn't rest.

He'd been instructed to bring her to Picasso Street on Sunday morning. Sophia and Paula raced around, arranging food on trays, and women's faces were lined up on the couch. Women from her job, and Miss Ralphine, Mrs. Tribeleaux. They smiled when he led Brenda inside, and she pressed her fingers into his arm. "Oh," she said. "Look at this."

After the women had gone, hours later, Darnell came back inside where his mother and hers sorted the piles of clothing. A stroller was parked in the corner. "All the ladies at work pooled their money to buy it," said Brenda, seeing him stare. "Strollers cost fifty dollars."

Darnell touched the gray canvas cover, the rubber wheels. He bent down and saw the metal plate. GRACO CHILDREN'S PRODUCTS: ELVERSON, PA.

Picking up a tiny sweater, he saw the label. Made in Philippines. The clothes were mostly yellow and pale green with ducks and bunnies. "You get yellow or green if you don't know boy or girl," his mother said. "You don't want no boy wearin pink." Yeah, Darnell thought. I guess not. But he was reading the labels. The rattle was made in India. The white booties in Taiwan.

I'm a hero, he thought, packing the stroller into the car. See, a man gotta carry all this heavy stuff. Damn. "We have to go to that Lamaze class tomorrow, right?" he said, driving, but she only nodded.

She went to bed, and he talked to her back. "Your feet hurt?"

"Just let me be for now."

She didn't move all afternoon, and when night fell, he went into the room to see if she was asleep. She was sitting propped in the bed. Her eyes were closed, but she pressed them tighter now and then, her lips and eyes only thin lines when she hissed in breath. She looked like her father for a moment, he saw, and he said, "The baby kickin hard?" That was how she breathed if the feet got her hard in the lungs or stomach.

She only nodded. He sat on the couch, watched TV, took the trash down to the apartment dumpster. Lights were on in the other five apartments, the curtains closed. Then he heard Brenda call, "Darnell? Darnell?" It was so soft he barely heard her, but her voice was high. He ran up the stairs and into the bedroom. She looked up, and he smelled sharp, watery vapor all around her. She closed her eyes, and he pulled back the blanket to see damp soaked everywhere.

"My water's broken, Darnell," she whispered. "I'm scared."

"How long, I mean, you think you're in labor?" he said, keeping his back stiff, sitting carefully close to her. He tried to remember Fricke's EMT stuff, the things he'd mentioned.

"All day," she said. "I was scared."

At the hospital, her contractions were only three minutes apart, and nurses surrounded her bed, moving things around, saying, "This is awful fast for a first baby, hon. This is four weeks early? Why didn't you call somebody? Let's see how far along you are."

Darnell stood in the corner near jungle-hung tubes and cords, waiting for her to scream, but she only moaned now and then. The nurse closest to him said, "This baby wants out fast. Did you do Lamaze, Dad?"

He stared at her, remembering the nurse at the doctor's calling him and all the men Dad. And the other nurse said, "Look at this impatient baby coming!"

An Oriental man stood by the bed, touching the inside of Brenda's thigh, pushing gently. "This is Dr. Liu, Brenda, okay?" a woman said, and the man glanced at Darnell. "You ready, Dad?" he said.

Darnell touched her forehead, the blood rushing at his ears, his back stiff, and her eyes were still closed. It was like he wasn't there at all. He heard them saying, "Push now, stop, now, push, now." Brenda's neck bulged, that tiny neck grew thick and her shoulders rose up under his hands. Darnell closed his eyes, too, at her face unrecognizable, a swelling mask.

"A girl!" Dr. Liu said, and the mewling rasp from the baby's slit mouth jolted Darnell. Brenda opened her eyes and tried to lift her head, but the doctor said, "Aren't you going to cut the cord, Dad?"

He grabbed Darnell's hand and pushed scissors into the palm; a suction descended over the baby's purplish face, and the frog-bent arms and legs were stiff. Darnell stared at the waxy-smeared covering, at the membranes shiny and wet. "The cord," the doctor said softly, and he put his hand around Darnell's as if Darnell was a child learning to cut construction paper for the first time. Brenda began a laugh-moan, a high catlike sound, over and over, holding out her arms for the baby. The cord pulsed and bulged, like Brenda's neck, and the metal sliced it where his hand was placed.

CONFINEMENT

"THE BABY GONE," Mrs. Batiste said from the doorway. "They already taken her."

"What?" Darnell felt the trickle of cold race in his hair. "Gone?"

Mrs. Batiste's eyes were red-rimmed, and she opened her mouth; he heard Brenda call, "Darnell? Is he back, Mama?"

"Gone?" he asked again. He'd driven to the apartment for more of Brenda's clothes and things.

"No, no," Mrs. Batiste said, pulling the bag from his arms, leaving damp across his chest, cold in the air-conditioning. "She too small, so they taken her to the . . . the place."

Brenda's eyes were all that moved when he went into the room. A nurse was taking away bloodstained paper, and he winced. "She's only four pounds," Brenda whispered. "Premature."

"So she impatient just like me," he said, trying to sound normal. His heart was still so big he had no room for breath.

Dead—I thought she meant dead gone. Maybe Brenda. "I can't touch you, huh?" he asked. But when the nurse disappeared with the gathered armful, Brenda nodded, her eyes blurred. He bent to cover her with his chest, feeling her shake underneath his collarbone.

"I was so scared when they started talking fast," she whispered. "Go see her, make sure she's okay. They won't let me get up yet."

He pushed off her carefully, put his lips on hers and tasted salt.

He'd been happy to run back home for her stuff; the blood, the placenta, all the people in the room bent over the baby, bent over the dark flow under Brenda's legs, made him faint and sick. The nursery was crowded, but he didn't see his name. When he asked a nurse, she pointed to neonatal intensive care, and he saw two babies, the same shade of pinkish-blue, with arms and legs thin and round as pencils. Charolette—that was what Brenda had whispered to the baby, no one else, when she held her and stopped laughing. Charolette. Her black hair fringed slick over her forehead.

For a week, Brenda slept at the hospital, on a cot. Charolette was too small and sleepy even to eat the first few days, and Brenda's breasts rose full, veins snaking along the skin, hours after the birth. Darnell couldn't watch when she pumped the milk, when the plastic funnel gripped her nipples. He stared at the too-tiny baby head, the pale lavender legs that Brenda said were filling out by the fifth day, the darker purple wells under Brenda's eyes and around her lips.

He listened to his mother's stories at her kitchen table; her cheeks trembled even now when she told him about how Antoine was small, how the twins had been so skinny, and how he was plump compared to Melvin.

His father only said, "You feel useful yet?" Darnell stacked the plum wood he'd brought into the yard, and Snooter came over to say, "I need a ride to Jackson Park, man, you goin home now?" Darnell nodded.

He dropped Snooter off, lingered to tell the men he had a new daughter, and they began in chorus: "You whupped by *two* women now," Victor said. "That sweat on your face or tears, boy?" Mr. Talbert crowed.

Darnell folded his arms, and Brother Lobo said, "Two queens."

"And a lotta cryin," Darnell said, relieved. "Brenda's happy, though."

Lobo raised his head. "That's her instinct, from the motherland. No—not a pun, I mean Africa. Her instinct is to populate the world with beautiful black children."

Victor said, "Seem like Darnell's instinct the one populatin." And when they all laughed, Ronnie began flailing his arms and imitating Whitney Houston, singing about children being our future. Victor looked over at Darnell and laughed.

"Shut up, man," Darnell said, grinning. "I ain't talkin about all that." But when Lobo smiled regally at him, he thought, Yeah, these guys ain't feedin nobody but themselves right now. And them pale green envelopes from the hospital comin soon—what if Brenda's insurance don't cover all this intensive stuff?

In a doughnut shop, he read down the list. Automotive Sales. Banking. Bookkeeper. He turned the newspaper page. Cable TV Sales. Cashier. Clerical. He thought of Brenda and the rustling women typing, talking. "Yeah, right," he said out loud.

Collections—plenty of those. Construction—Experienced. He'd been to sites all over Rio Seco and San Bernardino. Data Processing. Dental Assistant took up eleven squares. "Lotta teeth in Rio Seco," he mumbled. Engineering. He backed up to Driver and Delivery.

Fountain Park was another new industrial zone past Terracina. He drove there, saw the two blue-mirrored buildings reflecting the sky. Fountains, poppies, marble floor in the lobby. He went to the suite, filled out the application, and waited for the secretary to ask for the DMV printout. Damn.

Every time he applied for a driver job, he had to wait in line at least an hour for a DMV printout. He started up the El Camino, staring at the rippling light on the glass. Still windy and hot. Two men came out and got into a Lincoln. Black car, silver hair, gray suits. Three kinda guys, he thought suddenly. Guys movin paper around, talking on the phone. Guys makin something and sellin it. And guys cleanin up, cookin food, movin things around. What do they call it? The service industry—that's what Brother Lobo said. Welcome to Darnell's. How may I serve you today?

"You may get out the way," his mother said from beside the crib.

"Go on do somethin," her mother said. "You ain't confine." Her mother had been there two days now, making gumbo, Brenda's favorite, and people kept dropping by to see the baby because Brenda wasn't allowed out of the house for a month. "She need to be careful, cause the baby too early, too small," Mrs. Batiste kept saying. They were delicate; they had to do things the old way. Not leave the house for thirty days, neither of them—Mrs. Batiste had a whole regimen, a ceremony, for each new day, and Brenda only nodded, her eyes on the legs poking out from Charolette's diaper. She was watching them fatten; the eyes were already bigger, brighter, moving now, even though when Darnell leaned over the back of the couch, they still focused their blurred purple only on Brenda's face. She lived in Brenda's arm, tucked into the crook of her elbow, her head hidden in Brenda's shirt, sleeping draped over her thighs.

He picked her up, held the tiny skull, his fingers across her temples, pulse stuttering against the inside of his fingerprint. Afraid of her neck, spindly as a straw, he tried to look into her face, to see Brenda there, but he could only see the low down-crested forehead and the private features still blunt. The skin peeled back from her fingertips and toes, the blind eyes and her silty smell. "You women always talk about that baby smell," he said. "It doesn't get me."

"Don't need to get *you*, huh?" his mother said, rolling her eyes.

He held her against his chest, remembering something Fricke had told him. Baby prey were born able to walk, even run, with their mothers and their herd. Llamas, deer, horses. But predators were helpless for a long time, until they were fed, taught, trained. Wolves, lions, humans. She woke and right away rubbed her cheek against his chest; it was too hard, too smooth, and he didn't smell right to her, either. She opened her mouth to cry; he'd seen her naked, damp from the women washing around her navel, and she always took in such a deep breath to scream that a hole depressed itself into her chest.

"Give her back to her mama," his mother said. "You ain't got no groceries." They laughed, and he gave her to Brenda, who slid her under the blouse. "Go on, you don't need to clean up, I'll do that," her mother said.

Don't matter if I smell the baby perfume or not, he thought, going down the stairs. What the guys all say? Mama's baby, Papa's maybe. Nah—I seen that nose, and she mine. But she don't need nothin else from me but cash. Just like Pops said.

"You ain't findin nothin in there you ain't already seen," his father said, pulling a chair up to the wooden table and putting his coffee cup onto a wavery stain-ring. "Her belly button fall off yet?"

"Yeah," Darnell said. The clamp had held a green-black stick that went inside the navel, something Darnell couldn't look at. The hole in the center of her made him weak, but Brenda rubbed alcohol and something her mother gave her all around it, even over it, without flinching.

His father smiled. "Look at you, squinchin your face. I had four of you, and I never got used to seein that, either. Women don't mind." His father lifted up a heavy workboot and stomped his heel in better.

"Five," Darnell said. "You had five." His father stopped. Darnell looked back at the ads, knowing his father didn't even like to bring up Antoine.

"This one's exactly a month before you," his father said. "Hope you two don't have the same hard head. Yours ain't got softer in twenty-one years."

Darnell swallowed. He'd thought everyone would forget his birthday; he'd been hoping they would, since he didn't feel like partying. "Where you think I got my hard head from?" he said.

"I bought it for you at Woolworth's when you was Charolette's age," his father said, standing up. "I bought somethin else for you this week. You can come pick it up on your birthday."

He looked back at the newspaper. The article read, "Although authorities say the region is weeks from official fire season, firefighters have already fought two blazes in the riverbottom area near Dolo-reaux. Investigators say the fires may be attributed to homeless drifters living in makeshift shelters in unincorporated areas just east of city limits."

Paid reserve or volunteers helpin out on those, Darnell thought. I could put in my application. But Fricke said paid reserves get six-somethin an hour, and you might not get called much. Maybe in a drought year . . . But it ain't steady enough.

Darnell looked at the photo, the caught flames in a palm tree, orange boiling at the center of the fronds, and he knew it was just before the tree exploded. He touched the color with his forefingers. I used to be sprung hard over this—sprung just as hard as the zom-bies. He shook his head and stood up to go outside.

The gumbo had left a stain smeared in the sink, so he got out the cleanser and dumped on sprinkles. Not too many brothas even know how to do this, okay? Just us Nature Boys had to survive in the woods.

He turned the shiny can around and read: Calcium carbonate. He thought Brother Lobo had told them calcium carbonate came from Jamaica.

Man, quit this, okay? Who cares? You ain't gon make no Ajax. He scrubbed the stain. His father used to say he'd get stuck on one track, get lost in that groove and couldn't come out. When GranaLene kept him, all he did was talk about spirits and zombies and stare at his mother's stomach, at neighbor cats and neighbor ladies' stomachs. Then, with fire, he'd see smoke and gauge the direction from his bike, even when he got his young butt whupped with his father's belt for the disappeared hours.

The girls—all of them—came for the weekend. His mother, Brenda's, his sisters, and his two women. The living room was strewn with filmy-thin pattern tissues and pieces of material. They were knocking out a blitz of bigger-girl clothes for Charolette, a new outfit for newly thin Brenda, and the early planning for someone's prom dress. "It's at the end of May," Mrs. Batiste said. "You two went, Darnell."

"Remember?" Brenda said, grinning. "And me and Mama started the dress just about April."

"How would he know?" Mrs. Batiste said. And she leaned over to Paula and Sophia. "All boys care about is how much skin they can see that night."

His jaw hot, he said, "Well, I'm gettin out of here." He stopped to look one more time, heard the radio playing, saw Charolette sleeping on her belly on the couch, with pillows on the floor just in case. He remembered when a big wedding was coming up on the Westside, he and Melvin and his father were banned from the front room while the dresses were being made; their boots and hands were too dirty.

As they handed out the coffee in his father's driveway, a white truck full of PVC pipe and black irrigation tubing pulled up. "Ain't that your cousin Trent?" Darnell's father said to the Kings.

Nacho looked up from the tire he was filling, and Snooter called, "You slummin? My Grayglen relation—how you livin, up there in the hills?"

They'd given him a hard time since he moved from the Westside after his father died. Darnell remembered when he'd hung out with Melvin and Snooter in school; now he wore Dockers, moccasins, a

T-shirt, and his hair was old-style shag, thick at the neck. When he said, "Hey, Darnell, right?" Darnell nodded, surprised, and Trent said, "I thought you were a firefighter. You're here now?"

Darnell folded his arms. "Budget cuts."

Trent just nodded. "Some raggedy tires, cuz," he said to Nacho. Turning to Darnell's father, he said, "Got a woman with a pepper tree she's tired of. She wants me to redesign the yard. It's Grayglen."

"See, he don't cut grass like us," Snooter said. "He *designs* it."

"Shut up, Snooter," Nacho said. Whenever he and Darnell talked about the right color for the Spider, Snooter said, "Don't paint your boring landscape shit on it, and it'll be fine."

Trent handed Roscoe a piece of paper. "I told her you'd give her an estimate."

Roscoe said, "Wait. Darnell, why don't you go up there? We've got that tree to do for Mrs. Tribeleaux."

His father only said, "Don't underbid us, damnit. Go on."

In the cab, Darnell smelled the plastic hosing heated in the truckbed. Trent said, "So you working with your dad, huh? You got competition from the Samoan guys."

Darnell hesitated. Nacho and Snooter said Trent talked yang about guys who didn't leave the Westside, about their old trucks and equipment. "Not really," he said. "Just waitin to hear if I get called back for fire season." The lie sent jabs of anger into his ribs, and he went on. "He wants me to look for some gardening jobs. I heard you're livin large with your business. If you hirin any extra help, let me know."

Trent looked at him with a blank face. "Man, I just do the planning and landscaping. I'm not into maintenance. After the irrigation, I'm gone."

You ain't gotta get that polo-ass tone, *brotha*man, Darnell thought. He said, hard, "So you went to *college* for this, huh?"

"Yeah. It's landscaping. Not gardening." Trent sped up Hampton, and the sea of new red-tile roofs waved over the first, low hills. The stucco walls and bare windows were close together, and Darnell said, "They cram em in tight." His father always said he'd rather have his shack—at least he didn't have to hear the neighbors flush the toilet.

Trent said nothing. Darnell knew Trent's house was up here somewhere, but he didn't want to seem nosy. Brothaman might think I want somethin else. Each tract was enclosed by beige block walls, with an opening for entry and a sign proclaiming the name of the development. Grassridge. Stonehaven. Hillcrest Estates. The higher up the long slope they drove, the more elaborate the entryways became, until the last one: Grayglen Heights—the name Snooter mentioned when he talked about going to Trent's house.

"That's how he made his money," Mr. King had said. "Bought him a house in one tract, sold it, bought a more expensive one. Made a damn bundle each time."

The huge, sprawling development covered the base of the foothills with red and dark-gray tile. Darnell saw a few of the houses over the wall, some Spanish style, some Victorian with balconies, before Trent turned off on the narrow road that led to old Grayglen.

"We took out two carobs at this one," Darnell said when they passed the driveway, and before he laughed about Gasanova's truck, he saw the new wrought-iron gate. Trent wouldn't think that was funny, man, but Gas would bust up. She thought she IDed the brotha quick.

Trent wound around to the far side of the highest hill, where the eucalyptus and oak were heavy and gray, shrouding the land to give the area its name, and he relaxed. "Everybody hates carobs," he said. "All my clients do." He pulled down a long drive so hemmed in by tall spears of cypress that Darnell felt spiderwebs near his elbow in the window. Trent parked in the tight circular drive near two other trucks.

Around the back, Darnell saw piles of reddish dirt everywhere. "Mrs. Shaefer's got big plans," Trent said, unrolling the paper he carried. "She wants something half-English, half-California. To go with the Tudor-style house. She read about a garden called 'Controlled Nature.' A knot garden . . ."

Darnell glanced at the bluish paper covered with tiny circles and shapes, and the two white guys with cement-smeared pants came up from the pathway they'd been forming to get Pepsis. "Hey," said the older guy, with silver stubble. "You brought reinforcements, huh?"

"Just came to give a bid," Darnell said, nodding toward the pepper tree. He walked around it, at the far end of the property, figuring his father would say $575 to pull it out and haul it away. It was old, with huge gnarls on the trunk, the kind that were hollow and sometimes held bee or wasp nests.

"Drip system," Trent was saying, and he led Darnell to where the woman sat looking through garden catalogues. She was small and plump, eyes tiny-slitted with her constant smile, and when Darnell clenched his fingers nervously and gave her the bid, she grinned and said, "The sooner the better."

Beside the truck, Trent picked up circles of hosing and said, "Man, have you heard of hydroponic farming?" Darnell shook his head, and Trent said, "You can grow all kinds of vegetables and plants just using water. No soil. Life is liquid."

"Now you sound just like Roscoe," Darnell said, grinning. "Or Brother Lobo."

"Great." Trent smiled back, wider than before. "A street poet."

Darnell looked at the hard-packed ground, spat, watched his saliva stay in a dime-sized circle. Water. Spit. Brenda's milk, always leaking through her shirt, so he could smell it chalky sweet. Charolette's tears. He stepped on the circle to press it into moisture.

Darnell found a book at his feet when Trent drove down the hill. *Gardens of the World.* "See—that's what I like," Trent said, pointing to a page. A wall, old and beige, had gray-green plants spilling over. "That's Italy. I like those old gardens, with the rosemary draping over, and the white roses. Real subtle. I'm talking Mrs. Shaefer into some of this."

"Where'd you get this garden stuff, man?" Darnell said. "Your pops just cut grass, right?"

Trent shrugged, and Darnell could see he was embarrassed that he'd shown his enthusiasm. "Hey, for all I know, my great-grandfather was into landscaping. Maybe he designed Jefferson's garden in Virginia."

"After he worked in the cotton field," Darnell said without thinking, and then, trying to take it back, he went on, "I mean, most brothas ain't into flowers."

"I'm not interested in what most brothers are into," Trent said coldly. "Not Westside brothers. Sorry you don't consider it normal."

Darnell's neck was hot, and he thought of his own boots, of the fire station, Fricke cooking, and the smoke calling, and he said, "I wasn't trying to talk shit, man. I'm sorry."

"Yeah," Trent said. His wrists were rigid near the steering wheel.

"Snooter and them always call me Nature Boy," Darnell said. "I'm

the last one should talk yang." He watched Trent's hands loosen on
the circle of the wheel.

I missed the whole thing, he thought, pulling into the stall under
the darkened apartment. He didn't hear the TV. They probably woke
up, walked around, ate something, and went back to sleep.

When he opened the door, though, Brenda's mother was sitting in
the dark singing to the baby, who was almost hidden in her arm,
sleeping. Darnell heard the slurred-soft words. "*Fais dodo, petite.
Fais dodo, cher cochon.* Papa bring *gâteau, fais dodo.*"

She looked up at him, rounding her lips for him to hush, and stood
up to put the baby in her cradle in the bedroom. The cradle Brenda
had slept in, she said.

She moved the piles of clean, folded clothes from the table and
poured him the strong coffee. "What's all that mean?" he said. "My
GranaLene used to sing somethin like that, but I don't remember."

Mrs. Batiste smiled. "Means go to sleep—what else a granny gon
sing? It's a old song from *my* gran. From carceration time."

"Carceration?"

"That how she call slavery."

"And that Papa stuff?"

"Papa will bring cake."

Darnell kept his eyes on the coffee shine. Yeah, if he ever get some
ducats he will. If he get a steady slave. He heard his grandmother
singing her other favorite. "Hush, little baby, don't say a word. Papa
gonna buy you a mockingbird."

In the morning, he left Charolette a tiny beetle under the blanket,
Brenda curled on her side around the baby. When they were dividing
up the newspaper and debating about how early Mrs. Shaefer would
want them to start chain saws, his father handed him the classified
section automatically, taking the sports pages for himself and giving
the national news to Roscoe. "You got a floor jack?" Snooter said, and
Darnell went to get it. When he came back out and slid near the big
truck's tires with Snooter, his father said to his feet, "You stopped
hidin in the hills. Now you need to quit hidin over here."

Darnell sat up. "Ain't nobody hidin. Nothin for me to do at home."
He looked at Snooter. "I saw Victor and Charlton on the road camp

when I was up there. Hey, I could get me a job like that easy. All I gotta do is be me and drive in the wrong place. Get my ass arrested and get a place on road camp. Dig firebreaks, even work the big jobs."

Roscoe said, "You getting righteous with the wrong folks, son. I did my time on the road camp." Darnell looked up at Roscoe's half-lowered eyelids, his hard-held lips, and he slid back under the truck to breathe rusted metal. The night Brenda had gotten pregnant— the weekend police searched for Ricky Ronrico—officers had seen Louis walk into Roscoe's house when nobody else was out on the streets. It was the only time Louis had crossed the front steps since he'd quit college, and when the batons pounded the door, Roscoe refused to let them search the house. A few months later, he'd gotten so many tickets, expensive tickets, that he'd done three months by the freeway.

Darnell's father put down his cup when Darnell and Snooter stood up. "You think road camp is hard, huh? Job situation hard?" he said. "Lemme tell you about Mississippi, Louisiana, that levee down there."

Snooter said, "Oh, shit—Missippi story. Let me get on back to the crib." He rolled his eyes.

"Niggas all buried on them levees. White man need new niggas, he arrest you cause you was breathin wrong. You on the levee, you ain't workin hard enough or you talk shit, he shoot yo ass and the others cover you over in the bank. Bones make a good frame for all that dirt." He gulped down the last coffee. "My grandpa buried in there. Mississippi. He went on the chain gang for spittin in the wrong place." The cup was small in his hands. "See, you could swallow wrong, too."

Snooter said, "Them old-time days is gone, Red Man. I go down, somebody go down with me."

"Don't talk like that," Roscoe said, but Snooter went next door, and Darnell went to the sideyard in silence to look at the Spider's tires. I go down, I'm takin myself, he thought, and he swallowed, stared at the mountain dust still on the fender. Why you still thinkin that? Stall out with that. Carceration time—last night. Papa bring some cake. Incarcerated on the road camp, and doin the breaks. Serious memory lane.

He heard his father say, "Trent got a clean little Toyota, huh? But he does most of his work on paper." He rattled the newspaper, and then said, "Oh, hell, Roscoe . . ."

Darnell came back to see his father bury his head in his hands, gripping his forehead with long fingers permanently black at the knuckles. "Daddy?" Darnell said, dropping the chain saw he'd been checking, and his father looked up.

"Roscoe, they got Louis downtown."

It was in the sports section, because Louis had been a star basketball player in high school. "Louis 'Birdman' Wiley, who helped lead the Fairmount Falcons to two county basketball titles, was arrested yesterday for conspiracy to distribute cocaine. . . ."

Roscoe took the paper from Darnell and read it. Then he handed it back, put his tongue into his cheek hard, so that a lump traveled slowly back and forth, and walked to his house.

Darnell and his father were silent, taking Roscoe's big truck up the twisting roads to Grayglen, where they could barely scrape past the fences and trees. They worked on the pepper tree all day, and no one tried to knock on Roscoe's door until late that night. He didn't answer. "Maybe he went to Marietta Cook's," Darnell told his father when they walked back from the dark house. "You want me to go by her house?"

His father shook his head. "He don't want to see you. You still here."

By the next morning, the reporters had remembered more of Louis's career. They'd found his high school coach, his college stats, and gotten a quote from the college coach about how Louis had quit the team. Darnell drove to the pecan grove with the folded paper he'd bought. The grass was fine and lush in the cool air, the aisles between trees untrampled; the trees were blank, fern-branched with new growth.

No one heard from Louis. Darnell went to buy the newspaper for two days, not wanting to see it at his father's first. On the fourth page, in a few paragraphs now, Louis got three years at Chino. He'd pleaded guilty, quickly, under the new law that required arraignments in forty-eight hours to keep the overcrowded courts moving.

When Darnell handed the paper to Brenda, her eyes filled with tears. "Why would he say guilty?" she said. "You told me everybody said he wasn't even selling, he was just hanging out with Leon."

Darnell shrugged, but his temples felt congested, too. "What could he say? 'Yeah, your honor, I hang with these guys but I'm just a friend. . . . I don't make no cash slingin?' " He thought of what Gasanova had said. "Gas told me Birdman was trippin hard, like he wanted to self-destruct."

Brenda went to the bedroom doorway to look at Charolette, then folded her arms and faced Darnell again. "He used to talk to me, tell me how he was only playing basketball for his daddy."

"Louis liked you, he was always tryin to talk to you," Darnell said. "Always talkin yang about takin you away from me cause he was a hoop star. He said I didn't have no rep."

But she didn't smile. "Nobody ever listened to him, his daddy neither, and all you ever asked him about was basketball. He hated playing." She went past him to the stairs, to take the clothes from the washer.

Roscoe wasn't on Picasso Street. Darnell's father said Louis had never called; Roscoe had found out the sentence from the morning paper, too. Darnell worked beside his father all day, and after they'd brought thick logs of pepper wood home and stacked them, Darnell told his mother how the baby had slept, how Brenda was walking around looking skinny but complaining about the belt of fat at her waist. Then he went to the yard to see if his father needed anything else. Donnie Harris stood awkwardly near the El Camino. He was bigger, muscles pumped up from college ball.

"Hey, Darnell, this you?" he said, gesturing to the cab.

"Yeah, man, the Spider's on vacation." Darnell smiled. "Long time, homey. I heard you were back, just like me."

"Yeah, I ain't seen you in a year." Donnie looked at the house. "Uh, is Mr. Wiley around?"

"No, I think he's over at his lady's house."

Donnie leaned against the El Camino, moved a pepper branch away from his leg. "I came by to tell him I'm sorry. You know, he was always real cool to me, always takin me out to eat when me and Bird were seniors playin together. He used to call me and Bird the Gemini, remember, talkin about we were twin stars." He folded his arms. "But Bird was taller."

Darnell saw Louis's face in Leon's Bronco, the distant, unfocused gaze. "I don't know," he said. He looked at Donnie's black bomber jacket and badge. "So is that a security jacket, man? That what you into now?"

Donnie nodded. "Yeah, I'm over at the Hilton, the new one downtown."

"Big old ugly building, man."

"You ain't lyin. And now they got the new convention center right there, too, and they share this big parkin garage, so it's too much for me."

Darnell frowned at the badge. "They lookin for somebody, huh?"

Donnie smiled. "Gettin ready to advertise for swing shift. Why? You lookin for a gig, man?" He threw out his arms. "Come on, homey! We could cruise like the old days, but I'll be tellin *you* what to do."

SECURITY

THE SAME BLACK-WET smell rushed out at him from each parking garage he passed, the air permanently dark with exhaust and shadow. He didn't mind walking, like tonight when Brenda had come home from work at four and taken Charolette to the doctor for her two-month checkup. They were still gone at five-thirty, so Darnell had put on his jacket and headed across downtown.

Glad I got the jacket and badge, or I wouldn't be stridin like this, he thought. All the suits and heels gone home now, and the only brothas around are watchin somethin or lookin for somethin. I don't want Johnny Law thinkin the wrong thing. I take my jacket off and turn into the wrong thing quick.

The April warmth hung in the spaces between buildings, between garages, and Darnell felt the ring of sweat around his neck. The sky stayed light until after his shift started at six, and the windows on the tall buildings were silver facing east to the mountains, gold facing the low sun.

The Hilton's windows were smoky-black squares in the beige ce-

107

ment walls. The new hotels had fancy atriums and lobbies inside, but they were blank and impersonal on the outside. He walked under the giant mesh of white tubes sculpting the entrance and saw Donnie's little red Celica parked in its spot.

"You gon give me a ride home tonight, man?" Darnell asked when he got inside the tiny booth at the mouth of the garage.

"I don't know, man, it'll cost you," Donnie said. "You gotta go to the kitchen and ask Ana for leftover doughnuts. She can't stand my ass."

"You obnoxious." Darnell watched the people coming in and out of the entrance, heading for dinner.

"No, man, I think her and Sylvia are *fine*. Mexican girls got them big brown eyes and they know how to put on makeup."

"See? Mexican people are born in Mexico, fool. Ana and Sylvia were born in Rio Seco, man, up the street. They're Chicano."

Donnie folded his arms. "They speak Spanish, man, I heard them."

"So?"

"So I told them I can speak Spanish. *Burrito, tamale. Carnitas.*"

Darnell threw his head back and laughed. "They don't know you was a bighead ballplayer that didn't pay attention in Spanish class, man, they just know you don't know shit."

"Just remember to get the doughnuts, man, or you walkin home," Donnie said. "Go around the convention center, man, it's time. You still on part-time temporary status, brotha—Mr. Wilson might come by, and he love to remind you."

Darnell started walking the perimeter of the parking area, all the way around the convention center, through the no-man's land of loading docks, turning around at the high wall that hid the docks from view and cruising along the planters at the edge of the walkway. He looked at his watch, wondering if Brenda and the baby were home. Brenda was worried about whether Charolette had grown out of her skinny born-early body; she looked fat enough to Darnell, and she wanted to get inside Brenda's shirt every hour, it seemed. They'll be crashed hard when I get home, he thought.

His shift was six to midnight, Wednesday through Sunday, and he hadn't seen Brenda for more than a minute in the three weeks he'd had this job. Part time: he was technically only thirty hours a week, so he didn't get any sick days or benefits, but six bucks an hour was better than the six months of applications.

Darnell stopped when he got to the large central courtyard that the hotel and convention center shared, with banners flapping in the wind, hung from more white piping, and the fountain scattering drops from a long sheet of metal. The water flew off in a veil, making a strange sound, but two smaller fountains in the long, rectangular pool burbled the way fountains usually did. Darnell listened.

Donnie loved standing by the fountain, just hearing it, he said. When they were kids, Donnie's thing was water. Donnie grew up on Pablo, and Gas and Leon lived on DaVinci back then. All summer, they'd meet Darnell and Louis, living in the streets till dark on found oranges and candy they bought with fountain pennies.

Louis was already tallest, but Donnie was big and he had a big mouth. "All y'all come on," he'd say, wading into the city-hall fountain like he was just trying to cool off. "Louis watch for Adam-12 cause he chicken anyway."

With Louis looking for patrol cars, the others would follow Donnie into the water and feel for coins with their toes. Darnell used to hate the slimy bottom; Gas would say, "We gon get in trouble; we ain't suppose to take this money."

Leon would say, "Shut up, man, who else gon take it? You see the mayor comin outta there at lunch for some chump change?" They would all look over at the huge doors leading to the old city hall.

"You pickin it up, so that make you a chump, too," Gas would say, and they'd sling water all over each other.

Slingin. Leon wasn't getting chump change now. He was into distribution. Darnell circled the fountain. They all had their loves then, for a bunch of summers. Louis's was birds, Darnell's fire, and Donnie with his water jones always led them on serious excursions.

In winter, the canals that wound through the city to irrigate the orange groves were dry. The boys saw shopping carts filled with trash and mud, yellow grass and dried clumps like fur, shaggy animals pawing in the cement bed. But in summer the carts and rusted scrap from the railroad were covered with an endless ribbon of water that grew long, current-trembled grass.

Donnie led them all along the canals, even up past Hillgrove, where groups of white kids swam, jumping off a small wooden bridge. One of the greenish-pale boys in the water saw them watching and yelled, "Niggers can't swim here!"

Donnie yelled back, "We can't die! We ain't fools!" They'd all heard about the kids sucked into grates that suddenly opened to let more water rush down.

Along the riverbottom, they kept losing Louis, who would stop and stare at geese and egrets. They walked their bikes through the damp mud in the huge storm drain, where winos lived and tried to jack them for change. Leon threw rocks at them, his wrist snapping viciously.

Darnell looked off toward the cement, pinkish in the streetlights. He and Louis had always been the ones to wander away alone. Louis would go back to the riverbottom for herons when everyone else headed to Gas and Leon's, because their mother was never home and she kept Popsicles in the freezer. By late afternoon, when the wind had been blowing for a few hours and the earth was heated and ready, Darnell would see the smoke and take off toward the black scarf twining in the sky.

Walking toward Donnie, he breathed the exhaust in deep to erase the smell of fire season coming whenever he stood near bare earth. "I'm hungry, man," Donnie called.

Darnell said, "You ever think about goin to see Louis?"

Donnie leaned against the garage wall. "I called him once, man, but he didn't want no visitors." He looked hard at Darnell. "He probably pumpin, gettin them done-time arms. Be bigger than when he played ball."

"Your turn to hang out by the water," Darnell said, turning away.

He went to get the doughnuts at ten, when they were closing the restaurant. In the back, by the delivery area, Ana smiled at him. "How's the baby?" she asked.

"My wife took her to the doctor," Darnell said, the words "my wife" still strange on his teeth.

"Two-month checkup?" Sylvia said from behind her. Sylvia was older, around thirty, with a round face and mouth drawn full by red lipstick. "That means she got her puppy shots. She's gonna be grumpy tonight!"

"Great," Darnell said. "Every night's a party at my house."

"Here." Ana handed him the cinnamon rolls wrapped in napkins. "But I only wanted to give one to you. Not to him." She tossed her long hair over her shoulder, and her tall bangs swayed.

"Darnell's married, *mija*." Sylvia laughed.

"But he's cuter." Ana waved. "And quieter."

I'm safer, he thought, walking back to the booth. Ana like to flirt with the ones don't scare her. He handed Donnie one roll, saying, "This *ain't* for you."

"Oh, homey, she won't even give me the digits. All I want to do is call and talk, man." Donnie bit into the soft roll. "See, she kept it fresh for me."

"So you and Rosa ain't gettin back together?" Darnell asked. Donnie had gone out with Rosa all through high school.

Donnie shook his head. "She says she's movin up. She don't think I'm movin anywhere since I quit school."

They ate in silence. The garage was deserted. His father didn't think much of this job, but Brenda was happy. "You'll get on full time and get a raise," she said.

She said that whenever I last had a conversation with her, he thought. He got home after midnight, and she was always asleep. He was wound up from walking the lots, and he watched TV for half an hour, then slid beside her, watching her sleep, her shoulder gold in the light, her breasts pushed together in a deep-curved line, her foot pushing out from the sheet.

She still teased him about sleeping like a zombie, but now he lay in his envelope of sheet, she in hers, and Charolette was an extra bump. Three cocoons, separate, the smallest, by Brenda's arm, snoring like a baby VW engine. He couldn't believe she made so much noise—rev, snarl, rev, snarl.

She raised an eye like a periscope from the sheets at 6 A.M. He saw her swing her heavy head, the forehead rounder now, her hair in perfect snail curls. She saw his face watching, looked at Brenda's neck, and opened her mouth to yell.

Her mouth latched onto Brenda like she hadn't had milk for days instead of hours. He lay there listening to the noises in her throat; Brenda was half asleep, propped on pillows. Charolette's hand explored Brenda's chest, her collarbone—like a lover, probing, brushing with fingertips. He could see her eyelashes moving, roving over Brenda's face.

She didn't look at him again. After Brenda took her into the living room, Darnell lay touching himself, pulling the stiffness and scratching; then he tried not to think about Brenda's neck and the crease between her breasts, the soft skin inside her thighs. He folded his hands over his sternum, dozing until she said, "It's time."

Then he took her and the baby to his mother's. Brenda carried Charolette inside, bringing him back a biscuit. He drove her downtown while she said, "I'm so tired I look like hell. I don't even care what I wear. I don't even want to go today." She kissed him, lipstick waxy-sweet, while her hips moved away toward the car door.

The Spider looked pitiful in the drying grass of the sideyard. "Nowhere to park it at the apartment," he told Nacho. "But I miss it, man. The El Camino feels too clunky."

"Maybe your pops get you a new clutch disc," Nacho said.

The back room was full. Snooter, Mr. Lanier and Mr. King, Roscoe, and in his corner chair, Darnell's father. The dominoes were a jumbled whirl on the table, the plastic cups and beer bottles lining the edges.

"He grown now, and he finally showed up," Mr. King said, and Snooter raised his bottle of Canadian Club.

Darnell said, "Y'all don't look like you needed me to party."

"Do we ever?" Snooter said. "You ain't been around, anyway. Sit down, fool."

Darnell took the chair across from Snooter, and he, Nacho, Roscoe, and Snooter took seven each. Snooter poured liquor into a cup, and Darnell's father said, "He twenty-one today. He can drink now. What a milestone, huh, Roscoe?"

Roscoe shook his head. "Used to be a big deal. Eighteen you could vote, join the service, twenty-one you could drink. Now you boys can buy cocaine in elementary school." He slammed down a domino. "Dampens the celebration."

Darnell took a sip of the liquor, felt it harsh-hot in his chest. "It ain't like they vote, neither," Floyd King said.

"Who I'ma vote for?" Snooter said. "Who give a shit?"

"I don't want to hear that," Darnell's father said. "People died so you could vote."

"Oh, no," Snooter said, rolling his eyes, slapping down his piece. "Here we go again. To Missippi."

Darnell didn't want to hear them fight. He said, "So what you get me, Pops?"

His father stood up. "Take his place, Floyd, he losin anyway."

At the metal shed where he kept the chain saws, his father unlocked the door, pulling out a lawnmower and then a weed whacker. "I know you don't think doin yards is worth anything, but this'll get you some cash when you need it."

Darnell felt the heat from the liquor pull together and tighten in his chest. It was like when he played outside in the smog, as a child, and his chest was full of gray particles. The whiskey had cut through it, but now it just hurt more. "You think I ain't workin?" he said. "Shit."

His father's voice was quiet. "You only part time. You the last hired, first fired if somethin go wrong. It don't hurt to get a gig on the side, work for yourself. Then you ain't always dependin on somebody else."

Darnell shouted, "Why you always gotta remind me? Why you gotta expect the worst from me?" He took a breath, folded his arms, and said, lower, "You seen all them guys out there with a truck and a mower. You want me workin twenty-four-seven?"

His father kicked aside a piece of metal near the shed. "You got a baby now. You gotta feed her. When I had Melvin, I mopped floors and cleaned toilets after I was done haulin trees."

Darnell said, "I wouldn't care if I had a part-time job at the fire station, even volunteer or reserve. Just so I could be outta here, and up there." He turned away from his father.

"But you can't be up there!" his father shouted. "You can't be chasin them fires like you a boy. You got people to feed. Unless you want Brenda to feed em by herself." Before Darnell could answer that, his father walked back to the house. "Lock them things up," he said. "Rockheads stole my new hose last night."

Darnell pushed the mower into the shed. He stayed there, smelling all the metal gathering cool from the night, until Roscoe came out. "You better get your cake before it's gone," Roscoe said, touching his shoulder.

"He thinks I don't know shit," Darnell said, keeping his voice even, his lips careful.

"No. He knows the same things you do. Same things I do. How loud hungry kids cry. How loud women can get." Roscoe looked up into the sky. "New moon. Louis used to stare at the moon till I thought his neck would break." Roscoe paused. "He never ate much. Always skinny." Darnell bit his lips, and Roscoe said, "He won't be twenty-one until July. Hollie's five—she hasn't seen him since he left for college. Now she won't see him for three years."

Darnell said, "He wasn't even slingin. I know it."

"He's still a fool." Roscoe kept looking up. "I'm glad I don't have to see him by accident, riding around in that damn Bronco. His face is gone."

Darnell said, "Pops just called me a fool, too."

Roscoe brought his eyes down. "Your father just told me he could never offer Melvin a mower. He said he knew you had some sense. He just can't tell you." Putting his hand on Darnell's shoulder, he said, "You still got a face."

Marietta Cook was in the dining room with her grandson Freeman and Hollie. "Happy birthday," she said to Darnell. "Take a piece for you wife. She need she sweet, too." He felt his mother's arms twine around him from behind. "I love you," she said, holding him tight.

"Hey," Brenda murmured drowsily when he bent down to kiss her. Charolette was beside her elbow. Darnell left the bedroom to put the foil-wrapped cake on the counter. On the couch, he folded his hands, lined up his toes the way he always had to keep from falling off.

But she came out, carrying a box. Her hair fell in spikes across her cheek when she knelt next to him. "I know the season is about to start," she whispered. He frowned, and she said, "Since you miss the mountains, maybe you can take me and Charolette hiking up there sometime. If we ever get a day off." She put new honey-colored work boots on his chest.

He grabbed them by the heels. "Pretty good," he said, dropping them on the floor, "but I want somethin better." He pulled her on top of him, holding her by the hips, and put his lips on her neck.

He didn't wear the new boots to the mountain. He wore the old water- and ash-stained pair, pushed them hard on the floorboards up through the Sandlands. Windy, hot May. The grass on the slopes was already brown, still green at a few crevices and near boulders, but wilted dry in the open. He smelled the clean wind when he wound up the mountain, saw the dark chamise and manzanita purple on the steep banks.

They can't torch trails—we only got about three inches of rain. I remember four or five days, that's it. So they sittin up here waitin for the first one.

Only Fricke's old truck and Corcoran's Sidekick were parked on the dirt. Darnell slid his feet on the pine needles to feel them smooth, smelled the trees and dry chaparral all around.

He heard them inside, and he knocked. "It's Tucker," he yelled, opening the door, and they looked up from the table. Fricke was writing something. Corcoran was cracking peanuts. "Seasonal's greetings," Darnell said.

Fricke smiled. "I can't say we missed you, can I, Corcoran?" He laughed. "But we did notice you weren't here."

"More than I can say for home," Darnell said. "But that's just life in the flats. So what a large and merry crew we have here. You gon let the road-camp guys fight on the line, too, let em fly the tankers and drop the Phoscheck? They free, right?"

Fricke stood up. "We're as large as we have the money for. How do guys in your hood say it? We're living as large as we can." He got a cup for Darnell.

"Man, they don't say it like that," Darnell said. "So, Corcoran, you got the call, huh?" He felt his jaw shifting hard.

"Permanent crew, man!" Corcoran said, throwing out his arms. "I finished up EMT, academy, everything."

"We're operating with a skeleton crew," Fricke said, leaning against the kitchen doorway. "No seasonals. Just us. If we get a big one, we call for backup from the region."

"You don't look too skeletal to me," Darnell said, nodding at Fricke's stomach. "Still cookin, and you don't have Scott to poison you or Perez to eat all the grub."

"Come on outside," Fricke said. "Show you what we did during off-season." Darnell followed him to the garage, knowing Fricke wanted to talk to him alone.

"How was the biologist, or whatever she was?" Darnell asked.

"Interesting," Fricke said. "And far away, so she'll stay interesting. How's flatland life?"

Darnell looked at the engine, then walked toward the trees. "I'm married, man," he said, turning to smile at Fricke. "Got a baby— three months old."

For once, Fricke was silent. His mustache was still, and he wet his lips. "That was fast," he finally said.

"Neither one of em takes too long," Darnell said. "Long as off-season."

"What about your first love?"

Darnell broke off pine bark. "Hey, I ain't gon lie. I think about it all the time. The last one, man . . . " He stopped, the puzzle bark in his hand. The sound, the canyon. Darnell Tucker Canyon. "What kinda name is Fricke, anyway? Corcoran's Irish."

"Mutt," Fricke said. "My dad left when I was born, so I don't know." He bent down to pick up a pine cone the squirrels had frayed looking for nuts. "All you have to do is take the college classes. The budget freeze can't last forever. And you can go Corcoran's route."

Darnell shook his head. "I don't have the time or money to go all the way out to San Bernardino. They don't have Fire Science in Rio Seco."

Fricke's voice was sharp. "So you're gonna give me that 'I have to stay stifled and oppressed in the ghetto because I'm only into the short term' shit."

Darnell jerked his head from the tree. "No—I ain't sayin all that. The Westside ain't all ghetto, okay?" He crumbled the bark. "I know brothas that went to college; I talked to this guy named Trent the other day. All I'm sayin is I had to get a job, okay?"

"So what are you doing?" Fricke said, the words flat.

Darnell put his hands behind his head. "Hey, same thing as up here. We were just security up here, right, that's what you said sometimes. You were always sayin fires are meant to clear out the old chaparral, and we should let em burn, but people were stupid enough to build things where they shouldn't be. Like Seven Canyons."

"So you're a guard?"

"Guardin my life, man." Darnell smiled. "But I sure as hell miss torchin trails."

"I thought Brenda had a good job," Fricke said. "Plenty of women put their husbands through college." He smiled now under the brush of hair. "That word still scares the hell out of me. Husband. But that's how doctors and lawyers and professors are made."

"Not in my hood," Darnell said. "Home boy." He pulled off more puzzle bark, loose and dry, remembering Gas's favorite line: "When you live in my residence, you gotta earn them presidents." But Fricke would say, "Translate that shit, okay?" Fricke drew down his brows, and Darnell said, "We don't grow too many Nature Boys. That's what they used to call me."

"What do they call you now?" Fricke said.

Darnell shrugged. "Daddy Darnell, when they talkin yang."

"*You* keep her? Uh-uh, she doesn't even know you." Brenda came away from the phone. His mother had told her she and Marietta Cook were going to LA.

"She doesn't want to know me," Darnell said, watching Charolette watch him from Brenda's arms. That was how she liked to see him—from somewhere else.

But in the morning Brenda hovered around like a nurse, making Charolette a pallet on the living-room floor. "If you put her in the crib in our room, you can't see if she's breathing," Brenda said. "And she's moving around now. The doctor said she's really strong for her age. You can never leave her alone, cause she's trying to roll over."

"A new trick, huh?" Darnell said, smiling, but Brenda didn't find it funny.

"She's not a dog, Darnell." Charolette woke from the quick nap she always took right around eight; she lifted her head and kicked her legs like a frog, bowed and quick.

"I won't say it," he mumbled. "Come on, babygirl, you gotta get used to me," he said, reaching for her. Her tongue curled in rage, her head banged against his collarbone, and she got even madder. "No, I ain't got nothin soft and warm up there," he said. Brenda looked like she would cry, too, and he told her, "Go on. You said you wanted the exercise, unless you want us to walk with you."

"No," she said, and he stood by the window to watch her go down the sidewalk. "Your mama looks good," he said to the baby, whose eyes were slitted with her screams. He looked closely at her cheek in the sun, saw traces of glittery sparkle like she was wearing makeup. He smelled the skin. Brenda had rubbed her cheek against Charolette's, left perfumed shine. A girl already.

"What I'ma do with a screamin woman?" he asked her. "Snooter and Melvin always say nothin you *can* do. Just let em get done." She cried on the blanket and he gritted his teeth, sat right there on the

couch so she could see him. Phil Donahue ran from woman to woman
like a fly on a picnic table. Charolette's cries grew lower and more
pitiful, and he said, "Let's ride, babygirl. I'ma call you that till you
start feelin like it. Come on."

She screamed all the way down the stairs, her howls moving aside
the curtains in the Vietnamese woman's front windows. Darnell put
her in the car seat.

She was quiet then, watching the shifting sun and squinting. Her
eyebrows were feather straight like his, but more delicate, each hair
a tiny curved-in pattern. "You already got them thick eyelashes, too,
huh?" he told her. "Ladies love us both for that."

She stared at his mouth, and he said, "Oh, you want to talk, huh?
How come women always want to talk? Damn, that's what Scott used
to say up in the mountains. But I can't tell you what he wanted the
women to be doin instead. Nope. You don't need to know that. A
girl. Hmm. I don't remember nothin about Sophia and Paula when
they were babies except it was scary."

He stopped, but she was perfectly still in the seat. "Okay, so we
cool long as Daddy run his mouth. That's not really my style, you
know, but I'ma try it for you. Let's go check out Daddy's work." He
drove slowly past the Hilton, the garage's huge mouth even darker
in the bright sunlight. "There the big castle where I sit," he said,
pointing to the guard booth.

He took her to the city lake, carrying her to the water's edge to
see ducks and geese. They honked and swam closer, but he didn't
think Charolette could really see that far. She mostly stared up at the
shifting patterns in the pepper branches near the water. "Don't stare
at the trees!" He laughed. "Don't let your grampa see you lookin at
branches! He'll put you to work tomorrow."

At lunch, he told her sleeping face, "Watch this. Your mama gon
run out that door right there and start home, so she can see if you
still alive." He sat with the windows rolled down, Charolette's head
drooping low, her cheek so fat that it pushed against the seat strap
to squish her lips into a pucker. Sweat sparkled in her flat curls, and
he touched the moisture, watching for Brenda.

She came out with the other women and broke off toward the street.
"Look at her stridin," Darnell said to Charolette, who breathed even.
"Say, girl," Darnell called in his best Melvin/Snooter voice, leaning

his upper body out the window. "You lookin fine, baby. You want a man with a ready-made family?"

She ran toward the car. "What's wrong?" she said, not even glancing at him, going straight to the passenger door.

"Just kickin it," Darnell said. "Me and my daughter been cruisin, talkin about world politics and thangs."

Brenda perched on the seat. "Look at her sweating; you got her too hot."

"You know she sweats every time she sleeps, in the crib or on you, too."

"She been crying?" Brenda finally looked at him, and he saw her eyes and cheeks still sparkling in the light through the windshield.

"She was too busy havin a good time," he said.

She screamed when the engine started, and he said, "We almost home, and I'll get your bottle." But at the long red light, he couldn't stand it, and reaching beside him, he let her suck on his index finger for a moment, curling it up so he stroked the roof of her mouth. Her gums felt rough as asphalt. She stared at him over his knuckles.

On the pallet, she screamed for an hour. He'd tried holding her, singing, "Angel baby, my angel baby," real slow like it was coming out of a lowrider. He'd given her the bottle, and the milk had dribbled out with crying spit. He'd changed her diaper full of brown mustard, careful to dig in there and clean like Brenda told him to every time, but that was all long ago. Her mouth didn't move now, just stayed propped open while rhythmic yowls poured out. His ears throbbed, and his heart pounded—somebody was gon call the police about child abuse.

He lay on his back next to her. "Ain't nothin I can do," he said to the ceiling. "I'm tired, and I gotta go to work in a few." He watched, his temples numb, and she shuddered, her face toward him. Her eyelids fell, rose, fell, as she fought sleep, pulling her mouth back in an automatic yell a few times. He saw the lids half closed, and the deep brown irises dropping, rolling, and finally the eyelids eased shut over white.

"You one tough little chocolate Chiclet," he whispered. "Too stubborn to sleep. Now I wonder where you got that from."

*   *   *

The late July heat stayed dry, even drawing the dank cool from the walls in the bottom level of the garage when he walked. Outside again, he could smell perfume where women had just walked past the fountain. Then he smelled blank hot again, rising from the cement. He picked up a piece of palm bark, light as breath in his hand, and touched the spongy end.

Through the street-level lot, hearing the electronic farts and burps of car alarms being set, he stayed close to the fence. Black iron bars rimmed the rough cement block, tipped with spikes all along the top, winding around the lot and the hotel pool. He saw a few people swimming behind the hedge that screened the water from the entrance; the hotel was full for a jazz festival.

He heard a voice from the sidewalk. "Yo, brothaman," someone said. He turned to see Frankie Randall peering through the bars.

Frankie was always downtown, looking into open car windows at red lights, waiting in the center divider for pedestrians. "Brothaman, can you spare a dollar for a meal?"

Darnell looked right into Frankie's eyes, the deep street creases over the bridge of his nose. Frankie looked past him, to the fountains. He don't see me at all, Darnell thought. Played football with me in junior high, beat my ass up close and personal four times walkin home on DaVinci. Frankie's fingernails were curved thick, black, resting on the shelf of cement. Darnell pulled a dollar from his pocket and Frankie nodded. "Thanks, brothaman," he said, formally.

The palm fronds above Darnell rubbed hollow and dry, shifting noisily. His notepad and walkie-talkie were stiff in his pocket, the heavy flashlight clanked against his leg, and he didn't want to think about Frankie; he remembered the equipment he'd carried in the mountains, on the line. The Pulaski, the gear.

The fronds danced again. The old, dead ones waited for a strong winter wind to pull them off, and landed in the street cracking loud as gunshots. He'd always lain awake on the couch, listening. The wind would gust so hard around the house that the weather stripping, old and warped, would hum loudly, as if ghost mouths were breathing on the glass. In the morning, the palms like the ones above him would lean with their fronds all to one side so they looked like giant toothbrushes.

The summer he was six, the palm outside GranaLene's caught fire in the long, dead fronds gathered around the fat trunk like a hula skirt. He saw the tree smoking, breathing out wafts of gray like a huge man with a cigar. Rats lived in the palm trees; he'd seen them running the power lines, heard them rustling the fronds.

But with the next hard push of wind, he'd seen orange flames lick out from the heart of the tree, the place where the fronds began, and the fire engine came after GranaLene poked her head out onto the tiny porch and sniffed.

The men's yellow coats shone glossy, and the ruby lights twirled. The firemen weren't scary like the police; when they took off their coats, instead of guns he saw suspenders.

The tree breathed. The men uncoiled the hose from the humming engine, and Darnell saw the water blow in the wind, spatter on GranaLene's roof. A crowd of boys had gathered around Darnell then, and when the city truck brought a cherry picker and one fireman rode up to lean close between gusts that lengthened the flames, the boys all shouted. Darnell smelled the smoke harsh like burning trash in the vacant lots across the street.

He heard Donnie hollering, and he started. "Yo, man, you need to stop trippin when you on patrol, Darnell! I been callin you—hurry up!"

One of the ladies from the hotel had lost her car. Darnell walked with her all around the garage in a spiral square, until she found it on the third level. A maroon Sentra, like a hundred others. She smiled weakly and waved when she drove past the guard booth.

"Man, your pops was right. You lost in space sometimes," Donnie said. "I remember you used to wander off till after dark, and he'd whup your natural ass."

"I saw Frankie Randall, man," Darnell said.

"Man, Frankie don't know nobody. Only face he care to see is Washington's."

Darnell looked at Donnie's big hands holding the flashlight. "You ever miss ball, man? I mean college ball."

"You know I play ball all the time at the gym, man. Westside brothas are harder than anybody in college. I just hated school. I love playin ball now—no pressure, no coach hollerin."

"Yeah," Darnell said. "Your turn to walk."

"I'm goin. I ain't gon be dreamin out there like you. You hear the morning guy found two cars busted into by the center? Past the loading docks. See, they know it's two of us at night and only one old man in the day." He got up, but Darnell touched him with the pencil.

"So when they gon make me full time, man? I need some more money, some benefits, baby. I got dependents," Darnell said.

Donnie shrugged. "You gotta be patient, man. They wait to see if new guys are gon steal or let friends in. . . . " He walked toward the fountain, swinging the flashlight. Darnell stayed in the mouth of the garage. You miss fire, man?

Well, yeah, brotha, but I run out and fight one on the weekends, you know, I like it better, no other guys on the line hollerin at me to do this, do that.

Fricke had told him that Scott and Perez were living in Doloreaux, across the riverbottom from Rio Seco, and working as paid-call fire-fighters. They can afford to do that, Darnell thought, just go out and make ten dollars an hour when the call comes. Cause they only need beer and Taco Bell.

He filled his hand with water from the drinking fountain, wet the back of his neck and splattered the water across the cement, where it evaporated. Yeah, I just start a fire, do my own thing, baby, turn on the garden hose and listen to it sizzle and pop. I do a good job, too. He stared up at the gray waffle squares of the cement roof, the long tubes of fluorescent lights that left white bars inside his eyelids when he closed them.

"Same old story," Ronnie said. "I heard it. 'I walked ten miles to school, boy. Man, we couldn't even go to school in Oklahoma, they made us walk over the border to *Texas*. And here your lazy ass want a ride.' "

Darnell laughed at his perfect Pops imitation. "He think I'ma let his whole business go down while he gone for a week."

"Didn't he used to take all of you to Oklahoma?" Victor asked. "I remember Melvin hated that shit."

"Yeah, cause all they talk about is how hard they had to work, shootin squirrels for dinner. And then how Melvin and the young dudes don't know how to work cause they spoiled lazy." Charolette pushed her small palms hard against his chest to see around him to a dog. "My parents took Sophia and Paula, though, cause school don't start till next week. They wanted to see the funeral. Pops' second aunt."

"Man, take us to the park, homey," Victor said impatiently. He and Ronnie had worked with the Kings, who'd gone to the dump.

Charolette watched their hair pressed to the back glass. He'd had her all week, and he'd figured her out. She screamed when he stayed home and held her because she was bored. If Brenda held her against those soft bumps and that smell, she was in heaven, but with him— no, take me somewhere, she told him loudly.

She touched his lips now when he strapped her in the car seat. "So you ain't stupid," he'd said to her determined face. "And you like to drive. Cool."

Brenda didn't want her in Jackson Park, but Darnell said, "She's mine, too."

"All those guys selling stolen liquor, the cops going through," she started, but he said. "I got her, okay? Nothin's gon happen when she's with me."

On a hot day like this, men sat on broken couches, stood around the table, rested on lowered truck gates. Victor and Ronnie jumped out to where Brother Lobo was holding court on a folding chair. "Darnell!" he said, squinting. "And the littlest African queen!"

He took her carefully, as always, and kissed her huge cheek quickly before she frowned and twisted toward Darnell. The pride raced up his back—You, Daddy, I want you. I belong to *you*.

"Five more seconds," Brother Lobo said, before handing her back. "Look at that cheek—you could rent out office space in there, it's so big."

Darnell held her butt, the way he'd gotten used to, with his arm under it and her fist clenching a rosette of shirt; she brushed his ear in constant movement as she struggled to get down, to crawl. Her head bobbed, her arms flung upright.

"What a girl," Lobo said, watching her closely. "Her head moves around like Katharine Hepburn's, and her hand gestures like a flamenco dancer." He laughed. "Too bad she breathes like a telephone pervert."

"She uses a lot of air," Darnell said, smiling. Charolette did pant hoarsely, excited and smiling. Brenda said it was the smog, but Darnell knew she was in a hurry even to breathe. "She even sleep rough, move all around."

"Bad sign, brotha," Victor said, handing the bottle to Ronnie. "She sleepin between you and your woman, man, that means you ain't gettin no nappy, huh?"

Darnell felt heat rise in his neck. "Man, how you know? You ain't got kids."

"All I gotta have is ears, hearin how daddies like you don't get no time with your women." Victor grinned. "Brenda too tired, right, homey?"

Brother Lobo sipped his Dr Pepper and said, "African men had multiple wives for just this reason. Sex and new motherhood are separate by nature. In many African cultures, men cannot even touch a nursing woman."

Darnell felt strange when Brother Lobo talked about something like they were all still in junior high, even the grandfathers at the domino table. Lobo always sound like that, no matter who's around, he thought, except usually I ain't gotta hear about my love life.

He said, "I gotta get her a bottle." At the car, he thought, No, Brenda's chest still ain't mine. Tucked away safe in that thick nursing bra, no lacy push-up bras unhooked in the front. No easy access, baby.

She looked beautiful, too, her hips rounded now, her face fuller under the jaw, her hair thicker splayed out on the pillow. Her arms were softer around him, and when he put Charolette in the crib, if she'd finally stop screaming, Brenda would take him out to the couch for a few minutes. "You have to be quiet—the baby," she'd say.

Darnell held the bottle of juice for Charolette, who rested her head on his shoulder to drink. Maybe they done with sex and moved on to somethin I feel like hearin about, he thought, looking back toward the trees. But he saw Victor laughing, Brother Lobo talking so hard his head bobbed, and he slid her into her car seat. "It's all cause a you," he told her. "So let's do some day partyin, since my nights ain't mine no more."

At the day-old bakery, he bought three loaves for a dollar, and drove to the city lake. Holding Charolette tight, he tried to show her how to throw bread to the ducks, but she just held the squishy white center, pulling it to her mouth now and then.

"This used to be my homey Louis's favorite place," he told her. He saw three Canadian geese, the ones Louis said flew down here during the cold winter. "What you guys doin here so early? Or late," Darnell asked them. "You lost?"

The three geese stayed away from the others: the huge white geese that hissed and honked, the ducks, the small goofy black birds. What had Louis called them? Coots. Darnell pointed at the Canadian geese, and Charolette's eyes followed his finger. They were aloof, holding their long black necks still, the black feet paddling patiently, not frantically like the others.

"See, those are the brothas over there," he told Charolette. "They're cool, too cool to get in a fight. We gotta throw the bread all the way over there. Yo! Soul brothas! Time to grub!"

On Saturday, he had promised to help Roscoe. A woman had been waiting all week for them to take out her big jacaranda, and with Darnell's father still gone, Roscoe needed Darnell.

Roscoe had been quieter since Louis had gone to prison, spending most of his time at Marietta Cook's, and even though he still laughed in the back room and slammed dominoes, he didn't talk about poetry like he always had, didn't describe the moon or use the right word for the kind of heat or wind in the morning.

While the saws ripped and whined, Darnell watched Roscoe's forehead creased under the Dodgers cap. Roscoe had always worn hats, ever since Darnell first remembered him coming to the house. He thought about the way Roscoe had always been patient and gentle when he talked to Darnell, but gruff and short with Louis. And his father was more likely than Roscoe to listen when Louis named a bird in someone's backyard, but he was quick to holler at Darnell.

He was afraid to say anything, but when they stopped to rest in the midmorning heat, watching smog cover the hills, he looked over at Roscoe. "Charolette be checkin out the birds, just like Louis did," he said carefully.

Roscoe took a long drink of water from the thermos. "Babies love anything that moves fast," he said, tongue working inside his cheek.

Darnell brushed the crumbled dead leaves from his bootlaces. Charolette really loved trees—she'd started to stare at the pepper branches, the shifting silvers of eucalyptus, sometimes way up to the tallest, pencil-trunked palms, and he hadn't even known she could see that far. "I don't know," he said. "She's into trees, and birds in the trees."

Roscoe said, "Maybe your father can pass on the family business to her, since you're into security." He smiled.

"That's cold, Roscoe," Darnell said. "I ain't plannin to secure forever, okay? Maybe she'll be a forest ranger, or a fire lookout. Sit up high in a tower and stare at trees, watch for smoke."

"I thought you told me they were cutting all those jobs out because of low funds," Roscoe said. "But maybe she'll be a botanist. A tree surgeon."

"Brenda and Mama look at her eyes, them long old lashes, and all they say is, 'Oh, she gon be a model, a cover girl.' But I don't play that, cause the girl got a brain, I can tell."

Roscoe's face was suddenly shadowed when he dipped the hat brim back down. "You can't tell your children what to be," he said. "You of all people should see that, from watching me."

"Man, I didn't . . . " Darnell bit his lip, saw Roscoe's fingers clench the thermos. He remembered the tiny, distant sound of Louis's basketball on his driveway, remembered Louis hating every minute of practice in school. Roscoe'd had a few beers one night long ago and told Darnell's father about wanting to be a poet, about his own father laughing at him, saying, "You gon eat paper when you hungry?" And then Roscoe said the same to Louis, over and over, when he and Darnell were loading wood. "What can you do with birds? You gonna be an ornithologist? Lots of positions for that, yeah. Or maybe you can head the Audubon Society. Shit, Louis, you've got a forty-two-inch vertical. You can play *ball*."

"He didn't even call me from jail," Roscoe said now. "Finding out from the newspaper like that . . ."

"See, I couldn't even be havin this conversation with Pops," Darnell blurted out. "He never wants to hear about fire. Hell, he never wants to hear anything from me—just says, 'We ain't got time to chat. Get back to work.' I could always talk to you, but Louis couldn't." He paused, smelled the sawdust on his face. "Sometimes he talked to Brenda. And Brenda's daddy ain't spoke to her since we got married."

Roscoe bent to hand him the thermos. "It's like chess. Checkmate is a hard move to take back and do over." Darnell watched the grass stay flat even when he lifted his hand from it; the drought had made it limp. Roscoe straightened and said, "We better finish before the crows fly home." He smiled. "I watch them fly over us every evening, and it's almost like going back. Remember Louis with his face always up in the air like he was waiting for one of them to drop money in his mouth?"

He saw Trent that night, coming out of the convention center with a woman. "Darnell! This is my wife, Brichee."

She was light as Brenda, but her makeup was even paler, silvery dry at her jaw. She nodded. "That sounds French," Darnell said, uncomfortable.

"It is," she said, giving him a no-teeth fake smile, and moving off toward the garage.

Trent said, "She's from New Orleans." He grinned and shook his head. "She loves the weather out here, and hates my relatives. She comes from big bucks."

"I ain't your relative," Darnell said.

"But I got so many cousins, Snooter and all them, when she sees anybody she thinks . . ."

She thinks they want somethin, Darnell thought. He said, "How she get here?"

"Came out to go to college. Accounting. She works in LA." Trent glanced at her talking with another woman. "We were at the antique show in there." He nodded at Darnell's jacket. "So this is your gig now, huh? I thought you were going into gardening."

"Pops still wants me to work yards on the side. Lotta competition." Darnell watched the sparse crowd around the fountain.

"Better to work for yourself," Trent said. "Especially for a brother."

"Even a normal brotha?" Darnell said, smiling, and Trent grinned back. "Work for myself—you sound like Pops. Even Snooter."

Trent mocked fear, saying, "Don't let my wife hear that!" and he walked toward her, lifting his hand.

As the nights came earlier and the days got cooler, he went to pick up Charolette at his mother's around four o'clock. His father and Roscoe were just finishing by then, and clouds quilted the sky. He stood out in front with them the first week of November, Charolette on his thigh, where he propped it against a bumper, and they saw the moon come up so fast it left the clouds piled at its base.

"Brenda take the baby to the cemetery?" his father asked suddenly, and Darnell frowned.

"When?"

"On the first. Remember, Mrs. Batiste and Mrs. Dauphine and your mother all go over there." His father kicked a few twigs off the truckbed.

Darnell tried to remember what they did at the cemetery in November at the graves—was it flowers like Memorial Day? He'd been gone a few years—he heard pounding bass, and Leon and Vernon boomed by in the Bronco, lifting their chins at him. He wondered what they said about him. The drums knocked against his throat. Good boy. Square-ass brotha. Goddamn unarmed security with a walkie-talkie makin some spare change. Got him a spare job, they were laughing.

His father said harshly, "You goin to pick up Brenda? She shouldn't be walkin in the dark."

"Like I'ma let her walk downtown in the dark," Darnell said impatiently. "Me? Personal security for the world?"

Charolette pointed at the sound that had stopped at the end of the street. "Don't run your mouth, boy," his father said. "Get goin."

Roscoe stood up with them and said, "I'll come with you, Darnell, show you something."

He was quiet all the way downtown, and then he said, "See?" Darnell parked where he'd pointed.

They stood on the sidewalk, watching the sky. A handful of pepper was flung high in the descending gray, moving, wheeling; then it was a huge swarm of gnats, Darnell thought. But they swooped closer, the great flock of blackbirds looping together, shifting in ever-turning patterns. Charolette's mouth was open, her eyes following the flock for a long time. Darnell saw two mechanics watching from the gas station across the street.

"They live in these trees every fall," Roscoe said as the flock suddenly dropped onto the rounded, thick-leaved trees that lined the broad street. "Louis never did find out why. But they fly like that every night till dark." The birds all began to chirp and screech at once, and Charolette jumped at the noise that drowned out the traffic. Roscoe touched her back. "They're just birds, baby," he said gently.

* * *

The main ballroom at the Hilton was full of women. The Rio Seco County Women of the Year—dinner, awards, speeches. Darnell and Donnie went in and out of the lobby now and then to make sure everything was okay.

In the doorway, next to the ashcan with white sand on which somebody stamped the Hilton logo every night, Darnell looked at the tight circles of women. The chandeliers lit them up: their jewelry, glittering hair, shiny hose on their calves. Black women, white, Oriental, Chicana. Darnell stared at all the sparkling fingernails at the table nearest him. Women do all that for each other, he thought. Brenda put on makeup every morning to go to work, smear some of it on my face when she say goodbye, and then wash it all off the minute she come home. Take off them dresses and heels and put on her sweats. She don't wear eyeshadow for me. These women dress up for their friends. He saw an elderly woman at the table, with polyester pants and a shapeless blouse—her stubby nails were painted purple to match her shoes.

The shoes . . . heels so high they looked painful. Narrow, shiny, leather, snakeskin. He remembered Brother Lobo talking about black women and shoes. Even dudes who loved shoes. "It's simple. When we were slaves, we had no shoes. Sometimes we were *denied* shoes. We're still making up for that. It's genetic, by this generation."

At the table on the stage were the mayor, his mother, and other women giving or getting awards. Darnell glanced at them; they were part of the reason for the extra attention the hotel manager wanted from him and Donnie. Let me get on before Donnie holler into the radio, he thought. I'm up here trippin again, like he always says, lost in space.

Donnie walked, then Darnell. He saw a police car cruise past on Main as he neared the fence. Up and down the concrete stairs to all the parking levels, around the perimeter, down the center of the garage and up to Donnie at the booth. They were both heading to the main entrance when a group of women came out early, laughing, standing in the central courtyard by the fountain, digging in their purses. Lookin for the keys, Darnell thought. I hope they don't all lose their cars at the same time. They went down the stairs, and he heard somebody scream.

Donnie ran from the lobby toward the stairs; high shrieking from the garage echoed off the concrete everywhere. Darnell shouted to the doorman, "Call the cops!" and he ran after Donnie, his flashlight thudding against his leg. He took it off the belt and held it tight, hearing Donnie yell.

Screeching tires sounded behind him, and he ducked into the stairwell. Was somebody stealing a car? Or the cops already here? He saw two women kneeling over a third, who was sobbing on the ground, her shiny green pumps drawn up to her skirt. She was smaller than Brenda, and blood was smeared purple-dark under her nose, on her lip. Darnell saw the terrified faces turn up to him, and one screamed again. She think I'm the dude, she think I'ma jack her. "Ma'am!" he shouted. "Security!" Their eyes were blank. "Security," he said again.

"They took our purses," one woman cried, and the other added, "she wouldn't give him her bag, and he hit her in the face! With his fist! He didn't slap her, he hit her." She was standing now, facing him, screaming. Beads glittered on the ground by the curled woman's arm.

"Okay, we'll find them," he said, hearing the foolish words slow in his mouth and he took off down the ramp. He heard a car behind him again—no, on the street level—and he yelled, "Donnie!"

"Loading dock!" Donnie hollered, his voice muffled. "Darnell!"

The shout was fading. Darnell ran to the exit and saw two blurry dark figures and Donnie's wide-jacketed back. Black shiny windbreakers. Young dudes, one with a black cap, one bareheaded.

He heard the screeching again, right behind him now, and he ran faster. Shit, they got a friend in a car, gon run me down. Damn! He saw the two guys leap at the wall around the loading docks, and in the streetlight a long, floppy braid lifted behind one, the black hair glistening. Not a brotha, he thought automatically, and someone yelled, "Police! Freeze!" behind him.

The two guys were up and over the wall, and Donnie hit it hard. "Freeze!" the cop yelled again, and as Donnie turned, the flashlight in his hand, the shots popped out like exploding pine knots, echoing even louder. Donnie went down, and Darnell threw himself into the open stairwell.

"My leg! Darnell!" Donnie moaned. "Security!"

"You, in the stairwell, come out with your hands held away from your body. Now! Hands held away!" Darnell's body shook. The flashlight. His badge: metal shine like a gun. Shit. Shit. He shivered against the wall, smelling the filmy smoke on the warm cement. "He's not coming," he heard the voice say, and then the dog was upon him, the teeth buried in his leg, tearing pain into his calf, and his shoulders still shaking so hard his teeth chattered.

When the wet teeth lifted off, the heat rushed up from the concrete to his cheek, pressed into it, and he felt the flaming hot pouring from his leg. He could hear Donnie whispering, "It burns like, man, it burns," but Darnell kept his lips clenched shut until they were icy numb. He saw the helicopter beam knifing blue trails through the street toward them, and he heard the muffled click of paws moving away, the wet growing cool and sending streams of chill up his back, into his skull.

BURNING

CLOUDS PLAYED with the sun. Strong yellow light would fill the curtains and numb his eyes for a minute, then pewter would recede from the window. His head expanded, then shrank with the light until he turned over to get away from the shifting glare.

His leg throbbed, burned. Donnie moaning—it burns, man, it burns. The huff-rattling throat of the dog. The saliva hot on his skin. He pushed his face into the sheet, stiffening. The skin was tight as ready-to-split fruit, as dead possum belly in summer.

Darnell's stomach roiled, and he breathed into the cotton sheet, smelling Brenda's hairdress faint and sweet. The bites were in the flesh of his calf. He wouldn't turn his neck to look. He held his leg perfectly still. What color was calf muscle if it was infected—fever hot and pulsing with yellow? He'd seen the cloth rags Brenda's mother took away. His throat tried to hold down the bile. Bile was green. He ground his molars hard.

She heard him moving. He smelled the heavy tobacco smoke come in with her. "Your husband know you still here?" he said into the mattress.

"I ain't studyin him," Mrs. Batiste said. She straightened the curtains she and Brenda had made months ago. "Your mama went home for a while."

He stayed belly down, tensing. She pulled off the wet poultice, and the air against the swollen bites made tears press against his eyelids. He clenched his fists slowly so she wouldn't see the movement. He heard her blowing softly on the burning sugarcane stalk, and the charred-sweet smoke drifted over him.

"Do it itch yet?" she asked, between breaths.

"No."

"You hot." She didn't ask.

"Yeah."

"Fever workin. Try and kill them dog germs." She blew, blew, the smoke dancing over his legs, wisping lighter around his ears. He stared at the wall, the swirl of black.

"I been gone from the Westside so long I don't even know for sure that Puerto Rican man still have sugarcane grow by his yard. One dollar a stalk. He must be ninety," she murmured. She propped the reed in the tall jar by the bed; he heard the hollow clunk. Then she sat to make a new poultice with the strange tobacco.

"Stuff stink like no cigar I ever smelled," Darnell said.

She laughed. "That perique. Blacker than black. Only grow in Louisiana, by one place. You can't get it nowhere else in the world." She showed him a mashed weed. "And *la mauve.* From Louisiana, too. That pull out the infection."

"How you know all this voodoo?" Darnell whispered. His leg throbbed in the moving sunlight, like the heat swelled the skin worse.

"My granny was part Cajun," Mrs. Batiste said. "She was *traiteur,* a doctor for people in the country. She could pray better than me." He let his eyes fall on the string knotted around his wrist; another string held the ankle of his bitten leg. Nine knots in each string, and she'd whispered nine prayers. He couldn't understand the slurred words in any of them.

Her hands pressed the poultice on his leg, and he pushed his fists deep into the mattress. "We waitin for the itch," she said. "You tell me." She went back into the kitchen, and he thought she was finished.

He closed his eyes, but then she was beside him again, pulling at his arms. "I want that fever stay down in your leg, work down there. I don't want the heat work on your head." She circled his wrists, the insides, the pulses, with fresh-cut potatoes in thick bracelets.

He heard the TV in the living room, and the thump-hissing of the iron. She had washed and ironed all the curtains and bedsheets in the three days she'd been here. Brenda kept circling the bed at first, holding Charolette, crying so hard her chest shook tears from the baby's eyes, too.

He was still supposed to be in the hospital. The guys in the emergency room had said, "You're gonna have to stay here a few days, so we can drain the wound and watch it. Puncture wounds, when they're serious like this . . ."

"Fuck that," Darnell had said. "I'm gone." The doctor had argued with him and the cop who'd brought him. An ambulance had taken Donnie, but the older officer, who'd sent away the young cop with the dog, the K-9, had put Darnell in the front seat of his patrol car, then moved him past the crowds of waiting emergency-room faces and into one of the small cubicles, where doctors appeared. While they were alone, the officer had looked out the window, but Darnell could see his lined cheeks in the night-dark glass. "Damn," the cop said, his face twisting tight. "Why the hell didn't you two just follow procedure?"

Darnell said nothing. He saw the tiny woman, smaller than Brenda, the purple-dark blood under her nostrils, the glittering beads all around her; he heard Donnie's heavy shoes slap-fading into the garage. The cop shook his head, silver hairs like pins moving on the back of his head. Darnell stared at them, fascinated, imagining them flying off into his leg, his calf, which was screaming cold in the air-conditioned room. Shit! This damn uniform cost money. He ground his molars at the pulsing in his leg, and the cop said, "You guys have been watchin too many movies." He turned around, his voice soft. "*You* don't chase the perps. You leave that to us."

Darnell looked away, staring at the pale green wall while the doctor slid needles past him and muttered. Yeah, he thought. Next time. He heard the cop say to the doctor, "I can't make him stay, he isn't a suspect yet, not in this investigation."

The police sent Tommy Flair to the apartment. Short, bowlegged, he'd run track with Melvin, and he'd wanted to be a cop since he was a kid. Darnell had read about him in the newspaper last year, an article his father had saved: Tommy Flair had been chasing a drug dealer through alleys and outrun him, so the paper featured his old track-star photo beside a picture of him in the alley.

Tommy said, "Bangers are out there carryin Uzis, Darnell, man, you know that." His forehead creased, and sweat collected at his temples when he stood up from his chair beside Darnell's bed. The other cop, the older one, Sergeant Thomas, sat with his arms folded, smiling slightly. Tommy paced, and Darnell knew he was working hard for himself as much as for Darnell. "It's hard out there, man, gettin harder every day. Every night, man. Sue the department, and that ain't gonna get anybody anywhere."

Darnell was afraid to look at the sergeant's face; he stared at Tommy Flair's black shoes, thinking, It's hard out there, man. Every night when you drivin, or walkin to the store, you fit the description. Assume the position. He heard Tommy stop and he looked up. "Darnell. Look, Kleiser's a good cop, man, he's not, he's not like an asshole, man." Tommy kept his eyes hard on Darnell's. "I'm serious, Darnell."

Sergeant Thomas said, "But there's a lotta assholes out there, you know what I mean?" His eyelids were half dropped, he was still smiling, and Darnell reached up to rub his eyes like he was tired. The man's eyes—like when you were driving on the freeway or back from the Ville and a patrol car passed you.

Donnie had called after they left. Darnell had closed his eyes and felt his hips go liquid with the pain pill. Donnie said, "You got my back, Darnell? We gon sue, oh, most def. Big time. They send my man Flair over to your crib to talk?"

"Donnie," Darnell said. "I ain't into lawyers. You see people goin to court for three, four years on suits. And I don't want nobody callin me all the time for instant replay, okay? No—I'm serious, man."

Donnie said angrily, "So you ain't gon testify, man?"

"I got your back, okay?" Darnell said. "If I have to, I'll go up there for you. If you ever get up there. But listen, man, I can't live watchin for Rio Seco PD watchin me—see if I use my blinker when I turn, keep a eye on my registration, see how far I park from the curb. You know what I'm talkin about. And what if I'm drivin at night from the Ville and somebody say I was weavin in traffic?"

"Goddamn," Donnie said. "I can't believe you." But his voice was fading, and Darnell knew he was sleepy, too.

"Does it hurt?" Darnell whispered. "I mean, can you feel it?" He had his eyes closed, pictured the bullet resting in muscle like a seed, a peach pit.

"No," Donnie said, his voice lower. "But you know it's there. It's weird, I mean, it's by my hipbone and shit."

Hipbone connected to my thighbone, thighbone connected to my kneebone. Darnell felt his wrists thumping against the tight potato bracelets, and the milky smell rose to his face. The kneebone connected to the shinbone. Behind the shinbone was the other one . . . the tibia and the fibula. Biology class. Brenda sitting way in front—Batiste. Donnie trying to cheat off somebody's tests all the time. Louis daydreaming. The femur, the metatarsals. Darnell loved to recite them, loved to look at the skeleton, the huge life-size poster of the guy with his skin peeled away to show all the red-layered muscles, the tubing of veins and arteries. Blue blood, red blood. Put the skin back on the dude and sew it all up—take a hella lotta thread. Brenda's mother leaning over him that first night, when he'd left the hospital; Mrs. Batiste had put her face so close to the stitches, the four long wounds, that he could feel her breath on his skin, like the dog's, and he trembled. "I could have sew you better," she'd said. "I see much worse at home. In Louisiana." And she'd turned to Brenda's tear-shined face, his mother's ashen lips. "Go on outta here. Cryin like that and scare the baby, she don't need to know none a this. Go out to the couch." Mrs. Batiste had sent his father away, and Sophia and Paula, Snooter and Nacho. Everyone. She sent Brenda to his mother's with Charolette in the morning, told Brenda to drop off the baby and go to work.

Work. Procedure. The hotel had called him and Donnie. Proper procedure. Violations that jeopardize your probationary status. Report. Description. He slept. He felt her change the potatoes, colder ones for the warm rings he'd browned with his blood racing too hot. He knew when it was three o'clock by the clattering applause he heard. Oprah. Three o'clock meant Mr. Batiste would be gone to work.

When she came in again, he said, "Your husband know all these Louisiana cures, too?" He saw the contempt in Brenda's father's face that night, the thin lips and sharp-curved eyebrows and matching pencil-line edges of hair under the nose.

"Etienne?" she said, smiling a little, holding the perique tobacco in a pouch. "No. He don't have to know no more. He forget."

With the slamming door and women's voices came Charolette's high burble, and then he lifted his head to see her crawling into the bedroom, her mouth dripping a constant string of spit like a lead rope pulling her along the floor. Brenda's hands scooped her up, and his mother pushed splinters of ham into his mouth, because suddenly he couldn't even move his hands with their heavy potato jewelry. His eyelids were coated with heat. Brenda's lips pressed on his cheek, his neck—he could smell her, the scent inside her shirt when she leaned forward—and then the baby left a thread of saliva across his forehead.

The wedding cake was still half frozen when they put a forkful past his teeth. The crumbs were pellet hard, and he tasted the dye in the frosting flowers. Honoré's cake. The brotha bake like nobody else. And George do hair. My hair too long. I need to go see the man, get me a new fade, some serious razor cuts. Lightning bolts and shit in the back of my head, so somebody know me from behind. Like somebody could identify me from behind. Like Donnie and me if we both faced the wall and put our hands up. Both get a D on the back of our heads. We all look the same anyway, like gangbangers. That nigga probably slingin cane. Cane sugar—so sweet in my pipe—what them sprung brothas always say. Sprung dudes do anything for some rock cane sugar. Sugarcane smoke. The black whirls kissing his leg again, Brenda's mother pushing the veils of smoke over him now. Smoke crowning. Now! Fire comin over the ridge, man! Go, go, go! Get out your fire shelter. Head away from the flames, lie with your head away from the flames. No—you're dead again, you asshole, you lay down the wrong way—Fricke always yellin at Scott in practice. Your head's burned and your feet are okay, but with you there isn't much of a difference, is there, Scott?

Smoke in his eyes, burning in his leg, hands on his wrists to push them into the sheet's softness, keep them away so he can't touch the burning.

*   *   *

"The itch come now." She smiled. "You keep tryin to get your hands on it, we see you all night try and get to it."

Deep inside his leg, farther down than the heat, the itch began now that the pulse and fade of fire had stopped. Fierce, constant, like tiny ants chewing hard and circling frantically, the itch ate at his bone.

Brenda's mother spread the cool-mashed weed on again, covered his leg with layers of cotton cloth, and sat on a chair by the bed, sewing and humming. "You gon try and touch it," she said when he looked at her.

He didn't want her there watching. "No, I'ma be good. No lie. I'ma keep my leg up like this, like a good boy. No touchin."

She lowered her forehead at him and went out to the kitchen. When the phone rang, he picked it up right away and Donnie's voice sounded slurred, like he was on some serious tablets. "Darnell? Somebody wanna speak to you, man."

Darnell bent his leg at the knee. A strange voice said, "Hello, Darnell, this is Jerry Tarcher, and Donnie suggested that I call you to discuss possible representation for you, so that you can get some reasonable compensation for the terrible . . ."

"Say, man, lemme talk to Donnie," Darnell said, this voice thin as wire curling into his ear.

"Donnie has decided to pursue," the man continued, and Darnell gripped the receiver tight, rubbed the circle on his ear in anger.

"Yeah, look—you gon represent me when I'm in my hooptie at night? You gon speak for me when I get pulled over for bein under the influence? Look like PCP, sergeant . . . don't it always?" Darnell knew the voice didn't understand him. "Give Donnie back the phone, okay?"

Donnie's voice was faded-soft. "D., man, we need to get ours, man."

"You get yours, Donnie," Darnell said, bending close to the phone. "I don't want no drama."

He heard the sewing machine clacking. His mother used to sew at the kitchen table, when he was small, and her radio played the Supremes.

The trash truck rumbled down the street. Darnell heard somebody talking loud in Spanish in the courtyard. Itchin, man, you start itchin. That's what Ramon Morones used to tell Darnell about getting high. Ramon would stand around at Jackson Park, selling stolen meat from Lucky's, shaking his head and saying, "Man, you just start itchin and then your whole body kinda relaxes, you know? Your skin just tingles and shit, like you got a buncha fingers on you. Shit, *ese*, I can't tell you unless you already did it." Ramon was into brown-tar heroin from Mexico, the stuff that they sold down in Terracina.

Buyin some itch. Darnell pressed his palms over the cloth, tried to force the ants to move somewhere else, but they just went deeper, by his bone, to wait. *Mi vida loca*, man—Ramon's favorite saying. My crazy life. Man, I ain't into gettin high, but I have to move. I gotta get somethin.

He pulled on his jeans over the thick layers of cloth Mrs. Batiste had wrapped at his calf. Standing made the blood fall into his legs, and he waited until the room stopped tilting. The clacking paused, and he knew she heard him.

She stayed at the table. "You don't need to be goin nowhere now," she said, biting at a thread taut between her knuckles. "Walkin around in here okay."

Darnell shook his head. "I need to get some air."

She smiled. "If you gon go smell some Westside air, I drive you there. Brenda got the car at work and you ain't walkin all that way."

In her spotless Buick, Darnell kept his leg slanted off the long seat and smelled Armor-All. "How long you had this car now, ten years?" he asked.

"Eleven. Etienne keep it up. He like that."

Darnell watched the holiday banners flapping from the streetlights on Third Avenue downtown, until Mrs. Batiste turned and headed for the Westside. "Ain't no need to even look for a job till New Year's is over. I messed up Brenda's first Christmas with Charolette big time." Mrs. Batiste leaned forward slightly, concentrating over the big hood with her small self. "Why you didn't argue with me about goin out?"

She didn't look over at him. "You hardhead as your daddy. And you gon get yours, now, payback comin. Your daughter got a head like cement, too." She smiled, her lips nearly touching the steering wheel.

His father and Roscoe were cutting wood in the front yard. Darnell saw Mr. Lanier's big '49 Ford truck, the hood still shaking because he'd left the motor running like he always did. Mr. Lanier raised pigs, trading the meat for wood with Darnell's father. He and Roscoe threw bundles of cut wood, eucalyptus tied with cord, into the truckbed.

When they saw Mrs. Batiste, they all stopped. She pushed the emergency brake down carefully, took off her seat belt, and Darnell went around to open her door. But his father was already there.

"Geneva," his father said. "You given up on this boy and brought him here so we can put him out his misery?"

Mrs. Batiste folded her arms and said, "Roscoe. Lanier. John." She never called Darnell's father Red Man like everyone else.

Now they watched Darnell walk. He tried to bend the leg right, went straight over to the eucalyptus branches they were working on. "Darnell," Mrs. Batiste said.

"He all right," his father said. "He need to do some work, been layin up there in bed like a king. He gon forget how to work."

"He don't have the stitches out yet," she said. "He just get over the fever."

Darnell smelled the oil in the cut wood and steadied himself against the chain-link fence. "See, she the angel of mercy that saved him," said Mr. Lanier. "He need to listen to her, not you."

Darnell looked at his father's frown, the straight brows drawn together over the big nose, the way his father's long-fingered hands dangled in the air, gnarled, big-knuckled. His head spun, and he saw the fresh scratches on his father's forearms, the black-dried blood lines.

Roscoe said, "She knows best, Red Man," and Mrs. Batiste led Darnell to one of the folding chairs in the driveway. Darnell thought again of Roscoe's voice when he hollered at Louis.

"I'm gon visit with your mama," she said softly. "I didn't come to argue."

Darnell sat on the hard metal, his leg pounding with blood, and his father started to throw wood on the truck again with Mr. Lanier. He heard the screen door and his mother came out to touch his shoulder. "Why you up?" she cried. "You suppose to be restin still. If you were at the hospital, you'd be in bed."

His father yelled, "Bed rest only kill people. You see people retire and then they die. He need to get up here and work that leg. Work, period."

His mother yelled back, "You ain't hardly no doctor! Look at your finger if you got a short memory!" They all looked at the short middle finger on his left hand for a second, and then Mrs. Batiste murmured, "Always so hard."

His father could have saved the last joint on the finger if he'd gone to the hospital, but he refused. Darnell stood up and walked near the fence, and Roscoe said, "But Red Man did that to himself."

Darnell stopped, looked away from them, down Pablo. He didn't want them to start talking about the cops, about Donnie or the dog or anything else. The women were silent, the men chunked wood on top of wood, and Darnell said, "I'ma go inside for a minute."

He stopped at the doorway of his mother's room. Charolette lay on her pallet, scalp glittering in hot sleep. He headed for the back room and took the bottle of Canadian Club out of the small cupboard his father had attached to the wall. He poured a plastic cup half full and drank it down quickly. He steadied himself at the table, poured more, drank it. Fricke and them up there gettin looped at night, playin cards. Toe up. He lifted his foot, the bad leg. Daddy and them down here playin bones. He stared at the grains in the table, worn faint. Snooter, Mr. King, Roscoe—they would all be different around him now, want to talk about it, and how the hell could he explain? They'd say Donnie was a fool, or the cops were wrong; they'd talk about the K-9 painted on cars, the dogs' faces surprising you when you pulled up at a red light and stared out at teeth and tongue against the glass. They'd talk about suing.

One more drink. His head was warm, his ears felt long-lobed, and his stomach full of heat. He couldn't feel his legs. He walked carefully back through the sideyard and stopped to rest, his hand on the Spider's thick-dusted hood. Hey, baby. You miss me? You miss Brenda's ass in your seat? I do, man, I miss it big time. He touched the dirty passenger window. Yeah, the sun would shine through there, and she'd be wearin one a them camisoles. Nipples movin tiny in the cold.

Her neck, her collarbone, the pools of dark on either side where the hollows in her skin dipped above the bone. Clavicle. She had one hell of a clavicle. And the gold expanse of skin above her breasts, sheened with sweat when she leaned against the car door and he brought his lips close.

Yeah, now I'm really toe up. Half drunk, horny, fulla tobacco smoke and some kinda voodoo, strings tied on me and shit. He walked to the front, smiled carefully at his mother and Mrs. Batiste. "I guess I better get on back," he said, standing far from them.

His father said, "Plenty for you to do around here. Let Mrs. Batiste get on back to her work and I'll take you home later." He dangled a bundle of wood with one hand. Roscoe held the chain saw.

Mr. Lanier said, "Make sure you get healed in your heart and your head, too, son, not just in the leg." His elbow rested on the truck door, and he leaned out toward Darnell.

See, that's just the kinda shit I don't want to hear. Ain't nothin wrong with my head. Y'all trippin. All I got is some stitches. And the only thing I need to be healin is my dick. He smiled, still careful. "I want to get back home and clean up for Brenda."

He kept his face turned to the open window when he exhaled. Mrs. Batiste said only, "Your mama get a lot of orders for curtains lately." Darnell could tell that she didn't want to mention his father.

When she pulled into the courtyard, he had the door part open, saying, "You don't need to come back up. It's cool—I'ma rest up, so I can eat with Brenda and Charolette at the table." He was already outside, letting the whiskey blow off his words, and she held the steering wheel tight.

"If you need somethin to drink, take that itch away, ask me next time," she said. "I bring you somethin day after tomorrow." She didn't look at him, just backed out slowly, her face lifted to the rearview mirror.

The itch raced, burst under his skin like the silent fireworks that were always his favorite, the ones that sent sparkles flying outward wildly but didn't make a sound. He scissored his legs in the sheets and then walked around the apartment, the liquor draining down to his feet, leaving his head large and empty. The cuts seemed to follow him when he walked, the ants swarming until he thought he would scream. He grabbed his wallet and walked down the street to the liquor store, where he usually picked up milk at night.

The Canadian Club beside him, he lay in bed. Damn, first alcohol I bought for myself since I turned twenty-one. I could always get a taste of Pops' if I wanted some. He swigged the liquor. The heat traveled down to his leg again, drowned the ants, bathed his leg in numbness.

When he woke, the room was dark, the door was closed. He stood slowly, his smell rising to his nose. Serious funk, man—I need to take a shower, and Miz Batiste say I can't get these stitches wet. He put his palms on the door, opened it.

The front room was ghostly gray. He touched hardened macaroni curves on the table by the high chair. Brenda and Charolette breathed on the couch; he stood over them. Charolette was tucked between Brenda's arm and side, her open lips at Brenda's shoulder. Darnell slid his fingers under her stomach and pulled her up carefully; she curled onto his shoulder now, and he went into the bedroom, laid her in the crib that was always empty.

Brenda was propped up on the couch when he came back, touching her eyes with her knuckles. "How you feel?" she murmured. He draped himself on her, kissed her neck, the padded collarbone, and she put the heels of her hands at his armpits. "You been drinking? I can smell it coming off you."

"I can smell you, too," he said, moving against her. "Come on." He pulled at her clothes, the wall tight by his elbow, steadying his body on hers, on the narrow couch. Like old times, instead of the bed, when we only had the couch. You gotta stay tight-packed when you ain't got no room. He sank onto her, felt the warmth and wetness rise around him, but her fingers didn't pull him down by his neck, gripping the tiny hairs at the base of his head. Her heels weren't locked around his back, or pushing at his calves. He felt nothing but cool air on his body, his shoulders bare, his leg crawling in the empty space, like he was hanging on a cord from the ceiling.

When the phone rang, Darnell started, bolted straight up, thinking it was a night fire call. He felt the hard floor under his butt. The ringing cut through the dark again, and he crawled to pick up the phone. Brenda wasn't on the couch. He fell onto the cushion, said, "What?"

Donnie said, "Darnell, man. Don't cuss me out. I know it's early."

"What, man, what you want?" The living-room window was misted silver, but the sky was turning purple.

"I thought you might be workin a job with your pops, thought I'd miss you," Donnie said. Then he was silent.

"*What,* man? I was sleep." Darnell knew from the way Donnie's voice was low and cautious, not his usual smack-talking rush, what he wanted to do. He had called twice before like this. He wanted to go over every detail again, try to figure out what had happened, try to stop that moment when he spun and flashed.

"How's your leg, man?" Donnie began. Darnell rubbed his eyebrows, and Donnie said, "You remember when we were little, when they got that first K-9 unit, remember how we used to think that was Rin Tin Tin back there and shit?"

This was how he started; then he would start asking Darnell the questions about where and how long and then what. Darnell heard him breathing. "I can't talk right now, Donnie, man, I gotta get ready. I'm supposed to meet my dad, man, I overslept. Thanks for wakin me up, cause you know how he is when somebody late and shit. I'll check, all right?"

Donnie pushed air crackles into the receiver. "Yeah, homey, call me, okay? I need to get this straight, for when I gotta tell it."

"Cool," Darnell said, the phone already dropping from his hand. He rested his head against the wall, the cold hard on his skull.

Brenda came from the bedroom, pulling on her robe over her nakedness. He saw the soft mound of her belly for a second, the half-moon of her breast before she tied the sash. "What's wrong?" she murmured. "Who called?"

"Why it gotta be somethin wrong?" he said, moving over when she sat next to him.

"Cause every time the phone ring lately, it's bad news," she said, staring at him.

"Just Donnie," he said.

"What did he want? Did he find you guys a new job?"

Darnell smiled. "Yeah, right. Donnie ain't even lookin now; he's into this lawsuit."

She looked into the kitchen, so he could barely hear her. "You still don't want to do it?"

"It's no need to even bring it up, okay?"

She stood at the counter. "Darnell, what happened was wrong.

They were wrong. Maybe you could get some money. It'll still be wrong, but . . ."

"But I'll still be me," he said, turning to face her. "Well, yeah, baby, let's have our lawyer contact their lawyer." He made his voice businesslike. "And then I can wait for a year to hear somethin? While every cop in Rio Seco hates me, and I still ain't got a job cause I'm supposed to be sufferin whatever kinda anguish? Brenda, the only people can wait around for a suit can already feed themselves or they ain't got nobody to feed. They got the luxury, okay?" He breathed in hard. "If I had leisure time, I'd tried for five weeks of fire academy, okay? Then I wouldn't even be here," he murmured.

"Oh," Brenda said. "Then you wouldn't be here with me and the baby." Her voice was dull, her hands flat on the counter.

"No! I wouldn't be sittin here with my leg fucked up. I'd have a job."

"And you wouldn't be here," she said, in the same tone. "You'd be in the mountains. Or in another city."

He walked toward her. "And you'd be there, too," he said.

"I don't think so," Brenda said when he leaned on the counter beside her.

"Don't even bring that up," he said, and she touched the few straggly hairs on his breastbone.

"That's where we just started, a few minutes ago," she whispered. She kept her fingers on his skin, and he felt himself stiffen under the blanket he'd wrapped around his waist when Donnie called. The traces of her from last night, dried now on him, were like a thin web that broke on his tender skin.

"You always said the Indian in you was why you didn't have any hair on your face or your chest," she said. "Must be why you can't drink, either."

"Yeah," he said. "And the whole world gon be partyin tonight for New Year's. Look, so far I messed up our first Christmas together and our first anniversary. What you want to do tonight?"

Her hand stopped. "I have to work today," she said. She tried to move the blanket to see the cuts on his leg. "And you can't dance now, anyway."

"I didn't have no trouble movin around last night," he said, pressing close to her to keep her hands away from the wound.

"No, you didn't," she said, into his chest. But he knew she'd move away in a minute to get ready for work. Here we go again, he thought. She goin, I ain't. Unemployed—all non-void. "Mama's coming to take your stitches out tomorrow, too," she said. "I wish you'd go to the hospital."

"Gettin stitches out ain't no big deal," he said, bringing his hand to his eyelid, where someone had busted him open with a two-by-four in a junior high fight. Probably one of the Thompsons. He remembered the blood, remembered being just as scared to get the stitches out as when they were being sewed into his skin. "It's a minor procedure," the doctor had said to his mother.

Procedure. You didn't follow procedure. Minor procedure. He moved away, but Brenda touched the tiny zipper—that was what she'd always said it looked like, the thin scar just under his brow. She'd always whispered into his forehead right there, when they stood on her father's steps. "Be careful driving home," she used to say, and he would pull her hard against him, her lips at the corner of his eye. Here, in the kitchen, she was small, reaching up to trace the scar, and then they heard the baby.

When he went into the bedroom to get his pants, all he could see was the back of Charolette's head and the tiny hand roving from Brenda's exposed neck to her bare shoulder.

"Look at her, just slidin off your chest," his mother said when she saw them, and she hung up the last sheet on the clothesline in the back.

Darnell hiked Charolette back up and felt her fingers latch onto his ear again. "Nothin for her to hold on to," he said.

"Your daddy and them already left," his mother said. Darnell let Charolette hold the clothesline pole. "She crawlin so good now, tryin to stand up." She put Charolette in the empty laundry basket and draped her arms around the rim. Charolette laughed, eyes disappearing into her cheeks. "And you shouldn't be tryin to work yet," his mother said. "Your stitches ain't out."

"Tomorrow," he said, walking back to the El Camino.

The trash-can fire was high in the early-morning cool. Brother Lobo looked up from his game with Mr. Talbert and said, "Darnell! I'm glad to see you walking! We'd heard reports that you might have had nerve damage to the leg."

Darnell frowned. "Who said all that?"

"Leon and Mortrice, said they heard from some other people," Victor said. "You was the nigga of the news for a minute there." But even he stood awkwardly now that it had been brought up.

"I came to see if you want a job, man," Darnell said, hard, "not to talk about the past." Victor stared at him. "Pops might have a cleanup for the church on Sixth Avenue, and he said it'll take two of us."

"You sure you can go back to work?" Victor said, and Darnell sucked in his breath.

"White people with those civil-rights retrospectives on TV," Lobo said, "watch the dogs and the hoses, and they say, 'My God, those rednecks were vicious.' Who's doing a documentary on police dogs now?"

A young guy Darnell didn't know stood up from a couch and spat. "K-9."

"Eat brothas for lunch," Victor said.

Darnell opened his mouth, but Brother Lobo said, "It's been documented that the dogs attacked males of color more than ninety percent of the time, but . . ."

"Save it, okay?" Darnell said, loud, and his chest tightened. "I know all that shit." He had never spoken that way to Brother Lobo before; Mr. Talbert lifted his face to study Darnell, but Brother Lobo didn't even look at him. Darnell laced his fingers behind his head like he was stretching. "Sorry, man," he said, "I didn't . . ."

Brother Lobo scrutinized his two bones, held them lightly in his palm, and said, "You the man." Darnell heard the rebuke.

Victor said, "So your leg okay, huh?" He touched the ends of his braids, his hand curling around the back of his neck, and Darnell thought, He sound like he actually give a damn.

He didn't answer; he walked to the trash can to throw in the empty milk carton he held. The paper flared, the flame shaking the barrel and licking above, the pepper-tree branches touching his neck, the dominoes clanking between words. See, they all gon talk about it. They think this is it. If I mess up now, if somethin happen to me, they'll look at me and go, "Well, he never really got over that time when the K-9 . . . " Like Frankie and Tulane, them guys that walk the streets, and when Harris stepped in front of the train. Everybody got a story about why—"Remember when his brother hit him with that piece a wood?" Whatever.

Behind him, Lobo slapped down a domino and said, "I regret to inform you that it's over!" and then Leon's Bronco rounded the corner, booming DJ Quik from the windows.

Leon turned the volume down when he stopped by Darnell. "Homes!" Leon said, touching Darnell's palm. "You stridin fine!"

"You know it," Darnell said. He nodded at Vernon and Mortrice, who got out of the Bronco with Leon.

"We lookin for you to clarify somethin," Leon said to Brother Lobo.

Brother Lobo raised his eyebrows. "Oh—clarify, huh?" Victor laughed.

Vernon and Mortrice both wore big jeans, butts invisible in the square-sagging creases; both kept their baggy jackets halfway zipped. Always strapped, Darnell thought. Vernon said, "I need to know what 'perspication' mean."

Brother Lobo frowned. "You must have the wrong variant. You want 'perspicuity,' or 'perspicacious.' "

" 'Perspicacious,' " Leon said.

"What brotha you know gon talk like that?" Victor said.

Leon smiled. "White dude. What's it mean?"

Vernon raised his chin and said, "Mean the dude sayin Leon sweat too much, huh? He talkin shit about the brotha."

Lobo said, "It means that Leon has a clear and penetrating mind, that he's mentally alert, that he's very wise."

Leon nodded. "I knew he wasn't talkin shit, cause he had the word in a different context. Vernon don't hear when he think he listenin to this dude."

"What does this man do?" Lobo said, and Darnell chewed on his lip. Not a good idea to bother Leon about who he talk to, since he slingin cane now, he thought. Louis is doin time; Leon gotta be movin a lot of rocks.

"He a consultant," Leon said, looking straight at Lobo. "He into words. He into p-words this week. He called Mortrice 'peripatetic,' and homey took offense and shit."

"You say that word with resonance and just the right emphasis," Brother Lobo said to Leon. " 'Peripatetic' means that he travels a great deal."

Mortrice nodded. "Yup-yup," he said. "Like a rollin stone."

"Like you're rolling rocks, isn't it?" Brother Lobo said, and Victor and Darnell shook their heads. "Did this man teach you a word that describes your business? 'Pernicious.' Highly injurious, very harmful. Deadly."

Vernon looked at Leon and frowned. "Pernicious to talk yang. Somebody could smoke your ass."

Leon looked up at the weak winter sun, dime-sized in the sky, his arms folded, and Darnell's legs trickled cold. "Man, I remember you tellin us in school that bein a nigga is highly injurious. Ax my man Darnell here. He got some pernicious-ass teeth in his leg."

Darnell's mouth ran with saliva, and he swallowed quickly. "I'm off memory lane, man," he began, but Lobo cut him off.

"I never used the word *nigga* in my class, Leon," Lobo said gently. "And you're twisting a lesson for your own needs."

"That's because I'm perspicacious," Leon said. "And my man Darnell here need to hear somethin about bein peripatetic." He grabbed Darnell by the shoulder and led him aside, near the Bronco's bumper.

"I ain't suin, man," Darnell said, but Leon shook his head.

"I know. I seen Donnie. I ain't yangin about that. My brother told me you needed some cash to fix the Spider, but I see you still drivin the El Camino."

"I ain't into . . ." Darnell hesitated, not wanting to disrespect Leon. "I ain't into distribution, man."

"Neither am I, like you talkin about," Leon said. "I *been* moved up, man, and this dude, the consultant, he need somebody smart like you for special runs. Not no wild child like Mortrice or Vernon."

Darnell shook his head. "No, man, I can't hang."

Leon let his foot fall off the bumper. "That's cool, D.," he said. "So where you gon work?"

"I didn't start lookin yet," Darnell said.

"Brenda got that steady slave, that's cool," Leon said, and Darnell couldn't tell by his eyes what Leon meant. Before he could say anything else, Leon shoved him back toward the group with his elbow, and Darnell remembered all the summer days and evenings they had played football in the streets, fought in the fields.

"Homey a family man," Leon said, and Victor smiled hard. Then two girls came out from the alley beside the Gray Hollow houses, cocked their heads to hear the music thumping faint from the Bronco, and they walked toward the men. Vernon walked out to meet them; Leon turned his back. "I hate sprung females."

"You spring em," Victor said.

"Uh-uh, man, they put they own lips on the pipe." Leon spat. "I don't open they mouth and make em breathe. That's like sayin the farmer make you eat pig, brothaman. But you buy the meat if you want it. I don't eat the nasty pork."

"Choose your poison," Mr. Talbert muttered, and Darnell walked toward the El Camino, cool pulling off his shoulders like spiderwebs under his shirt.

He lay listening to the crackle of gunfire, regular now even though it was ten minutes to midnight. A shotgun—booyaa, booyaa. Then silence. Brenda's feet hissed across the sheets when she moved. Charolette's breath rustled in her throat, her arms thrown above her head, her mouth open.

Darnell lay still, hands folded on his chest, his leg tingling against the cotton bedspread. It only itched at night now; in the day, he put on a cream Mrs. Batiste left for him. He was too hot inside the covers. He heard a few car horns, a few faint shots, then the yells. He imagined the giant ball dropping on TV, like he and Brenda used to stay awake and watch.

The shotgun went booyaa, booyaa, booyaa. Then he heard the sharp report of pistols—.357s, a .38. Then stuttering fast and continuous. Automatic. Ooh. Uzi. Somebody real happy.

What you do on New Year's you'll be doin the rest of the year, people always say. Partyin, fightin, dancin, makin love. He heard the gunfire mixing in sound and texture, heard more shouting and laughing and car horns. Cool—I'll be hearin bullets fly, and I'll be itchin. Baby, I can't scratch it.

The Uzi sounded alone, chattered like shivering teeth of a big god, one of those long wood masks with scary mouths and fangs. Darnell didn't hear the helicopter or any sirens. On New Year's, the cops in Rio Seco parked under shelter, just before midnight. Usually they waited under a freeway bridge or in a parking garage to avoid the raining bullets that could pierce car roofs and pedestrians' heads and the teeth of children's upturned faces, bared to the sky.

Parking garages were the safest. Underground. Dark, layers and layers of asphalt winding above you. A guard booth at the front. Darnell rubbed his leg back and forth on the sheet, just an inch either way so he wouldn't wake Brenda or Charolette. They didn't even stir with the gunfire. Brenda slept through earthquakes, sirens, shots, but let Charolette cry for a second, and even if Brenda was downstairs at the washer with a Harley idling beside her, she could hear the baby. And Charolette heard every creak of the floor if they tried to leave her in the crib and escape to the living room; she heard every tiny laugh Brenda let out with Darnell. But they both lay motionless now except for their lips, trembling with air and dreams.

The Uzi was the last to quit. Finally the sound Darnell and Louis and Nacho had imitated all through childhood, the doo-doo-doo-doo through their teeth, rough sticks thrust forward in their hands, stopped. The sky was silent. Darnell saw himself hiding behind trees with the others, shooting their mulberry branches at cars until their tongues were tired.

When Mrs. Batiste pulled at the black thread, his skin pulled, too, as though tiny veins were sliding out. He pictured the veins and arteries again, felt her clipping and gentle tugging. Brenda watched silently behind him. He felt stupid lying down on his belly on the bed like this. The women bent over his leg, and then Mrs. Batiste said, "Finish. They heal okay, but the wound still not all closed up. You could wear a loose Band-Aid for a couple more days."

"You can still see the cuts," Brenda whispered to him. "Look."

"That's okay," he said, moving off the bed. He didn't want to look at the back of his leg, or at Mrs. Batiste's face.

"I made some coffee, Mama," Brenda said. Darnell felt wetness on his foot, and he jumped. Charolette leaned over his ankle, a heavy tremble of spit at her chin.

Her mother went into the kitchen, and Darnell picked up Charolette to let her look out the window. The back of his leg tingled. "This coffee ain't strong like you daddy like it, huh?" Mrs. Batiste said. She watched Darnell bend his leg. "I taken more stitches out Etienne many time when we stay in Gray Hollow." She smiled at Darnell's face. "Oh, he use to fight all the time. And my uncle, in Louisiana, oh, he worse. We sew him up, too."

"Your husband?" Darnell said. The stiff-held crescent of mouth, the line of mustache?

"I remember," Brenda whispered. "One time he bled on the sidewalk, and you were so mad, Mama, cause the city just poured the cement. Blood came all out his arm."

Mrs. Batiste's face was still now. "Didn't nobody cut him," she

said. "He done poke his arm in a broken window. Someplace he
don't need to be." Before Darnell could say anything, she sipped her
coffee and turned to the sink. "I finished at the store now, huh?"
she said.

Brenda said, "That where you told him you were? Did you go out
last night?"

"What you think?" her mother frowned. "You know your daddy
don't go out. Not no more." She let the lines fade from her forehead.
"Darnell, you can drink the rest of this dishwater. Brenda, you lucky
he like that Winchell Donut coffee."

Darnell remembered the smell of heavy black grounds, floating
way out to the steps at Brenda's when he came to get her. "Guys
from Louisiana do everything hard, huh?" he said. "Even gotta wake
up hard? You need to pack some food in a bag, so he believe you?"

Mrs. Batiste smiled. "No. You want me to pack you some medicine
in a bag, so when you go out you don't bother that wound?"

"No," Darnell said, seeing her eyes narrow with concern. "I ain't
choosin that poison."

Wrapped in a blanket on the couch, he held Brenda on his chest.
A faint scrabble of itch started in his leg, tiny legs and antennae
crawling under the skin, and he put his lips on hers, touched his
tongue soft to her front teeth and the inside of her lip. She put both
hands on his temples and pulled back to look at him.

"You sure you okay in the head, too?" she said.

"Why—I gotta be hard like your pops?" He smiled. "You think if
I drink some knockout Louisiana coffee and start smokin cigarettes,
I'll be okay?"

Brenda kept her eyes gold on him. "I never was into danger,
Darnell."

"What? We talkin danger?"

She shook her head. "Hard guys. Some girls like danger—you
know that. If I was into that kinda man, I'da gone out with Victor or
Leon."

He raised his brows and grinned. "Oh, you would?"

Brenda bit her lips to stop a smile. "You weren't hard. Not dangerous to anybody except yourself. So I'm just asking," she said, her
fingertips pushing his jaw toward her again.

"Hey, it's dangerous women, too," he said. "I never was into them. But you could let that dangerous side out now and maybe scratch me up a little." He bent to her neck. "On the back."

He sat up when the phone rang. This late he knew who it was.

"You get your stitches out?" Donnie whispered. "You go to the hospital?"

"It's a minor procedure, man," Darnell said, feeling his tongue tap the roof of his mouth when he said the words.

"Man, suin ain't nothin minor," Donnie said. "Take forever. I ain't even heard nothin yet from this lawyer."

"Make sure you follow *proper* procedure, man, right?"

"Why you want to say that, Darnell?" Donnie said, and Darnell paced in the living room, watching Brenda get up and go into the bedroom.

"I don't know, man, I gotta go," Darnell said, but Donnie whispered for a while longer, about the bullet, where it still rested in his leg, and Darnell stared at the shadowy light in the courtyard.

Brenda was curled under the sheet when he hung up. He said, "That don't look dangerous," into her ear.

"I'm not dangerous," she murmured. "I'm tired, and I have to go to work in the morning."

The white cotton shirt was ironed. He touched the label at the neck. Made in Macau. Where the hell was that?

He raised the glass of water and saw the tiny letters engraved in the bottom. Indonesia.

The application procedure still had three parts. The application. An aptitude test. An interview. Ten other men always waiting in the office. At the temporary agencies, he fit pegs into holes while a stopwatch ticked, to prove manual dexterity for assembly work. He waited for printouts from the DMV, watching the people behind the counter, their cubicles plastered with memos, photos of children, greeting cards. Brenda's work space had photos of him and Charolette.

He went to his father's house after the day's rounds, and she watched him help Roscoe cut and stack wood. She squatted to pick up a heavy wrench from the driveway and tried to stand up straight from her haunches. She rose and dropped the wrench, bent to try again.

"She's walking early," Roscoe said, when she staggered toward Darnell with her stiff-legged, slanting gait.

"She walk like she toe up," Snooter said, and Darnell caught her in his arms. Toe up. His boots heavy, the trembling fire roar pushing fast . . .

"She gon be a year old pretty soon," Darnell's father said. Darnell touched the soft-twisted braids caught up in her pink headband. She was getting her color this spring, being out in the sun. She was redder than he, lighter. Clear copper-gold as a new penny, her hair thick and wavy, springing loose after her bath.

"She sure is beautiful," Roscoe said. "I remember Hollie when she was little like that, all soft cheeks and bright eyes."

"She looks like you, Pops," Darnell said.

"You tryin to compliment me, boy?" his father said. "Hell, you ever hear any adult call a baby ugly?"

But everybody mentioned how much Charolette looked like Darnell and his father—her skin, her small spaced-even teeth, her eyebrows. "Her hard head," his mother said, laughing.

"Take that wood on over to Mrs. Theus," his father shouted. "You ain't doin nothin."

Darnell took Charolette with him. "Maybe Mrs. Theus be too busy cooin over you and won't ask me the question," he told her. "Where you workin, baby?"

His father gave wood away to some of the old people whose children were gone, to Mrs. Theus and the others. Darnell put the wood on their screened-in porches or by the back steps, smelling the close, old-people air floating in the doorway around their faces, and they reached out to touch Charolette's hair, her nose. "Got that Indian in her," Mrs. Theus said, and Charolette turned her face to his shirt.

His father put a bag of oranges in the back; his mother handed him a stack of collard leaves, already washed, and he drove home thinking, Yeah, like I'm charity, too. Shit, I ain't doin this application gig forever. In one of the glasses Brenda brought home from the thrift store he read "Italy," and when he set it down, she said, "Look at the pattern. I found three of them, only fifty cents each."

*   *   *

"You really miss that firefightin slave you had, huh?" Victor said when they'd been at the church lot for a few hours. "Crazy nigga loved bein up there in the mountains with them cowboys."

"No, man," Darnell said. "It wasn't about the other guys. I just liked it up there."

"I seen two of your old buddies at that fire last week," Victor said, and Darnell stopped pulling at a half-buried bottle to look up. "Remember the riverbottom went up?"

Darnell said, "Yeah. It was only a couple of acres." He hadn't seen it, since it was late at night. "What were you doin over there?"

Victor made his face a mask. "I had business." Darnell knew Victor had stayed there for a short time in the summer, before he started sleeping in Ronnie's broken-down car at Jackson Park. Now he and Ronnie had a room in an old house near the park. Victor said, "I seen the big-mouth white dude and the Meskin guy."

"Scott and Perez," Darnell said. "Perez had a busted ankle when we did the field with you."

Victor nodded. "They was hosin that baby down the other night," he said. "Workin hard." He lifted his chin at Darnell. "How come you ain't doin that?"

Darnell bent and kicked out the thick-bottomed glass. "Cause they're just paid call—they only make money when they get a job. And they ain't got people to feed."

"I told you about usin them jimhats." Victor smiled. "But you a daddy now."

They pulled at the skeletal tumbleweeds and disintegrated cardboard in the huge hard-dirt lot behind the church, shoveled bottles and disposable diapers into piles. Darnell saw the rough brush where he'd dug breaks, the red-barked manzanita and dark greasewood. Now and then he let his vision blur while he tore out the dried weeds, and when he raised his head he was surprised to see cars rushing past him on the avenue.

After they'd come down the long dirt road from the dump, Darnell gave Victor $50 and kept $50 for himself. The dump fee had taken the rest. He waited in front of Tony's Market, and when Victor came out with the gold forty-ounce bottles of Olde English, he said, "I can't hang out today."

Victor said, "Take me by Esther's, on your pops' street." His braids were rough, clouded between the rows. Sometimes he let them go for weeks before he could pay Esther to redo them. "You go home to baby bawlin, man, and I'll be chillin out, eight-ballin." He took a big swallow.

But when Darnell had strapped Charolette in, Victor came back to the El Camino. "Esther ain't home," he said. "Drop me off at the park."

Darnell let Charolette stagger on the sidewalk near the domino table, and Brother Lobo smiled. "Wasn't she born premature?" Lobo asked.

"Yeah," Darnell said. "But she was still walkin before eleven months. Brenda was tellin anybody who would listen." He stopped Charolette from heading toward the sparkle of broken glass. "Now you a year old, huh?" he said, picking her up. He saw the patrol car ease around the corner, and the men were silent, faces stone, until the brake lights faded and someone said, "K-9."

Darnell's breath rasped in his throat. Were they watching him? Charolette elbowed him in the neck, and Lobo watched her struggle. "She's baby Darnell Junior, with that face. She's you."

But Darnell didn't want to hear. He let her take a few more steps at the curb, and then he called, "Let's jam, babygirl." She smacked into his knees, and he remembered when she was round-bellied and short-legged as a horny toad crawling from a rock. Almost a year— another fire season coming. He looked at the whisper-thin dried grass at the edges of the lot.

Back home, he sat on the couch, and Charolette wove herself in and out of Brenda's piles of clean, folded laundry. After Charolette's bath, Brenda sang, "I'm goin to Kansas City, Kansas City, here I come. They got some crazy little babies there and I'm gonna get me one." Charolette screamed when Brenda buried her nose in her wet neck.

"That's a man's song," Darnell said, remembering Roscoe play the record.

"I heard it at your dad's," Brenda said. "She loves it."

Shit, ain't no need for me to be here, he thought, and he went downstairs to lean against the El Camino in the carport. In the stall used as a wash station, somebody's clothes circled behind the dryer door, clicking and falling, and he saw a small Mexican woman in a shawl lean over the railings to see if the washer was free. He listened to the passing cars and whisper-whirling clothes until Brenda came out to call him to the phone.

The job would only last a couple of weeks before Easter, the woman from the temp agency said. Swing shift. At two-thirty he drove the El Camino to the parking lot closest to Brenda's building and caught the bus to the industrial park out in Terracina, on the south edge of the city.

The warehouse was huge, and they'd hired four guys to move inventory. Darnell carried boxes, waiting for the guy with the forklift, pulled more boxes out of trucks in the windy parking lot. STARCREST ENTERPRISES was painted on the building, in a maze of tiny streets lined with other warehouses and paint stores and wood-product wholesalers and electronic suppliers.

When his shift was over, his arms ached, and he watched the other guys get into their cars. He'd only really talked to one, Jesus Sotelo, but he lived all the way out in San Bernardino, and Darnell didn't want to ask him for a ride. The bus stopped running way out here at midnight, so he walked toward the stop on Washington, past the long expanses of short-clipped grass and what Roscoe always called "industrial shrubs," the spindly gray-green junipers and evergreens.

The second week on the job he was walking with hands jammed in his pockets and jacket collar turned up against the April wind when he heard a loud muffler following him. From an old Impala, three Chicano guys stared at him.

"Shit," Darnell said. "Terracina *vatos*."

Most of the walls and warehouses were sprayed with graffiti that said TERRA RULES and LOS DEFIANTES DE TC. He'd heard Terracina was fighting a Westside gang, Sixth Avenue Loc Special. He walked faster and was heading toward an old house at the corner of the main drag when he heard the car rounding the corner again. Starting to run, he fixed on the black wall of bushes, the square where a path cut through to the yard. "Where you from, homes?" somebody yelled from the car. Yeah, like I got time to tell you. Westside—no set, man, just my hood. I ain't in a set. Let me get there. The pops sounded like cap guns. Twenty-two. He couldn't count the shots. He threw himself into the gap and fell through the sharp-branched yew, the piney smell all around him, the car still moving and two more shots before they shouted, "Terracina, homes."

Darnell lay behind the hedge, smelling the dried stems and dead grass under him. He brushed the rough twigs from his ear. "Fuck this shit," he whispered. "Fuck it." He turned on his back and looked at the house. The windows stayed dark, and he wasn't sure if anyone was home or whether they were all lying on the floor. Like him.

When he started walking again, he threw out his arms. "Come on," he said softly. "Step to me. Come on." He knew they were somewhere else now, laughing. He passed the bus stop and walked down the long, bright avenue, past all the 7-Elevens and McDonald's and apartment buildings.

It was two o'clock when he opened the door, and Brenda was waiting on the couch, her head thrown back in sleep but snapping up when the jamb cracked. "Where the hell you been?" she said, instantly furious. "Why you didn't call?"

"I was workin overtime," he said, feeling the last thready twig of yew fall deeper into his collar. "I couldn't take a break to call."

She stood, steadied herself, pressing her fingertips on the wall, and said, "Don't *ever* do that again. You got a mouth—you can speak into a telephone. Don't ever make me live my life around that window waiting for no cop to knock. No. Don't." He saw the drapes open, the shadow of high wires striping the wall behind her, and when he went toward her, she moved out of the glare.

"I wanted so bad to just sleep with Charolette," she whispered. "Like I could keep a hand on her back. And I made myself come out here, cause if you gon leave us, it's just gon be me and her forever."

Now he caught her and smelled the sweet hairdress at the part in her hair. "Damn, Brenda." He stared at the headlights raking the wall from the street. The light, high pops of the twenty-two—I damn sure can't let Terracina take the heat for this one. Sometimes you hold the truth? That what Mama said? Or Melvin? Said a white lie is okay sometime. But this a black lie. "I thought you'd be happy about the extra money," he whispered. "I'm sorry, baby." He guided her shoulder to bed.

Gasanova was the only one he could ask. He went to the Holiday Inn, drank coffee, and said, "Man, I don't want Brenda without a car, in case the baby get sick or somethin. And I don't want to tell Pops about it, cause he'll trip and start worryin. What time you get off?"

"We close at eleven," Gas said. "I'll come and get you until you save the Spider."

But he couldn't tell Gas, or anyone, about Brenda's face. Staring at that window. He had to lie. When Gas picked him up in the parking lot at the warehouse, no sounds booming from his truck's rolled-up windows, Gas said, "Some dude over here figure if you leavin Terracina now, you must be gettin some hoochie. Some Terracina coochie."

"Yeah, right," Darnell said. "I ain't gettin hardly none at home, and now I gotta get smoked for some *imaginary* lovin?"

But they both watched the narrow side streets and the red lights. "Dudes wanna smoke somebody just for the hell of it. Got a new piece and want to try it out—make sure it shoot nice."

Darnell looked at him. "Leon like that?" Leon had always fought, but he'd been careful about his battles.

"No, Leon into dinero, strictly business. But his boys—man, they serious mental, always lookin to gat somebody."

They drove on Washington toward downtown; Gas kept the music down low so they could hear gunshots or shouts or throbbing pipes.

But the red light came before the quick drone of siren. Gas said, "Here we go," and Darnell's breath clotted in his throat. Don't move. Don't move. We ain't packin. Gas was still; Darnell's shoulder blades were hard against the seat until the p.a. system from the patrol car blared.

"Passenger, display both hands outside the window and get out of the vehicle." Darnell felt the muscles in his neck, sore from loading, stretch when he dangled his palms over the door edge without moving his upper body.

When he and Gas were lying on far-separated squares of sidewalk, a cop stood beside each of them, looking at their side-turned jaws. In the long silence while Darnell waited for the man to ask for ID, he lay with his cheek against the still-warm cement. The chain-link fence surrounding a parking lot beside him was fringed with green, and he stared at the weeds. Been a drought, he thought, but they came up anyway. He breathed even. Ask me for ID. ID these plants. Okay—the tall one is wild oats, still got green in it, but not much. I see some filaree, makin them corkscrew seeds. If I spit over there, the seeds gon start to unravel in the wet.

"ID," said the man whose shoes were near. Darnell slid the wallet out of his back pocket. He could hear Gas answering the other cop. "We had reports of gunfire in this area last night," the cop said, flipping open the wallet. Then he said, "Darnell Tucker." Darnell heard his voice change, go higher in his neck. "I thought you drove an El Camino."

Darnell stretched his neck slightly to look up. He saw the pale toothbrush-sized mustache and green eyes, all he remembered from that parking garage, when the cop had leaned over him for a second before he got into the car.

"Why you doin this?" Darnell said, low. "I ain't suin."

The mouth was clenched, hesitant, and the face came closer when the man lowered himself into a squat. "I didn't call this stop," he said. "This isn't—I'm subbing for somebody."

Yeah, Darnell thought. No K-9. He kept his eyes straight at the wild oats now, the stems trembling when cars passed on the avenue in rushes.

"I saw you a couple of times," the cop said. "I didn't want to stop you, you know, to try and—because you might not think—" He stopped, looked at the other officer moving toward him. "I feel bad," he said, low.

Not as bad as I do, Darnell thought, but he couldn't open his mouth against the porous-heated sidewalk.

The other cop said loudly, "His story match up? This guy says he's givin him a ride home from work." He leaned slightly. "Where you work?"

"Starcrest Enterprises," Darnell said. "Warehouse."

"Okay," the older cop said, turning, and his shoes ground the tiny pieces of sand on the asphalt.

He and Gas started up the truck slowly. Midnight. We ridin under the moon, and we blacker than a thousand midnights, Darnell thought. Gas said nothing, either. He blasted the speakers and drove home, the drums loud enough so that they wouldn't have to talk.

He bought a tiny, airplane-sized bottle of Jack Daniels for his coat pocket. When he started the walk, he stopped behind a hedge after a few cars had passed him, and he drank deep from the tiny glass mouth, the heat pouring onto his tongue. He rubbed the smooth, hard lip right there again. Brenda's nipple—right there was where it used to rest. He walked down the sidewalk past the warehouses, slipping the empty bottle into his pocket.

She'd be asleep tonight when he got home. This morning, she'd said, "How's Gasanova?" when Darnell sat at the table, bleary-eyed.

"Cool," Darnell said, resting his head on his arms, pushing his cheek onto the cold table. "He's cool."

"Darnell?" she said.

"I'm just tired, baby," he said. "Real tired." He spoke into his arms. "You take the El Camino to work, cause I ain't goin nowhere today. Not till swing time."

Come on, he thought, walking fast. He felt the heat travel down to his knees, loosen the joints warm with his stride. Even his elbows were full of liquid. Like workin the fire line. Come on. Smoke me— yeah, no flames this time, just that bit a smoke you see from the gun barrel. You got a shottie? Twelve-gauge? They make some nice smoke—bitter powder-black. Come on.

He was down Washington now, past the weed-edged chain link he'd studied last night, and he said aloud, "Come on. Bring K-9. I'm drinkin my intoxicants in public—I done drank em. Come on."

He'd called Gas, told him yesterday was the last shift and he didn't need a ride.

Walking so fast, in the night-cool air, made the sweat moisten his back and shoulder blades under the jacket, and he strode long as he could, pushing himself like those women race walkers he'd seen in Grayglen. Yeah—that's me, just out for some exercise. Lemme hold my arms right. But when the sweat spread to the nape of his neck, he stopped stepping funny and remembered the glow of water across his forehead, his whole back, when he worked a night blaze. The cool hitting heat, under a layer of cloth, the dark air pulled deep into his lungs. By the time he climbed the stairs outside the apartment, his skin felt bubbled with heat and alcohol.

He lay in bed with their breath rising all around him, their night breaths webbing thick in the closed room, and he folded himself into position to lie awake for a long time.

"Okay, guys, thanks. Come pick up your checks in two weeks, or we can mail 'em to you," the warehouse manager told Darnell and the others. Sotelo shook hands with Darnell and drove toward the freeway; the other two men stood beside their trucks, talking, while he headed for the street.

No tiny bottle. No job, now, he thought. Damn, I ain't tellin Brenda, not this week, not till I get somethin else first. He stared ahead of him at the sidewalk lit chalky white in the moon, and heard booming bass behind him. Come on, he thought, but he hunched his shoulders, tired from last night.

"You lyin fool, I seen your dad's truck in the driveway when I got off work," Gas said from the open window. "Sit your ass in here."

They drove slow when they got downtown. "I need the Spider, man," Darnell said. "Have some dashboard and glass between me and everybody else."

Gas smiled. "Man, last dishwasher job they opened, the Inn had thirty guys apply. And you know they hired a Mexican guy, about thirty, with kids, cause he gon work his butt off."

"I got a kid." Darnell rested his head against the seat and saw the wrought-iron railing in front of his apartment.

Gas laughed. "You don't look—I don't know, you ain't got no belly. You don't look comfortable."

"I ain't," Darnell said, getting out.

He told Brenda to take the car in the morning again, and he lay in the empty apartment, smelling Charolette's milky spit wet on the sheet beside him, feeling the warmth Brenda had left outlined. All day he slept in the hard white light.

At three-thirty, he sat on the couch and swigged from the bottle of Canadian Club he'd bought for the ants in his leg. He stared out the window at the closed door directly across from him. Where I'ma go? he thought. She'll pick up Charolette and come home by five-thirty. If I get toe up, I can't drive, but I could walk over to Jackson Park and act like somebody who know how to drink. He put the bottle on the coffee table; the liquor made his head full, right behind his eyes, and when his legs didn't move, the heat seemed to stop at his neck.

When the face peered in the big window and pulled back, he felt wires shoot tight through his back. But it was Mrs. Batiste, who let herself in with her key.

She went straight to the kitchen and put a foil-covered bowl in the refrigerator. Then she sat in one of the kitchen chairs and pulled an

Easter basket, green-plastic grass springing from the sides, out of a shopping bag. "You think Charolette ready to find eggs?" she said casually.

Darnell looked at the bottle and then out the window. "She pretty big. Pretty nosy. I guess so."

"But you ain't plan to be around, huh?" she said, still conversationally. "You still got a itch. Brenda told me you come home late now. You see that fire, huh?"

"What fire?" Darnell kept his spine deep in the cushion.

"Was a big fire in the riverbottom the other night—same night you come home so late. Brenda call me, cause she worry. I tell her who knows." Mrs. Batiste put the Easter basket on the counter and stood in front of him. "Now I see you still got that itch, try to drown it, maybe try burn it out. You ain't go to work today?"

"Ain't no work," he said. "Job over." He stared up into the soft chin and flat cheeks, always flushed perfect with makeup, and the eyebrows like commas, dark and neat. Brenda's eyebrows, he thought. But Charolette got mine.

"Then come on help me for a minute," Mrs. Batiste said, putting the bottle in the kitchen. "You ain't done this in a long time."

She drove slowly and carefully like always, peering over the wheel, and Darnell felt the big bench seat covered with blue velour bounce slightly when they got to the cemetery. Shit, he thought. She bringin me here? She right—been a long time.

They drove off Olive Road, on the other side of downtown near where the freeway stretched over the riverbottom, in the deep, constant shade of Pedregal Hill, named in Spanish for the white rocks covering most of the small hill.

Darnell watched the newer graves, flat-shined squares in the last section closest to the street. He knew Mrs. Batiste was headed down the dirt road winding narrow through the cemetery, to the older part where the pepper and olive trunks surrounded weather-rounded headstones.

When his grandmother was still alive, she brought him here on November 1st, All Saints' Day, on Christmas, and on Easter Sunday. His mother came then, before the girls were born, and they drove Mrs. Dauphine, who had no car. Here, Mrs. Batiste and Brenda would be waiting, near the row of small white stones.

Antoine James Tucker. Jadette Geneva Batiste. Samuel Pierre Dauphine. Darnell helped Mrs. Batiste carry the little hand shovel and the bucket. He walked over to the tap way down at the far end, and when the water spilled inside, the chalky-white mixture she would brush on the headstones frothed. He stood there, watching it settle a bit. His mother used to pack up a whole bag on Christmas: wrapped toys, tinsel, a tiny tree in a red-foil-lined pot. She and Darnell would arrange the things on his brother's grave, while Mrs. Batiste and Brenda laid dolls, a tiny necklace, and each year new black patent shoes. Darnell was four or five; he only remembered Brenda as another pair of shiny, dark shoes that eventually gathered slivers of damp grass around the edges. Then Mrs. Batiste would sit her on a blanket.

GranaLene used to whitewash the headstones for all of them in the row, the people from Louisiana, even Mrs. Revelle, who had moved back to Bogalusa. Mr. Theodore Revelle. Darnell passed his grave. He came closer to Mrs. Batiste, bent over the grass, and near his brother's stone he touched Zelene Marie Dupree. Taking the brush, he scrubbed the pitted stone around her name.

"You mama only come by on Memorial Day now, huh?" Mrs. Batiste said softly, breathing hard from the work.

"Yeah." Darnell's father, and all the Oklahoma people, had a big Memorial Day party in Rancheria Park, nearby, and then people visited graves and brought flowers.

"Your daddy never liked us comin here," she said. "Didn't like Catholic, either."

"He and GranaLene used to argue about it," Darnell said, watching her put tiny foil-wrapped chocolate bunnies on Samuel Dauphine's grave.

She saw his eyes, and said, "Miz Dauphine so old now, don't have much money, so I do hers for her." She paused. "Her boy was only two month—but she was too old then to have a baby."

He watched her go next to his brother's grave, and he thought of the evenings here with GranaLene, when his mother would sit silently and GranaLene would say to him, "That who your middle name for. Antoine. So she don't lose all of him. Oh, but he gone." GranaLene would pause and stare at Darnell. "Mama can't think like that, no, and she can't think on the other one go from her while you still restin inside."

She knew his father hated her to talk like that, about what she thought was a twin. "Sometime twin call from the other side for they brother or sister to join em," she would say, holding him tight to her smoky-smelling dress, the skin too soft, like bruised peaches shifting under their velvet. Darnell would hold his breath and wait. "Don't let nobody call you to go early, you gotta be careful, cause spirit want a beautiful boy like you. Don't listen."

"Darnell," Mrs. Batiste said sharply. "Bring me that." He carried the brush to her, and she started on her daughter's grave last. "I know you rememberin, now," she said. "You go to that fire the other night?"

"No," he said, his chest full of the whitewash smell and the pepper branches swaying slightly, the afternoon already dark here. "I might as well walk right into some flames," he said, "might as well go down there, cause I was busy gettin dead anyway. Might as well get it over with." He walked to the next row, where the stones were dark gray, veined on the blank backs.

"Yeah," Mrs. Batiste said. "Only men choose to die. Do it to they own self." She knelt on newspaper, didn't look up from what she was doing, but she spoke clearly. "Women do that—drink to death or so—they not truly women."

Darnell pulled his shoulders back hard, squared his collarbone. "Women drink. They smoke rock. They die, too." He saw the zombies, strawberries, on their porches.

But she went on as if she hadn't heard him. "A man see a fight, he *know* he gon die, but he say somethin, the right thing to start, he pull out his knife. He buy a gun." She paused, brushed grass from her hand, her hair shaking dark. "Somebody else kill a woman. A man kill her. Or he die and she got kids to feed, and she get old too quick." She looked up at him now, her lips set square, her chest rising hard with breath.

"Your husband ain't dead," Darnell said, folding his arms.

"Oh, but that don't mean he ain't try," she said. "In Louisiana, he try whole lotta time. And when we first come here, when he get out the service, he looked for fights in Gray Hollow. Drink every night at the bar—that courtin death."

"He ain't dead," Darnell said.

She let her brows rise slow and her eyelids drop halfway, just like Brenda, and said, "I whup him in my own way." Then she dropped back onto her palms on the grave, to pull a dandelion from close to the stone, and he couldn't see her until she stood up to get the last basket. "My first baby," she said, and red suffused her pale face like a nectarine. "Baby girl. We didn't have no money for a good crib, and she was sleep. It broke in the night, but it didn't make no noise, just slid on down and push her so she can't breathe. My first baby." Light gathered in the corners of her eyes and slipped near her nose. "We live near your Granny Zelene, and she bring me here. Say you have to keep her like this. Not Etienne, not you father. They never come here. They don't want to hear. And you ain't want to listen." She walked toward the faucet with her bucket, leaving him with the glinting foil eggs near his feet.

TO ASK

"WE FINISHED EARLY tonight," he said. Brenda was still sitting on the couch, folding washcloths into squares. Charolette was rearranging her own pile of dishtowels.

He went into the bathroom while Charolette ran to bang on the door and yell at him. He splashed water on his face, dried the beads that clung to his hair. He'd told Mrs. Batiste he'd walk home, and she frowned. "Bullets don't choose people," he'd said, but it didn't come out right. "Just don't tell Brenda I wasn't at work, okay? Let me tell her."

When he came back out, he lay on the living-room floor and let Charolette ride the dip in his back that she loved to squeeze until he bucked her off. "Ahee! Ahee!" she yelled, and Darnell said to Brenda, "Sound like she's speakin Spanish."

Brenda smiled and rested her elbows on her knees, fingers framing her face. "It took me a while to figure it out. But she points at the pictures of horsies in books, and she goes crazy when the Wells Fargo commercial comes on TV, the one with the stagecoach. It means horsie."

He bucked Charolette off gently and she screamed with laughter before she raked her fingers across his shirt to climb back on. But he caught her on his chest and said, "What kinda first word is that? I thought you were supposed to start off with 'Mama.' "

"Ahee!" she shouted, burying her fingers in his hair.

Brenda said, "She says 'Daddy.' Pissed me off—I spend all the time with her, and she says 'Daddy.' Somebody at work told me 'Daddy' is easier to say than 'Mama.' " She poked Darnell's leg with her toe. "She calls you, and you haven't even been home. It's nice to see you."

Darnell swallowed through the webbing in his chest. "Hey, Daddy's supposed to be gone, supposed to be makin that dinero, right?" He turned over with the pushing of Charolette's tiny palms.

For three weeks, he had taken Brenda to work and Charolette to his mother's. He worked with his father sometimes; other days the men were already gone, and he was glad he didn't have to keep his face right around his father. When he left, Charolette would cry and cry, pushing so hard at his mother's chest that her hand sank into the soft front. His mother had said, "She want to be with you all day. You must show her a good time when y'all drivin around."

"Later, babygirl," he'd said, watching her tears drip down with her spit to leave a tiny puddle on the cement slab by the clothesline. Now he'd drop the car at Brenda's job, after he'd put in a few applications.

Driving down the street, he thought, I wouldn't mind hangin with her all day, but I can already hear Pops and Victor. Women's work. Oh, yeah.

He saw Leon parking the Bronco in front of his mother's. "What up?" called Leon, getting out. "I been lookin for you, but you been hidin out."

"Just workin," Darnell said.

"Shit," Leon spat into the street. "Baby bruh told me about Terracina. You need a hooptie, brotha." He leaned into the window. "So that's why I was lookin for you. You want to do that?"

"Why you want me to do it?" Darnell said. "You settin me up for somethin?"

"Shit," Leon frowned. "You trippin or what?"

"No, man, but I was gone awhile, I came back, and you ain't even hardly seen me."

Leon said, "Look, Darnell, we hung out a long time ago. But you were smart way back then. Donnie and them never had no brains. You, you hear somethin once and you never forget it, right? Ain't too many smart brothas left. Half of em *been* done smoked their parts— remember when we learned the parts of the brain? Cortex and some others."

"Cerebrum, cerebellum," Darnell said.

Leon smiled, his teeth small and perfect. "See? You the smartest one outta all of us."

Darnell stared ahead to the avenue. Yeah, I can name you all the plants that grow after a fire, he thought. I can see where to torch trails. Name you the birds that'll move seeds. Birds. He saw Louis, neck arched, and said to Leon, "Louis was just as smart." He'd wanted to visit Louis, to tell him about Roscoe, but he'd been afraid to know what Louis had done.

"Shit," Leon said, pushing himself off the window. "Louis act crazy and never even smoked no product."

"So I ain't interested in doin whatever he was doin for you."

Leon propped his elbows again. "He wasn't doin nothin," he said. "Go see his ass out there in Chino and ask him, man." He glanced down the street again and said, "Look, Darnell, this don't have nothin to do with rock or the street." Darnell held the steering wheel tight. "My man need somebody to make a run, one day is all. He need somebody to figure out the travel, and I told him you been all over fightin fires. I heard you been in a damn helicopter." He smiled. "See, Vernon and Mortrice and them, they don't even know where San Diego is. Vernon messed up his last errand big time."

"I ain't into carryin product," Darnell said, putting the car in gear.

Leon smiled harder. "Neither am I, anymore. You movin clothes, man. Look, meet me at Del Taco at ten, man. You ain't gotta promise nothin. But it's on *me* to get somebody good." He lifted his fingers from the door. "He payin five hundred for one day. Unless you trimmin money trees with your dad, you can't laugh at that."

When he and Leon pulled down the long driveway of the house in the historic district, Darnell recognized the bunya-bunya trees. A few grew near the county courthouse, and they made huge pine cones that hit pedestrians on the head. This guy had called Darnell's father to trim his two bunyas right away; he remembered it from when he was twelve or thirteen.

Darnell stood near the fence, listening to the dog pace, the wide-chested growls sending cold sweat through his scalp. Leon said, "Rottweiler, man, he gotta put him away." Steps crunched on dead leaves and returned to the house. Leon pulled open the gate. The rest of the trees were huge, gloomy ash and ancient jacaranda. Darnell remembered how dark the house and yard had been, private and shaded. "Let's go, man," Leon said, tapping once on the back door, where Darnell had stood waiting with his father for the check. And the same face appeared in the window, holding back the lace curtain, smiling when he saw them.

He wasn't sure where to look. With Fricke and the others it had taken a long time before he knew enough about them to look straight into their faces. His father always said, Look too hard in their faces, they get nervous. But look away all the time, you're lying. Darnell was young, and he was never sure how to talk to the older white ladies, the men, the people who watched them trimming and asked questions while they wrote a check.

This dude used to Leon. Vernon, too. Come on. Chill, look around like it ain't no big deal. Darnell saw the man sit deep in his leather couch; the huge living room was dark, with mahogany-paneled walls and heavy drapes. A wide-screen TV flashed colors on the walls, and the consultant watched Darnell. "I love MTV," he said. "Each video is like a little movie, and you can watch a hundred of them in a hell of a short time. Some of them are riveting, and the bad ones are much funnier than sitcoms. Faster, too." He sat with his knees wide, palms over the round bones that poked through his khakis.

Darnell glanced at the consultant. To consult—to ask, to inquire. Like the guys hired by the county. He was afraid to inquire why the man called himself that. He'd only said, "Darnell, right? I'm a consultant for several entities, and Leon tells me you might be interested in a part-time position."

All the right words—the same words he heard in the personnel offices. But this man said them like a joke. Darnell nodded now, took a sip of the mineral water the consultant had offered him. Leon drank a Seagram's Wine Cooler, but Darnell didn't want any alcohol.

I can't be drinkin no more, anyway, he thought. Makes me trip too much. He blinked. You trippin now, just like Pops says. Thinkin about the wrong thing. He looked at the consultant, at his yellow-gray teeth, square in his tanned face. His eyes were not as blue as Fricke's. "Well, Darnell, the word is 'peripatetic.' Do you know what it means?"

Darnell looked at Leon, remembering Brother Lobo. "Yeah. Travels around a lot. A great deal." Leon smiled and turned toward the TV again, and Darnell could tell he was glad the consultant was surprised.

"Good. Are you ready to fulfill the definition?" the man said, his brows pale-bristled. "Jeans. I have some jeans to deliver."

Darnell waited, tried to look relaxed. He looked right into the man's eyes. Some famous actor—that's who he looked like. Square ridges of heavy skin starting to fall slightly, nudging inside the eyebrows, at the corners of the mouth, under the neck. Robert Redford. "Jeans," Darnell said.

"I need a—I guess it would be an odd-job man," the consultant said. "And Leon tells me that's what you're doing right now." When Darnell frowned, the man went on. "But you used to be a firefighter, up in the San Jacinto Mountains, right?"

"Yeah." Darnell picked up the glass of mineral water, but at the metallic smell he put it back down.

"I don't see how you can stay down here after that," the man said. "I used to have a cabin up in the Garner Valley—you know where that is?"

Darnell nodded. He and Fricke had gone out there a couple of times. "I used to have some Matilja poppies up there," the man said. "You know them?"

Darnell smiled, flared his fingers to stretch them. "Yeah, like a bunch of fried eggs noddin in the sun," he said, and then stopped, embarrassed, when Leon shifted impatiently by the TV. Darnell saw the huge, flat flowers, white petals with a large yellow center.

"I have to get them at the nursery here, because you can't start them from seed," the man said.

Yeah, Darnell thought, they need fire, too. They only germinate off ashes and heat. He stayed still. He'd forgotten for a second why he'd come, thought he was sitting at the station, around the table with Fricke telling him something. He said as evenly as he could, "Look, man, we here to talk about poppies?"

The man smiled wide. "Yeah, I guess we are. A poppy product, sort of. Did you know there are hundreds of Hmong tribesmen down there in Banning? You had to drive through there on your way home?"

Darnell shook his head. The consultant's mouth was straight, and the ridges of skin nudged harder toward his chin. "You know the way, though. It's so rare that I get to talk to someone intelligent. Leon told me you were quick."

Leon said, "I don't play. Not after Birdman."

"Birdman is a strange one," the man said, his knees bobbing gently now. "What does Vernon say? Mental—he cost me money. He cost *Leon* money." He paused. "Leon brought you here. If you fuck up, it's Leon's problem. Immediately." He smiled.

Darnell let his chest rise slowly. "Yeah. Mine, too." He looked at the dark blue eyes. "Keep talkin money."

The consultant said, "Yeah. Leon told you. You'll be gone a few hours. Rented car, okay? Mountain scenery—you're going up north." He grinned. "But payment's when you get back. Hey, you might like that landscape and bail, so we'll check you on this one, and then we can talk about future jobs."

Yeah, just like probationary status, Darnell thought. Follow procedure, right. He watched his knuckles bring him the bitter water. But this is a one-time errand, cause all I need is the five hundred to get the Spider runnin. Jeans. It ain't cane sugar. He raised his eyes and nodded.

TRAILS

A MINOR PROCEDURE. The young man's blond hair gleamed green-ish under the murky fluorescent light. "Can I help you?"

"There's a car waiting for me; the reservation was already made," Darnell said. "Marcus Smith." He took out the wallet Leon had handed him.

The man showed no change in expression. "Let me see what we have," he said, tapping the computer keys. "Lotta cars gone for the holiday. Credit card?"

Darnell laid the American Express card on the counter, his heart pounding blood to his ears. Just like a fire, remember the sequence. Head away from the flames. Everything taken care of. Leon said the consultant got boys everywhere—at the DMV, here at the airport, all over. He don't call em boys. Associates. Like Vernon. Why Leon have to send Vernon, too? He always talkin smack in the street—he probably gon yang all the way up to Tahoe.

The blond guy slid papers across the counter. "Lincoln Town Car waiting for you on the lot," he said, watching Darnell's face.

"Uh, that's a big car," Darnell said. Shit—a Lincoln? I'll be hella conspicuous.

"Memorial Day's comin up," the guy said. "But you got a problem?"

Darnell shook his head. "No, man, not if that's what you got." He signed the name carefully, like it looked on the back of the card.

Virgin gray carpet lined the trunk. Trunk bigger than my damn apartment, Darnell thought, his hands dangling empty. And no suitcase. He closed it, hearing the car pull the metal down all the way with a soft, hollow buzz. He slid onto the huge leather seat, and the car breathed wild cherry scent, so strong his nostrils felt coated with the chemical cleaner. The engine trembled, and he drove carefully around the narrow airport roads toward the exit.

I can't believe this brotha gotta come with me, he thought. Leon tellin me to look college. He rubbed the corduroy ridges on his thigh. Vernon got that big Raiders jacket and a gangsta light in his eyes. Vernon had stopped at the curb near the rental-car counters, saying, "I ain't parkin in no damn airport. What if a damn plane crashes right now? Come get me at the exit." He drove off in a Honda Accord Darnell had never seen.

Peering into the morning-gray dark, he saw the square-coated figure past the parking booths. But another shadow stood next to him. Shit! Darnell thought. This is why I ain't into Leon, cause people be lyin all the time. Who the hell is this?

A white guy plopped hard into the front. He had short red hair, freckles big as cornflakes floating in milk, and a shiny satin jacket with tigers and names embroidered on the back, like military guys wore.

Vernon got in the back, lifting his chin and grinning at Darnell, but he didn't say anything. The white guy smiled wide at Darnell and said, "Thought I was never gonna get a ride to San Berdino! Everybody on my flight was goin to LA. And I seen your friend here. Glad you're goin my way." He stuck out his hand and said, "Brad Riddle, man."

"Darnell," Darnell said, watching the cars behind him, and then, "Marcus Smith." He heard Vernon snort in the back. "I go by Marcus."

"Hey, movie stars in California all got three names, right? So this is lovely Ontario, huh?" the guy went on fast. "I'm originally from Michigan. Went to Germany and the Gulf in the Navy, flew a lot out here. I love some parts of California, you know what I mean? The women. The beaches."

Darnell looked in the rearview at Vernon, who just smiled, sending hollow gashes down his cheeks. Man, is Vernon plannin to yoke this guy up? He ain't carryin nothin—just like us. He took a breath, nodded out the window at the rows of eucalyptus windbreak ghostly along the freeway. "No beaches out here," he said to Brad. "So why you need a ride, in California?"

"I live in Seattle now. You ever been there?" He stretched his face over his shoulder to include Vernon. "No? I work for this big Chevy dealer, and I'm goin out to San Berdino to pick up this van. Loaded— stretch wheel base, air-conditioner and heater, Kenwood stereo, the works."

"You're gonna drive a van all the way back to Seattle?" Darnell asked. The freeway headed east, and the dawn was just a pale breath at the edge of the San Bernardino Mountains.

Brad stretched his arms. "Yeah, well, this customer wants a real specific model, with all these extras, and he's got the cash for it right now. So my boss called around, and he couldn't find it anywhere. But this guy I knew from the Navy, he's a dealer in San Berdino, so I said let me come on down and pick up this model. See, I'm not makin much on this deal, with the plane fare. But I'm new on the lot, and even if I just make a grand on this sale, this guy's the kind that's gonna come back and buy somethin else down the line. And he'll send his relatives to me, and his friends. In the long run, it'll be worth the trouble."

Gotta be a salesman, cause he love to talk, Darnell thought. Brad said, "You guys are savin me cab money, I really appreciate it." He nodded, looking at Darnell's clothes. "You're goin to Palm Springs, right?" he said, slanting his voice back to Vernon. "College break?"

"Yeah," Vernon said, grinning wider, and Darnell thought, Vernon's gonna jack this dude, he just playin with him. The nervous cool trickled down his neck.

"Yeah," Brad said. "Man, the military's better, in my opinion. I learned a lotta shit I never woulda learned in college. I was on a aircraft carrier for two years, man, you wouldn't believe the shit I learned." He reached his arms to the roof again. "This Lincoln's a great car. What kinda car do you usually drive?"

Darnell blinked hard, flexed his hand by his leg. "El Camino."

"Good, keep buyin American," Brad said, nodding. "See, our mini-vans are doin great, cause people know they want to buy American." He bent over his bag, and Vernon leaned forward fast to see his hands. "Wait till you see the new sports model," Brad mumbled, pulling out a magazine.

"San Bernardino," Darnell said, looking out at the dim buildings.

"I'm goin to the Chevy dealer on—here," Brad said, showing Darnell a business card, and suddenly Darnell was tired of the talking, of wondering what Vernon was planning. He drove a few more exits, his face heavy as wood, and got off on the wide commercial strip lined with auto dealers. He stopped at the silvery-lit sidewalk, keeping his eyes half closed, and Vernon's hand came over the seat between them. Brad shook the hand, saying, "Hey, bro, you really saved me some time and money." He wrapped his dry fingers quickly around Darnell's hand and laid two business cards on the seat. "Come on up to Seattle, and I'll get you a deal on a car. Anytime."

"Later," Vernon said, still grinning, and Darnell watched the dragons on Brad's back.

"What the hell was that shit?" he said while Vernon got into the front seat, his jacket rustling.

"Dude came up to me when I was parkin the car." Vernon didn't look back at Brad. "You know how you can look at his mouth and tell he talks a lot? I like to hear white boys like that, they always make that spit by their mouth. Like bubbles. I knew he was gon talk. You ain't never got nothin to say."

Darnell held his jaw tight. "We ain't goin to Palm Springs," he said, wanting to get out of the city. On the ramp, the Lincoln's power lifted his stomach like an elevator, rushing his chest forward, rising.

"Who give a shit?" Vernon said. He closed his eyes. "Just pick up the jeans."

Darnell drove against the heavy traffic coming out of the east to commute to LA. No one was headed to Banning. He saw the chamise thick, the ceanothus blooming pale-blue high up on the slopes of the pass. This was the other side of the ridge from his old route, to the station. He breathed evenly, scanning the arroyos, dry and sandy. No water this spring, but the season ain't started yet.

Another fire last week—a column of smoke had risen thin and dark on Saturday, a day he didn't have to walk around all afternoon to pretend he still had a job. The smoke blended into the air already gray-thick with smog, and Darnell could tell from the black roil it was the riverbottom again, where the homeless men were still cooking.

He'd squatted in the hot shade on the balcony, where Charolette insisted on playing, winding threads in and out of the wrought iron, and he knew Brenda's eyes were hard on his back. But when the pillowy smoke thickened, he didn't tell her the car needed gas or he could run to Thrifty for ice cream. No, Brenda, I ain't gon chase the smoke.

Just before Banning, he saw the field where they'd cleared the tumbleweeds. It was already plowed, the furrows powder-dry, the ditch thick with ashes.

"Wake up, brotha," he whispered to Vernon.

At a boxlike stucco duplex just off the freeway, a man was watching for them from the open front door. His face was moon-pale and round, his eyes and mouth thin crescents of dark. He pushed forward a large box, sealed with tape, the mailing labels torn off in rough smears; Vernon didn't get out of the car. "Put the box in the back," he said, barely glancing at the man. "The money been took care of."

When Darnell looked back at the duplex from the street, he saw tiny faces bobbing around the man's legs, and a woman came from the yard in a long, wrap-around skirt. He said, "I read in the paper that Hmong families got lots of kids."

"Just like niggas," Vernon said, his eyes half closed again.

Darnell got back on the freeway. "Why you always say 'niggas'?" he asked, trying to keep the anger from his voice. "Why you can't say 'brothas'? Or 'Africans,' like Brother Lobo?"

"Cause it ain't no difference. Unless you a nigga wit a attitude." Vernon's voice was hard. "Rio Seco niggas. Not me." He lifted his chin toward a gas station and minimart at the next exit. "Stop over there and get your shit."

Leon had said, "Banning your second home, right? The man say get a map for the rest. That's why you goin." Darnell pulled into the station, and Vernon said, "Get me a Choco-dile. Brotha."

The sun was up fat and hot already. Seven o'clock, rush-hour traffic, Darnell thought, looking at the map on the front seat. He'd stopped at the turnoff just before the exit to the station. He looked up the mountain at the winding highway. How bout if I make a quick run up there and tell Fricke hey? Yeah—he and Vernon can talk about travelin. "You want to go through LA?" he asked Vernon, looking at the three possible routes on the map. Interstate 5, through LA, cops everywhere. More towns on Route 99. No-man's land on 395, through the high desert.

"You don't know shit about LA," Vernon said. "You wouldn't know how to get to my hood."

"Where you from?"

"Fifty-first and Denker," Vernon said, turning his head slowly to look at Darnell. "Fuck LA, too. I ain't there no more."

"We could go through the high desert and cut back in at Bakersfield," Darnell said.

"Who give a shit?" Vernon said. "Just go."

Darnell drove in silence, watching the brown mountains rise up before them. Look like fungus killin off some chaparral on the south side over there, he thought. Like this brotha want to hear that. I got a driver job now. Just two dudes on a shift—but at least Donnie talked. I can't say nothin to Vernon. I'm just a chauffeur. Until a cop see me. What if they got them drug-sniffin dogs, and they can smell somethin in the jeans? Damn. He took a bite of the doughnut, drank from the milk carton. Looking at the back from habit, he saw Adohr Farms—Chino. Still trippin on that. The candy bar from Hershey, Pennsylvania. Who cares where? Chino—milk and prisons. Where Louis is now—for doin what you doin. The Lincoln's powerful, smooth thrust didn't shiver, up over the Cajon Pass. The way Pops came down from Oklahoma. Don't think about that, either.

He looked at the desert below, twisted ridges of brown with deep chasms cutting through, expanses of dirt and rock with lighter road strips crisscrossing. The Helitorch, throwin down lines like that for the deer, he thought, trying to calm himself. Fricke up there talkin about how thick the chaparral was, how the animals live better after a fire cause they can get that new grass shootin up from the ashes. Trails—not this year, home boy. He couldn't help it—his eyes filmed blurry, and he slammed the stem scar against the window to make his knuckles sting.

Vernon jumped. He must have fallen asleep, because his shoulder had started to lean against Darnell's arm. He jerked his head, closed his mouth, and Darnell saw the wet shine of drool at the corner of his mouth. Darnell swallowed hard, thought, This dude sleepin closer to me than Brenda. Breathin my air.

"Big-ass car put me out like a baby," Vernon mumbled, rubbing his lips with his wrist. He stared at Darnell. "Don't fuck up, okay?" He clenched his jacket closed with one fist and his head came at Darnell when he slid himself over the seat into the back. "I'ma sleep like a baby, man."

Vernon must don't have a baby if he talkin about sleepin like one. Darnell stared at the mountains all around, their flanks studded with sparse brush. Babies thrash around. He'd lain awake most of the night, worrying that he'd sleep past the time, preparing what to say to Brenda if she heard him dressing. But she didn't even hear the mockingbird, the torrent of sounds that poured through the cracked-open bedroom window. Charolette had struggled to stand and slap the wall beneath the window. "Irdy," she said.

He remembered Louis saying that mockingbirds fought by singing, guarding their territory with sound. "What the hell you guardin over here, homey?" Darnell whispered.

He'd left a note. "Nacho picked me up for a big job. Be back real late." He stood near the window, panicked. He'd forgotten change to call her from the road. And the warbling only stopped when Vernon pulled up. Louis used to tell them to listen when the mockingbirds looped their singing through the air, and Darnell remembered what Leon would say, while they all crouched near the riverbottom or the gullies of Treetown. "You can yang and woof all you want with niggas, but you gotta thrown down eventually. When you from the Wild Wild Westside."

Over Tehachapi on 58. Through Bakersfield and up 99. Louis went to school up here somewhere. He was always talkin about the cotton and the birds. Vernon sleepin more like a dude with a hangover. Lotta towns between here and Sacramento. Turn off to Tahoe. Hundreds of tiny towns that don't sound California—that's what Fricke used to say. Darnell glanced at the map, at the tiny veins of gray roads that crisscrossed huge areas between red arteries of free-way. His eyes went distant on the asphalt for a minute. Lucky there's no arteries or veins in the area where he bit you, the doctor said to the back of his head. Darnell's cheek was pasted to the thin paper on the table. I've seen some guys get bit in the groin, near the femoral, and I saw one guy with serious bleeding near his inner arm.

He felt his scars tighten when he lifted up on the accelerator, looked in the rearview for highway patrol. Sweat slid his fingerbends down the wheel, his stomach lit with fireworks. The Lincoln had been doing seventy-five and he didn't even feel it. No shaking like when Roscoe's old truck got going too fast, no jerking, nothing, just a big boat floating down the river of freeway, smooth like surrounded by water. No—this is an artery, and we floatin in blood. Hellafine car. Turning on the radio, he said softly, "You in a serious hooptie, fuckin up your life in style."

The automatic scanner found stations, sound floating from good speakers. But Vernon didn't stir, his head cradled in the neck of his jacket. Darnell heard the country music on every station. "All my exes live in Texas . . ." Darnell smiled, forgetting the fireworks in his stomach, thinking of his father and Roscoe and Mr. King working a big job, bringing a radio to play country all day. Mr. King loved this song. Snooter would argue with him, and Mr. King would say, "I can hear what these guys sayin! This is music, boy!"

At night, his father and Roscoe listened to blues in the back room. "Big Joe Turner! Eddie Cleanhead Vinson!" his father would shout. "Singers!"

"We got Big Daddy Kane! Redhead Kingpin!" Snooter would holler right back. "They can sing, too, but y'all can't understand cause your ears too old."

The song ended and a woman's husky voice wound around a new set of guitars. Brenda was probably singing to Charolette right now in the car, happy he'd gotten a day job. Her voice would travel up sweet in her throat, coming from far down in her chest—under the tiny nipples, the apricot collarbone where he'd left purple circles before the baby. Her throat—the first time she'd made sounds when he moved inside her, so long ago, in the car—had tightened him up inside like nothing else but hillside flames. Brothers used to sing "Do the Tighten Up" when he was little. When she let those low, long sounds bubble up from her throat, and he bent down to catch them with his tongue, his skin was filmed by a thousand tiny threads pulling slow.

Now, if he talked her into coming home at lunchtime so the baby wouldn't be in the apartment at all, she was silent in the bed, breathing high and hard at the back of her teeth. And they couldn't fall asleep with skin sealed together.

Darnell felt the long space beside him on the seat, the brush of air under his arm when he held the wheel. No Charolette crammed in tight—her fingers on him, cookie and juice melted into that baby coating he smelled on her palms.

He looked at the map again. He had to stop for gas soon. Names jumped out at him. Manteca. Somebody named a town after the Spanish word for lard? Copperopolis. Strawberry. He shook his head. No, I ain't gettin no sex from a strawberry. Folsom. Where Leon's cousin Terrell was doing his time.

South Lake Tahoe. The guy would meet them after they called. He stared at the highway, surrounded by green fields. Jeans. Poppies. This is just a job, not an adventure, like the commercial says for the Navy. Brad Riddle, huh? Yeah, I could join the military, but then I'd be long gone from Brenda and Charolette. Like if I tried to get on a hotshot crew, fight fires all over the country. Shit—don't even think about it. Just get remuneration for the delivery, like the consultant said. "I can't wait for the R words," he said. Go home, get the Spider fixed, and start lookin again. Start the procedure all over.

"This gun might want to get a body," Vernon said idly, pulling out the pistol. "I don't know. I just got it."

"Man, don't pull out no piece," Darnell said. They had called the number and were waiting in the parking lot of a Denny's. The air smelled sharper, woody, up here. South Lake Tahoe.

Vernon smiled. "Semiautomatic. *Brotha.* Three-eighty a okay size for today." Vernon looked over at Darnell. "You don't know what they got."

"I don't know shit," Darnell said. "Don't want to know." He saw the two guys then, driving a yellow Volkswagen bug, motioning to him to follow. "Man, I got a kid."

"So do I." Vernon smiled. "So?"

From the backdoor of a wood-shingled house two men came toward him on the dirt drive where he'd parked. Vernon sat completely still, expressionless. "What's up, bro?" said the taller one, with round wire-rimmed glasses and blond hair curled onto his neck. He had wide, talk-a-lot lips like Brad's.

The other guy was nervous. "Let's go," he said. His skin was yellowed like the fingertips of someone who smoked too much.

"I'ma pop the trunk," Darnell said.

"But once he do, he ain't for frontin," Vernon said toward the open window. Darnell stood outside while the taller one picked up the box and carried it inside. He followed the short one into the shabby kitchen strewn with paper plates. The short guy knocked a pizza box dotted with grease spots off the table, and Darnell took the fat manila envelope with money. Before he could say anything, the short one began taking the jeans from the box, saying, "You didn't fuck with us, right?"

"How's the Oriental dude gonna get the stuff out of em?" the blond guy interrupted. Darnell saw Vernon leaning against the Lincoln, watching through the open door. "Way too chemical for me," the blond guy said.

The waxy-skinned man said suddenly, "He doesn't even know what he'd do if we didn't take these off him. He couldn't extract it."

Darnell folded his arms. "I ain't worried about it. I don't mess with my brain cells." He turned toward the door.

"Opium doesn't fuck with your brain," the waxy-skinned one said. "It relaxes the brain, and it's a natural substance, not like crack. That fucks up your people's brains."

The blond guy pushed his friend, and Darnell made himself smile. "I wouldn't know, man. I'm strictly business." That was what Leon always said.

In the car, he drove quickly back toward the highway, his temples hot with the disdainful voices. Think they woodsmen and shit, cause they live up here. Come on out to fire camp with me, boys. Me and Fricke burn the hairs off your little *cojones*. You don't know shit about me.

Vernon said, "You gotta get back on five, man."

"I know."

"We ain't goin home yet. Brotha. We gotta make one more run."

Darnell looked at Vernon. "What the hell you talkin about? That was it."

But Vernon shook his head, slumped low, still wearing the big jacket. He looked out the window, his face just above the edge like a periscope. "I'm tired, man. But we gotta take somethin to Portland. Get some grub at Mickey D.'s and let's go."

"Hell, no, Vernon, I ain't drivin to no Portland. That's hours."

"It ain't that far." Vernon still stared out the glass.

Darnell looked at his watch. Almost six. "You playin, huh?"

Vernon smiled. "Leon don't play. Neither do I. Check the map— that's your job, man. That's why you drivin."

Darnell blinked to try and clear his head. "I don't need to look," he said. He remembered Corcoran and Fricke talking about northern California, Oregon, about taking five all the way. "Shit," he said.

"Mickey D.'s up there," Vernon said, grinning. "Coffee break."

He went to the bathroom, and Darnell ordered cheeseburgers, fries, coffee to go. He asked for five dollars in change and got a dirty look with the quarters. The phone rang and rang, but no one answered. She must be at Pops' house. Damn.

Vernon came out behind him. "I don't drink coffee, man, tastes like shit."

He stopped at the liquor store. "You buy it, get me two forties," Vernon said.

"You go in, man," Darnell said, eating fries.

"I'm seventeen, man. I ain't gettin IDed up here in the boonies and shit."

Darnell stared at him, went inside and brought out the heavy bag with the fat bottles. When he pulled out of the parking lot, Vernon said, "You went to school with Leon, so I know you twenty-two."

But Darnell didn't want to talk. He swallowed the coffee, which tasted like soapy water. I ain't got nothin to say, Boss. The coffee stung his throat. Coffee part of the cure, too, Mrs. Batiste had said, making him a pot of the strong black Louisiana stuff. Brenda—he gulped more, burning. She gotta come home soon.

Driving north, he tried to keep his eyes steady, breathed in the too-sweet cherry that had faded into their smells. Vernon took out a Kool and pushed in the lighter on the dashboard, raising the glowing circle. Darnell shook his head when Vernon proffered the cigarette. He drove faster, hitting eighty, heading into the gathering grayness. How the hell they get the opium in the jeans? Somebody gon smoke that. Who cares? Just drive. That's what you do.

The freeway passed thick stands of trees and a few streams, even some standing water in fields now and then. Dead animals were sprawled on the roadside: a needle-bellied possum, several raccoons, one just a flat round of skin with the striped tail full and pretty, like a Daniel Boone hat. The kind Gas used to want. Then he saw the ears of a rabbit, pointing straight up, with the body nearly disintegrated. Finally he saw a live animal poking into a hole by a field. It was hump-round, brown-furred, but he couldn't see a tail. Maybe it was a beaver, with all this water around.

The gas gauge was low. Vernon still slept, in the front seat now, slumped with his chin hard on his chest. Darnell said, "I'm gettin gas, man. Wake up."

He stood at the scarred counter inside to pay. An older white man with traces of red veins on his cheeks took his money and said, "Stays light longer now, huh?"

"Yeah," Darnell said. He wanted to ask the man about the animals. He looked up at the white hairs curved back from the forehead, afraid to say anything. Turning to the door, he thought, Yeah, I can see it when the cops ask about me. Colored boy, drivin a Lincoln, asked me about beavers or porcupines.

At the phone booth, he watched the abandoned farmhouse across the street. No answer. He hung up and got back into the car.

He saw the falling-down barns, the few abandoned buildings, even a brick building that had empty, yellow-boarded eyes. In the twilight, he saw another possum, saw a squirrel sitting on a fencepost. His father and Floyd, all the men telling stories about hunting. "Ain't no squirrels, no possums, nothin left in the state, man. We ate every movin thing in Oklahoma. No rabbits left, nothin."

They told stories about mules that wouldn't plow, about banking sweet potatoes for winter and stewing them with possum. His father's grandfather had walked across two states when he was freed and bought an abandoned farm. His mother's grandfather had married a Creek Indian woman.

Darnell looked at the falling wood barns, the gray-wood fences. Yeah, I'll bring Brenda and Charolette out here, buy me a farm, buy Vernon's .380 and shoot me some squirrels. What I'm supposed to cook with squirrel?

When Vernon woke up, as the sky finally turned purple-black, it was like he'd heard Darnell thinking. He pulled out the .380 and started shooting into the darkness of the mountain range. They passed over the border to Oregon, and on the long stretches with no lights to pierce the black landscape, he fired off into the trees now and then. "I like how it sound, man," he said.

"Stall out, Vernon, you might hit a cow or somethin," Darnell said, peering into the rearview.

"Then somebody could have steak tonight," Vernon said, smiling.

"Vernon, man, that ain't necessary."

"You never know who could be in Portland, man," Vernon said. Darnell shook his head. "Clint Eastwood might show up."

"I ain't even supposed to be up here," Darnell said, smacking the window. "Shit!" He looked over at the pistol in Vernon's lap. "This ain't LA, man."

Vernon shrugged. "Portland could be buck wild. Rio Seco might get buck wild, too." Then he seemed to lose interest, and he closed his eyes. "Depend on how shit go. Like what's in the air. My auntie use to say that. You can't stop it if it's already floatin in the air."

Darnell looked out the window, but he couldn't see if the forests were thick, if the geography was different, if he could recognize chamise or trees. He smelled the last trace of smoke from the gun. *If I die, man, I ain't even me. All I got is a comb and a wallet say I'm Marcus Smith.* "What if somebody look real close?" he had asked the consultant.

The man had shrugged. "Who ever looks close, real close, at a young man like you? A cop, if he wants you, he doesn't have to *look* at you. If he does, you probably look like Marcus Smith to him."

No trippin. Vernon pointed the gun out the window and then brought it back in, nodding at Darnell. "You just like your homey Birdman—always starin at the trees. We almost there?" he asked. Darnell stared at the freeway, a twisting dark artery through the next pass. No animals, just yellow eyes reflecting now and then in the night.

North Side. *There was always a side,* Brother Lobo said. *East Side. South Side. The Westside.*

He sat at a table in Rob's apartment, watching two girls in the living room. Rob passed him a small brown cigarillo. "Swisher Sweets, man, try these," Rob said. "Make cigarettes taste like trash."

Darnell lit the cigarillo and smelled the pungent sweet smoke rise into his face. Honeyed brown poured into his chest. Rob smiled. "So Leon been tight with you since baby days, huh? I didn't move to the Westside till I was about sixteen, man. My moms from Terracina."

Darnell pulled in the smoke, felt it circling through his blood, drifting into his head. "Terracina bangers tried to cap me a little while ago," he said, his voice far away. "Impala." He felt the weight of the tiny gun Vernon had slipped into his jacket when they found the apartment. A Raven Arms .25. "You wanna die up here?" Vernon had whispered. "I ain't takin your ass home."

Rob cocked his head to listen. "Them *vatos* from Terra are bolo wild," he said absently. Then he called to his boy, a Portland brotha with a shaved head, "Go see who comin." The girls watched. Darnell glanced toward the bathroom, where Vernon was. The Portland boy mouthed a name to Rob, and Rob nodded.

Five more people came into the apartment, and Rob huddled with the two guys to do business. Darnell closed his eyes and sat back in the stiff kitchen chair, letting the sweet smoke curl around him. All Vernon had remembered was a bridge, but they'd found the place. And in the bedroom Vernon had taken product out of his huge jacket pockets. Product, cane sugar for glowing embers. Darnell had begun to pant, his throat so closed with anger. "You had that in the car with me? *Damn*, Vernon, that's big time at the government gym. Shit! That for Leon or the consultant?"

"For sale." Vernon had smiled, and Darnell had punched the wall, splitting two knuckles that stung in his mouth. This ain't procedure. He went back to the chair where he sat now, staring at the blank wall. Rob didn't have a phone. What time was it now? She was already asleep. Hey, baby, I tried to call you, but . . .

He felt the smoke slow his breath, his pulse, and he knew he'd have to sleep before they started the drive home. About twelve or thirteen hours, Rob said.

Rob frowned at one of the girls, who was getting loud. Another one, across from him in Rob's chair, smiled at Darnell. "So you from LA," she said, her voice high and sweet-slow. "You gon stay with Rob?"

Darnell took the cigarillo from his mouth and shook his head. "Not hardly," he said, his voice echoing in his ears.

Rob was leaning over her shoulder then. "Hell, no, Quelle, he ain't stayin. He lucky. Man, I told Leon I ain't into the cold and shit. Can't keep no kinda nice hooptie out here, no place to cruise."

Darnell closed his eyes, put his head on his arms. When he yawned, he felt gravel spread behind his ribs. "You want me to get you somethin to eat?" the girl said, close to his ear. He thought of Brenda, standing at the stove with her neck bent, and tried to shake his head. "It's always warm down there where you stay, huh?" she went on, leaning over him. "And y'all got all kinda clubs, not like here. I always wanted to go to LA."

"I'm from Rio Seco," Darnell mumbled, moving his eyes to see her face.

"That sound even better," she said, and he saw the way she held her lips, like she had a secret inside the slippery part, smiling with just a lifting of one corner. "That your Lincoln?"

Darnell didn't answer. She had stars beside her eyes, those tiny moles gathered in a loose cluster at the top of her cheekbone. Brown skin, and the small black dots moved when her lips pushed the smile into her cheek. "You gon get some rest before you go?"

He stood up, head draining to blank, and said, "I'm goin in here and sleep for a minute, Rob." He nodded at everyone, including the girl, and Rob followed him to the door of the bedroom. "That hoochie yours if you want it," Rob said.

Darnell looked at the bathroom door, still closed. "I need some rest, man," he said, but when he was in the bedroom, lying on his stomach in his T-shirt and boxers, he knew he would hear her come in.

His head rang so loud and fuzzed from the cigar that when he turned to see her his eyes felt left behind his forehead. He had slept for half an hour; his mouth was coated thick. She sat beside him on the bed, leaned down suddenly to press her soft chest into his shoulder blade. "You relaxed now? You drivin a long way home, I know you want some company."

Darnell felt her mouth hot on the back of his neck, her tongue sliding wet. "I could keep you awake while you drivin," she whispered, and her hands slid under his hips to touch him. He felt her breast shift, her mouth along the back of his arm, and he knew he would turn over.

Her voice rose suddenly. "Ooh, you got cut back here?" Her fingers

touched his leg. "This one look like a turtle." Darnell lifted his face
from the pillow to look behind him, at her hand moving off the scar.
Round-humped shiny, the scar was long as her finger. He had never
seen it. "And this one even longer, like one a those worms, you know,
with all the feelers?"

A centipede, with stitchmarks splayed like tiny legs. Where the
teeth tore when the cop pulled the dog off; the jaws wouldn't open,
the voices yelled, because he wasn't lying still enough. His shoulders
were suffused with cold now, and she said, "What kinda girl gon cut
you down here?" Her lips were on the scar then, wet breath-hot, and
her teeth were hard behind the softness pushing. He jerked up off
his stomach and said, "You gotta go, get off me. Get out, okay?" The
scars pulsed cold now, air hitting the wet. Her mouth trembled, the
moles still, and he pushed her back toward the door, carefully.

"When you leavin?" she whispered, and he shut the door, knowing
Rob wouldn't let her come back in if he'd sent her out.

He curled on his side under the sheet that smelled of other people,
shaking. The teeth raking his skin, the shouting. "You're moving!"
The burning in his leg, the air on open wet tissue, the voices cracking
sharp on the radios. Donnie calling out to him, the warm oil-scented
cement under his face, the exhaust lingering in the air. Darnell heard
Vernon talking through the wall, and his heart beat too fast. He
smelled sweat. Reaching over to the pack of cigarillos by the bed, he
broke one open and rubbed the tobacco on the dirty sheet all around
him, the curly-sharp bits clinging to his hot palms.

Shouts came from the living room, and he pulled on his pants. Rob
was arguing with another man who'd come in, and Rob's boy was
standing with arms folded, hand deep in his armpit. Darnell saw
Vernon sitting on the couch with Quelle, smiling as usual. Rob smiled,
too, and nodded at the girl standing next to his customer. "All I said
was she hellafine."

The man glanced at Darnell. The girl wore a short dress and ankle
boots; her hair shone in loose spiral curls. "Yeah, but Hellafine with
me," he said. "Hellafine here is *mine*."

"She could be with him, man, if you was elsewhere. Like a grave,"
Vernon said softly, enjoying himself. Darnell kept his eyes on the
man's hands, held too still.

"So you strapped, nigga?" the man said. "So who ain't?"

"If y'all gon do the pow-pow bang-bang, step to it," Vernon said, pulling out the .380, and he held it slanted loose. "I ain't for playin."

The man backed up, reaching for the door, and Darnell saw that smoke filled the whole apartment now. Rob laughed, and the man pulled his girl out the door. But Vernon pointed the gun at the door and held it. Rob said, "I hate sugar cane. They either beggin or they all wild and shit."

"I'm gone," Darnell said, buttoning his shirt. He grabbed his jacket and felt for the wallet. The manila envelope with money from the jeans was in the bedroom, in a small bag, and when he came back out, Vernon still sat on the couch, the gun loose again in his fingers. "I'm gone," Darnell said again, glancing at the girl with half a constellation near her eye.

"No, you ain't," Vernon said. "Cause I ain't ready."

Darnell walked toward the door. "Shoot my ass," he said. "Then you gon have to catch a plane, okay?" He pulled open the hollow, flimsy door. This ain't procedure. I ain't getting yoked this time. I'm quittin before I'm terminated.

OKLAHOMA REMORIAL

THE APARTMENT COURTYARD was hot by the time he got home. One of the Mexican women from #3 stood at the washer, pulling out wet, tangled clothes; she heard his shoes on the concrete and turned, but she smiled when she recognized him. She always touched Charolette's chin and whispered, "*Muy bonita.*"

Darnell stared at the El Camino, running his tongue over teeth coated with coffee and Swisher Sweet smoke and Vernon's sleeping breath. Damn. She should be at work. One o'clock. And he had no money.

Vernon had awakened in LA, taken the envelope in Pomona, and said nothing until he dropped Darnell at the corner. Then he mumbled, "Come to the man house at ten. He want to talk to you."

Darnell climbed the pebbly stairs, sucking his furred teeth, his head large as a balloon. He couldn't say, "Look, baby, I was doin that big job with Nacho way out past San Bernardino and the truck broke down, so we had to stay with the equipment all night, but I got *paid.*"

190

No cash—and smellin like a party. His hand stung at the heated black paint of the railing.

The living room was immaculate, the piles of folded laundry that usually covered the couch and coffee table gone, and the apartment was quiet except for the radio in the bedroom. He stood near the gleaming clean counter and small table where they ate.

She waited. When he went into the bedroom, she was sitting on the made bed in a silky flower-printed dress, sewing the little snaps that always came off Charolette's pants. Lunch break, he thought, and she didn't look up. He stood by the doorway and waited, too.

"Apartment looks good, huh? You can pack your stuff and go. It'll be easier to keep everything clean without you tracking dirt and making laundry anyway," she said conversationally. "Go on and sleep at her house tonight, too."

Her elbows jerked with the thread, and he didn't want to go closer. Just piss her off more. He folded his arms, leaning against the wall. "I didn't do that, Brenda."

"Was she good?" she whispered, head down. "She do it for three hours and hang upside down and holler? I know you don't get it when you want it here. She didn't give a damn what her kids thought—or she didn't have no kids. She didn't have to go to work this morning, either, huh?" She bit off a thread and finally looked up. Her eyes were whiskey-dark, her skin pale, and gray nudged the inside corners near her nose.

Melvin and Snooter always say, Just let her finish talkin when she mad. Females hate when you interrupt what they done already planned to say. They always got it planned out. Darnell closed his lips, breathed through his nose, and she went on. "Cause you weren't workin with your dad or Nacho. No, I didn't call em up. I wasn't about to say, 'My husband didn't come home.' Not me, Darnell. My mama did that. I don't do that. No. Uh-uh." She stared at him. "So I went over there late to tell your mom I needed a seam ripper and thimble. Yeah, so I could see Nacho in back with your dad, Roscoe, all of em. And they said, 'Darnell home sleep, huh? Lazy brotha.' " She bent her head to the snaps again, the tiny silver circles. Her hair was brushed flat and shiny against her small head. He swallowed bitter tobacco. It take a while sometimes, man, Melvin said. Just let em finish.

"And I even went by Jackson Park. No, you weren't hanging out," she said. "Charolette thought it was a party; I had the radio on and I was singing to her. And I came home, put her to bed, and started waiting. Still waiting now, for the cops to come and tell me the bad news. Or you, to come in here with some kinda lie and your dick soft." She whispered, "One of the girls at the park, they'll do you for five dollars."

"Damn, Brenda, you don't talk like that," he said, but she laughed.

"Marlene and them always do," she said. "They got left—now I got left." She lifted her head again. "When I took Charolette, your dad said how come you didn't need the car, and I said you had a job with some guy. But she musta dropped you off, huh? What kinda car she got? She must be real good if you walked."

"I didn't sleep with nobody, Brenda," he said, feeling the tiredness spread back out to numb his forehead, his scalp. "And I called coupla times, but you weren't here." He sat on the other edge of the bed and rubbed his eyebrows. Melvin probably right—this works for him cause he messes with dumb women, and they give up fast. He looked at Brenda, tried to keep his voice casual. "Nothin I can say, right? Look at me, Brenda. No hickeys on my neck, no perfume. What you want me to do?" She put down the red corduroy overalls and covered her eyes, shoulders starting to shake. He thought, I can't say the truth. I was workin. I got close to this woman, but I freaked. Then I finished up the shift. Just touch her—maybe that part of Melvin's plan right.

He moved over on the bed and said, "Brenda, come on. You know me better, you know I wouldn't do that." He put his arms around her neck and pulled her face into his shirt, and she wouldn't look at him. She spoke into his neck.

"I ended up hoping you were with somebody else. Cause if not, the cops would come. I stayed out there on the couch, watching for the lights, and then after I took Charolette this morning, I decided I couldn't sit out there all day waiting for them to find your body." She wiped her eyes on the overalls, pulling away, and folded them. She touched the darker wet spots. "You need to pack your stuff, Darnell. I won't live like this. I know where you were now."

"My body, Brenda? What you talkin about?"

She stared at him. "All that time you were gone, I waited for them to come and tell me they found it."

"Damn, Brenda, why you want to dream me like that?" he said, looking away from the shimmering film over her eyes.

"I don't dream you like that. It's just in my brain, like in the cells. Like I inherited it from my mama." She twisted the rings on her fingers. "She probably had it in her brain, too," she whispered. "That's why I want you to just go. I can't even see you a couple of hours late and I don't think somebody got you. The good guys, the bad guys. Whoever. A fire."

"What I'ma do at a fire now?" he said sharply.

But she went on like she hadn't heard him. "And everything scares me, Darnell," she said, looking at his collarbone, her eyes blurred. "Everything. When you take Charolette with you, I see accidents. I see her in the *street*, after somebody was chasing you. I see a branch flying off in a yard. I see her hand, it's so small."

"Brenda, Brenda," he said, cutting off her deepening voice. "You scarin me now, too. If I thought like that, I'd never get out the front door again."

"I can't help it," she said. "That's why you need to go. Back to wherever you were last night." She stood up, holding the overalls, but he pulled her back toward him.

"You don't know," he said. "Look, if I was with somebody else, could I do this?" He kissed her, said into her ear, "You think I'm that bold, I'd be doin this?" He pulled at the skin between her neck and shoulder with his teeth, gently, smelling nothing, no perfume or smoke. Just skin. She didn't push him away, she pulled him down onto her, hard, her palms holding on to his shoulder blades through his shirt, and when her dress was off and her nipples were hard against his chest, she didn't keep him at wrist's length with her fingers splayed against his collarbone, like she had been doing since Charolette.

She collected half-moons of dark under her fingernails. When she lay on her stomach, her head turned away from him and resting on her arms, he saw the crescents edging the white of her nails. She had his skin, loosened with sweat and scraped from his back, where crisscrossing lines glowed warm now. He felt his heart slowing down, thought maybe Melvin was right, always saying fights made sex better. "You gotta get they blood racin somehow—trust me, young boy," he used to say, laughing.

"I'm sorry I scared you," he whispered, and she turned her face toward his.

"I know where you were," she said. "You were with your other lady. You went to that fire. You were with the lady you still love more than me—ain't no difference." She swung her legs slowly over the bed and pulled on her dress. She smoothed her hair, twisting it back tighter. "I'm going back to work; I'm late from lunch," she said. Then she knelt over him on the bed. "Darnell. Why you still want to get lost in the flames? I love you—why can't you stay?"

"I'm here, right?" he said, sleep dissolving the sand behind his brows.

She put her nails fierce and close to his eyes when she laid her hands on his face. "I don't know where you are," she whispered, hard. "I love you." He thought she was gone, but she came back in to lay the newspaper on his chest. "But this is what you love," she said. "This is your lady." She ran her finger across her wet cheek and turned to go.

He heard the jangle of keys dropping on the table, and he knew she was walking back to work. The door clicked. Wrapped in the damp sheets, the wetness beneath him from when he pulled out of her, he looked at the picture of flames in a riverbottom palm, the orange boiling at the center of the fronds, and he knew it was just before the tree exploded. The text read: "Although authorities have postponed an official declaration of the county's fire season due to sharply reduced funds, firefighters have already fought two blazes in the riverbottom near Doloreaux. Investigators said the fires, near the freeway, could have been caused by discarded cigarettes, but last year many fires were attributed to homeless drifters living in makeshift shelters along the river."

He lay staring at the ceiling's rough plaster, remembering the cupfuls of water he'd poured over his hair, the wood popping like gunshots. I want to be out there like I'm *sprung*. Like they say—it just comes up through your neck and into your head like fireworks. Like sex. He closed his eyes.

Charolette was nestled into her pallet of sheets on the floor, arms thrown out on either side like she was flying in her dreams. Her fingers curled loose, her breath snarled in her throat. He swallowed, his own throat tight, and backed out to close his mother's bedroom door.

She was pulling the hem of a dress from under the silver foot of the machine. Earrings swinging, she looked up and said, "We ain't seen you for a couple of days."

"I had a job," he said, and when she frowned, he kept walking. He heard wall-shaking bass. Gasanova was cruising toward his mother's house.

"Hey, homey, you get that waitress yet?" Darnell said, glad to have someone else to talk about.

"Tamiko," Gas said, shaking his head. "I'm serious this time, but she says, 'You gotta wait awhile.' I say, 'Yo, the while has been *waited*.' She says, 'We gotta take some time,' and I say, 'Yo, that concept is out*dated*.' " He smiled.

"Listen at your sorry rap!" Darnell laughed.

But Gas looked embarrassed. "I think I might be ready to buy the ring, man," he said.

"What? You? Kick your homey Kreeper off shotgun?" Darnell said. "Hey, rappin don't work the same when you married, let me tell you that right off."

Gas shrugged. "But I gotta try it to know, right? Maybe you just can't say it right. You never could—that's why Brenda the only fine woman put up with you."

"Give me a break," Darnell said, and he heard Charolette screaming with joy, staggering onto the lawn in front of his mother.

"Here come your other lady," Gas said, smiling wide.

Darnell shook his head, laughing still, and he couldn't believe the watery vapor that rose in his chest, flooded his cheekbones. "There your daddy," his mother said, and Charolette slammed her palms down on the sidewalk when she stumbled. But she pushed back up, came at him with her arms outstretched, her two front teeth lonely in her wide-open mouth, her dusty hands reaching for him.

She held a tin pie plate in front of her like a shield, going around and around the coffee table, ducking under Brenda's legs stretched out to rest on the top. Darnell lay on the floor, and she pulled at his hair to turn over his face, stuck her index finger deep inside his ear until he shivered and said, "I still got brains in there somewhere, babygirl!" He caught her on his chest, and she said, "Daddy! Daddy!" pointing to the telephone wire glinting in the low sun. "Irdy!" she said, like it had been just this morning.

"She always looks for you," Brenda said. "She never wants to cuddle or sit in my lap anymore. Too busy."

"Just like you," Darnell said, looking at her upside down. "You always too busy to cuddle, too."

Brenda smiled when he reached for her leg, but she said lightly, "You ain't taken your boots off yet. You planning on going somewhere?"

Darnell let Charolette bounce on his chest. "Pops wasn't home when I picked up wild thang here, and Mama says he got a job for me." He hesitated. "I need to swing by and pick up my money from the last job."

She looked at him. "Yeah. I know how long it takes to get there and back."

Darnell sat up, swallowed. "I know you do. So you want to come?" He raised his eyebrows, put his hands palm out.

She looked at Charolette, then back at him. "I would if Sophia and Paula was there, but they have practice for some school play." She rubbed her eyes. "Tomorrow's Saturday, and I have to go to the store."

Darnell stood up, Charolette holding a crease in his jeans leg. It was almost eight. "Oh, no," he said, seeing the baby's face gather redness at the temples, the bottom lip turn under like a red, fat moon. Brenda scooped her up, and she began to cry.

The courtyard was deserted, but all the doors were open and the railings fluttered with drying clothes and upended mops and Charolette's fluttering pieces of yarn. Darnell heard the televisions and clinks of washing silverware, and he sat in the El Camino, smelling Brenda's perfume, coconut hairdress and Charolette's baby powder. The car seat was inside, because somebody might steal it, but he felt Charolette crumbs with his palm. This ain't even my hooptie no more, he thought. I gotta get the Spider fixed. He looked at the dashboard; his screwdriver and coffee cup were gone. On the floorboards, he saw two of Charolette's sparkly hair ties, and in the pulled-out ashtray was a tiny bottle of pink lotion. He rubbed some into his bare arms and started the engine.

His father and Roscoe were alone in the back room, drinking Miller's and watching an old Western. "Quiet in the front," Darnell said when they looked up.

"Sophia and Paula gon get to yammer in front of a whole audience now," his father said casually. "They good at it—never forget any lines."

"Where you been for the last few days?" Roscoe said.

"Workin." Darnell looked at the grayish cowboys on the old black-and-white TV. The truth, he thought. "I had a job for a dude downtown."

His father frowned. "One-man job? What you doin over there?"

Darnell said, "Just movin stuff around."

"He let you use his equipment? I didn't see you come over here to borrow nothin," his father pressed.

"Yeah, I used his." Shit, this was too close, Darnell thought. The truth. Nothin but the truth.

"Well, shit, one-man job and he got the equipment, why he didn't do it his own self?" his father grumbled.

"Why, when someone will do it for you?" Roscoe said, watching Darnell.

That's enough, Darnell thought. I hate this shit, tryin to keep stories straight. He said, "Mama told me you got a job."

"Mrs. Panadoukis, the doctor's wife up there in Arroyo Grande, she's got a bank full of dead iceplant and two dead pine trees. She wants it all cleared out right away because she's planning an anniversary party," Roscoe said.

"You and Victor and Ronnie could knock it out," his father said, looking at him hard, the long nose pulled over his mouth. "Y'all can take the Chevy so Brenda won't be without a car. She been talkin to your mother about the grocery bills. Maybe this extra money cheer her up."

Darnell closed his lips tight and drew air in hard through his nose. Don't even start that shit—I ain't in the mood, he thought. I know— I ain't about nothin. I don't know what hard work is. He stood up.

"Early, boy," his father said. "Not no leisure hours—it's gettin hot." Darnell said nothing, walking to the door, and his father said, "You been hangin around with Donnie Harris?"

Darnell stopped by the door. "Why?"

"I asked you a question."

Darnell heard the wire in his father's voice. "No, I ain't seen him."

His father's eyes were hard in the window's reflection. "He come around here yesterday, lookin bad. Say he need to talk to you. He smokin that shit?"

Darnell thought of Donnie's ragged voice on the phone. "I don't know," he said. "I'll check him out." He pushed the screen door, but Roscoe spoke behind him.

"Donnie always asks me, every time," Roscoe said. " 'How's Birdman doin?' I have to tell him I'm the last person to answer that. If he's doing fine in prision, I must have prepared him for that."

Darnell paused in the sideyard, touching the Spider's dusty hood, his toes deep in the high grass around the tires. He remembered Roscoe telling his father about the drive up to Louis's college, the same route Darnell had just taken. "You'd think the boy be excited about the team, about ball, but all he did was look for egrets," Roscoe had said. "I don't understand how his brain works."

What's Pops thinkin about my brain? He ain't supportin his family— he's wanderin around dreamin about somethin he can't have. He straightened from where he'd peered into the Spider's interior. Let me go get paid, he whispered to the headlights. Odd job. I ain't goin home broke. And I'm tired of walkin.

"You weren't nervous, were you?" the consultant said, settling back on the leather couch in the dim living room. MTV looked garish and jumpy in the darkness, and Darnell pushed himself back in the easy chair.

He hesitated. Look into the man's eyes. You know him. He gon pay you now, just like they do after you rake up the trash and stack the wood. "I don't know," he said, concentrating on the heavy laps of skin by the mouth. The truth is the easiest. Why lie? You ain't doin no more odd jobs for this dude, so who care if he think you ain't got no *cojones*? "Nervous about cops. And Vernon actin a fool."

"Couldn't have been as nerve-racking as fighting fires," the consultant said, and Darnell frowned. He smelled the cigarillo smoke rising from the ashtray—that's where Rob got it. Smoke. No. Darnell glanced at Leon in the other chair; he raised his chin a half inch. The consultant said, "Judgment calls, quick decisions—just like firefighting." He paused. "Those jeans are really hot in that flower-power-revival crowd. My postal connection might get some more soon." He smiled at Darnell. "Weird to see all those Hmong just down the mountain, huh? Did you know they're totally different from the regular Laotians?"

"You learn all that in Vietnam?" Darnell said without thinking, glancing at the Spandex-shimmered breasts on the dancers.

The consultant's voice went up. "Who told you that?"

Leon's face froze, and Darnell's back prickled cold. Pops, he thought. Pops was talkin to this dude, about bein a pilot in Nam. The man stared, waiting. "I just guessed," Darnell said, shrugging. This dude don't remember no tree trimmers—don't nobody actually see you when you out there workin.

Leon spoke up. "Darnell ain't stupid," he said. "That's why you wanted him." He looked at Darnell. "How's Rob?"

So the consultant know about the sugar cane, Darnell thought. Think I'm just like Vernon—a delivery boy; wasn't no need to tell me about the schedule change. Damn. He lifted his head. "Rob ain't thrilled about the clientele. Neither was I."

"Hey, nobody likes working directly with pharmaceutically deprived individuals," the consultant said.

"Sprung assholes," Leon said. "Everybody hate sprung assholes, except Vernon. He love strawberries."

Darnell tried to erase the image of Vernon smiling at the door, eyes narrowing when he held the gun tight. He looked straight at the consultant. "I'd rather take my chances with fire and rattlers than have some pharmaceutically deprived dude smoke me. Or some pharmaceutically drowned dude kick my ass."

The consultant's eyes glowed red-rimmed blue. "You were Marcus Smith then. But you live in Rio Seco, on the Westside. Those things could happen to you at any minute. For free."

"Nothin's free," Leon said.

Darnell smiled. "But I ain't Marcus Smith."

"You're going back to firefighting?" the consultant asked.

Darnell shook his head. Leon said, "What you gon do for dinero, D.?"

"I have plenty of odd jobs," the consultant said.

"I'ma do some landscaping work," Darnell said, thinking of the mower, of Trent, of tomorrow.

"Oh," the consultant said, leaning back again. "You know, you need a license for that."

"Yeah," Darnell said. His father and Roscoe always complained about the yearly fee.

The consultant grinned, really enjoying himself now. "As long as you pay, the government doesn't care what you do. Roofers, painters. Pilots." He nodded at Darnell. "The market for pharmaceuticals isn't any better. You have to pay tariffs, just like everything else. My shit isn't any more dangerous than Halcion or Xanax or Prozac." Darnell stared at his mouth—now he sounded like a combination of Fricke's hard-clanging voice when he talked about government funding and Brother Lobo lecturing in the park.

"Government assholes like those chemical drugs—legal narcotics, you know, college boys with labs and beakers and FDA approval. Same old country-club shit," the consultant said, dreamily. "They don't like messy farmer drugs. Poppies." He looked at Darnell for participation.

"Coca's a leaf," Darnell said. He saw the embers of rock pipes lighting.

"You're quick," the man said, smiling. "Hey, you know how the Hmong grow their crops, right? Slash-and-burn farming. All those flames, all that ash really make the soil rich." He squinted hard at Darnell. "You guys should really just let the forest burn—that's the natural way."

Darnell stood up. This ain't the station. This ain't Fricke. He wondered where the riverbottom blaze had been; from the photo of the tree, he thought it was near Treetown. He focused his eyes back on the consultant's heavy-lined face, the fifties in his hand.

"I'll see you in a few weeks," the man said, smiling.

In the Bronco, Leon said, "Why you get into all that palaver if you wasn't gon do nothin?"

Darnell shrugged. He knew he couldn't explain Fricke to Leon. Leon hated most white people, and he said, "I don't spend no longer in there than I have to. The man yang about anything. Stay up in there and watch cable all day, think he know everything. Always wantin to talk about Bobby Brown and Public Enemy. Palaver." Leon's sharp-trimmed hairline was minky black when he turned to look at Darnell. "And you wanna go back to manual labor and shit."

Darnell looked out the window at the Jack-in-the-Box, at the El Camino in the parking lot. "I need somethin steady, man, maybe get me some yards for every week. I don't know."

"License." Leon smiled. "Gas don't have a license to cook. He could kill you with some bad meat loaf, cause he thinkin about Tamiko." He smiled wider, like they were finding pennies in the fountain, and Darnell bit the inside of his lip, seeing them run the sidewalks, the gullies and drainpipes. Louis—Louis had sat here. Working. His chest flooded with cool, and he shook his head.

"Damn, Leon, you makin me feel old," he said.

"Not as old as you gon be when you start workin with your pops," Leon said. "Man, you a fool; just wait a while and you gon get tired a that."

"Homey, you don't know me," Darnell said, touching Leon's palm. He stood in the parking lot. "Hey, like your baby brother just told me: the while has been waited."

Pine-sharp ammonia scent drifted down from the balcony. He lifted his face, saw the door open. Damn, it's almost midnight, he thought. She ain't sleep.

She sat on the couch, staring at the window, the mop propped in the kitchen. The checkbook was open on the coffee table, and her fingers twisted a pen cap. She didn't look up; her hair was glossy flat near her ears, and he saw her give a quick shudder, like she'd been crying.

"Brenda?" he said, bending near her, and her face, when she raised it, was swollen, her lips twisted square like a mask. "You worried about the money? Look—" He dropped the bills on the table. All I was thinkin about was the Spider, he thought. This my paycheck, and I'm supposed to give it to my wife, like all the guys joke about.

But her mouth went even wider, and her voice came out rubber-flat around her sobs. "You want to die—go on and do it away from me," she said. "Take your gun and go, Darnell. I love you too much to see it."

He turned to where her eyes went, and he saw his jacket, the small silver-and-brown gun like a chocolate bar lying in foil. "I picked up your jacket to put it away, and I thought you forgot your wallet," she said. "And Charolette coulda gone in there and found that! Darnell," her voice gulped air. "I can't live like this. I wish I hated you. I wish I could sit around with all the other women and talk about how it ain't no big deal you're gone. But I can't see it—I can't wait for them to bring you home." She buried her head on her folded wrists.

"Brenda," he said, his fingers on her elbow, but she wouldn't lift her face again. What can I say—it ain't mine? Hella old line. He knelt, and Charolette's voice came from the bedroom door, her palms pushing it open.

"Daddy!" she yelled, and Brenda whipped her head around to look at Darnell, her eyes smeared with tears, her mouth a sharp crescent, tight now. Keeping his face away from Charolette, he grabbed the jacket and dropped the gun into the pocket.

On the sidewalk, he heard Charolette's clotted screams, high-pitched as an animal caught in burning chaparral, and then the door clicked shut.

In the cold corridor between government buildings and banks and law offices, he passed windows and metal railings and garages. The street people were parked near doors with their shopping carts close; they lay in the landscaped areas, arms sprawled over their foreheads against the lights. In the winter, they had huddled here for warmth, old white women with street-sunned faces, ashy thin brothers, riverbottom-wrinkled men so dirty they were no color. The security guards looked past them unless they were noisy or on the property. Securing the lines, patrolling the boundary. Following procedure. He knew they watched him walk past, hands deep in his jacket pockets.

Step to me, he thought. Bangers. Sprung dudes. Po-lice. Whoever. I'm strapped. The gun rubbed against his palm, and he took his hand out. Vernon's property. Might not even have bullets. I ain't checkin.

Brothas don't need no help—that's what Lobo and the older men used to say when they read about the three suicides in Darnell's last year of high school. All white kids, senior boys, faces he didn't remember ever seeing in the huge streams of passing kids. Brothas don't do that, Leon and them said.

Cause we do it to each other, Louis said. Darnell rarely saw Louis then, by senior year. Louis and Donnie were athletes, hanging on the hill with the other jocks. Leon was running weed and pills in the parking lot; Gas was under the hood of someone's car. And Darnell was off in the corner with Brenda.

He saw the green of go arrows, the same green as Brenda's letters and arrows on her computer, pointing him ahead in the last street before the buildings gave way to stucco apartment boxes. Like the one where they lived. Where Brenda live—I ain't payin rent, I ain't nothin but a guest. He walked faster, like he had somewhere to go. Was Brenda asleep now? Was Charolette curled into her ribs, calm, dreaming?

Death wish. Same thing her mother said. Brenda think I want to go out like that. He walked down the incline to the cemetery's gravel road. He'd always thought Brenda was scared. She was afraid of Marlene and most of the Westside girls, and she refused to let him park too close to the fires; she glanced at them nervously, the glow reflecting in her pupils. But she was tougher than he was now—going to work, taking care of Charolette, watching him. When I start trippin, I drink somethin nasty, drive around, act useless. She get upset, she clean the house. She never stop workin.

He walked slowly along the line of headstones until he saw the faded glow of the ones Mrs. Batiste had whitewashed. The eggs and gifts were gone, but remnants of shiny green grass had gathered in the brownish blades of lawn, and the silk flowers were still bright.

Here I am. Antoine. GranaLene. All the spirits she said were callin me. She said my twin was callin me. Sometimes twins only share one soul between them, his grandmother had whispered to him sometimes. You keep you soul tight about you. Don't let it wander.

He sat there for a long time, listening to the faint wind in the branches. This gotta be dangerous—I'm in the graveyard after midnight. If zombies want me, they can come on, too. I already called everybody else. Step to me.

His brother's headstone was nubbly-warm against his back. He hadn't slept for days, and the leaves rubbing and turning made a whispery sound that echoed in his head. He let his chin dig into his chest until a stick high above him broke sharply and he jerked awake. Bird. He widened his eyes, moved his shoulders. GranaLene said your soul wander at night, when you dream.

Pops always hated hearin that. He was always yellin, "If the boy work hard enough during the day, his soul be too damn tired to crawl."

He stood up and hunched his shoulders. Yeah, I know Pops could have me come along every day, keep gettin me these side jobs. But that's less money for him and Roscoe. All the Samoans and Mexicans doin trees now, he got serious competition. He don't need deadweight.

He looked back at the headstones, stepped over the new glossy markers. Yeah, Moms and Pops want Sophia and Paula to go to college—that way they can run their mouths even better and faster, Pops always jokin. Have more to say. Pops don't need to be feedin me, too.

He tried to walk fast toward the Westside, to keep awake and moving. At the street that led to the bridge over the river, a voice came up behind him. Darnell wheeled around to see a Mexican man in worn-heeled boots and a straw cowboy hat. "Excuse—the freeway sixty is this way?"

Darnell slipped his fingers off the gun. They'd fallen there without his thinking, noticing. He breathed hard. "Pretty far."

The man nodded. "How far?"

"About three miles," Darnell said, nodding down the avenue.

The man smiled with one side of his face. "Oh—so not far." He ducked his head in thanks and started walking. Darnell watched him for a minute and headed the other way.

The fire at Jackson Park was only a smear of orange hanging below the barrel rim, and the cars were all dark, with men sleeping on the seats. Darnell saw two women peer out from one of the porches, and he looked away. Their faces slipped back into the darkness under the overhang. The domino table was pushed close to the pepper tree, and the chairs were all gone for the night, stored in the ancient wooden shed one of the men kept locked.

He stood in the lit phone booth at the stone-walled store, the metal shutters blind over the windows. She answered the phone quickly, her voice thick with sleep.

"Like high school, huh?" he whispered. "When I used to call you all the time and try to rap."

"You okay, Darnell?"

"Brenda, I ain't dead." He stopped. What to say—wait for me? Tired rap. I'll be home soon, baby? He heard her rough breathing in the receiver. "Sssh," he said when she started to speak. "Don't wake up babygirl." He hung up and walked again.

Crawling into the cab of the Chevy, he lay curled on his side to breathe in his father's Tareyton smoke and sugared coffee and motor oil.

*   *   *

When the wrought-iron screen clanged hollow, he sat up quick, trying to look fully awake. His father walked to the curb and looked at the slice of risen sun, and Darnell opened the door, set his shoulders casual. His father turned, eyes narrow, and then he nodded. "You finally ready to work, huh?" he said. Darnell threw his jacket into the Spider and went inside.

His mother heard him in the kitchen and came in frowning. "I didn't hear Brenda—she don't want no breakfast?"

He shook his head, and she looked at his face, his neck, his boots. He turned to reach for monkey bread on the counter, and his mother was in his face when he turned back, bumping the coffee cup against his chest, spilling a few drops to burn his wrist. "Brenda the best girl you ever find," his mother said, dead quiet. "You best not mess up. Cause if you do, you ain't comin back here. No. Uh-uh. I won't let you get out of it that easy." She glared at him and left the room.

He hadn't heard the Apache rumble up to the curb. Roscoe and his father were looking at the load of branches and refuse, and Darnell said, "You need some help? I see y'all didn't make it to the dump yesterday."

"Get up in here," Roscoe said, motioning with his head to the Apache's cab, and Darnell climbed into the huge, high cave he'd always loved when he was small. The engine stuttered, and the truck shuddered up the back roads to the county landfill, where the bulldozers nudged the trash up into graded hills. Darnell looked for the shack near the edge of the dump, just over the county line, where an old man with skin dark as tires used to live. Now five or six trailers and shacks crowded the property, and Darnell had seen Mexican men combing the piles when no one was looking.

A short line of trucks waited to be weighed. Darnell kept his eyes on the exhaust pipe in front and said, "You and Louis's mom broke up before she died."

Roscoe nodded. "I wasn't doing what she thought I should. I didn't want to work a nine-to-five, every-day gig. I wanted to write poems." He waited, knowing Darnell had heard the story. "You didn't go home last night, right?"

Darnell shook his head, watched the trucks move up. "Man, if I could get a nine-to-five, I wouldn't even think about the mountains.

I'd try. But I go to the damn offices, fill out the papers. A hundred other dudes in the waitin room and the parkin lot."

Roscoe frowned. "You never heard of the Depression? Black folks didn't even know it happened—your dad's told you that one many times." But he touched Darnell's wrist. "But marriage is the same for every generation." Darnell turned away again. "Yeah, it's all about compromise. You don't believe me. You think it's about money and sex. Compromise. I couldn't do it, even though we had Louis. But you need to think long and hard. When you go home, you have to bargain. And when you two start hollering, don't forget you can't really take spoken words back." Roscoe gripped the steering wheel harder. "When your daughter gets older, you're gonna see it's the same with children. Compromise. When they're little, it's food, clothing, keeping them safe. Then they get grown, and you fight about different things." He waited for Darnell to look at him. "I heard someone say you can only be friends with your kids once they get grown themselves. I can't see that—Louis is gone from me."

Darnell put his laced fingers behind his neck. "I'ma go see him."

Roscoe set his lips. "What could you tell him now?"

"I want to ask him somethin," Darnell said. Roscoe held his eyes, and Darnell saw the tiny pieces of mica from the floating dust sparkling on Roscoe's forehead. He thought of Charolette's cheeks, the makeup sheen Brenda left there. "Roscoe. I can't talk to Pops like this. And I'm grown. Damn, I got a kid."'

Roscoe slanted his head and shrugged. "The parties involved are hardheaded. Your dad and I have known each other a long time. Maybe you need to have Brenda for your friend."

"You and Marietta Cook friends?"

"Yeah. Never thought I'd say that about a woman." Roscoe put the truck in gear. "Not in my life."

They pushed off the tight-stacked eucalyptus branches, the leaves and scrap cement and wrecked plastic slide from yards. Darnell swept out the ridged bed. On the way down, Roscoe took the lower road through the wealthy part of Hillgrove, where Darnell saw the historic houses with huge sloping lawns. He and his father had trimmed some trees here, when he was just eleven and learning to use the chain saw. He saw the porches shaded and cool, wrapped all the way around the houses, remembered the smell of sap in his father's shirt, the wicker furniture while they waited for someone to answer the door.

At one old yellow house, ivy hanging over the porch and roses thick beside the walkway, he saw three Mexican guys ripping out a huge circle of ivy on the lawn. They talked, chopped with machetes— big curve-bladed machetes that swung loose. Their radio blasted Mexican music, horns and swinging voices going so fast Darnell imagined them playing at 78 speed. He saw a shadow at the front screen, a bent gray-haired lady coming out to watch the men from the porch, and Roscoe pulled away from the stoplight.

"You go ahead and climb, Mountain Man," Victor said from the bottom of the slope.

From the front yard of Mrs. Panadoukis's house in Arroyo Grande, Darnell had seen the bruise-brown pall of smog drifting toward the city from LA, but in the backyard only the huge bank rose before him. The iceplant was mostly dead, and the woody, tangled mesh tore from the dirt easily, but he had to dig his boots into the steep incline.

He didn't look behind him at Victor and Ronnie. He bent to pull another webby mess of stems up in a thick mat, but he wouldn't let himself see manzanita or creosote. He kept seeing the Mexican man's face from last night, under his hat, and the men laughing over their machetes today, but he couldn't figure out why.

The piles of iceplant were heavy. Victor and Ronnie raked and pushed the heaps onto the burlap sacks they'd laid out at the base of the bank. They took off their shirts. Darnell remembered that they didn't have anywhere to wash them unless they were springing for a motel room or boarding house this month, something they usually did when it rained or a vicious Santa Ana came through.

"I don't go nowhere without my jimhat," Victor sang along with Digital Underground on Ronnie's radio. "Yeah, my man Darnell didn't use no jimmy, and now he doin the daddy thang. You gon have some more if you keep up the sex with no Latex, man.'"

"When you desperate for some ass, man, you don't care," Ronnie said, and Darnell heard a scraping step on the cement. He saw Mrs. Panadoukis, her face frozen, standing by the back sliding door with her purse. She clenched her lips tight and fumbled with her keys. They were silent, the music thumping loud.

When she'd closed the glass door, her neck curved toward them, Victor busted up. Darnell saw her held-tight cheeks. He bent to the pile of iceplant and saw the machetes flashing at the ivy. The Mexican guys had been laughing—he looked at Ronnie's chest, Victor's braids touching the nape of his neck. The Mexican guys could be saying anything, talking dirty or yanging about the lady they were working for, but it would be in Spanish and they'd sound happy; their radio was jolly, funny, that bright, quick music spangly as mariachi suits Darnell saw at Rancheria Park. Ronnie's radio. Uh-uh. The bass was low, shuffling around her, and the drums slapped her in the face. Booming.

"You ready?" Darnell said, and they went back to the far end of the bank to tear out the last patches.

Victor was steady making them laugh. "Darnell, you just graduated a couple years ago, man, you remember Mr. Rentell, that drivin teacher we had? Serious redhead, always talkin hip. He came by the park the other day, saw me. 'Victor, is that you?' He start storyin bout why was I hangin out, couldn't I do better? I told him, 'Man, I can still *drive*, don't worry—let me have your car, I'll show you right now.' " He threw iceplant down the bank to Darnell.

They loaded the Chevy in the front yard. Mrs. Panadoukis had already come to the front door and handed Darnell a check, her eyes averted. Darnell thought, Sorry we don't look good. He saw a Baggie on the lawn and bent to pick it up, thinking it had dropped from the truck. But someone else had put it on the grass; he saw a flyer inside and a small rock. Looking down the street, he watched a silver Toyota truck stop for a second at each lawn. A hand threw out Baggies. Darnell saw rakes and shovels and mower handles in the truckbed.

"Nguyen's Oriental Gardening Service," the flyer read. He spread it out on his lap in the truck, and Victor said, "Come on, man, it's hella hot."

"Let experienced Oriental Gardeners keep your yard look neet-clean & nice. Professional. Mowing, edging, trimming, and cleaning up for only $60 four times monthly." Darnell squinted. They gon come every week, he thought. The printing look nice, but they shoulda proofread this baby. The note had been printed on a computer, and a picture of a bonsai tree was in one corner. In the opposite corner was a stone lantern and a curved bridge. Darnell turned the flyer over and saw a phone number. Below it he read, "Also Sodding and Relawnscape. All the Works Guaranteed."

"Darnell, man, quit trippin," Victor said, running his hands over his braids. "Hit the bank."

Driving down the hill, he saw the city shrouded now in smog, brown with dust raised from the wind. I can't see Hillgrove or Gray-glen, but all those new houses gotta want gardeners. Landscapers. Trent makin a grip up there, he thought. He felt the little rock in his jeans pocket. Nguyen—he remembered Don Nguyen and Tom Bui, two Vietnamese guys who talked to him in biology sometimes. Ngu-yen—Don had explained that last name was like Smith in Vietnam. "Like Johnson for brothas," Gasanova had said, laughing.

His father and Roscoe were stacking wood. "Y'all finish the doctor's wife's job?" his father said.

"Yeah," Darnell said. "Iceplant was dead anyway."

"She pay you? She love to talk when she get started," his father said.

Darnell looked at the spirals of gray above his father's temples. "She didn't get started with us," he said. His arms and back ached, his chest was fist-tight with smog. When he drank the warm Coke he'd carried, the liquid trickled through the gray dust webbing his lungs. Avoiding his father's eyes, he said, "Roscoe, can you drop us off?"

After the Apache had turned the corner and Victor headed to the store with Ronnie, Darnell started the walk to Treetown. When he got to the olive groves, instead of turning down the street to the Thompsons' barn, he followed the arroyo to the riverbottom, where the deep-gashed banks flattened out to a sandy fan of jimsonweed and wild grapevines.

The river itself was a winding strip about twenty feet wide, but the wild flats extended half a mile between the banks, which were covered with wild tobacco in bending plumes, the flowers like long yellow macaroni tubes, and stiff-stemmed arrowroot.

Darnell walked along one of the narrow paths, sand shifting under his boots, to the cottonwoods and wild palms and vine-draped giant cane that hid the water. The shadows were full of the day's heat, and he looked for smoke, for the old fires' blackened earth. Good day for a fire, with a nice dry wind steady off the desert. If Scott and Perez show up, I could just grab the hose and go—maybe check out their captain if he comes.

Maybe I'll see the dude that's startin these little conflagrations, he thought, ducking under a curtain of wild grape that hung from a stand of cane. He touched a thick stalk—arundo, the giant cane taking over the whole swath of land from here to San Bernardino. Fricke said the only way to get it out was burn it deep and then take a dozer to the rest; you'd still have to dig some clumps. This stuff burns good and hot, he thought. He stopped, hearing voices behind the stand.

Bamboo grew near the cane, the greener, thinner stalks shaking now when two people walked out from another tiny path. The old woman stared at him from under her pink umbrella. Her wide, square mouth and small eyes were still, and he saw that she was afraid. Vietnamese. He looked at the boy, about ten, and recognized him from one of the chopped-up houses near his apartment. "Hi," the boy said, smiling shyly, and Darnell nodded.

"What you doin?" he asked, looking at the plastic bag in the boy's hand.

The woman stood very still, but the boy held out the sack. "Bamboo shoots," the boy said, embarrassed. "My gramma won't eat em from a can."

Darnell remembered Fricke showing him a can of pale squares, and he smiled. "Grammas never do," he said, and the boy frowned, puzzled, when Darnell kept walking.

He found the ashes and charred cane trash around the next bend. The fire had stopped abruptly at the edge of one path leading to the river, and the concrete-chunked levee on the other side only had sooty licks up a few slabs.

Darnell wandered around the blackened earth for a long time. Why would anybody want to be an arson investigator? he always wondered when he walked in already burned places. The carbonized tree branches and thick-scaled trunks, the headless palms, the ashes wet and muddy in old puddles. He sat on a flat chunk of concrete and stared at the burn swath. Plenty more fuel down here. The river-bottom stretched for miles.

When the cement grew cooler with evening, he started walking toward the freeway bridge. I guess I ain't bustin no wild pyro arsonist today, he thought. Damn, and I was sure if I was the hero the fire department might give me a job. He breathed the last traces of carbon.

Near the concrete pillars of the bridge, covered with graffiti, he saw two guys carrying water jugs. The brotha was dressed in green fatigues, and the white guy was shirtless, his back burned deep red. Darnell frowned. Those guys lived down here, and they weren't going to start a fire until now, he thought, when it was cooled off and dark. But none of the fires this year or last had been at night. Must not be homeless guys. He stared at the men disappearing into the stand of trees near the bridge.

Three Mexicans about his age looked up when he crossed the dank path under the bridge; they wore only their undershorts, and he saw their clothes drying on the scrabbled cement beside them, a trail of soapy water dripping down to the tiny stream that ran parallel to the river here.

When he came up out of the riverbottom past the bridge, at the street that led to Rancheria Park, he picked up a long stick and jabbed it into the shoulder of the road. His arms prickled cool. The evening had turned purple, and the packs of wild dogs that roamed the river-bottom would be cruising now. When he and Louis used to finally meet up after going their separate ways, for wings and flames, they'd run in the dark, afraid of the dogs, the other boys long gone home. Afraid of the callused palm, too, his father's big-knuckled hand hard at his ear when he'd make it home in the true dark smelling of smoke and ash and sweat from racing.

He called her from the same phone booth as before. He could hear Charolette talking near Brenda, saying, "Mama! Mine! Mine!"

"So what did you want to be, when you were a kid?" he said to her. "See, this is my rap. I didn't do it right in high school, when I used to call you."

Brenda was silent, and he heard forks drop into the sink. "A nurse," she finally said, hesitant. "A model, but I was too short. Get married and have kids, I guess."

He stared at the empty playground, the black skeletons of slides and swings, and the fire beyond, with shadows of men crowded in the lot. Dudes ain't like that. "You ever hear your brother James say, 'I'ma get married and have kids?' " He paused, watching a car cruise past. She was silent. "Remember what Leon used to say? 'Whatever

I do, I'ma get *paid.*' And Donnie talked about playin ball. Louis used to bug hell out of us with that word—ornithologist." He heard her rough breath in the receiver. "Me—you think I'm out here dreamin about smoke, and I mean, I am, but that ain't why I'm gone."

"Are you gone?" she whispered.

"I ain't comin home broke, Brenda. That's all I can say. I got some plans, but . . . " He threw his head back to stare at the weak gray light in the ancient booth. "Everything I say sound like a joke. I'll call you back." He hung up, slamming the stick into the curb.

At his father's house, he lay on the couch he'd sometimes imagined was a boat, rocking through the living-room air, or a coffin open around him while he stared up at the night ceiling and heard the embers glisten. GranaLene would say, "I hear that nose, you," and he would be afraid of his snuffle-wet nostrils, the prickle in his throat.

"Cold turn to pneumonia and take you on," she would say. "Get up here by the fire." And she'd hold him in her lap, wrapped in a blanket that smelled of sour coffee.

He slept hard and woke with his fingers trailing the carpet, his other hand pulling the stiffness between his legs, moving it in his jeans till he could breathe. Like high school—stretched out here thinkin about Brenda, hearin Pops snore. Music chattered slight as crickets from behind his sisters' door; they had always slept with the radio on, since they couldn't stand voiceless silence.

A dishtowel slapped his neck, and his mother snapped, "Get your hands off your pants, boy." He jumped, sat up with his back hunched and rubbed his face. His mother sat in the old chair across from him. "What the hell you doin sleepin here?" she said. "You don't live here." Her face was creased with anger, dark in the dim morning light through her drapes, the heavy drapes she'd made and kept perfect-pleated.

"Ain't no need for me to be there," he said, but she cut him off with the flat of her hand across the air.

"Don't give me that. You're—you're a man of color, like Melvin used to go on about. A black man. Negro. You got no business staying out all night. Brenda thinkin you dead! And you done did this before, call yourself showin up early for work."

He stared straight at her. "I ain't workin hard enough for Brenda."

"Please. Don't even try my patience with that."

"So what can I tell you, Mama?" He looked past her furious eyes, her swinging earrings, to the creamy drapes, the lining he used to touch, satiny, holding the daylight away now.

"Why y'all get married?"

He straightened. "Not cause she was pregnant. I didn't even have to do that. We woulda got married anyway."

"So?"

He rested his head on the couch back. She had gone to the mountains with him—he couldn't even ask any of the other girls. She'd say she wasn't into the nature-girl thing, and she cut her eyes sideways for snakes, but when he tried to explain the north-side vegetation and the chaparral, she didn't fold her arms and stick her chin out. And down in the flatlands—in the theater, biting her cool neck, watching her go into a dressing room and come out with a tight miniskirt on just to show him when he was helpless in a store full of women. Her face through the windshield while he watched a fire, waiting.

"You two was young for nowadays," his mother said to his chin. "But I was seventeen. Your daddy was nineteen. We had us some long tussles, but I told him, You ever stay away all night—I don't care you call and say you in bed right *now* with some woman and be home soon—but you stay out till the sun come up, I'ma do my best to kill you when you come through that door. Cause it's no justification for that. Your daddy drink with Floyd and Roscoe and whoallever he want, and I don't always like it. But he have *always* honored me by comin home."

"Maybe Brenda don't feel like that. Maybe she glad I'm gone, so life'll be easier." He looked at his boots, heard Fricke's drawl. "Maybe we ain't metaphysical soulmates."

"You fulla crap," his mother said. "Who you gon find better than Brenda? Huh? You ain't got nothin to say. Look, me and your daddy was in love. That gotta be obvious, cause I *still* gotta put up with my floor. We been married twenty-nine years, and he know how much a clean floor mean to me, but he and Roscoe tramp in here *daily* to get a coffee or some Pickapeppa. Leave mud worms everywhere."

She paused, and Darnell saw the brown tubes, the dried dirt from their boot soles, intact on the floor.

His mother flicked the towel toward him. "He always talkin about, 'This my house—my feet.' " She bent to lift his face up with her gaze; he couldn't look at her, remembering his father's shouts.

"That's what I'm sayin, Mama. That ain't my house. I can't even pay no rent—Brenda does that."

His mother bit her lip hard, reached out as if she would touch his face, then dropped her hand. "Brenda's mama love a clean floor, too. You don't know how hard Brenda come up with her daddy like he is—me and her mama don't even know how hard he come up. But Brenda don't need to be barely survivin, all alone with that baby, worryin about you all night." She tried to smile. "Me and your daddy showed you marriage is fightin and hollerin. Sometimes. It ain't no Brady Bunch."

He had to smile at that. Melvin had watched that show when they were young, and she'd grump around the room telling them to turn off that garbage. He heard his father's shoes thump heavy on the floor now from behind the bedroom door, and his mother said, "Go on and walk home, cause she makin a 7 Up cake for Memorial Day."

"Damn—I forgot," he said, and she frowned.

"You owe her to take her round and pay your respects," she said.

From the doorway, he could feel the oven pouring heat into the already-stifling kitchen, and Charolette had flung ladles and wooden spoons on the floor. When Brenda turned, eggs cradled in her fingers, she stepped on a metal edge. "Darnell!" The knife-thin cords rose taut from her collarbone. "Daddy!" Charolette called, waving her spatula at his knees.

The mountains were missing, hidden in the gray shroud, and he passed the listless, dusted palms lining the street to Rancheria Park. "Gon be hot as hell, and sticky down there by the lake," he said, keeping both hands on the wheel.

Brenda was silent, the foil-wrapped cake on the floorboards between her feet, and he saw her arms gold against the white tank top, her thighs smooth in the denim shorts. Charolette's spiral-twisted hair brushed his arm when she turned to look past him to the crowds in the park.

The Sunday before Memorial Day was unofficially Oklahoma Day. Everybody in Rio Seco who had people from that state gathered for the day and half the night, and barbecue smoke drifted thick above the tables. Oklahoma people—some from LA and San Bernardino and Indio, but most from Rio Seco—profiling, looking, eating, and talking serious yang while they caught up for the year. Then they went as families to visit the graves.

I don't even want to do this, he thought, looking for a space. Gotta see Donnie, and he'll just give me that "Homeys gotta have each other's back" cause I don't want to sue. Gotta see all the rest of em— "Where you workin?" A whole day of palaver, like Leon call it. Yeah— I can tell em Leon got jobs lined up for me.

"Look who gracin us with their presence!" his father shouted from the crowded picnic table shared by the Tuckers and some of the many Kings. Donnie, his brother Three, his mother and Great-Aunt Rosa. Darnell's mother nodded at him and held her arms out for Charolette, who smacked into her with lips trained and ready. Brenda sat with Sophia and Paula in the small lawn chair they'd saved for her, bending her head away from him, and Darnell stood, hearing the voices swirl around him.

"D., I ain't seen you around," Donnie said, standing next to him to touch his palm.

"You ready to get your ducats yet?" Darnell said, figuring to get it over with. "You gettin prepared to live large?"

"Shoot, man, court take forever," Donnie said, looking off toward the lake. His face seemed softer, vague, and his eyes darted from place to place. Darnell saw why his father thought Donnie was high, but Darnell could tell by the new plumpness around his waist that he wasn't on the pipe. Sprung guys were skeletal every time.

Donnie's mother said, "They givin him the run-around; that system take its own sweet time."

"This baby sleepy," Darnell's mother said, cradling Charolette, and Brenda reached over with the juice bottle, watching Darnell with half-mast eyelids.

"I'ma check my nephews by the water," Darnell said, moving off.

"I'll come with you, man, see if they still got crawdads," Donnie said.

They caught up with Lamont and Clinton, who were poking sticks into the water. "This man used to be the crawdad champion," Darnell told them, and Donnie stared intently into the murky water.

"No bubbles," Donnie murmured, and Darnell popped Lamont

and Clinton on the backs of their necks. He and Donnie turned back to see the people laughing around tables.

"Still rappin hard to the females, huh?" Darnell said.

"Who—them two?" Donnie said, nodding at the girls he'd been talking to before. "They from Terracina; they remember when I played ball."

"You gon get some later?" Darnell teased him. "Oklahoma Day cool for you, cause you still young and single and love to mingle."

Donnie's face had that same softer, slipping look again, like he wasn't hearing right. "No, man, I can't do it no more," he whispered.

"What you talkin about, man?" Darnell said. "You got shot in the leg."

"In my hip," Donnie said. "But I can't make love no more, I mean, I got close with this one girl, and then, you know how your heart start beatin real fast?"

"That's the point, man," Darnell said, but Donnie frowned.

"See, like, if my heart beat that fast and my blood start racin around, it might move the bullet."

"Didn't the doctors tell you exactly where it is?" Darnell couldn't look at Donnie's face.

"Yeah, they said. But, they could be lyin, D. Maybe the law paid em off to lie so I'll mess up and the bullet move. Then I'd be dead and can't go to court."

"Donnie, man, you can't trip like that." He hated the way Donnie always brought it up, always made Darnell feel the tight pull of his scars.

Donnie stared at him. "Yeah, man, I can't play ball no more, nothin. Like, what if it come loose and get in my bloodstream? I can feel it, man, I can feel it in there."

"Go see another doctor," Darnell said, walking beside him toward the crowds.

But Donnie shook his head. "Man, you just got the scars. Not the lead. It ain't the same."

Darnell felt the anger rise to his face, but he didn't want to scream at Donnie, yell out what he thought. No, man, it ain't the same. Nobody dependin on you—you just floatin. But he felt the balls of his feet warm from all the walking the last few days. "Let's get back before I get in trouble," he said softly, and Donnie was quiet when they reached the table.

Charolette was awake, and Brenda rose up fast. "Let's go visit," she said, glancing at him.

Yeah, he thought, walking. You got the baby, so you can talk about what she eat, her hair, all that. But all the brothas—I ain't got nothin good to say.

Brenda let Charolette run ahead to find a pine cone, and she said, "See? Nature girl. That's what they all gon say right now anyway— 'Look like Darnell spit her out his ownself, like you didn't have no part in it, girl.' "

Darnell took her arm, smelled her coconut-sweet hair. "That's the only thing I can take credit for right now," he said.

She turned her eyes up to him, her brows low. "She cries for you every morning. You're the one likes to wake up early—you always took her out for doughnuts. She knows you're gone."

"I ain't gone yet," he said, and she jerked her head away.

Charolette called, "Ba-by!" at the toddlers staggering near them, picking up fallen potato chips. Women sat in the folding chairs, men stood near trees, and foil was folded back over the spicy-coated hot-links and drumsticks and ribs, the baked beans and potato salad, the huge pans of peach cobbler and sheet cake. The women always made enough to offer anyone a taste. They'd hand out a paper plate, then the questions would begin.

"I hope you still ain't up there messin with them fires," Mrs. Rentie said.

"You ain't got on with no fire department yet?" her husband asked.

"He still wearin his cowboy clothes," Marlene said, smiling crooked, her arms folded. "I see you had a female Darnell junior." She nodded at Charolette.

"Look just like him, huh?" her mother said.

"Long as she don't act just like me, she's cool," Darnell said, but Charolette struggled in Brenda's arms, clutching pine cones and ja-caranda pods.

"She act just like him," Brenda said, resignedly.

The rounds took forever, even though he moved around the park quickly. "Where you workin? Why you ain't signed on with the city? Why you didn't go back to college—you got hella good grades, I remember. Oh, man where the Spider? I'm doin window tint now, got a shop downtown—totally legal. You workin with your dad? He kickin your natural ass? You see in the paper about all them fires?

Some pyro gone crazy. Too bad you can't have your own firefightin service, huh? Yeah, like tree trimmin. Shoot, you ain't got enough business, just strike you a match."

Yeah. Too bad. Because just before the sun started to fade under the weight of smog and early evening, a sharper scent of smoke cut through the rich, fat-laced spiciness around the grills. Darnell saw the hook-and-ladder and another engine circle the park and head for the riverbottom entrance, where the lake drained into the sandy bed and the jungle of vine-draped trees stretched to the flow of water.

Homeless guys cookin early? he thought, and when people realized there was another fire, Demetrius Thompson handed him an empty soda bottle. "Here, brotha, fill this up at the fountain and get busy. Got a fire down there."

"Forget you, Demetrius," Darnell said, smiling, but his chest flared hot.

Brenda sat back on the lawn chair slowly, Charolette lolling on her chest again in sleep. Darnell looked around at the groups of people walking toward the street that led to the cemetery; a few more families got into their cars, because their people were buried at the military ground.

I ain't goin with Mama and them to the graves, he thought. I did that. He remembered GranaLene saying, "I go on Easter. That my day. But I go on that Oklahoma Remorial, too." He saw Brenda close her eyes, lean her head back, and a thumping moved into the parking lot. Gasanova—Midnight was booming. Right behind him Leon's Bronco played the same station.

He said, "I'll be back," and started walking before Brenda could look up. Leon and Gas approached the crowd of men near Floyd King's huge '49 Ford, and Darnell heard Donnie beside him now. "They gon have the what-is-a-damn-truck argument," he said.

They were hollering, but Trent King stood next to Darnell's father, talking about a job. "What up, D. and D.?" Gas said, and Leon met Darnell's eyes.

Darnell's father saw him. "Come here, we talkin about this teardown."

Floyd King said, "Better you than me. Them damn Grayglen people always gotta find somethin wrong when you work, gotta look over your shoulder. I'll take a construction teardown any day."

Trent smiled. "I'm Grayglen, now, Uncle Floyd. Be careful."

"Sheeeit," Floyd said. "You *think* you Grayglen. But tonight, when you goin home, watch your back. You still blacker than a thousand midnights."

"When Johnny Law see you, he see one color, man," Snooter said.

"Donnie and Darnell already know that," somebody said, and then they were all quiet for a long, uncomfortable minute.

Trent jumped in, saying loudly, "I'm bidding on the landscape contract, but they're taking forever with the permits."

Darnell saw his father glance at Leon, saw the forehead dropping into a glare. I ain't in the mood, he thought, turning, hearing his father say, "We supposed to know next week, just in time for some real ass-kickin heat. Your favorite kinda day, huh, Darnell?"

He moved further away, keeping his mind blank, and Donnie said to Leon, "Y'all must got some serious car alarms with them systems." Darnell shifted with them, away from the older men, to walk toward the music coming from the car windows.

"No—I got Vernon." Leon laughed, and Darnell saw Vernon's head moving to the beat. He sat in the passenger seat, tapping his fingers on the door frame.

Donnie peered into the Bronco. "Let's cruise, man," he said, a faraway look on his face, and Darnell glanced back. His father opened his mouth to shout something. I ain't in the mood to get yelled at about no damn trees, Darnell thought. But Donnie's trippin. He ain't right—he want to ride with Leon?

"Come on, D.," Leon said, motioning with his head to the front seat, and Vernon leaned forward to let Donnie in the back.

"Man, I gotta let Brenda know I'm leavin," Darnell said, looking toward the veil of barbecue smoke wafting low. "The baby's sleepin, but . . ."

"Oh, man, you pussy-whupped now?" Leon laughed. "You a captive and shit? We'll be back in a flash—before you in trouble with your woman."

Gas stood beside his truck, and Darnell met his eyes, asked, "You comin?" Gas shook his head slow and opened his own blue-scripted door. Midnight. Leon sucked his teeth sharp, and Darnell felt the bass when he turned up the sounds. "Let's go, homey." Darnell slid into the pounding beats that tapped his heart.

*   *   *

"What you drivin?" Leon asked Donnie. "Still got the red Celica?"

"Yeah," Donnie said. "That's me. No Bronco."

They drove around the lake, and Darnell leaned out the window to smell the wet ash-smoke from the fire. Damn—this is where Brenda's gon think I am. "Go over the bridge," he told Leon, and Leon grinned.

The swath of riverbottom was fading gray now, the green disappearing under the late-day smog and smoke. From the bridge, Darnell could see the glow of fire deep in the cane and bamboo. The bright orange was lighter than chaparral fire, flickering and jumping from cane to palm instead of racing solid red lines up a hillside. Leon cruised slow off the bridge, and Darnell saw the trucks and coats gathered at the sandy off-road parking area. He stared, told Leon, "Hold up for a second right here." When he opened the door, Vernon said, "Naw, man, we need to hit the liquor store."

But Darnell was walking fast toward Scott and Perez, standing near one of the trucks. Their faces were ash-streaked, tight, not seeing him, and he called, "You supposed to keep your head outta the flames, man!"

Scott grinned, yelled, "Tucker! Long time, bro!" Perez poured a foam cup of water over his head, and his lashes stuck together spiky when he smiled at Darnell.

Darnell nodded at their blackened hands and gear. "Paid call got you workin hard, huh? CDF still ain't got no money."

"Who needs Forestry takin part of my check?" Scott said. Darnell heard the truck humming behind them, pumping water through the fat-belly hoses. He smelled the fumes, the steam.

"Not much progress," he said, seeing the smoke rise still dark, not white.

"Hey, it's just that bamboo cane, man—let it burn, the city says, long as it don't threaten anything. Just street assholes," Scott said.

"Arundo," Darnell murmured, watching the flames leap into a palm down the riverbottom. "Arundo cane."

"Yeah, you were always into names—just like Fricke," Scott said, and Perez laughed. "I'm just into work. You should apply for paid call reserve, man."

Darnell shook his head. "Not enough money."

"Hey, ten bucks an hour is cool with me, with a drought like this," Scott said. He threw his hand out at the fire and Perez laughed again. "Plenty of work now, man. Cane all up and down the river."

Darnell heard the horn sharp, and the beats thumped loud against the pumpers. "I gotta go," he said. He made his voice hard. "My *home boys* are waitin for me."

"Yeah, our break's over," Perez said, and they started toward the thick cane lining the sandy path. Darnell lifted his chin and went back to the Bronco.

"I'm thirsty, nigga," Vernon said. "Oh—sorry. Brotha. Let's go."

Leon headed back over the bridge, faster this time, and Darnell saw the thin silver stream of the river. Paid call—if it's winter, if we get some rain, I couldn't even buy groceries, he thought.

Vernon was looking at the park. "Oklahoma, huh?" he said.

Leon said, "Yeah, Mama's over there partyin with the Tulsa people."

"Where was your pops from?" Darnell asked.

"LA," Leon said, short. His father had been killed when the boys were young. Shot in LA. Darnell remembered Gas and Leon wearing little black suits, getting into a car down the street.

Leon said, "Brenda's daddy from Louisiana, right? Used to tell me get my sorry black ass out his yard when we tried to shortcut, re-member? And Gas hit his hooptie with a football, he went ballistic. Face got all red."

"He ain't spoke to Brenda since we got married," Darnell said, staring at the green line pulsing with the drumbeats on the stereo.

"Lucky Brenda got her mama's personality," Leon said, and Darnell thought, Not all the way she don't. She hard enough—she buyin the groceries, makin it without me.

At the liquor store, Donnie went inside with Vernon. Leon said, "So the consultant want to know, man. You gon do that or what?"

Darnell kept his eyes on the light. "No, man, I ain't interested."

"It's no big deal, homey. It ain't slingin—just odd jobs, you know. Like you doin now."

"Yeah," Darnell said. Vernon and Donnie got in the back with the paper bags. "That's what I'm doin now." Half-steppin. Scrapin. "But I set my own schedule, okay?"

Leon shook his head. "Keep that shit in the bags till we get there,

Vernon. I ain't up for no open-container stop." He drove toward Sugar Ridge fast, and Darnell remembered hurtling through the dark in the Lincoln, the black leather cool, asphalt and nothing beyond it but faint now-and-then lights.

They were visiting the graves now, he knew. I did my remorial, GranaLene. Darnell heard Vernon laugh at something Donnie mumbled, and he saw the riverbottom fire just a smear of orange in the narrow belt of dark vegetation from way up here.

In the foothills, they checked out the other cars first. All white guys, in four-by-fours and two old junkers. Teenagers in a crowd by the pepper trees. This used to be a meadow, Darnell thought. Collected rain. Now it was packed hard by car tires and feet. Vernon opened the bag, and they stayed in the car, windows down, the bass booming softly. The white guys had their car doors open, and their speed metal music thrashed out fast.

He looked at the label on the forty-ounce Vernon handed over the seat. "St. Ides," Vernon said. "Kickin, homey, better than 8-Ball." He didn't hand one to Leon. Leon pulled a bottle of San Pellegrino water from the glove compartment and took a long swallow.

"This stuff slow my blood down," Donnie said. "Make me relax." Darnell sipped the heavy malt and held the fat bottle between his legs. Huge boulders were gathered across the field, holding pockets of taller brittlebush like the one that had sent the drifting, glowing stem to his hand. He couldn't see the scar in the dim light now. He saw the brittlebush was already dry, finished blooming. Drought had kept the other brush down. These hills too low for true chaparral, he thought. Facin north. No trees except peppers. Chaparral side is south. Pine forest north face—if you in some true mountains.

He drank again. Leon was silent, watching the white guys. Vernon said, "Darnell, man, reach under the seat."

Darnell ran his hand in the space, felt the gun, and straightened. He held it for a moment. "My nine," Vernon said, palm waiting, and Darnell laid the nine-millimeter there. Vernon held it loose, drank long and deep. Donnie bent close to see the gun, and Vernon said, "Yo, man, I got a baby-nine back here, too. You could have it for cheap."

"Where you get it?" Donnie said.

"Off some sprung nigga," Leon said, spitting out the window. "Man, I'ma be glad when I'm off the street."

"I love sprung niggas," Vernon said, smiling. "They got a lotta stuff."

"Yeah, and you keep messin with them strawberries, you gon get a lotta stuff," Leon said.

"Let me see it," Donnie said, and Darnell looked back at him quickly. He saw Donnie holding the .380 revolver tightly, the cheap striped etchings above his thumb. "What you want for it?"

"Not much," Vernon said. "It got bodies on it."

"I know that's makin your blood move too fast, Donnie," Darnell said, his heart racing. "Give it back to him, man."

Vernon looked straight into Darnell's eyes. "Sometimes a gun want a body, man. You seen how that shit happen."

"See, Darnell," Donnie said, his voice soft and slow. "If you'da had a piece, you coulda shot the dog before he got you."

"Fuckin K-9," Leon said.

"Yeah, and the cops woulda smoked me *too* fast," Darnell said. "Don't trip like this, Donnie. Too many brothas gone—Max Harris gone, Tiny gone, remember?" Donnie held the gun stiff-slanted across his leg.

Vernon stared at Darnell still, the grin gashes long beside his mouth. "When your time come, ain't nothin you can do. Outta your hands, when your time come. Brotha."

"Shut up," Leon said. "Let's hat, man. I hate hearing that metal music." The white guys leaned against their doors, staring at the Bronco. Vernon pointed the nine-millimeter to the glass and said, "Take out the speakers?"

Leon said, "Stall out with that, before one of em got a daddy on the force."

"They can't see in the dark," Vernon said. Donnie drank deeply and dropped his bottle on the floorboards.

"I gotta show you somethin," Leon said to Darnell, pulling out of the dirt lot and heading down the road toward the air base. He got onto the same highway Darnell used to take down from the station. Leon was silent, and Donnie and Vernon talked blurry in the backseat, too low for Darnell to hear. When they got closer to the base, Leon said, "You see the ramp?"

"Yeah," Darnell said, looking at the freeway bridge rising over the route they were on. Leon went up the long, gentle slope. Darnell saw two Mexican guys standing next to a beat-up Monte Carlo. Leon passed them, and Darnell saw the base spread out over the valley, the planes, buildings, runways.

Leon said, "Mexicans and brothas always breakin down, right, cause they drive sorry-ass old hoopties." He spoke softly, and Vernon didn't stop telling his long story in the backseat.

"So?" Darnell said. "They need a ride, I guess."

Leon smiled. "No, man. They workin for the consultant's friend, watchin for when the DEA plane take off. They got a phone in there, and they call up."

"Damn," Darnell said.

"See?" Leon said. "My man got all bases covered. You could keep makin cash ducats. He like you cause you know all that geography, and you adaptable. Like me." Leon was back on the freeway now, cresting over the hills they'd just left, and through the mist of smog Darnell could see Rio Seco like he used to when he came home from the station. The four powerful beams of the auto dealerships' searchlights circled the sky on the eastern end, and the silvery-blue finger of the police helicopter's beam traveled the Westside.

"Yo, man, what the fuck you doin?" Vernon yelled, and Darnell and Leon both looked back to see Donnie put the small gun to his ear.

"This baby-nine got bullets?" he asked dreamily.

Leon pulled off the freeway at the next exit and said, "Stall out with that shit, Donnie. Give Vernon the gun."

Darnell was afraid to reach back there, Donnie staring at the ceiling of the Bronco, the muzzle touching the tiny ridges inside his ear. Vernon said, "Give me the gun, fool."

Leon pulled over to the side of the street, and Darnell saw past Donnie's face that it was the main residential avenue in the Ville. He said to Donnie, "Don't trip, man. Come on. Give it up."

But Donnie pushed the seat forward and got out of the car, stood on the sidewalk with the gun in his mouth, then moved it to his thigh. Then he pushed it into the soft skin between his eyes, hard, and Darnell could see the circle of a dent. Donnie pointed the gun at Vernon, who had gotten out, too. "You didn't tell me, man. Do it got bullets?" Donnie whispered, and Vernon's face contorted with anger.

Donnie turned and threw the gun in the sewer. It clattered into the low hole in the curb and they could hear it land in the dry, hollow space under the street.

"Fuck you, nigga!" Vernon yelled, pointing the nine-millimeter at Donnie, who stood, his face blank.

"No bullets, huh," Donnie said.

"Why you throw away my cash, fool?" Vernon yelled, and Leon stayed put.

"Donnie," Darnell said, but he didn't move either. His knee pressed against the door frame, and he hung in the open space. "Donnie."

"What you gon do," Donnie whispered, "shoot me?"

"I should bust a cap off in yo ass right *now*," Vernon said. "I ain't for playin."

"So?" Donnie said, smiling. "I already got one bullet. You got some more. So?" He spread his hands, palms out, and said, "Come on."

Leon got out, stood by the hood, and said, "Shut the fuck up, both y'all. Vernon, put the damn gun away or I'ma smoke your ass my own damn self. I ain't for playin, neither. Get your ass in the car before five-o cruise up here. We in the Ville, nigga. Y'all both gon get us killed."

Vernon looked down the street, then shook his head. "You trippin," he said to Donnie, getting back into the Bronco. "Sit your ass up there, cause I don't want to see your face."

"No," Leon said. "You walkin, Donnie. Cause I can't have you gettin me busted. Later."

Donnie smiled and started walking down the sidewalk into the Ville. Darnell looked at Leon, turned the handle. Leon shook his head. "Man, talk to your boy," he said.

"Talk to *your* boy," Darnell said, low, so Vernon wouldn't hear.

Leon gunned the engine and said, "I'm tellin you, you need to get paid, Darnell. The man ready to see you."

"Yeah, see ya!" Vernon said, leaning out the window. "Glad not to *be* ya!" The Bronco pulled away, and Darnell followed Donnie down the sidewalk.

TRACKS

THE VILLE STREETS were wide and pale, houses set far back on blank squares of lawn with tall palms shooting up in the sky, Charolette's favorite head-thrown-back palms: the ones whose trunks he'd leaned against to pull Brenda onto his chest for one last kiss, in the dark, away from her father's front door. Brenda was home now, sure he was with some other woman or at the riverbottom fire. And Donnie was winding around the streets.

He ran down the slope after Donnie, who kept his head down to watch his feet. The sidewalk was white as chalk. He stopped running, stared into a dry dark sewer opening, low and long. Would the baby-nine wash away, if it ever rained? "Donnie!" he said, but Donnie didn't pause, even when Darnell clamped his hand onto the wide shoulder. "Man, we can't be stridin around the Ville at night. We got no vehicle, nothin on us, look suspicious as all hell. Come on—I gotta get back."

Donnie went up Brenda's parents' street instead. "Brenda's mama took care a your leg, huh?" he said, dreamily. "Maybe she can fix up my leg."

"Man, it ain't your leg," Darnell said, passing the New Yorker in the driveway. The light was on in the back, which meant her father was working on the patio. "Been a long time since you came up here with me," he told Donnie.

James came to the door, holding a schoolbook with his forefinger jammed into the pages to hold his place. "Darnell?" His thin face was all eyes under the baseball cap.

"Hey, James, can you get your mom for me?" Darnell said.

"My sister sick?" James said, working his tongue in his mouth.

"No, man, I just need to ask your mom a favor." Darnell squinted in the glare of the porch light.

"What's wrong, Darnell? Brenda ain't called." Her brows were drawn together tightly. "Y'all go to Oklahoma Day?"

"Yeah," Darnell said. "Brenda's at home." He heard a faint tapping of metal from the back.

"Etienne fixin on a water heater," she said, seeing his hesitation. She looked at Donnie. "What's wrong with you, baby?"

"I know you fixed Darnell's leg up," Donnie whispered, staring at her so hard that Darnell heard her breathe in. "My leg ain't healed."

Darnell said, "Maybe you could give him some a that tobacco." He looked at the street. "We gotta go, Donnie." Behind her, he saw the familiar baby portraits of Brenda and James, hung on the entry wall. Brenda's roomy beige cheeks—he thought of the dark-welled circles under her eyes now. She ain't called her mother to talk about me. I have to call her.

"I can't do nothin standin here like this," Mrs. Batiste said, but Donnie's face slid shapeless, and she said, "Wait." When she came back, she handed Darnell a string with knots. "Remember?" she said, looking into his eyes. "That one already got prayers on it." She paused. "I don't know if they worked for you anyway, Darnell."

He couldn't look at her, and he saw Mr. Batiste come out from the back gate, his face moon-gray in the sensor light that snapped on in the driveway. "Hold this," Darnell told Donnie, giving him the string. "Come on."

He let Donnie keep up or fall behind, passing the circled glare of each streetlight, the wheels speeding past. No force tonight, he thought. No bangers. Come on. Through the groves, past his father's street. Can't go to Pops' house unless I want to answer some questions. Can't go home yet.

"Why y'all even make a fire when it's this damn hot?" he asked Victor when he reached the small blaze in the lot at Jackson Park.

"Old dudes like to cook on it," Victor said, nodding at the three older men who sat on the couch under the pepper tree, eating something out of cans. The crowd of younger guys around the abandoned porch was thick with liquor and sweet weed-smoke and hollering. Darnell took a sip of the 8-Ball Victor handed him and looked at Donnie, who had slumped into the front seat of someone's car. Brenda had been slumped like that with Charolette on her chest when he left the park. Donnie sleepin, and how I'ma get his big self out the car and to his house? Brenda ballistic-hot by now. Darnell took another drink and handed the bottle back to Victor. He felt the liquor line his head with warmth, the heavy film sliding behind his eyes. I don't see how these guys drink every day. Like Pops' song, this give me a virus called the blues. Ronnie came to sit on the curb and get a taste.

The string, knotted, was clutched tight in Donnie's fist, resting on his thigh. I hope it works, man, cause I'm about to get my sorry butt in trouble for you. He said, "Keep a eye on Donnie, Victor."

At the pay phone, he said, "Brenda?"

"What."

"You take the El Camino home?"

"No. Santa dropped by."

"Brenda. Donnie freaked, he went off and tried to kill himself. But he's sleep now, and I gotta stay with him, okay?"

"How he try to kill himself?"

He took a breath. "Vernon had a piece."

Her voice shot up. "You went with Leon and Vernon again?" Then she whispered. "Then you aren't coming home, huh? It's worse than a fire." He could hear cries in the background.

"Charolette ain't sleep?"

"She slept too long at the park, while we were waiting for you." She was silent, then, listening to Charolette cry, too. The howls were regular, high circles, tiny sirens that raced around the bedroom walls.

"Darnell," she said. "It hurts worse. It's not just me waiting now, like when you were in the mountains. You have to go or stay, because she knows."

Darnell looked out at the shadowy figures walking in the park. "You could find somebody better."

"No," she said. "I wouldn't look. I would think about you.'"

Victor was standing when he walked back. "You see Andretta—remember that fine body from school?" he asked, raising his chin toward the house, and Darnell saw her talking to two men. She smiled—four of her front teeth were missing, and the white bottom teeth were a straight line like a cigarette lying in her mouth.

"She looks bad," Darnell said.

"She still got a body, but she sprung now, so don't nobody want that," Victor said. "And ain't no problem with her teeth, cause they just get in the way for what she gotta do."

Darnell watched her leave, go into the alley with the men. Her back was so thin, exposed by her halter top, that her shoulder blades stood out like wings. Darnell lifted the bottle to his mouth, closed his eyes.

Ronnie laughed. "Feel better than the nappy, and you ain't gotta worry about no babies."

Victor said, "Darnell like babies. Huh, Daddy? You just check on yours?" He narrowed his eyes. "So she almost one and a half, right? Y'all gotta whup her yet? She a stubborn chick, that's what your pops say."

Darnell stared at the asphalt, seeing Charolette's face wet with tears now. "But she smart, too. I had to pop her hand about dangerous stuff, like the stove and the chain saws, but she ain't into pain. She don't do it a second time." He put his palms over his eyes. But me— I ain't got no sense.

Victor said suddenly, "You talkin about whuppins. Man, my stepfather used to beat my ass." Darnell opened his eyes, saw Victor's pupils glassy-hard. "Beat my ass every day. Nigga beat me for breathin wrong. For chewin too fast. For lookin at him."

"All kids gotta get whupped," Ronnie said, frowning nervously.

"Not mine," Victor said. "Cause I use the jimhat every time, don't care who the hoochie is. I heard Robin Harris, man—any baby get through the Latex, you could name him Samson. And then he could whup my ass." He drained the malt liquor and threw the bottle into slivers against the curb. He and Ronnie headed down the street.

Donnie's breath filled the car, so Darnell kept the door open and let one foot dangle in the gutter. He stared at the small fire, the stacks of scrap lumber piled near the tree. Two fire seasons gone, and

I ain't never gettin called back, he thought. No cash. No insurance. Brenda the one with everything. She could sit around with all the other women, always talking about "triflin brothas ain't about nothin." He remembered sitting in the dark yard one night while his father and Roscoe talked about someone who'd driven into a tree. An older man, laid off. Eight kids. Insurance.

I could get me some insurance. I got the .25 in my jacket in the Spider. No—you don't get money if you do it yourself. Get Vernon to smoke me. Yeah. Icy brotha probably laugh silly and do me in a second. In a shot. He stared at the pepper branches melting dusty into the dark sky. But then I'd be a "known associate of criminal elements," like they say in the newspaper. Probably wouldn't get Brenda no cash.

He pushed in the cigarette lighter idly, pulled it out to watch the red circle pulse and fade. He used to love pulling it out on cold mornings for his father to light a cigarette. A baby dot of fire, in a little tube. Fire—that's a better way. Like in the mountains. I could set a fire and be tryin to put it out. Or the riverbottom. Like a hero. Then Brenda could be right. You want to get burned, huh? she always said. She never saw me in the mountains. You gotta know the fire—like Fricke said. Yeah, like he sayin to somebody else now. Hey, I remember everything Fricke said. Not like Scott. Like the poison oak. If I was doin a fire right now, and a mat of poison oak went up, the smoke would scorch hell outta my lungs and knock me out. And I wouldn't even feel no flames.

Donnie's breath shuddered loud in his throat. Darnell walked back to the phone. Brenda said, "H'lo?" in a sleep-deep voice.

Darnell watched the pulsing knot of embers in the vacant lot. No one was near the fire now, and the circle was growing smaller in the pit. "Brenda," he said, tongue thick.

"Darnell?" she whispered.

"Brenda. What if I don't come home and some other brotha can take care a you guys? Somebody makin serious ducats, right, and plus you ain't gotta worry about him. Right?" He held his mouth close to the receiver, smelled thousands of other breaths.

"Darnell," she said. "Come home now. Or stay away. I still love you, but you the one running."

"You gon let some other dude beat on my girl?" he whispered, leaning his forehead on the cold metal. "You gon let some other dude touch you?" He heard her breathe in sharp, and he said, "You ain't gotta wait." He hung up.

The fire was dead-gray now, the sky lower, dropping late night. The car's windshield was silver-webbed, and Donnie's eyes opened when Darnell pushed his shoulder hard. "Yeah, brotha, near bout midnight, time for you to go home. Wake up your brain, man. You acted a fool."

Donnie stared at the ceiling, blinking, silent. He didn't lift the hand that clutched the string. Darnell sucked his teeth impatiently. "Here, man. Lemme show you."

The string was warm, damp when he took it from the fingers. Donnie watched as Darnell tied it around his ankle. The dark skin was ashy at the anklebone, above Donnie's flip-flops. "It got prayers on it," he told Donnie. "And the gun got bodies on it. Make up your own damn mind, okay?"

Donnie's mouth trembled loose. "Thanks, D.," he said. "Thanks, brotha."

He walked to Picasso Street alone, opened the door of the Spider to get his jacket. A window creaked at the sideyard, and he froze, but then he heard nothing else.

Through Treetown, he kept striding fast, listening for booming or sirens. He heard footsteps a few times, but when he turned around, he didn't see anything. He'd left Donnie sitting in the car. Walking faster, he found a narrow path before the arroyo, and he slid down the riverbottom embankment. No concrete here, just the steep slope of loose dirt and dry straw-stemmed wild oats packed thick under his boots. At the bottom, he sat on a downed trunk, feeling the tingle of heat across his shoulders in the cool night air. Not since the mountains, he thought. I'm never out at night workin now. Except with Leon—that ain't workin, that's just drivin.

I could get to work right now. Go off into that big stand of arundo cane, start a little conflagration, and be the first one already workin hard when the crew gets here. Cane go up in a wall. He heard coyotes howling in the distance, heard the answering barks of dogs close by, and he stiffened. Wild dogs? Still, he listened to crackling in the cane, in the vines, but it was light bird rustles. Maybe rats running in the palm fronds overhead. Then he heard heavier steps, moving branches aside, coming down the path that led from the arroyo.

The steps were slow—they stopped, began again cautiously, and Darnell felt the fan of heat flush his moist back. He reached into the jacket pocket and felt the gun, pulled it out slow, his movements silent on the crumbling wood where he sat. The gun felt so small in his hand, not an ax or shovel or hose, and he trembled. Don't trip on that shit. The squared-off barrel nudged sharp at his knuckle when he gripped it, cupped the hand and gun in his other hand, pushed it into the air in front of him.

A panting breath came from the other side, from the cane stand, and he saw a flash of yellow eye. He swung to the right, pointing the gun at the small cavelike entrance to an animal run in the green, and a voice said, "Darnell."

It rang low from the arroyo path. "Darnell!" it came, sharper, like whenever his father called him twice and he hadn't answered the first time.

He lowered the gun between his shivering legs, and both hands, still gripping, scraped on the rough trunk at the little fingers. He pressed harder, feeling splinters when he rubbed slightly, rocking back and forth, and his father came around the bank, shoulders hunched in his workshirt, eyes darting around the narrow clearing.

His father sat a few feet from him on the trunk, and Darnell kept his eyes on the bark. Old pepper tree, gnarled, deep-cracked. "What you huntin?" his father said, staring off into the cane.

"Nothin," Darnell said. He looked sideways at his father's hooked Indian nose, the jaw working. His father nodded.

"Not much down here worth killin," his father said. "Raccoons and possum and rabbit, but you don't need to get none a that. You can buy you a whole chicken at the store. Frozen rabbit, already cut up."

Darnell chewed at the inside of his lip, thinking, Here come another Oklahoma story.

But his father didn't frown. His face raised up to the top of the cottonwoods further down, and he said, "Game everywhere when I was a boy. Eighty acres, on my uncle's place. We hunted all the time. And we went all up in the woods. Everything belong to the government out here. You gotta have a permit to catch one fish. Rangers out lookin for you." He looked at the gun in Darnell's hands. "You got a huntin permit for that thing?"

Darnell shook his head, and his father reached out and pulled the gun close to his face, studied the barrel. "Cheap little Raven twenty-five. Made in USA." He squinted at Darnell. "You know where they make these things, these cheap-shit guns? Chino," his father said. "Convenient, huh? Go right down the street and you can be with Louis."

Darnell stared at his father's twisted mouth. "You always got a Oklahoma or Mississippi story. But you don't want to hear no Rio Seco stories, right? They ain't good history."

His father's knuckles moved like stones under the skin of his hands when he examined the gun again. "Yeah, seen you go out the drive-way; I couldn't believe all the walkin you been doin lately. Followed you all the way down here, and you was walkin like you ain't rode all your life. All us old men—King, me, Thompson—we plowed with mules, walkin behind them mules, so once we got out on the road, twenty-five miles wasn't nothin. Shoot, your ancestor walked across Mississippi and Arkansas to get to Indian Territory."

"I know, Pops. You told us every time it rained and me and Melvin wanted a ride to school," Darnell said, trying to make his father shift over to Melvin like usual, talk about Melvin's lack of responsibility. And his father looked up again, the long nose and cheeks stiff with anger, the flash of lighter, redder skin near his neck.

"I don't know what's goin on with you and Brenda, but I know you ain't been home. You think marriage is so hard? You never walked twenty-five miles just to visit some girl."

"I walked fire lines," Darnell said. "All up and down the mountains."

"And while you was doin that, Brenda was workin hard at the county, waitin patient," his father said. Darnell flinched, turned his face toward the wavering cane. "You kept sayin if you worked seasonal a few years, they'd hire you full time. It ain't no mystery what happened. It ain't no new story. You actin like you the first one ever got disappointed." He thrust the gun toward Darnell. "What you gon hunt with this piss-ass thing?"

"I forgot to knock off a coupla rats at Jackson Park for her dinner," Darnell shouted, looking away from the gun. "I came down here to try and hit some lizards or somethin, so she can cook em up good. Make a stew." He stared out at the blackness. "I know—I ain't had no car fulla Oklahoma rednecks racin me down on a country road,

throwin bottles at me. I heard that one. I got brothas and *vatos* steppin
to me, cappin hard. Got five-o force packin."

His father said, "Speak English, boy."

"Rio Seco stories ain't about shit, right?" Darnell shouted, louder.
He felt the back of his neck trembling; he'd never screamed at his
father like this, his shouts disappearing into the round, thick stems
and rustlings near them. "Young boys don't know shit, right, got no
excuse? Look, Pops, let me do what I gotta do—I'ma kill a possum
and cut up some a these bamboo shoots and make my dinner, okay?"

His father raised the gun and fired it into the cane. The pop-pop
sounds Darnell had heard in Terracina, the round explosions he'd
heard in the Lincoln, were bigger than this blunt tapping that dis-
sipated fast in the current of air over the riverbottom.

"That's what I miss," his father said softly. "I miss my guns. Followin
you, I was thinkin about trackin, walkin miles with my friends to find
some game. Just walkin, your thoughts all in your own head cause
you can't talk, like tonight, and then you see it move and all you hear
is the shot." He handed the warm gun to Darnell. "I miss it all the
time when I'm workin trees, especially in one a them big estates that
almost look like woods." He nodded to Darnell. "This is what you
gon miss—the woods, the fires, bein outside at night. Cause if you
start workin yards, you gon be done by dark. Unless you still plannin'
to die soon."

"Plannin don't seem to get me nowhere," Darnell said.

"Didn't look like you planned on gettin into Leon's loud-ass four-
wheel-drive vehicle which he don't never take further than the liquor
store," his father said, a slight grin forming. "Shit. Boy drivin a Bronco
through the rough terrain of his apartment complex." Darnell felt his
cheek go deep to hide his own grin, but he swallowed, looking at the
gun. "I wouldn't pay ten dollars for that," his father said, nodding at
it. "I miss that beautiful twelve-gauge I had."

Darnell remembered the huge stock, the rich-whorled, rubbed
wood, the fine-meshed etchings on the wide barrel. His father kept
the gun hung in the living room when he was small. "I forgot about
that shotgun."

"I sold it when times got real tight," his father said softly. "Right
after your sisters came. It was antique. I got it in Oklahoma." He
stood up. "What you gon do with yours?"

The faint smell of cordite was gone, and the gun was already cooler to his touch. Darnell threw it into the cane, and it made no sound for a second. Then they heard it rustle its way to the bottom of the stand. "It ain't mine," he said.

"You ain't even breathin that hard," his father said when they neared the driveway. "I guess all that firefightin left you in good shape, for a lazy ex–security guard."

"You find out about that teardown?" Darnell said.

"Not yet." His father leaned against the truck. "You know what's down there in the riverbottom, right by your tree trunk? You seen that hollow? Fox—I used to see gray foxes down there all the time."

"Yeah," Darnell said. "And? I gotta go."

"They got a new tract up there in Grayglen, call it Fox Hollow." He folded his arms. "Only canine they got up there is watchdogs for them new rich houses." He watched Darnell. "You ain't followin me. Got all kinda yards—I still think you should get you a route."

"I'ma get some sleep," Darnell said, heading down the driveway. "I still gotta walk a ways."'

He heard his father spit. "You call that little distance a walk?"

MIGRATION

HE SAT NEAR the railing and took off his mud-crusted boots to leave them outside. The apartment was dim when he went inside, trying not to wake them, but he heard something rustle in the bedroom. He paused in the doorway, saw Brenda curled around Charolette's body. He bent, thinking he could slide his upturned palms under Charolette's little self and move her to the crib, but he saw Brenda's eyes already open, staring at him, and she whispered harshly, "Don't." When she uncoiled herself slowly, not jerking the bed, and slid her legs out carefully, he saw the knife glint in her hand.

In the kitchen, she put the knife down on the counter and got a glass of water. "You scared the hell out of me," she whispered. "I thought you were somebody breaking in."

He sat at the table, and she sat across from him, like they were going to play cards, he thought. "You were sure I wasn't comin back," he said, frowning.

"Hey—you got your hat again, right?" she said bitterly.

"What?" He leaned forward, felt the edge of the table in his stomach.

"I'ma get my hat," she said, imitating Victor. "I'ma book, man. Time to vacate, homey. We gon jam or what? You ready to roll, brothaman?" The phrases spilled out of her in perfect tones, like she was singing a guy's part in a song.

"Yeah, I know all the ways to say it," he said. "I hear em all the time."

"I know you do," she said, rubbing the sweat from the glass. "I gotta make a run, baby. And then the guy never comes home." Her thick braid ended in a sparkly elastic from Charolette's collection, and a wedge of bangs leaned sharp over her forehead, where it had been pushed by sleep.

"I'm here, right?" he said.

She shook her head. "You guys have so many ways to talk about leaving cause you got so many ways to do it. But you—you just do it half-assed, Darnell. You can't make up your mind."

"I left my boots outside," he said. "I'm home." He stood up and went to the kitchen to get something to eat, and the knife gleamed on the counter. "This for me?" he said, trying to joke.

She didn't smile. "I was by myself at night. Somebody told me to keep hairspray by the bed, cause I could get him in the face." She raised her chin to look at him. "But I felt better with the knife. I've cut up a lotta chickens and it didn't bother me at all."

"Thanks for sparin me," he said, leaning on the counter, but she still didn't smile.

"I hope you made up your mind this time," she said. "Cause I was getting ready to make it up for you." She went back into the bedroom, and he stood in the dark kitchen for a long time.

He emptied his pockets in the morning, getting up from where he'd slept on the couch, when Charolette slapped him in the face joyously. "Daddy!" she yelled into his ear, pulling at his eyelashes.

Brenda sat at the table, trying to get a knot out of Charolette's shoelace. "Hey," he said. "I'm still here."

She raised her eyebrows. "Thrilling," she said, but she smiled slightly. "Who wouldn't stay for breakfast?" She saw Charolette picking up the things he'd put on the coffee table—some loose change, four dollar bills, the Baggie with the flyer and rock inside. He frowned at that himself—he still had that? "I can't believe you gon let her hold two things anybody could tell you a child shouldn't have," Brenda said when Charolette clutched the dollars and Baggie. "Money's dirty, and Baggies could choke her."

"Mummy," Charolette said, holding it tight to her chest. "Mine!"

Darnell watched Charolette take the blackish rock out, put it back inside the Baggie. "She ain't gon put it in her mouth," he said. "She's too smart."

"Come here and put some food in her mouth," Brenda said, going to the kitchen. "If you're really going to stay."

"Shoot, every dude with a truck and a mower runnin around callin himself a gardener," Floyd King said in the driveway, sipping his coffee. "Lotta competition for all them new tracts up by Grayglen and past the hills. That's why we gettin more into the construction cleanup."

"More money per hour anyway," Nacho said, nodding at Darnell.

"He could start, though," Darnell's father said. "Build up a clientele like we did."

Darnell let Charolette pull him toward his mother, in the doorway. "I gotta go; my boss says break is over," he said. He avoided his mother's eyes, handing her Charolette's diaper bag, and Charolette held tight to the rock, Baggie, and dollar bills. "Can I keep my pennies?" he asked her, and she cocked her head to look up at him.

He waved at Mrs. Tribeleaux, sprinkling her grass, the sun glinting off her rhinestone-framed glasses, and at Snooter, standing in someone's yard talking. "Grayglen," he said aloud.

The circling streets, houses all laid out in curves of red-tile roofs behind sandy block walls, were baking in the heat. At one intersection, Darnell saw a crew of Mexican guys building new walls around the raw-scraped land for another tract: five short Indian-looking men with bowed legs and straw hats loaded blocks and laid them in place, while a white guy with thick, sun-reddened forearms watched.

Grayglen Heights was Trent's tract, he remembered, going into the single entrance through the walls, past the sign. The lush gardens of these established homes were immaculate, and Darnell knew these people already had gardeners, but he wound slowly up and down a cul-de-sac and said, "What the hell—gotta be some shaggy grass and dandelions somewhere. Gotta be one yard somebody forgot in this maze."

He parked at the end of the next cul-de-sac and walked. In the already-hot morning, no one was out in yards, on driveways, even in open garages. All these garage doors were closed, the slatted mini-blinds tight, and the grass was blank. No wagons or toys or shovels or firewood or kids. "They must got hella big backyards," he said to himself, ringing the first doorbell.

But no children yelled from backyards, either; central air hummed at each house, so the windows were closed. He waited, hearing the echoes of bells inside each door, but all he saw were occasional shivers at the blinds or drapes. Nothing as obvious as a face peeking out or retreating, but a faint trembling. He kept going, trying all the homes, and at the last corner house, he saw a station wagon with vacuums and buckets in the open rear. He rang the bell, knocked, and was about to turn away when a woman bumped into him coming out of the door.

She was small, brown, with tilted-up eyes, and he said, "Excuse me, I was wondering if you had anyone doing your yard already?"

She shook her head, looked down at her mop, and said, "No inglés. Please." She went back into the house, leaving the mop, and returned to pass him, picking it up and carrying it straight before her to the station wagon. Another woman stood in the doorway now.

"Hi, I'm a gardener and I wondered if you needed your yard done today or on a regular basis," Darnell said. He remembered his father's words, back when Darnell had been small enough to stand on cool porches and listen.

"I gave you five dollars yesterday," the woman said impatiently, looking back into her house, and Darnell raised his eyes from her ankles. She was about forty, her lips more invisible than most white women's—no lipstick, he realized, just when she said, "I can't afford another donation."

"I wasn't here yesterday," Darnell began, but she was adding loudly, "And I don't need anything done today."

"You didn't give me five dollars," he said into the sudden silence, finally looking at her eyes, rimmed with dark green shadow.

"Oh, I'm sorry, I—your hat," she said, fingers holding the collar of her robe. "A man came by yesterday, he said he was out of work, and I—he had a hat."

"Yeah," Darnell said, hard. "Another Raiders fan." He walked back down the pathway, this one brick, and stopped by the fancy iron mailbox to wait for the maid to back down the driveway.

The white-painted cast-iron mailboxes were lined up and down the street. Where had he stood next to one before? The Bridgeport Casting Company—where had he read that? On the U.S. mailbox, he remembered. So who makes these? Who gives a damn? He didn't look up at the station wagon or the still-moving miniblinds.

He drove, swerving through the streets, trying to find an opening in the block walls. Uh-oh, let me get on out before goddamn armed response hear about me. Lookin for a job? Yeah, right. The tires slipped on loose dirt at the corner when he headed back up another street, and he remembered all the times on the mountain when Scott would piss him off and he'd race the Spider through the sharp curves to blow the words away with rushing air.

Three new custom-built houses were going up on this slope, and the bellied, blond construction workers hammering and laying brick looked up at the El Camino when the tires screeched again. Born that way, he thought, his tongue hot. Come out with hair like that, trucks with toolboxes behind the cab, stomachs already big enough. They get the job—just like I can dance. But Charolette's car seat rattled empty against his elbow when he scratched the tires on the asphalt at the stop sign, and skidding around the corner didn't make him feel any better. He looked at the crumbs crushed deep into the corduroy chair.

Driving down the hill toward the Westside, he pressed the crumbs to his tongue. Graham cracker. He thought about going by Jackson Park, talking yang with Victor, but he slowed at his father's street. "Daddy here!" Charolette screamed from the tiny porch, and his mother looked up from her hand sewing. "Ain't this crazy?" he thought.

"They wasn't in a hurry all these weeks we been waitin to hear on the bid, and now it's June, hot as hell, and they want it done in a week." His father stood looking at the lemon trees, the huge elms and overgrown hedges, the pile of junk behind the small wood-frame house.

Darnell followed his father and Roscoe around the house. The contractor was in back with the guy who'd bought the property. It was an old home buried in the side of the hill on Grayglen, and Darnell thought that somebody had been just waiting for an old man to die or move out so they could build a big new house on the land. The man held a roll of plans down on a picnic table and bent his head over the writing Darnell glimpsed, squared like miniature graffiti.

The small lemon grove had to go. He was keeping a few trees, "ornamental," he said, but the new house would be three times the size of the old one, so everything else had to be leveled. "We're anxious to get started," he told Darnell's father. "It took so long to get the permits and the financing. Clear it out as fast as possible, okay?"

"Yes, sir, get you some flat land soon as possible," his father said, and Darnell watched the too-wide smile he'd always seen when his father talked to clients. When the contractor had taken the man back into the vacant house, Darnell's father said, "Shit. These lemon trees ain't even dead. Good Meyer stock, ever-bearin." He shook his head.

Darnell smelled the oil in their leaves when they walked around to count the trees. The grove was small and thick, lemons still heavy on the dusty branches. "If they were dead, like the groves up there where they built Mr. Batiste's house, we could just plow em over with dozers," he said.

"Those trees were just wood by then," his father said, and Roscoe nodded. "Crew's supposed to show up tomorrow and pick these clean, and then we can start on the grove. You gon have to get Victor and Ronnie in the morning, cause if he want all this clean, we need two guys loadin." His father spat into the dust. "Gotta split that way, make you less money."

Darnell looked back at his father's stare. "I can find some lizards and rats up here," he said. "Take a coupla these lemons home to Brenda, too. She been cookin some hella stew past few nights."

His father chewed on his lip and brushed his arm when he turned. "Might as well do the junk today. Maybe finish that up."

They sorted through the rusted pile, throwing the scrap iron into the truck for Leo, the man who collected it. Darnell felt his muscles lengthen and stretch in the warmth, watched the alligator lizards undulate into the tall grass when he moved a piece of bumper or old pot they'd slept inside. He worked his way toward his father by the late afternoon and said, "Pretty shady up here. This close enough to the woods for you?"

His father didn't look up from the ancient radiator he was lifting, and Darnell helped him. When it was on the truck, his father said, "Nothin close enough." He wiped the water from under his cap. "You see me worryin about bein fulfilled? You see a lack of food on my table?"

"I get it, Pops," Darnell said. He hesitated, though, before he moved back to the scattered pile. "I thought Brenda was gon try to save me," he said, keeping his head down.

His father looked toward the lemon grove and Roscoe, wandering between the rows. "She was busy. She was feedin her own child. I was worryin about losin another one a mine." Then he turned and walked back to the work still waiting.

Darnell watched his father in constant motion, dragging another abandoned radiator to the pile of machine parts. "Mr. King comin to pick up the metal?" Darnell said.

"Soon as I tell him where it is."

"Wish we could just burn the rest of the trash, instead of haulin it to the dump," Darnell said, looking at the pile of boxes and broken furniture and planter boxes.

"I bet you do," his father said, laughing. "But you ain't Fireman Fred—and ain't no burnin allowed up here in Grayglen. Too much brush."

"Too much money," Roscoe said from behind him.

"Yeah," Darnell said. "These people don't need feed trails."

"What time?" Ronnie said, leaning back on the couch under the pepper tree.

"Early," Darnell said. "You know Pops. And they got a Mexican crew comin to pick the lemons."

Victor half grinned. "Contractor went out to Terracina, huh?"

Ronnie said, "They all go over there and hire Mexicans now. I mean, when you talkin day work, old guys like your pops and Mr. King and them still come by here, but all them white dudes go by Terracina Avenue."

"Mexicans underbid anybody, man," Victor said. "Hundred guys sittin out there all day, waitin." He leaned against a car parked at the curb. "Man, you can go by there at three and it's still twenty guys squattin." He called to Ruben Sotelo, who sat at the other end of the couch. "Ruben, man, how do you *vatos* squat like that, I mean, for hours? How your legs do that, *ese?*"

"Damn, Victor," Ruben said, smiling. "It's genetic, *ese*, like you guys can jump and run. We like to squat and talk, okay?"

An older man Darnell had seen around laughed and said, "Remember when Leland Emerson came down here and got four dudes to do his mail route?"

His buddy laughed. "Man, back then they didn't drive—they walked every block. Leland been out with some girl, tired as hell. Told each dude to take a batch and a street and hurry up, so he could get back to the girl. Them old white ladies on his route never noticed the difference. And these dudes looked *scruffy*. But some old sista, live-in nurse or some shit, she called the post office right quick, talkin bout 'Leland got some winos messin with the U.S. Mail.' Got his ass fired."

Darnell grinned. "So the brothas all looked alike, huh?"

But Victor sucked his teeth. "Yeah, well, contractors goin over to Terracina cause brothas too much trouble. They can pay them Mexican dudes anything, talk shit to em. They can't talk shit to a brotha."

Ronnie said, "That Italian guy still comes—Cacciotti. He buys lunch, too. Remember we did that cleanup last month at that minimall?"

Ruben looked over. "Somebody say Cacciotti? I'm starvin, man, where is he?"

Victor looked at Darnell. "So you sleepin at home again, huh? That mean we usin your El Camino and you takin the big cut?" He smiled. "It's every brotha for himself around *this* fire."

Darnell remembered the tumbleweeds piled in the ditch so long ago, the road-camp guys working while the station crew watched. Why Victor bringin that up now? he thought. I ain't been a mountain man a long time. "Whoever can handle the shovel, brothaman," he said, staring right back.

"Darnell," Brother Lobo called from the domino game. He stood up and moved slowly from the table to a chair set alone in the dirt. When Darnell came close, Brother Lobo pulled out a folded-soft newspaper clipping from his pocket. The soft clicking of the new players mixing the bones stopped, and Lobo said, "I thought you might want to see this."

WOUNDED POLICE DOG RECEIVES GET-WELL GIFTS, the headline on the small article read. Darnell frowned. "Blaze, the German shepherd shot in the shoulder last week, is being showered with attention as he recuperates. Floral bouquets, doggie bones, and cards have been received at the Rio Seco Police Department since the dog was wounded in a confrontation with an inebriated lawyer enraged that party guests at a neighboring estate had awakened him. Blaze's handler, Officer Rick Kleiser, said the dog is resting comfortably."

Darnell refolded the clipping and gave it back to Lobo, who held it loosely, squinting up. "Thanks," Darnell said. He didn't want to talk about dogs.

"Lobo," his new opponent called, and Darnell was glad to help Lobo back to his chair.

He stood watching the game for a minute, and Lobo said, "I hear drumbeats—a distant army approaching." His head was cocked to one side, his hand reaching out to the pile of extra dominoes.

"You just tryin to distract them from the fact that you goin to the boneyard *again*," Mr. Talbert crowed, his glasses sliding. Darnell saw the Bronco pull up, Leon's sunglasses glinting in the low-slanting sunlight. He and Vernon got out, leaving the music loud, and a guy on the dark boarded porch said, "You jammin the new House of Pain?"

Darnell stretched his sore arms. That's me—house of pain. Let me get on home to my crib.

"Just chillin?" Leon said, working his way over to Darnell. Darnell turned his back, so Brother Lobo's eyes wouldn't watch him. "You want to ride over there and talk business?"

Darnell took a breath. "I still ain't interested, man."

Vernon said, "How's your homey? He still serious mental and shit?"

"Donnie's okay," Darnell said, looking over the vacant lot to the church across the park, where GranaLene's candles flickered. "He got some prayers, and he gotta figure it out for himself."

Vernon snorted. "Prayers? Nigga, you bad luck. First your homey Birdman fuck up and lose money and then your other homey lose my piece."

Leon said, harshly, "Save it, Vernon. You don't know Donnie."

"Rio Seco niggas," Vernon mumbled.

"Yeah," Leon said impatiently. "I'm fixin to hat up, Darnell. You gon come palaver or what?"

Lobo turned, regal, blind for a moment, and then his eyes fixed on Darnell. Darnell said, "I'm cool now, Leon. I got some jobs lined up."

Leon folded his arms. "You ain't interested, huh? Do the man got competition?"

"Why I gotta be all that?" Darnell said, lifting his chin. "You know me better than that, man."

Leon threw back his head and stretched his neck. "Sorry, homes. It's just somebody floatin around here, and I can't figure it out."

Darnell shook his head. "I been floatin, damn skippy, but not like that."

"I don't know. I heard some LA bangers tryin to front over here cause they think Rio Seco like virgin country. Somebody said they got a tall, light-skin dude for a enforcer, pack a AK. Hard toast." Leon ran his eyes over the vacant lot. "Damn, for all I know Birdman mighta got out early, want some payback."

Payback for what? Darnell thought. Did Leon set him up? But Vernon said harshly, "I hope he do try. Cause he know I'ma be toastin his ass for what he did."

Darnell saw the burned-pale weeds near the fence, the wild tobacco sprays the only green left.

In the driveway at his father's house, he sat in the folding chair with Charolette's hand on his knee, feeling the sweat and iron dust on his neck. "Moon," she said, pointing to the faint yellow wedge sitting high in the east before the sun had even set.

"Yeah," he nodded, and Roscoe watched the sky silently, leaning on the Apache. All the years of sitting here with Roscoe, he thought, hearing what the different-sized moons could be compared to when Roscoe made up poems. All the old ladies on the street, when he was little and they'd be trickling water onto their roses and telling him, "Blood moon tonight, boy, you better go on home and get out the streets." Even Fricke standing with him outside the station, peering through the pine needles to see the new moon.

He could hear a truck booming, the beats still far away, and Roscoe said, "Thumping like a telltale heart." The truck passed down DaVinci

Street, and Darnell listened to the pounding fade into the heat. Leon, or Gas, or Cartunes—a truck that goes boom. He thought of Louis riding long ago, Roscoe hearing the drums, Leon driving somewhere now looking, looking. I need to check Louis, he thought, watching Charolette bend to pick up a penny. Did the consultant turn Louis out, cause he didn't want to do a job? Everybody says Louis wasn't even carryin cash or slingin cane—just hangin out with Leon. Charolette pulled at his jeans by the ankle. "Mon," she said, curling her fingers up, telling him she was ready. Roscoe was silent, his long legs crossed and the heavy workboots slanted on the driveway, his eyes staring into the darkened asphalt.

All the way home, Charolette put the rock inside the Baggie, folded the flyer, slid it next to the rock, and took them both out. "Mine," she said, when Brenda tried to take it.

"You should be tired of that," Darnell said.

Brenda said, "She loves anything you give her, cause you're a special visitor, remember?" She stared at the dark cave of the parking stall.

"Not anymore," Darnell said. "Here I am."

He'd thought she would smile, but she didn't look at him. "I'm tired," she said, carrying her shoes up the steps. Inside, she sat down, keeping her eyes away from him. "I'm waitin for you to give me those old lyrics again: 'I'm goin through changes, baby.' 'Just let me get myself together.' 'Give me some time.' "

Darnell sat in the chair and took off his boots. "Yeah, but I ain't the one that sings. You are." He touched the hair starting to clump long at his neck. "And George do hair. I need to change my specialization." He looked at her frown. "I'ma get big cash at the end of the week. And check the palms." He held them out, and she reached to put her finger on the pillow-round calluses.

The Mexican crew was already set up, dropping lemons into crates. Five guys, all sun-dark, with red bandannas in loose circles around their necks, climbing ladders, laughing, reaching for the fruit. Darnell stood beside Victor, watching. Their music swirled from a radio in their truck: horns lassoing swirled air, guitars and voices high and fast. Darnell's father came up beside him. "Did you get a bag for Brenda and your mother? They want to make fresh lemonade."

Darnell nodded. He'd filled a paper sack and put it on the truck floorboards. Victor and Ronnie got chain saws and shovels, and Darnell's father said, "Damn. If this guy wasn't in such a big hurry, we could take it slow and split three ways. But he gotta have it now. After gas and dump fees, we're lucky to clear decent change."

"Victor and Ron are only fifty a day," Darnell said, "and you'd be cryin if this was a ten-grand job."

"How much is your day-labor fee?" his father said, raising his brows. He thrust a chain saw into Darnell's hands.

Darnell worked near Roscoe, cutting the branches off the fallen elm. The clinging dust stayed with him in his own small cloud, and Victor and Ronnie dragged refuse to the trucks in their own stream of brown. The Mexican crew left by early afternoon, and the elm tree and dried hedges were stacked tight in the truckbeds.

"At least another day of this before we can get a dozer in here, if it'll fit up these narrow streets," Roscoe said, sweat streaming from under his cap. "Smell that—it's like a thousand lemon meringue pies."

"I smell a few hundred dollars disappearin if we don't get this done fast," Darnell's father grumbled. "It's three o'clock, and we still gotta hit the dump." He squinted up toward the road. "And we gon have to clear out this driveway, trim all them overgrown hedges, if we gon get a small dozer down here."

Darnell saw the owner's Lexus pulling slow down the narrow space. The man parked down by the house, and Darnell said, "What does this guy do for a livin?" His father didn't hear; he was walking toward the man.

Roscoe said, "He told me he's an importer. Coffees, teas, exotic beans from all over the world. Coffee's the big thing now." Darnell saw the man walking around the house, looking at the dirt near the foundation. His tan chinos were pressed and his gold-rimmed glasses sank low on his nose. Imports. Well, hey, I was just learnin about distribution a while ago. I had another job offer, with this consultant. You got any openings?

His father came back, shaking his head. "Gon be one big house. And got all this privacy, so nobody gon be able to see this big house unless they invited." Darnell looked at the trucks, all three with plywood gates straining with the stacked wood and refuse, and the narrow, sloped driveway. Victor and Ronnie sat in the cab of the El Camino, and Darnell said, "See you tomorrow. I know—early. You ain't playin."

All morning, they chain-sawed the trunks of the lemon trees, the pungent wood and leaves flying, then dragged the wide round-topped trees to the cleared space to reduce them to branches and firewood. Victor and Ronnie were still clearing the perimeters of the land, carrying rocks, chicken wire, scrap. The heat floated with the dust and lemon oil to coat them all. At noon, Darnell threw water onto himself and wiped his neck. "Come on," he said to Victor and Ronnie, throwing Charolette's car seat in the back with the scattered leaves and sticks and the two shovels they hadn't used.

"The government gon get you if you don't provide me with a lunch break, man," Victor said to Darnell's father, who shook his head.

Darnell took them to the little store all the way down Woodbine Avenue, at the base of the hill. No little markets in Grayglen, he thought. Nobody walks. He said, "Drink up, man, I ain't in the mood for no open-container stop."

Victor and Ronnie downed the malt liquor and two hot dogs each. Darnell ate a hot dog and steered. His father and Roscoe would be resting in the shade, drinking hot coffee from the thermos and eating sandwiches.

"I'ma try this one," Darnell said, and Victor looked up. "I need a steady route, man." He pulled into the gap in the block walls where the sign read Woodhaven.

"This ain't Trent King's hood?" Victor said, and Ronnie grinned.

"Uh-uh," Darnell said. The houses were slightly smaller than in Trent's tract. The streets were laid out the same way, though, circling and ending, and Darnell tried to park somewhere that didn't block a driveway.

Victor said, "Damn, Trent packed in close up here in Grayglen. With the gray men."

Darnell heard the derision in his voice, "Hey, homey's just tryin to make it. He seem okay to me.'"

"He ain't nobody's homey," Ronnie said. "Don't try to borrow no change."

Victor was peering outside. "They got three-car garages, so ain't no need to park on the street." He sat back. "Hurry up, man. I hate it up here."

He left them at the corner and trudged up the cul-de-sac. Same as before—nobody answered doors, no garages were open with men inside and tools whirring. No kids played in sprinklers.

"Everybody at work, earnin that dinero to pay the house note," Darnell said to himself. "Or they way back in the formal whatever room."

The trees were broom-sized, poked into lawns and staked against the wind, and the yards were all the same: new sod, cast-iron mailbox, brick or cement walkway. "They ain't openin the door for nothin," he whispered, staring at the grass. That flyer was cool. They ain't even gotta open the door. See it on the grass—they ain't gotta see me. He headed back to the Chevy, saw Ronnie's head resting against the window.

"Let's get back up the hill before the boss goes ballistic," he said, and Victor laughed. Darnell tried to find the exit in the walls, and finally he was on the avenue. The police car came around the corner behind them, and Darnell said, "Damn. Where y'all put the bottle?"

"In the back, man, under the burlap," Ronnie said, his lips tight.

Darnell looked at Victor. "Be cool, all right?" Victor only smiled.

The cruiser had parked, and Darnell held himself still. "Don't get ready yet," Victor said, still grinning. "You know he gon take his time."

The officer talked on the radio; Darnell could see when he moved his eyes to the rearview. Checkin registration. Okay. The man got out slowly, and he called, "Hands outside the vehicle, please. Move slowly."

Darnell dangled his palms from the window; Victor leaned over Ronnie to hang out the other side. The man approached slowly and said, "You guys have been cruising for a while, knocking on doors. You got a reason?"

Before Darnell could open his mouth, Victor said, "Tools in the back, man."

He didn't care who he was talking to. Darnell felt his neck prickle cool. The cop leaned slightly to look in Victor's face. "Didn't you do some time this year?" he asked.

"I like the government gym," Victor said. He flexed his arms without moving.

Darnell said, "We were lookin for gardening work." The cop transferred his eyes to Darnell's face.

"Who's the vehicle belong to?"

Darnell stared straight ahead. "It's in my father's name."

"What's his name?"

"John Tucker."

"Address?"

"Twenty-eight ninety-seven Picasso."

"You're pretty far from the Westside now."

"We're working a job up the hill."

"I thought you were looking for jobs."

"We're on lunch break from that one. My dad's up there." Darnell kept his eyes on the palm tree, tiny new, to the left of the man's shoulder.

"Almost one o'clock," the man said, turning his wrist to check his watch.

"Thanks," Victor said. "Appreciate it." He smiled, his eyes fixed on the officer's face. The man turned and went back to his car, and Darnell pulled away from the narrow curb slowly. "Have a nice day!" Victor shouted into the glass.

It was already so hot by 7 A.M. that the pepper branches hung limp, heavy with dust, and the cars where the men rested, sitting up, filled with bright heat. Darnell stood in the dewless weeds, the men squinting at the heat shimmering off the asphalt near their feet.

"About ninety-five today," Ronnie said. "That's what I heard."

"And your old man gon be goin hundred miles an hour tryin to finish," Victor said. "Man, this the last job I want till next *week*. Don't you know black absorbs heat?"

"You know you broke," Darnell said. "Today's payday."

"Hey," Victor said. "I get to keep my own money, brothaman. And it last longer. I ain't gotta work every day, like you, Daddy."

"Let's go," Darnell said, rubbing the edges of hair behind his ears. He smelled the pink lotion Charolette had rubbed into his ashy forearms. She'd done it every day, and the sweat washed off the faint, rosy scent. "I'm whipped," he told Victor. "What can I say?"

Driving, he thought, Let me get today over with, get some dinero in my pocket, and get pink lotion rubbed on me by my two women. He smiled to himself. After Charolette's tiny palms were finished smearing the drops into his arms, marveling at how they disappeared again and again, he could get Brenda to rub the smell on him with her wrists sliding around his neck.

The importer hovered around the property, pacing, talking to someone on a cordless phone. Darnell paused to wipe the sweat off his eyes when he'd dragged a long branch to the clearing. He wondered if Trent had gotten the contract to do the landscaping.

At the dump, he stared at the Mexican men unloading trucks alongside his father's. Two small men, their eyes slanted toward their temples, their straight hair short, raked roofing material from the bed of their truck. They looked almost Oriental, he thought. He pushed the trash off the gate. Why you trippin? he thought. Accordions— that's what you keep hearin in the music.

By dusk, the packed-hard dirt was strewn with wood chips and sawdust, and Victor and Ronnie were sitting in the empty bed of his father's truck. Roscoe and Darnell stared at the raw land, the stumps. "Dozer comes tomorrow," Roscoe said.

Darnell's father came from around the corner of the house. "You gonna need a new tire for the Apache," he called to Roscoe.

He held the check, and Darnell saw his fingers leaving brown smudges on the blue paper. "I'ma head to the bank with those two," his father said. "Darnell—you goin to get Charolette? I'll be home soon." When Darnell turned, his father said, "Wait. This guy's got a friend on the other side of the hill wants some tree work. Go up there tomorrow and give him an estimate, cause I'll be here for a few hours."

Darnell stared at his father. "Tree work's yours. I'm workin on a route."

His father looked away, and Darnell thought, I don't want charity. Roscoe said, "Well, do him this favor. You owe him one, right?"

He checked the address twice, but when he'd parked at the gravel space beside the long driveway that led down into the property, he didn't see any signs of life. Standing at the curb, he looked across the circular yard to the trees. Maybe just trimming, and he and Pops could knock it out this afternoon. The sun glinted off the broken glass in the steep bank across the road, and Darnell heard an engine. A minivan with a bearded guy at the wheel and two boys in the middle seat came up from the garage, and Darnell saw the surprise on the man's face. He stopped. "Are you out of gas?" he said cautiously. "Or can I help you with something?"

"I'm up here for an estimate," Darnell said, keeping his face blank. "Tree trimming. I tried the bell."

The man's forehead opened up. "Oh, yeah, my wife called. Sorry— we were in the back room." He yanked the brake on the van and got out.

Darnell walked across the lawn with the man, who peered up into the branches of a huge old jacaranda. "Did you want them all trimmed?"

The man frowned. "Well, to tell you the truth, they're a hell of a mess. We've got the three jacarandas here dropping flowers and big seed pods all over the grass, and in the back there are two huge olive trees. We put in a new cement patio and a redwood deck and they're covered with blotches from the olives."

"We can take them all out, if you want," Darnell said. "But you'd be losing a lot of shade."

"Well, we'd replace them, yeah. I'm not from here, we just moved from Orange County. Newport area," he said absently. "It's cooler there, and I'm not sure what trees do good here. Some color would be great in the fall—like real New England style."

Darnell nodded. "I know liquidambar turns colors. It's real popular."

"Is that the one planted all over downtown, like by the museum?"

"Yeah," Darnell said. "They're everywhere."

"But my kids say they make stickery balls, some kind of sharp seed balls."

"Yeah," Darnell said again. He and Melvin used to throw them into each other's hair while they were supposed to be raking.

The man shook his head. "No, I wouldn't want to worry about those with the kids playing in the yard."

Darnell smiled politely. So tell the kids to clean em up, he thought. The man said, "You know what would be great? Trees that turned colors but didn't drop all their leaves. Yeah, like that bush we've got over there."

Darnell looked at the low nandina bushes lining the driveway—
bushes Trent King had showed him at that lady's house. A landscaper's
favorite, he'd said. "Tell you what," he said to the man, who was
checking his watch. "I'll check with this landscape architect I know,
and I'll give you a call tonight." He squinted up through the ferny
jacaranda leaves. "But if you buy baby trees, you're gonna have a
long, hot summer."

"Well, let's find some full-grown ones somewhere," the man said,
smiling.

Darnell left the steep, winding road and passed the tiny trees along
the development block walls. He knew Trent wouldn't be home
now—he could call and leave a message. When he neared the Westside, he saw the dark mass of old trees hovering like clouds over the
neighborhood. Everyone had fig trees, lemons, persimmons. His
mother had apricots and nectarines. Marietta Cook had the best plum
tree on the Westside. Darnell turned down Picasso Street. Trees did
things for you, his father would say, so you gotta do things for them.
Rake up their leaves, cut their branches, water them. And then his
father would frown and throw in an "Idle hands are the devil's work-
shop." All my life, he thought, in the trees. In the Conservation
Corps, we cut down the old ones, the diseased stands that were fire
hazards. Burned them sometimes with Fricke. He parked and closed
his eyes for a moment. Two fire seasons gone. I'ma be workin in some
domestic, tame forests now.

In the yard, he saw the piles of wood. Deciduous. Trees like the
jacaranda, dropping flowers, like the maples and liquidambars that
turned spectacular colors and then dropped leaves—they were more
work. Like people that are changeable. Full of temper. Me. My pops.
Charolette. Harder to get along with, Brenda says. Hey, I'm tryin to
be very convenient. Make some money, come home on time.

He called Trent's house, thinking, What the hell kinda tree is
convenient? "I need your help, man," he said to the answering machine. "Come by my pops' crib soon as you can and lend me some
knowledge. Oh—this is Darnell. Peace."

He musta been pissed when I said he wasn't normal for a brotha,
Darnell thought hours later when Trent still hadn't come by or called.
Darnell had cut up the eucalyptus wood, stacked the blind-eyed
branches and logs. Charolette held up a cracker for him from the

blanket by his mother's feet in the front room. "Go on up there, cause your father gon want that estimate done," his mother said.

He was surprised to see Trent's dark face look up from his driveway, and he stopped in front of Trent's white mailbox. Shit. The drapes on your street gon be jumpin now, brothaman, he thought, seeing Trent's blank, neutral glance.

He was unloading the PVC pipe from his truck. "Hey, Darnell," he said, counting sprinkler heads, not looking up.

Darnell leaned on the heavy head of the mailbox and saw flyers poking out from the slit, a whole handful of colored pamphlets and folders and paper. He pulled them out and pretended to study them. "Hey, Trent," he said, "just stopped by to see your crib." So if he ain't gon mention I called, I guess he don't want to do me this little favor. Cool. Victor and them always say he grinnin and skinnin in your face, turn around and act like he better than you. "You got a lotta mail here."

Trent reached down into the truckbed again awkwardly. "That's not mail—just ads. We get em every day, since we're in a new house."

"Latvian housekeeper," Darnell read. "Neat, clean, reference. European cleaning." He looked up, and Trent had to smile at his accent. "That better than Mexican cleaning? Cause I seen a maid just now looked like she was workin hard."

"I guess it depends on who you think you are," Trent said, folding his arms and smiling wider. "Latvian, huh?"

"Don't ask me," Darnell said. "I don't need a maid. Here—Custom Miniblinds. Custom Pool. Home Security—Armed Response. Say, brothaman, you need this one, cause everybody in your neighborhood seen a shaggy-lookin black guy driving around knockin on doors yesterday. Real suspicious."

Trent frowned. "What are you talking about?"

"I went door to door tryin to get some yards," Darnell said. "Pops been on my ass for weeks to do this. I'ma have to break it down to him that on memory lane white ladies always opened the door."

Now Trent had to laugh. "So you didn't meet all my neighbors?" he said, mocking surprise. "And it's such a homey neighborhood. Come on in and get a drink, before we're two black guys in a driveway and they call it a gang."

In the entry, on a table, Darnell saw the phone, saw the red lights blinking. "So why you didn't call back, man?" he asked Trent, who pushed the button.

"You called?" Trent said, frowning, when the first voices began to play. After two calls about home loans, Darnell heard his voice, his message, and Trent laughed again. "That's why. Cause Brichee was already here, she's been home, but when she heard your message, she stopped listening to you after the words 'help' and 'lend.' She didn't call me on my pager because she thought you were someone like Snooter."

"*Like?*" Darnell said, looking at the tiled floor of the entry, the marble fireplace.

"Like Snooter, who always calls to borrow money." Trent looked at the pink notepad beside the phone. "Brichee went to the gym and then she's going to some accountants' meeting, about new tax laws." He looked up. "So what did you want?"

"Hey, all I need is some names of clean trees," Darnell said.

Outside, Trent got in the El Camino, saying, "Clean trees, huh? He must have jacarandas. Or carobs."

"Yup," Darnell said. "Jacaranda and olive."

Trent shook his head. "You know what? You can't get another tree with the look and the dimensions of jacaranda, that light, airy quality. And these new guys hate em. The landscape crew comes once a week, you know that, and they want the grass pristine every day."

"They payin for it." Darnell shrugged.

Trent said, "Yeah, I remember mamas used to go out every evening, rake up the carob pods or the jacaranda pods, the figs. They'd keep an eye on us, talk to everybody, stand there. The grass would be sharp." He looked out the window, then back toward Darnell. "Now everybody's in the house. Ghost town."

"Your town," Darnell said. "You've bought what, three cribs up here?"

Trent stared out the window. "These people want beauty all around them, but they don't like all the work," he said suddenly. "I do."

Darnell shifted. "Long as you get paid big dinero for what you like," he said. But he looked out, too, at the tall palm trunks turning dark, the narrow tunnel of road. Seem like I'm drivin up some Grayglen street every day. I miss my old landscape—drivin home through the Sandlands, seein Rio Seco all laid out for me. Brenda waitin, the palm trees all up and down the streets.

"Looks like nobody's home," Trent said when Darnell parked in the street. "Sprinklers are on timers. Windows are dark."

"Hard to tell," Darnell said. "It goes way far back." The water misted in circles under the trees. He walked down the shined cement drive toward where they'd come out this morning, and the Doberman lunged at him from the shrubbery before the wrought-iron gate, the deep-throated snarl trailing slowly from the teeth when he missed Darnell's thigh. The chain pulled him back at the neck, and he leapt again and again, his saliva flying toward Darnell's fingers, where they were splayed on the concrete. Darnell was on his knees, seeing his fingers fanned wide, his face getting closer and closer to the sweet ozone smell of watery vapor.

"Man, I've never seen a guy faint," Trent said, still breathing hard. "I didn't think I could get you up here and in the seat. Damn!"

Darnell felt the seat back sticky against his neck. He heard the dog's high-pitched barks. They'd been sitting here for a few minutes now. He'd thrown up in the bushes—the grassy-hay smell of the dog's mouth so close to him.

Trent's voice was still different, higher, not so careful. "Damn, Darnell, you just *fell*. That ain't normal for a guy. I've seen women faint."

Normal. "What's normal for a brotha, man?" Darnell said, feeling his stomach fill with warmth now, when he tried to laugh. "Brothaman."

But Trent only frowned. He didn't remember. "You okay now?"

Darnell breathed the damp air wavering from the yard. "Yeah." He sat up and saw the patrol car cruising. He shook his head. "Here we go." The car drove past them, the lone officer bending his head to stare, and then he turned slowly into a driveway up the street to come back the other way. Darnell leaned back to wait. At least Trent wouldn't talk shit like Victor.

But Trent's mouth opened wide and he started yelling, pounding the dashboard with his fist, his other hand gripped around the edge of the vinyl. "I am a goddamn fucking resident!" he screamed, while Darnell saw the officer squinting. "Okay! A fucking resident of the area!"

"Trent, man, stall out!" Darnell said. "He'll see the equipment. Me and Victor and Ronnie got stopped up here yesterday, I told you, it ain't no big deal if you stall out."

But that only made Trent's voice higher, and he screamed, "I'm not Victor, goddamnit! I am a fucking resident!"

Darnell grabbed Trent's flailing hand at the forefinger, at the last knuckle, and pressed hard enough to cause pain. "I'm not gettin shot cause you don't like gettin GPed," he said quietly, watching the cop pull away and head down the street. Every brotha looks General Principle up here.

Creamy—the whole house was creamy. Cold. High ceilings, open space. The bathroom was the color of apricots. Brenda's skin. He had to call her.

Trent sat on his beige couch, two empty Coronas in front of him. He poured from the silvery bottle of vodka. "Man," Darnell said, "you thirsty, huh?" Trent didn't smile.

Darnell picked up the clear bottle and said, "I saw guys drink Stoli up in the mountains. Way too hard for me." He could tell Trent was getting drunk fast. Toe up. He looked at his boots, knocked them gently together on the rug. Toe up. Normal behavior—Fricke didn't think so, back at Seven Canyons.

Trent said suddenly, "See?" He'd been leafing through papers, and he handed Darnell a printed flyer. "Mannheim School offers Protection Dog Training! Handlers will train members of the public and their dogs! Your trained dog protects your family and property better than a gun! Also, imported trained dogs for sale."

Darnell stared at the picture of the German shepherd, tongue hanging, in the upper corner. Like the bonsai tree, he thought, but Trent said, "I hate dogs, cause they mess up flower beds, they crap all over my work." His speech was slurring, and he downed another shot of Stoli. Darnell slid the flyer onto the floor. A tiny shard of rock stuck to his palm, from the long driveway. He nudged it in harder, so he wouldn't have to think for a moment.

Trent kept on, almost whispering now. "Brichee wouldn't like you cause you too black."

"What was your first clue?"

"You wear that Angels hat. Your hair—you got razor cuts. You don't wanna talk right on the phone."

Darnell said, "She a sista, right? Can't never please a woman on the phone."

"You know what I'm sayin," Trent said. "She don't wanna hear 'hooptie' and 'crib.' " Trent's eyes closed, and he leaned against the couch. "You scared the shit out of me, man," he whispered, softer.

Darnell saw the masses of flowers in the backyard through the huge window: they glowed in the garden lights. Yeah, Trent ain't supposed to like flowers. Not normal. Always talkin Latin names. What was the one he told me for baby's breath? Gypsophila-somethin. Charolette's breath. Charolette—pretty name. If it was a boy, I wasn't gon call him Darnell Junior. The colored give em a name like that, it's a burden. Tom Corcoran, Billy Scott, Josh Fricke. Those are okay. He reached down to the pile of flyers. Latvian. The dog's triangular ears. The papers were dimpled from dried moisture. The Baggie is a smart idea. The flyer can't get wet. And the rock keeps it from blowin away.

Oriental Gardeners. People see the tree, the lantern, they're thinkin of those perfect Japanese gardens and small, quiet guys trimmin and rakin.

Darnell's Expert Landscape Service. Professional Brothas. Yeah— that'd go over like Darnell Tucker Canyon. He saw the ravines again, the wall of flame, and he stood, shaking his head. Trent was snoring slightly, and Darnell could tell he fell asleep like this frequently.

"Stay black, man," he whispered, grinning, and he pulled open the etched-glass and oak front door.

"I'ma take her and do the shoppin," he said to Brenda on Saturday morning. Brenda lay in bed, her arm over her eyes. The heat streamed in through the curtains.

"Don't get all that weird stuff we never need," she murmured. "Get some chicken and a bag of rice."

"You get some rest," he said, taking Charolette's hand.

She put her forehead against the railing so hard dents printed into her skin: she was looking for the Kawasaki that always revved the engine. "Do-do-si-cu!" she said proudly, pointing at the motorcycle.

"That's Daddy's girl," Darnell laughed. "Goin for the ride already."

When they passed the county building, Charolette pointed to the gleaming glass and said, "Mama."

"Yeah," Darnell said. He stopped at the tiny Oriental market, in an old wood-frame house near the building. Brenda had come here with a Chinese girl from work, Connie Lee, and she was addicted to some strange shrimp chips. He carried Charolette inside. Manufactured by Hanmi, Tokyo, Japan: he read the back of the bag. The store smelled of salt and ginger and fish. He looked at the jars of spices and bags of dried mushrooms and seaweed. Fricke probably loved stores like this. Curry powder in a tiny can—he recognized it. India, the back said.

But Charolette found M&Ms by the front counter, where the woman smiled at her and gently took the money from Darnell. She recognized him from the frequent chip trips. "The eggs very fresh," she said, motioning to a rack. "Come from Chino."

Chino. What else came from there? Someone had told him. The gun. He froze, hearing Charolette say, "Bye! Bye!" to the woman. His father had fired the gun, lifted his lip in disgust. Darnell jerked his shoulders with the trail of cold across his neck. Louis was doing his time in Chino.

"Mon!" Charolette urged, pulling his wrist. "Mon."

He stood by the curb, looking back at the faded wooden sign with both foreign characters and English letters: NGUYEN'S ORIENTAL MARKET.

At the grocery store on the Westside, she rode in the cart, and he stared at faces. He kept thinking of Tim Bui and Don Nguyen, how the teachers in school had looked at them, nodded at their pronunciation, but he looked around the store, seeing Mexican faces, too. The guys on the crew that had picked the lemons, the guys working on the block walls. Almost as many Mexican families lived on certain streets in the Westside as black families, and he watched the men outside the store, tying plastic bags filled with food to their handlebars. Ten-speeds. The men carried whole chickens, stacks of tortillas, chips, fruit. There were groups of five or six, one guy guarding clothes in the laundromat while the others stood in line at the store. These were the guys who lived in trailers and converted garages behind houses, the guys who stood on corners waiting for work, the guys who rode the ten-speeds up the hill to Grayglen every morning.

He watched their faces while Charolette rode the horsie three times. She was amazed that he kept producing quarters without a fight. He saw a mariachi band walk through the parking lot and into the schoolyard of Our Lady of Guadalupe, where Donnie and Louis had gone to school. Their huge guitars and glittering suits fascinated Charolette, who pointed when the horsie stopped.

But Darnell looked back at the men on the bikes, their eyes and hair, knowing that he was missing something. "Come on," he said. "We gotta get Daddy's equipment."

His father was working on a chain saw in the sideyard. "Hey," Darnell said. "I'ma check the gas and oil in the mower. I need it for Monday."

His father said, "Whose yard you doin?"

"Yours. Roscoe's. Brenda's daddy's." Darnell wheeled out the mower.

"What the hell you up to now?" his father said, straightening his back. Darnell saw the deep lines, four of them, cut into his forehead.

"I ain't sure yet," he said. "What you doin with that spoon?" he called to Charolette, who stood over a fresh-dug hole.

She clutched the spoon to her chest. "Mine!" she said.

All weekend, he kept hearing the music again, turning the radio to the Mexican station. "What are you tripping about?" Brenda said, folding the laundry that lay in drifts on the floor. Charolette moved washcloths from the couch to the table.

"Nothin," Darnell said, listening to what he thought was an accordion. He smoothed out the flyer, the pink paper ridged with dirt at the creases, and Charolette snatched it from his fingers.

"I need that," he told her, pulling it back.

On Monday, he drove slowly past the corners where they always gathered, the crowds of Mexican men waiting for day work. And he saw the shortest, Indian-looking guys. Their eyes were slanted almond, their hair thick and straight, their legs short-curved.

The men shifted and scattered when a construction truck stopped at the curb, crowding around the driver. Darnell watched five guys jump in the back of the pickup. Some of the disappointed ones stared at him, and he tried to recall what he could of his high-school Spanish. All that came to his head was *"Como se llama?"* and *Hermano, hermana. Llantería:* the used tire shop where his father and Roscoe were friends with Mr. Sánchez, the owner. He licked his lips while he leaned out the window. He said, "I need a guy who can speak English."

Three guys came over. "I speak English, bro," a skinny dark guy said, and Darnell knew from the teardrops tattooed near his eyes that he'd been in prison.

"I'll give you ten bucks to help me out here, man," Darnell said. "I need two dudes who know how to mow lawns, and I want them to look Oriental, you know, like those guys over there." He pointed to the short, slim men.

"He wants *los indios*," the guy said, muttering to the men. Several of the Indian men gathered around him, and he brought over four with anxious faces and small, tilted dark eyes under thick brows. Darnell thought of Charolette's brows suddenly, how delicate and straight they were, like the youngest guy's in front of him.

"You guys can do gardening?" he asked. They all nodded, and he said, "But I gotta get somebody who speaks English—even a little."

The youngest guy said, "I try speak *pequeño*. My brother not so much." He gestured to the older man next to him, in a baseball cap.

"Come on," Darnell said, gesturing, and they got into the El Camino. The other men melted away, then ran toward another truck, and Darnell handed a ten-dollar bill to the tattooed guy, who lifted his face and said, "Later, bro."

The two men were so small compared to Victor and Ronnie that air still flowed through the cab to touch Darnell's shoulders. Their shoulders were thin. No government gym. "Where you from?" he asked.

The young one said, "Mayco."

"Yeah—where in Mexico?" Darnell said.

"Wahaka."

Darnell frowned. Wahaka? "Write it down, okay?" he said, and the guy printed *Oaxaca* on the back of the pink flyer.

"O-sa-ka?" the guy said, trying to pronounce it differently, and Darnell smiled. Wasn't that a city in Japan? He'd heard the name. It was Rio Seco's sister city; every summer, there was some ceremony downtown, and college students went back and forth to study. Osaka. The younger guy shrugged and smiled, and the older one stared straight ahead.

He watched them work on Roscoe's small front and back yards.

Anyone could mow, and Juan, the younger one, did the front while José weed-whacked the back. Darnell blew the grass off the sidewalk. It took twenty-five minutes for José to finish mowing under the fig tree.

They were sweating, watching him. "Let's go," Darnell said.

He pulled into the Batistes' driveway. The New Yorker was gone. He told Juan to start mowing the front, and he knocked on the door. Brenda's mother opened it, frowning. "Darnell," she said.

"My crew," he said. "We're gon do your yard, to say thanks for curin me. And Donnie. Mr. Batiste at work?"

"No," she said. "Just runnin some errand. Come in here."

In the kitchen, he heard the whining mower and the zipping of the weed whacker starting and stopping. He watched José move around the backyard. Mrs. Batiste's sewing machine was hot; he touched it, on the table. She came back with a bagful of clothes for Charolette.

"I ain't came by cause Brenda haven't call me in two weeks," she said. "What been goin on with you?"

"Just been busy," he said, looking into her soft-rimmed eyes. "I had to take care of some things, and Brenda been workin too hard. I'm cool now, and I figured my crew could do your yard every week. Mr. Batiste still won't hire a gardener, so we'll come for free. Okay?"

She shook her head. "You know he do his own yard," she started, but Darnell smiled.

"So he'll have more free time to spend with you." He waited, and she smiled and shook her head again.

"Don't get smart," she said, and turned him at the shoulder toward the kitchen. "Go on get you some coffee."

He saw Juan pushing the silent mower down the long driveway toward the backyard. Juan caught his eye at the kitchen window and pointed; Darnell nodded his head. He touched the sheer curtain, remembered Brenda's face in the glass, framed by the lace. Next time, if there was a next time, if his plans worked out, he'd make sure the New Yorker was here.

After José cut the tiny grass plot in Darnell's father's frontyard, while his mother peered out the screen and frowned, Darnell took them back to the corner. "Next Monday," he told them. "In one week. Be back here, and I think I got regular work if you want it. Five bucks an hour."

"Every day?" Juan asked. "All day?"

Darnell said, "I hope so, man. Where you learn English?"

"I went in college one year," Juan said. "I love English."

"Well, here's some dinero," Darnell said, handing them the cash. "Ducats. See you Monday."

He wouldn't tell Brenda what he had in mind, and when she said, "You driving me crazy with that little planning smile and won't give up no information," Darnell just smiled it again. "Oooh, I'm drivin you crazy, huh?" he said, wrapping his arms around her from behind and rubbing himself against her.

"Not right now you ain't," she said, turning around. "Where are you going?"

"I gotta find Nacho," Darnell said. "Maybe I can make some more money."

"The suspense is killing me," she said, rolling her eyes. "You have big money one night, and none the next week."

But he smiled again. He found Nacho and Snooter sitting on folding chairs in their yard, doctoring a cracked hose. Darnell said, "Nacho, come in the back with me, man. I gotta show you somethin." He didn't want Snooter to see the flyer, to make fun of his idea. He hadn't even said it out loud to anyone.

Sitting at the scarred table in the back, Darnell laid out the sheet for Nacho.

"You the artist—can you make me a flyer like this, one I can copy? I figure half a page—like this." He laid his sheet out next to the pink one, and when Nacho read the message he laughed hard.

"You serious, man? You want me to print or script, like calligraphy?"

"Print," Darnell said, "cause it's gotta be easy to read. But make the letters kinda exotic. And put a picture in opposite corners. I think one a those little incense burners, like you see in a Japanese garden. Like in the garden downtown, for the sister city." He thought for a minute. "The little bonsai tree is cool, but I ain't into stealin. Make the other picture a bridge, like in the sister-city garden, too."

"Curved?" Nacho said, sketching.

"Oh, yeah!" Darnell said.

He had three hundred of the flyers printed on light blue paper, then he went to Trinidad's Building Supply down in Treetown. The other flyer had been held down with a nondescript gray pebble. Darnell chose the small, sparkling white rocks in bulk. Baggies at the store, with orange juice and cereal. He'd need the Corn Pops in the morning.

He took Charolette with him, long before dawn. She was sleepy for a few minutes, but he whispered to her, and she said, "Dark, Daddy?"

He said, "We're cruisin in the dark, baby. I got your breakfast in a jar right here." She loved the plastic honey containers from his mother's. She shook the cereal in a swirl, and he said, "Watch out for trains."

He drove up the long avenues, remembering when he'd been in a hurry to get to Brenda's house and got stuck behind the long trains that came through the Westside. Now they both leaned forward at each track, looking for the headlight on an engine; he always lingered before the tracks, because Charolette loved to catch a train and listen in wonder to the clacking wheels, wave to the engineers.

"Choo-choo," she said sadly now. They went to Grayglen first, Darnell driving on the wrong side of the street to drop Baggies on lawns. He pitched two onto Trent's grass, laughing. Charolette couldn't throw them far enough from her open window, and he gave her a pile to wreck so she wouldn't cry.

"My door-to-door marketing strategy just wasn't gettin it," he murmured, looking at the blank, dark squares of window and door, the grayer shades of lawn. "Get me a sentence."

"Daddy?" Charolette said. "Papah?"

"Nosy girl. These dudes ain't even up yet, but they gotta go to work soon, and then they'll find this when they get the paper."

"Noo-papah." She always heard the paper fly against the apartment door, and she had to run out for it every morning.

"You got it." They twisted through all the new streets, then went to the Ville and dropped some more. Darnell watched her forefinger curl into the corners to extract the rocks, which she put carefully into her lap. "There your grandpa's house," he said when they drove up the Batistes' street. He stopped for a long minute, looking at Brenda's window, and threw a Baggie as close to the hedge as he could. The arch over the porch was dark.

The sky was turning gray, and he said, "We don't want nobody to see us, or we turn into pumpkins. The wrong color." She scattered the rocks off her sleeper and held her hands out for the cereal.

His father laughed silly. "Tuan's Oriental Landscape Maintenance Service," he read out loud to Roscoe. "Boy want to be a damn gardener, talkin bout maintenance." He frowned at the flyer. "Expert landscapers will mow, edge, fertilize, and maintain your property with weekly service for only $50 a month. Call now to keep your landscape beautiful." His father turned to him. "Who the hell is Tuan?"

Darnell said, "Nuh-uh. It's Juan. And José. If I get enough calls this week, I'm hirin two Mexican dudes."

Roscoe said, "You know, he isn't crazy. There's a cachet to that image. But I don't know how you'll pull it off when they see your ugly face."

"They ain't gotta see me," Darnell said. "Just send the check here, to your address." His father raised his eyebrows. "In case we can afford to move eventually."

"Where you movin to?"

Darnell shrugged. "I don't know yet. Someplace with two bedrooms." He turned to look at Charolette pulling down dry laundry with his mother. He wanted her to have a room, so that he and Brenda could have their bed back. I been on the couch all my life, he thought. I want to make love in a big bed. If I can afford one. He took a deep breath.

His father frowned. "You realize you're encroachin on Floyd King and Nacho's business?"

"No, I stayed out of Arroyo Grande and downtown," Darnell said, lifting his hands. "I'ma go with the new tracts and the Ville. Grayglen. Nacho said he and his pops are concentratin on construction sites, cause they pay better. Homey wouldn't have done the flyer if he was mad."

"You thought all this out," Roscoe said, nodding.

"He had plenty time to think, since he ain't been workin," Darnell's father said, and Darnell stretched out his arms.

"But I'm good to go now!"

He practiced his voice in the bathroom. Brenda was at work. He tried to remember Tim Bui's words, the clipped-short sound, the way each word was exact and separate. He sat on the couch, watching Oprah with the sound off, remembering the wall by the gym, the older guys leaning there. Victor and Trent and Ronnie and Melvin. Melvin laughing at Darnell when he'd first come to high school, laughing at his lack of imaginative rap. He remembered when Tim Bui was allowed to stand there, too, because he could dance as good as Leon and Donnie to the suitcase-sized radio near the brick. "Dude dance like a brotha," Leon would say, laughing. Darnell drank his soda, sweated, watched the shroud of smog rise to envelop downtown, where Brenda was typing at her computer, thinking about what he was doing. On the third day, the phone rang, and he was ready. A woman said, "Tuan's Landscape?" and he said, "Yes, ma'am, I can help you."

"Are you reliable?"

"Yes, ma'am, very reliable. We will come every week, and we do a careful job." He chopped the words off cleanly, his heart racing heat all the way to his ears.

He talked to Juan for a long time. He told him that they'd have to comb their hair straight back, short, and no straw hats. He took them to Kmart for white T-shirts, dark-green Dickies, and work boots. "And no talkin, I mean if the people are around watchin you," he said. "I don't want them to hear Spanish."

Juan frowned. "But if they say, speak to you? If they want different? The flower or *semilla?*"

Darnell said, "*Semilla?*"

Juan looked around in the front yard of Darnell's father's house, where everyone was gone and José leaned against the El Camino, watching. Juan bent low to the ground and picked up a sunflower seed. "*Semilla,*" he said, placing the seed in Darnell's palm.

Darnell frowned now. "Okay. Just say like this, 'Please call my boss; he can help you.' "

Juan looked at the flyer closely again and smiled slightly. "I am Tuan?"

"Maybe, man," Darnell said. "Maybe I am."

But he felt strange staying home the rest of the day, waiting for the calls in the empty, stifling apartment. June had burned into July, and the shimmering bells of the Mexican ice-cream carts passed on the sidewalk below. Darnell went to the bathroom mirror, pulled at his eyes to make them long and narrow. He touched the new haircut he'd gotten from George. A fade, with three lines above each ear. His father hated the razored cuts, said, "What the hell? Look like a damn mower got *you*."

He stared at his face in the speckled glass. "Homey, doncha know me?" He'd seen Victor at a stoplight last week, near the park. Victor's eyes were half slit and hard. "Work been *slow*, huh?"

He knew Nacho would have told Victor about the flyer, about Tuan's. He splashed water onto his face and neck, ran his wrists under the tap. Cold onto the veins. Cold potato bracelets that Mrs. Batiste had given him. You feverish, boy? Thinkin this shit gon work? Cause if it don't . . . Homey, doncha know me? His chest was clotted with warmth when he sat on the cold edge of the bathtub. "What you planning to do if somebody doesn't pay?" Roscoe had said.

"Go over there and collect."

"Who you—Tuan's bodyguard? His butler?" His father had laughed.

"Shoot, whoever I gotta be, long as I get the cash." But he was shaking.

"I was just testing," Roscoe said gently, touching his elbow. "But I have a suggestion. Get a beeper, so you don't miss calls if you still want to work with us or get side jobs. Beepers are cheap now."

"Yeah, and I'll look like a dope dealer," Darnell said, turning away. "Ain't that what I'm supposed to look like anyway?"

He paced around the living room now, the bells fading, and he turned up the radio to pound the walls with music.

PROPER CARE AND MAINTENANCE

"SEE, MAN, I told you she was gon do it. She pimpin you, Darnell." Victor shook his head and watched Charolette hang out the window of the El Camino. "She pimpin you big time."

"Daddy!" she yelled, her round face bobbing furiously above the door. "Juice-juice!" She disappeared for a moment and then pulled herself up again. He could see her fingers curl over the doorframe as she threw her empty bottle onto the asphalt.

Darnell turned back to Victor and Ronnie, sitting on folding chairs around the cold, blackened trash barrel. "I'm fixin to go check this lot behind that Catholic church near downtown, the one close to the riverbottom," he said. He was sweating, looking into Victor's eyes. He'd rehearsed this.

Victor raised his chin a half-inch. "*Brotha*man, do that mean you need to borrow a shovel?"

"Man, I ain't seen you for damn near a month," Ronnie said.

"Need you guys for the job," Darnell said, waiting. "Cleanup, brush and tires, all that usual junk."

"Homey, doncha know me? I'm just a nigga wit an attitude," Victor said. Ronnie and a man near the pepper tree laughed.

"Yeah, but are you still good to go?" Darnell folded his arms. He could hear Charolette screeching behind him.

Victor smiled. "I heard you was hirin illegals, man. Word is you don't need no brothas."

"If I don't want no brothas to work, then I better kill myself, too," Darnell said. "I been workin with two Mexican guys, doin yards. I'm tryin to get them on a route, so I can do regular side jobs when I get em. But Victor, man, I *gotta* be sweatin every day. I ain't like you—I can't wait till I'm in the mood." He made his voice hard, thinking of the tumbleweeds, of the balls of flame merging in the ditch.

"Man, you think you big shit," Victor said. "You been yangin with Trent King too much." He smiled harder, no teeth showing, his lips curved full, and Darnell suddenly remembered Marlene and her friends saying how fine Victor was. Scary fine, they said. "At least I ain't no strawberry," Victor said. "Do anything for a few presidents. Or some rocks."

Darnell breathed in through his nose, seeing the sparkling white stones in the Baggies, the chalk-pale rocks in Vernon's hand when he'd turned his head. "I ain't a strawberry," he said. He hesitated. He had practiced this, too. "I'm just whipped, like you said, by two women. They kickin my natural black butt. Hey, you always talkin bout 'Brothas ain't meant to be out in the sun, absorbin all that heat.' " He turned to watch Charolette, who threw his sunglasses out the window. "Victor, man, proper care and maintenance keep your ass from shrinkin and fadin, okay?" He waited. "You gon be ready Saturday?"

Victor ran his hands over his braids, glancing at Ronnie. "Damn, homey, I might be a stockbroker by then." They all laughed, and Darnell started back to the car.

He put Charolette back into her car seat, and she said, "My *bottle*, Daddy." She watched out the window, pointing to the trash barrel. An older man had arrived, and he threw something inside, dropped a match. "Fire, Daddy."

"Yeah. Smoke." She looked triumphant, sticking out her chin.

She'd seen the smoke rising into the sky several times now when he stood at the apartment railing watching the billowing dirty-cream explosion, the scent traveling with the sirens. On the last weekend in August, when the riverbottom went up again, the west wind blew the ash thick as the light snowfall they'd gotten up at the Conservation Corps camp, and he sat on the balcony with her, pointing to each flake. He reached out to smear a piece of cane bark. Brenda said, "It blows this far?"

She sat behind them, her chair in the open doorway, sewing torn overall straps. "Yeah," he said. "Rides the air pretty far."

She was still watching him. He thought, I'm not goin to search them out now. Not right now. He'd never been alone in the mountains, he realized, breathing in the scorched-cane smell; with all the other guys in the station or the corps, laughing and farting and talking smack, it was loud and elbow close. But when they worked the fire line or bent to scramble up the slope, every man was by himself with his protective gear and his own circle of chaparral.

He was never alone now. Brenda was silent behind him, only a faint click from the thimble and needle. Charolette worked purple yarn into the wrought-iron railing. Her favorite was to drop the ball all the way into the courtyard when he stood by the car, to watch it roll on the cement near him, and then pull the endless string back up forever.

"What you want for breakfast?" he asked Juan. They sat on a hill in Grayglen, the sun just up, white in the September heat. There were only a few flyers left at their feet in the El Camino.

"I have at home a *bolillo* and *café*," Juan said. He had been trading words with Darnell for several weeks while they worked, his small eyes watching Darnell's lips from under thick-arched brows. Darnell thought about Charolette and her new words, murmured and shouted over and over. He and Juan speaking slowly, awkwardly. José never spoke at all.

"I got *café*," Darnell said. "*Bolillo* a doughnut?"

"Not a—the hole," Juan said, frowning. "Like a bread. Little."

A stream of cars was leaving the tracts along with them when Darnell cruised down the slopes. He'd picked up Juan in the dark, and they hit three developments so new that most of the yards were still bare, tamped earth with tractor marks. Only mountains I get for now, Darnell kept thinking. The dirt fronts were dotted with signs that read CUSTOM POOLS and CUSTOM FENCING and CUSTOM SECURITY. Darnell had looked for Trent's name under a few of the CUSTOM LANDSCAPE DESIGN signs, but it was too dark and he was moving quickly while Juan pitched the Baggies.

"A biscuit?" Darnell laughed. "We can get that from my moms." But they drove to a Mexican bakery on the Westside, because he didn't want to see his father yet today. He didn't want to say how many yards he had on the route—still only two days' worth. He looked up at the bakery sign: PANADERÍA. Juan brought back coffee and small plain buns. "*Bolillo* boring," Darnell said, chewing, and Juan smiled.

"You like the sugar," he said. "I see you this." He handed Darnell a flaky, heart-shaped pastry.

"*Gracias*," Darnell said.

They picked up José from the tiny garage that had been converted to an apartment, on Twentieth Street. Juan and José shared it with three other men. José was silent, as always; he nodded and sat by the window.

Darnell headed to Hillgrove. He was giving them each the straight $5 an hour for all of Thursday and Friday. After gas, dump fees, the used mower he'd bought from Floyd King, and paying for more flyers, he'd only cleared a few hundred this month. Not enough yet, but he'd worked a few jobs with his father, too.

"Remember, everything's on timers and drip system," Darnell told Juan when he'd seen that no one was home at the Stephenses', the first house. He pointed to the thin black hosing that circled each bush and tree in the backyard. Looking up for a moment at the flat brown hills above them, he tried to see the dark spot etched into the side where he'd parked that night with Leon and Vernon and Donnie, where the ground shimmered with broken glass and evaporated liquor.

"Timers," Juan said, squatting to examine the hosing. "I see everywhere." José stood watching, waiting for later when Juan would translate; he kept his eyes on Darnell, his thin lips folded.

Darnell glanced at the mountain again and pulled his eyes back to the yard. "Yeah," he said. "Automatic, right, so nobody's asked you to water?" Juan shook his head. "You never stand around with a hose, then. Cool." And the homeowners aren't hanging around sprinkling all the time, so they don't have to see me or you two, he thought.

In the one circular flower bed by the patio, they knelt to weed. "Baby palm tree," Darnell said, pulling up the straight blade, thick as a knife. He held it up, and the tiny seed clung to the single root. "The *semilla*, right?"

"Yes," Juan said. His shirt was soaked transparent across his thin shoulders. He said, "We will plant trees, too?"

"We gon go out with my father and Roscoe pretty soon and plant some trees. Best time to plant em here is late fall. We're supposed to get rain in the winter to get baby trees established." He shrugged. "But that's not the way it's workin now. Serious drought. I think it's, what, five years now?" He remembered Fricke laughing: Drought piss.

Juan nodded. "This we have, in Mexico." The word still slurred Mayco to Darnell's ear. "In my home, farm was very dry and no growing."

"What do you guys grow?" Darnell said, going around to the front, pulling at the milkweed rising among the flowers along the walkway.

"*Maíz, chiles.*" Juan went to the border along the street, sitting back on his heels to weed. "José and I put money to my mother. My uncle help at the land, but no water."

"You got any sisters?" Darnell asked.

Juan nodded. "Three sisters. In school, the small school."

"Elementary?"

Juan shrugged. Darnell said, "So we all givin our paychecks to women. That's the way of the world, man." Juan moved to the edge of the planter and yanked more weeds. "You pretty good at that. I guess it's like bein a farmer, weeds are weeds."

"The *pequeño* field," Juan said, but his smile was crooked.

"*Pequeño* is little. Yeah. But do you want your own farm?"

Juan shook his head. "No. I want to go to college, learn English."

Darnell looked down the street at the empty driveways. "Anybody try to talk to you when you workin?" he said. He waited every night for the call, the voice that said, "I saw a black guy out there today, writing something down while your guys were working. I was worried about . . . security."

Juan stood up. "They say, 'Are you Tuan?' One man say this. I say, 'No, my boss. He work another place today.' " Darnell smiled, but

his shoulders felt tight when he pulled out a knife-blade palm seedling. Juan said, "A few lady talk, but I say, 'My English no good.'
And one say, 'You take ESL, English Second Language.' "

Darnell squatted on his heels, seeing Juan's hands move in the air
excitedly. What if this whole thing didn't work? José came silently
down the slope from where he'd been raking a few dead bougainvillea
flowers on the lawn. Darnell pointed to the clay pot with the gera-
niums by the door. "What's that again?"

"*Maceta*," Juan said. "Flower pot."

"*Maceta*," Darnell murmured, pulling another palm. Why you
care? he thought. So you knew all the names of the typical chaparral
habitat. So Scott don't know it's arundo cane down there while he
workin it. But he said it again. "*Maceta*. Okay. Let's get on to the
next yard, cause it's hella *caliente* out here by lunch."

Juan nodded, his eyes disappearing when he grinned.

If he was never alone, he didn't have time to think about the season
ending, about what Fricke and the others were doing in their down
time, about how the chaparral was turning colors on the slopes. He
drove Brenda to work, took Charolette to his mother's, picked up
Juan and José, unloaded burlap-wrapped trimmings and trash at the
dump with Roscoe.

Some days, he picked up Victor and Ronnie, and he had to listen
to Victor's long-running yang, his Spanish and yuppie imitations, for
the first few hours; then Victor settled into himself and bothered
Darnell about his women.

And when he got to his father's house, Charolette was halfway to
Honolulu. They walked around the sideyard, and she looked up, her
cheek smeared with dust, a cloud of misty fringe around her forehead
where her braids were worked loose. Roscoe's Hollie, who was six
now, was bent over the shallow ditch.

"Hollie and Charolette are diggin to Honolulu," Paula said. "Hollie
told her they could dig to Honolulu and Cincinnati, and you know
Charolette doesn't understand, but she loves hearin Hollie say those
words, so she's goin at it with her little shovel."

"Daddy! Shov-a!" Charolette cried, and Sophia rolled her eyes.

"Don't even think about takin that spoon away from her," Sophia
said. "She freaks if you even look at it."

She held the tarnished soup spoon tightly, but she pressed her face to his shirt. "Daddy!" she said. "Dutty!" She slapped at the dirt on his chest.

"You filthy, too," he said.

"Check this chick naggin my man already," Victor said, leaning in the doorway of the back room.

"She my runnin buddy," Darnell said, smelling grape juice and clay dust at her neck.

Victor shook his head. "You weak, man. She what—goin on two? You supposed to let *grown* females pimp you."

He took her to the McDonald's downtown, near Brenda's office. He sat at a table in the play area while she tried to climb the forest of hamburger flowers, running back to him every few minutes for a sip of vanilla milkshake. Bigger kids tumbled down the slide, and Darnell took a bite of cheeseburger; he remembered the McDonald's off the freeway when he drove with Vernon, the cheeseburger, and the air-conditioning rippled up his shoulder blades. Tuan's gotta work, he thought. I'ma get this truck, and it's gon work. My schedule. All the proper procedures.

Charolette's mouth was open like a bird's—her milky white teeth were squared and separate on her bottom gum, like baby tombstones, he thought when he tried to push some soft bun onto her tongue. She snapped her mouth shut and grabbed the bun. "Myself," she said, frowning.

He carried her across the plaza near the county building. They were early. She leaned over the edge of the fountain, and Darnell stared at the sparkling drops. Every time he sat here, he heard Donnie's voice, Donnie who'd called him last week to say that he was leaving. He was going up north to the college where he'd played ball, to look for some friends he hadn't seen in a while.

"Be careful, Darnell, man," Donnie had whispered. "Okay? Watch your back, cause they don't like it when you sue. They know you, too."

"You okay, Donnie?" he'd asked.

"I'ma get away from all this stress, man. My lawyer says stress . . ." He paused. "You ever trip out when you see a cop? Or just, like, a K-9?"

Darnell couldn't answer. Yeah. But I can't afford to trip. I gotta feed people. He finally said, "Uh-uh, man. I don't think about it."

He looked up to see a guy in a gray suit come out of the county building. See—the dudes go home early, he thought. An Oriental dude, young, like my age. Check the suit—sharp.

"Darnell?" the guy said, coming close, shading his forehead.

"Kenny!" Darnell said, standing up. Kenny Matsumoro had graduated with him. They'd talked sometimes in Biology, and Kenny had run track with Darnell freshman year. "How's your distance, man?"

Kenny shook his head. "Just run from the parking lot to the office," he said. "How's your four hundred?"

Darnell smiled. "I just run after this little chick." He pointed to Charolette, who was chasing pigeons.

Kenny sat on the bench. "You waiting for Brenda? I saw her on the elevator twice, and she told me you guys got married. I just started here two months ago."

"What are you doin up here in mirror land?"

"Intern in county planning, man, that's what I'm going to school for." Kenny looked at the heat coming off the windows. "You still firefighting? I didn't ask Brenda. September, about ninety today— good day for a fire."

"Yeah, maybe, but I won't be up there. The funds got cut. You should know about funds." Darnell saw Kenny nod, and he didn't want to say it. Yeah, Brenda been feedin me until this past few weeks. "I gotta come down here and get a license pretty soon, matter of fact. I got my own business."

"Yeah?"

"Landscaping—lotta work out there in the new developments."

"Yeah," Kenny said. "I went home last week and my mom showed me this ad she got in the yard."

Darnell remembered that Kenny's father had died last year. "You still live up the street from Brenda's mom?"

"Yeah. Boring Street. But man, this ad was funny. We've gotten two different ones. This was Tuan's Oriental Something. Mom didn't even see anything wrong with it."

"What was wrong?" Darnell's forehead was cool with sweat, and Charolette brought him a penny she'd found.

"Like, Oriental is old school, man. Oriental means east, when you take it down to the Latin root. Like Oriental is east and Occidental is west. It's only the Far East if Europe is the center of the world, man. And that's old shit."

Darnell was silent. "So, your mom wasn't pissed?"

Kenny laughed. "Old people don't want to make waves. Remember I used to tell your friend Donnie my name's Japanese—a bunch of syllables, okay? Chinese names are shorter. My mom was born here, my grandma was born here. I'm sansei—third generation." Kenny's face was flushed. "Where'd your parents come from?"

Darnell said, "My parents are immigrants from hell, I guess. But I get the point."

Kenny said, "Calling me Oriental is like me calling you colored. Or Negro."

"Not as bad as nigger," Darnell said. "Or gook. So what's the right word?"

"Most people prefer Asian American," Kenny said, thoughtfully. "Every time Donnie saw me, he'd yell 'Hai karate!' "

Darnell laughed, stretching his hands hard behind his head so he would feel pulling muscles instead of buzzing sadness. "Donnie picks up a few foreign words here and there," he said, remembering the long nights at the hotel. He looked up at the building's glare. "So where do you get a license?"

Kenny shrugged. "Upstairs somewhere."

Darnell nodded casually. "So did your mom call the number on this ad?"

Kenny said, "Shit. I'm still her son—I gotta mow the lawn every Saturday for the rest of my life."

Charolette watched him walk toward the parking lot and said, "Daddy? Juice?"

"Here comes Mama now," Darnell said absently. Asian. He watched the earrings flash and swing toward them.

He got two more calls that night, and then he sat at the table, looking at the flyer. He crossed out Oriental and stared at the words. Tuan's Landscape Maintenance . . . Tuan's Asian . . . No. He wrote on a new sheet: "Tuan's Landscaping Service, with expert Asian landscapers to mow, edge, fertilize, and maintain your property weekly. Only $50 a month will keep your garden beautiful. Call now."

He stared at the words again. Trent had told him how much classier the word "garden" sounded compared to "yard." Like "yard dog," "yardbird." My pops always tellin Moms, "Give me another piece of yardbird. You did a hell of a job with it tonight."

Asian. Where the hell is Asia, then? Brother Lobo said all peoples came from Africa or Asia: they think the first people over here came on a land bridge from Asia, and that's who the Indians were. Are. Dude called Juan and José *los indios*. Indians. Pops is part Creek— Red Man. So I'm part Asian my own damn self. Can't you see it? Right here around the eyes? The hairline? The color?

I'ma have to get Nacho to change this up, he thought, taking the flyer to the couch and sitting beside Brenda. She was reading a magazine. He leaned over to see the newspaper beside her, and when he grabbed her around the waist and pulled her arm on top of his, she laughed. Charolette was sleeping on the floor, her blanket puddled around her, and Brenda said, "Shhh!"

Darnell lined up her soft, pale forearm with his. "Hmmm," he said. "I can't see the Asian in you, baby."

"Is that right?" she said, her teeth showing long, gleaming, before she ducked her head, and he pulled her face toward him, his fingers in her hair. He pressed his mouth on hers, curling his tongue under to feel her teeth, to tickle her just behind them.

"You come over here just for that?" she said into his neck. "Cause I haven't even seen you lately."

"I came over here for the classifieds," he said, and to the frown on her forehead, he went on, "I might need a new truck."

"You think we can handle the payment on something? Why can't you fix up the Spider?" She kept her hands on his chest.

Darnell shook his head. "Man, I ain't even thought about the Spider in a long time. But the truck ain't for me. It's for Tuan."

She rolled her eyes. "Every time you say that, I think of the film critic on *Living Color*, the bald guy, you know? I crack up."

Darnell threw back his head and laughed so hard Charolette did her periscope imitation from the blanket on the floor. He picked her up and took her into the bedroom, laid her in the crib on her side. Her temples were smooth, new-penny clean from her bath, almost pink under the thin skin.

He closed the door and went back to the couch, where Brenda had moved the newspaper to make room for him.

*   *   *

He began trimming the long-arched branches of bottlebrush that streamed out from the peel-bark trunk, remembering the red sprays of bloom and how he and Melvin used to tickle each other with the brushy flowers, leaving pollen yellow on each other's necks. Tiny wooden knobs lined the stems; they would break those off for ammunition. Darnell rolled a few between his fingers. Charolette would love these—probably call em little biscuits for her Barbie or somethin. I shoulda brought her today, cause this is just a two-hour job.

He was trimming bushes at an old house in Grayglen, one of his father's customers. He'd meet up with Juan and José after he was finished. He raked the bottlebrush trimmings and moved to the two huge oleanders. Dusty, spear-shaped leaves. Poisonous. His mother had always lectured him and Melvin: "Stay away from those bushes; don't even breathe the dust while your daddy cuttin them." But when they got to the job, his father always said, "Hell, they'd have to eat a whole handful of leaves to get sick. Go on and rake that up."

That was mostly what he and Melvin and Louis had done. Raked, pulled the heavy piles of stem and branch and leaf all around the grass and dirt until their shoulders and forearms ached from joint to skin. Roscoe worked the chain saw, and Darnell's father was always the one in the tree, climbing agile and loose, only paying attention to the best way to cut the branch or reach the limb. His thin legs wrapped and propped against bark, and Darnell would stop to hold his breath, when he was very small, first coming to work. A splintery piece of bitter bark had fallen into his open mouth once; Melvin had laughed.

He loaded the trimmings and sat in the El Camino a minute to cool off.

Juan and José were in the back; he heard the mowers. This was the Stonehaven tract, where they had the most yards so far, and the houses had wedge-shaped lots with tiny front yards. "I'ma edge this one," Darnell said to himself, and he was standing in the driveway, concentrating on the spinning wire of the weed whacker, when he saw the shadow across the cement.

"Excuse me," the man said. His face was pale and unshaven, and he wore slippers. "Do you work for Tuan's Landscaping?"

Darnell's heart boomed like Gas's speakers were inside him. He nodded toward the El Camino. "Yeah," he said to the frown, making his voice deep.

The frown deepened, and Darnell was tempted to look down the driveway or at the man's feet, as he always had when someone talked to his father, but he raised his eyes to the short hairs on the jaw. "I thought his workers were Oriental?" the man said hesitantly, and Darnell thought, *Cojones,* just like you talkin to Vernon.

"You know, he doesn't really like that word. Oriental. It's the opposite of Occidental, and that means, like, Europeans gotta be the center of the world. Callin somebody Oriental isn't as bad as, like, nigger," he said, looking into the gray eyes. "But it's not really acceptable, you know what I'm sayin? The guys prefer Asian."

"Uh-huh," the man said, sweeping his eyes over the grass, looking at the truck.

"The Asian dudes are in the back," Darnell said. "But I could help you with somethin specific." The man met his eyes and nodded slowly.

"I guess I'ma have to use that one again," he told Roscoe, in his father's back room. "Can't tell if it worked until somebody call up and complain. And then they gon be talkin to Tuan." He grinned. "I guess I could say, 'My worker's black? I had no idea!'"

Roscoe narrowed his eyes. "Don't get too full of yourself."

Darnell closed his mouth. "Yeah. Okay." He saw his father's shadow in the doorway, and he took out his wallet when his father sat at the table with them. Darnell had come early, to try and catch them before the other men finished eating and came over to cool off in the driveway. "Here," Darnell said.

"I knew you weren't a bad risk," Roscoe said, when Darnell handed him the hundred dollars.

"First installment," Darnell said. He watched the twenties in Roscoe's hand. Brenda hadn't asked him at all about what he was making now; she saw him pull out twenties for milk, diapers, garlic salt. He needed to give this money to Roscoe so he could ask his father the next question.

"You gon cosign with me on a truck?" His father was working mink oil into his boots; he always complained about how new ones fit, and tried to hold on to each pair forever.

The knuckles glistened slightly, didn't stop moving when he said, "You ain't got that many accounts yet."

"Gettin there," Darnell said. "If Juan and José got a truck, I can paint the name on the door, send them out. And I can use the El Camino for side jobs with Victor and Ronnie."

"You serious, huh?" His father's eyebrows stretched wide under the forehead lines, and Roscoe sat back, folding his arms.

"Serious as a heart attack," Darnell said. "I need to get this goin. I'm still gettin calls, and you see the new tracts. Everybody runnin from LA out here."

His father was silent; just the dry-husking sound of the fingers brushing dust off the boot heel before the oil went into the leather. Darnell said, "Just like Nacho told me, they all want their yards done Friday, so the weekend is cool for them. Maintained." He paused, staring at the vapor sliding up into the air outside the open door, the heat rising from the cement slab. "Most of these dudes call at night, so you know they're hardly ever home during the day. I heard half of em do their shoppin and eatin in Orange County or LA. Bought the house out here cause it was cheap, but they don't even like to claim they live in Rio Seco. Nobody's out when I cruise Grayglen. They don't care who's cuttin the grass—they don't even have to look out the window, just hear the mower."

"Juan and José." Roscoe shook his head.

"Hey, I don't look like you guys, like you used to," Darnell said, hard. He rushed on, before his father could speak. "These guys, in these tracts, they want somebody . . ." He ran his tongue over his teeth. "I showed Juan and José how to fertilize today. Got some a that granular stuff from Nacho."

In the long silence, they could hear all the swamp coolers vibrating in the backyards, even this late in the fall; they could hear Sophia and Paula laugh at Charolette, who was talking to ants near the sidewalk. Darnell's father said, "Now I gotta cosign for a damn truck. I ain't never finished."

"And I'm just startin, okay?" Darnell said. "So give me a break."

Charolette and Hollie played in the bed of the Toyota truck. Darnell had kept it parked in his father's driveway after work, since there was no room at the apartment complex. He and Roscoe leaned against the Apache, watching the girls. Charolette sang out, "Mit-su-bi-shi!"

"It's a Toyota," Hollie said scornfully, her braids falling over her shoulders when she bent over the gate to touch the big letters.

"What'd we look at? A Ford, Isuzu, the Mitsubishi and this one," Darnell said to Roscoe. "And she didn't care about the prices. Just the words."

"I like her instincts," Roscoe said. "The sounds are important."

Darnell sat in the shade, watching the girls. Their hair glistened when they bent, heads together, to line pebbles on the rim of the truckbed. "Daddy throw rocks," Charolette said. He couldn't believe how much she talked now, imitating everything his sisters or Hollie said.

"No, he don't throw no rocks," Hollie said. "You ain't allowed."

"Little rocks," Charolette said, her head disappearing.

Darnell drank his soda. He heard his father talking to someone in the back. Don't get bigheaded. His heart had felt too large for his chest long after the man had gone back inside. Who cares? We got more yards now, Juan and José happy cause they workin three days, and I ain't gotta do much more with them cause they know enough. Almost time to trim trees with Pops, plant bare-root fruit trees. Roscoe said trees are dyin cause of the drought, and people want unthirsty ones.

He ran the condensation from the can around his hairline, cool circling. You know you were scared, man, he thought. Don't try to front. His father came through the sideyard then, and Charolette yelled, "Pop-Pop!"

His father gave her a hug and stood looking at Nacho's lettering on the truck doors. Tuan's Landscape Maintenance. Above the words was the small lantern, and below was Darnell's phone number.

"Go on in the house with Granny," his father said, lifting the girls out of the truck. "Me and Daddy be right back," he told Charolette.

Darnell pulled out of the driveway, his father listening to the engine. "You gotta pay their worker's comp," his father said shortly. "Go on down to Jackson Park."

Darnell headed that way. "Yeah, I checked out some papers Brenda brought me."

His father spat out the window. "Taxes and all that don't mean nothin to workers like your guys," he said. "They want to go back home to Mexico someday, huh?"

Darnell shrugged. "Maybe José. But Juan wants to stay."

His father nodded. "Right now, they ain't in the system, they ain't gettin no benefit from taxes. But it ain't fair to leave somebody hangin if they get hurt workin for you. You gotta set somethin up."

"Yeah," Darnell said. He cruised slowly up to Jackson Park, going the back way by the church, and his father said, "Stop here for a minute."

When they got out, his father looked into the church door, and Darnell saw the dancing candle flames in the dim inside beyond his father's shoulder. He turned away to see the evening start to gather in the pepper trees across the park, where the fire was already started.

His father was watching him. "You ready to take your Asian truck over there? Lotta black eyes to see you, read that paint."

Darnell folded his arms. "Yeah. Victor and Ronnie gon see it. If they don't want to work no side jobs with me, I can get another brothaman."

His father mashed his lips tight, working his tongue into his jaw. "How long you gon keep up this lyin?"

Darnell cocked his head to the side. "All them years when I went with you, every time Mrs. Panadoukis or somebody came out, you was smilin like you had gas, noddin and sayin, 'Yes, ma'am.' That was a lie, cause you wasn't in a good mood. I didn't see her tellin no funny jokes, but you was just grinnin away."

"Wasn't no lie when I got the check," his father said.

"Then you know what I'm talkin about. And ain't no lie when I get my checks, neither."

"Come over here," his father said, walking past the low wall toward the vacant lot. They crossed the dirt, stepping on the fist-sized clods left by the city tractor when it plowed the weeds under. Close to the boarded-up houses where the zombies had peered out at them, the last two houses in the gapped row, his father stopped at a faint square left in the dirt from a crumbled foundation.

They stood in the center of the tiny rectangle, the concrete rim around them, tall weeds still untouched from here all the way to the men around the fire. The dozer couldn't hit all this concrete. Darnell looked at the church in the falling light, and he realized where they stood. He hadn't been here in a long time.

"Your Granny Zelene's old house," his father said, nodding. "Remember when they bulldozed them three houses, the ones they condemned? Long time ago."

Darnell squatted down on the square where the old fireplace had been. It looked so small under his boots. "I forgot how little it was," he said. "Cause I was little."

"You used to hang on her every word, and all she talked about was death," his father said, bending on one knee, too. "That was her specialty. Roscoe always talkin about poetry, and I never said much about nothin. But Zelene could talk about death for days. She was sure a twin got lost when your mother was pregnant with you, and she had your mother so scared she was afraid to move, afraid to eat anything Zelene didn't like her to."

Darnell looked down at the dried wild oats and filaree, burned brown, near his knee. He remembered the altars, the candles, the flowers, and smell of wax and pollen.

"It ain't all downhill from here," his father said sharply. "Don't go thinkin you smart and you pullin it all off. Lotta men smiled on the trains. Your great-uncle was a Pullman porter, and he smiled plenty. You smilin different, but you ain't done."

"Never said I was," Darnell started, but his father kept on.

"Zelene used to work sugar cane in Louisiana. You ain't worked hard as her, and she was a woman. Sugar cane kill you," his father said, staring off toward the church.

Cane sugar, Darnell thought. Leon's product—all these faces hidin in the porches down the street workin hard for some cane sugar. Rock cane candy. Sprung hard. His father motioned him over to where he'd walked, just outside the cement foundation marks.

"I ain't sure where it was exactly, but I know it was in the yard somewhere," his father mumbled, and Darnell saw him stand near a baby tumbleweed growing new-dark in a circle. "Your mama was still in the hospital; you were just a few hours old. I had been workin some job out in San Bernardino, and when I got home Zelene was there. She said she helped your mama at the hospital, cause it was just county ward and didn't nobody pay much attention to her. Zelene was talkin about this twin; she was sure a twin got lost, but she said you had a caul over your eyes when you was born."

Darnell frowned, looking down at the tumbleweed again. "A caul?"

"Somethin like, I don't know, I never seen one, but it's supposed to be like a smoky kinda web over your face, over some babies' faces when they just come out." His father stroked his jaw with black-rimmed fingernails. "Zelene said she took it, said she seen a sign in it, and she buried it in the yard out here by her house." He paused. "She did things the old way, like my granny did. She buried your navel string here, too. That's how they used to do, for luck, for the spirits they believed in."

"What was a caul supposed to do?" Darnell tried to imagine how it would have looked, but all he could remember of Charolette's birth was the blood, the red smears on her body, on the bed, on Brenda's thighs. He winced, feeling saliva trickle in his throat.

"Caul was supposed to mean you could see things other people couldn't," his father said, standing up slowly, clenching and unclenching his hands. "I never seen you act strange except around a damn fire. I ain't countin that night down in the riverbottom."

Darnell tried to keep his voice steady-light. "Can't see much fire right now. Only smoke comin out the mower, that lousy old one."

His father still stared at the baby palm tree near them. "You see somethin special when you were up there? In the canyons?"

Darnell shrugged. How could he explain the sound, the tremble, the flash of warmth that ran all the way to his knuckles? He glanced at the figures moving through the alley on the other side of the park. Ask one a them sprung guys—that's probably how it feels. His father looked at him, and he said, "You saw the newspaper: CDF laid off seasonals early this year. October. No money."

"So you applyin for next year?" his father said.

Darnell held his face flat, still. "Maybe—I was thinkin of applyin for paid call reserve. I can't go seasonal, but if this business works out, my funds are cool, I might get the papers."

His father lifted his eyes to the crowd of men near the trash barrel and the domino game. "You ain't out the woods yet," he said, grinning slightly, and Darnell shook his head.

"I hate when you and Roscoe do them puns," he said.

"We gotta talk to Victor," his father said. "You want to walk over there, so they don't see the truck?"

Darnell looked down at the crumbled cement, picked up a chunk. "Hell, no," he said, starting back toward the church.

The gray lump on the dashboard, he drove up to the small street near the domino game, leaning out the open window. "Victor!" he called, and Victor strolled over to the truck, checking out the doors, the cab, leaning into the window.

"Brothaman," he said to Darnell. "Mr. Tucker," he said.

"Need you to take out a eucalyptus," Darnell said. "Where's Ronnie?"

"He went to LA to visit his gramma," Victor said. He looked down at Darnell. "So who hirin me? Tuan?"

Darnell's father laughed. "One-day job. Andrew Jackson hirin you. And I'm talkin be here early—not no leisure hours."

Darnell stuck out his hand, and Victor touched his palm lightly. "See you then," Victor said, his eyes half closed. "Homey."

"Can you drop us home, Pops?" he said in the driveway. "Brenda took the El Camino so she could get her hair done after work. I can't park the Toyota on the street downtown."

"She can't ride in the big truck," his father started, but Darnell held up the car seat he kept in his mother's living room now.

"She's portable," he said.

She chattered all the way home, and Darnell held leftover monkey bread wrapped in foil on his lap. His father was quiet until he pulled into the courtyard of the apartment, and then he squinted at the threads and yarn dangling from the railing. "What the hell is that?"

"Charolette," Darnell said, and she grinned, pointed up. The threads were fluttering from the bars, tied in knots, and the purple yarn was in bows. Brenda had been showing her bows.

His father frowned. "I saw somethin on TV, some show about a mountain country, and people tie rags on trees and bushes. Like that. They supposed to be prayers." He shook his head. "I know your landlord ain't thrilled. Y'all need to get a house. With a yard."

"I gotta get out the woods first," Darnell said, pulling Charolette out of the cab. He lifted her to touch the threads moving slightly in the breeze, the ends that dangled dancing above the carport.

Juan drove the truck around the corner, and José dropped the gate and walked the mowers down the wooden plank. They worked systematically through the tract, and on the last street Darnell helped them load the burlap sacks of trimmings into the back. He put the edgers and blower into the El Camino and sat in the cab to mark the schedule while Juan and José loaded the mowers. Darnell saw Trent's white truck pull in behind him, and he got out.

"Tuan!" Trent said, smiling, and Darnell set his mouth carefully, waiting. But Trent said, "I can't believe you, man!" and shook his head admiringly. "I didn't think you had it in you. Nacho told me about this flyer, and I remembered getting a few. Hey, did you get those two new jobs way up in Grayglen, back in the big-money hills?"

"What two jobs?" Darnell said, still cautious, remembering the vodka and Trent's slurry voice talking about haircuts, voices.

"I just did two custom jobs, and when I was done, I told the people they should hire Tuan's for the maintenance. That Asian stuff cracks me up—they love it." Trent opened his palms to the sky, leaning out the window. "You're an entrepreneur, got the pager and all."

"Just tryin to make it," Darnell said. "Thanks for the referrals."

"I'm glad to see you aren't into self-destruction like your old running buddies. Man, Louis, Donnie, Leon, all of em pitiful." Darnell drew his head back from the window. Brothaman, he thought, your definition of . . . But before he could speak, Trent went on. "I got something big for you and your crew, if you want it. Mrs. Shaefer, the big property? She wants a drought-resistant garden installed."

Darnell folded his arms. "I usually do side jobs with Victor and Ronnie, man. Anything off the route I stay with that crew."

Trent wrapped his hands around the steering wheel and looked through the windshield. "Hey—that crew isn't really comfortable working with me, okay? It's your choice. Can your guys here plant? I mean, have they done it?"

Darnell pictured Juan and José planting rows of chiles, corn. "Yeah," he said. "This crew can plant."

When Juan and Trent had both driven off, he sat for a moment, staring at the list of names and addresses, thinking of the money. He started up the El Camino and headed out to Woodbine. But the engine stalled after the second stop sign, and he couldn't get it to turn over again. Damn—the El Camino had gotten vapor lock a few times. He threw his head back and stared at the stained material on the ceiling. And Juan got the good hooptie. He grinned. Tuan's truck. He slammed the door and started walking.

Cars sped past, and he stayed far to the shoulder near the block walls of this development. No phone booth for a long way—not till I come to the commercial strip down there. He trudged along, heard a car cruise to a stop. Gots to be patrol, he thought.

He heard the radio. "What's wrong with your El Camino?" the voice said.

Yeah, I know you were scopin it hard, Darnell thought, turning. It was Kleiser, and Darnell couldn't tell what was in the grin.

Kleiser ducked his face low to see Darnell. "So the other guys got your white truck?" he said. "Lemme take you to a phone booth."

Darnell stared at the patrol car, heard the radio spitting. "I can walk, man, if you got things to do."

"Come on," Kleiser said. Darnell sat in the front seat, staring at the ribbon of road, trying not to see the eyes of approaching drivers. Shit—Pops happen to see me in here, he have a heart attack. "You got a beeper, huh?" Kleiser said.

Darnell stiffened. Yup—there it is. You know what, man? The hospital rents out beepers, for your wife's last month. I remember. But me—no, I'm slingin, huh? Rock daddy. Normal for a nigga. Kleiser spoke again before he opened his mouth. "I saw you, saw the truck. But you don't spell it like your middle name."

Darnell felt the web of tingling lift from his scalp. Antoine. He know my middle name from the reports. He glanced over at Kleiser's half-grin. "I spelled it different."

"Yeah. I got one of the flyers, too, and I put it together. I live in Stonehaven, man, so I had my wife call. You guys been doin our yard for a few weeks now." Kleiser's teeth showed full now. "Your using your middle name is slick. I got a friend with a tow truck uses a different name."

"Oh, yeah?" Darnell said carefully. They pulled up at the 7-Eleven at the bottom of the long slope, and Darnell scanned the parking lot, but no one looked at him when Kleiser got out, too.

In the phone booth, Kleiser said, "Here he is. Just who you need. Check it out—Aaron's Towing." Darnell looked at the ad. "When you call him, this guy named Jamey Wilson will answer. We went to school together, out in San Bernardino. If you go, 'Is Aaron there?' he'll go, 'No, he's out, but I can help you.' Cause his name is Wilson, so he'd be last in the phone book, but now he's first. You guys are pretty slick."

Kleiser backed out of the booth, looking around the lot. "I gotta go, but I'll cruise up past your El Camino so nobody steals your stuff. Call Aaron's, man, he'll get you." The grin faded, and Kleiser looked

down at the trash-littered asphalt. "Hey, I heard your friend left town
for a while. I won't tell nobody I saw you, okay?" He glanced back
again. "I'm real sorry, man, I still am."

Darnell stood inside the phone booth. What am I supposed to say?
It's a scar. I fall out sometimes. That drama gotta be over. He heard
wheels turn into the street, and he looked down at the A names in
the yellow pages.

On All Saints' Day he took Brenda and Charolette to meet Mrs.
Batiste. Charolette clutched her plastic pumpkin with the few pieces
of candy she'd gotten from touring the apartment complex. Brenda
and her mother cleaned the headstones, their voices too soft for him
to hear. He stared at the etched name growing blurry. Antoine.

Brenda held up a pecan. "Guess who been finding these everywhere?" she said, and her mother took the pecan to smell it.

"I ain't been to the riverbottom for pecans in so long," she said,
and Charolette held out her hand with another one.

"Daddy! Birdy drop." He looked at the pale brown shell with
lengthwise tiger stripes, remembering how Louis always held the first
few nuts in his huge palm. He hadn't realized how many months had
passed since Louis had gone to prison. Charolette dug through pine
needles, looking for more pecans. Louis used to watch the flock stream
over while they were raking leaves and stacking wood after school;
he always said the pecans weren't ripe until the crows hid the first
fat ones for later, pushing the nuts into loose piles of dirt and stems.

He ate the soft gold nut, but Charolette spit it out. "Birdy eat,"
she said, brushing off her tongue.

He held the jagged edges of the shell. "Me and Mama's friend used
to watch the crows. They fly real high and drop the nut on the street
so it'll crack."

"Then they can get the nut out with their beaks," Brenda said. She
looked at Darnell. "I guess Roscoe's gonna be sad now, all fall, with
the crows and the blackbirds."

Mrs. Batiste nodded. "He done lost a child for a while."

"No," Darnell said. "I think Roscoe feels like him and Louis might
never talk again. Like they strangers now."

"Like me and Daddy," Brenda whispered, and her mother's eyes
filled with tears.

"That's my fault," Darnell said. "But it ain't gotta be like that forever. I know he gotta come around." He tried to change the subject back to Louis. "Remember Roscoe was so hard on Louis? My pops hard on me, too."

But Brenda's face was blurred with sadness, and she scooped up Charolette, tucking her head near Charolette's neck. "Pop-Pop hammer," Charolette said, still holding another pecan.

On the next Saturday, his parents and his sisters followed in the big truck, and Darnell drove toward the grove, pointing out the window so Charolette could see the riverbottom. Brenda said, "Your mother said she doesn't remember the last time she was out here."

"Been a long time," Darnell said. The bridge over the river was sharply outlined farther down, and when he came out on the dirt road that ran along the levee, where the concrete chunks were high, he could see the thin strip of water, narrow from the drought. The cane and arrowroot had been pushed back, bulldozed by the city, to keep the fire hazard down, but already they were creeping across the sand again, almost as lush as when Leon had driven him here to see the fire.

When they had parked in the dirt clearing and begun to walk, Sophia grumbled, "We need to be walkin at the mall, not out here in the dirt."

The huge, arching branches came into view, and Paula said, "Okay, now I remember. We used to bring picnics sometimes, right, Daddy?"

Darnell's father said, "Your mama used to make a lot more pies," and she glanced at him sharply.

"Your mama used to be shellin them pecans way into the night like a fool," she said, and then she and Brenda laughed as Charolette ran forward waving her hands and yelling at the crows.

Other families were in far parts of the grove. Darnell saw a few old, dark women with broad-brimmed straw hats. Mrs. Strozier, from DaVinci Street, and her sister. Even Nacho's Aint Rosa was way down the line, with one of her nieces. And Mexican families were everywhere, the women filling transparent plastic grocery bags, the men poking with long sticks, the kids running over to look closely at Charolette, the way kids did.

His sisters went on ahead, holding Charolette's hands, and Darnell's father said, "They didn't even want to come, cause two things missin: boys and clothes hangin on a rack. Now look."

They squatted beneath one tree in the long rows, probing the leaf litter, and Charolette held up a long pecan like a prize.

Darnell's father sat in the dappled shade, his back against a trunk. "You used to always do that, all three of you," he said to Darnell. He nodded toward the boys facing a tree at the far end of the grove. "You and Melvin and Louis loved to pee behind a tree."

Darnell watched the boys disappear into the brush that led to the river, the dry arrowroot that had grown taller than them. He stared at the dead cottonwood, gnarled black trunk and stark branches, in the brush, and he couldn't help wondering whether the fires would start again in late spring. I'ma apply this year, he thought suddenly. It's time. I'ma try for paid call reserve. He heard shouting, and Brenda's face, above Charolette's, turned toward him. His mother was covering her mouth, shoulders shaking with laughter, and Charolette's shirt front was stuffed bumpy with pecans.

The first serious wind came through a few weeks later, when he was helping Roscoe trim an old fruitless mulberry in the historic district. His father was in the tree, cutting the long, arrow-straight branches off, leaving huge fist-blunt knobs on the trunk. "She ain't had this tree done for three years," Roscoe grumbled.

"Pops swayin around up there," Darnell said, his head thrown back. The gusty wind tore away the sound of the chain saw.

"Gotta have wind before rain," Roscoe said.

"What?"

"You can't mop a dirty floor—not before you vacuum it. Wind clear all the big trash out, and the rain wash it down."

Darnell said, "I didn't know you was into housework, man. Must be your female nature tryin to sneak out."

But Roscoe gave him a hard look. "My father nature, fool. Who you think cleaned up after Louis—the fairy maid mother?" He walked over to a bundle of branches and tightened the rope.

Darnell thought, How can I tell him? He had another pecan in his pocket; Charolette kept handing them to him now, every day. He'd been looking for the right moment to hand it to Roscoe. But toward afternoon, whenever Darnell saw him, he was watching the crows with his tongue pushed far into his jaw. Sometimes he seemed happier, softer around the middle, because of Marietta Cook, but whenever Darnell tried to talk about Louis, Roscoe said the name like it was only a memory.

Darnell said, "You know when Louis gets out?" He thought of Leon, saying that someone who looked like Louis might be cruising the streets, packing a serious weapon.

"How would I know?" Roscoe said evenly. "The newspaper doesn't write about young black men coming out. Only going in." He went to the Apache for his coffee.

Darnell watched his father move his boots around in the tree, step lightly for position, and heard the whine of the chain saw again. He said, "I want to ask you somethin, okay? Don't get pissed." Roscoe nodded, his mouth on the cup, his eyes half hidden. Darnell licked his lips. "If you lose somebody, like all the way, is it better if you forget or remember?" Roscoe was silent, and Darnell rushed on. "If I lost Charolette, like I dream about somebody takin her and I'm not watchin, and if she was gone, I wouldn't take away all her pictures and toys and stuff. I'd want to think about her every day. Like, pass the trees she always talks about, stop at the trains, and keep the soup ladle. Say 'Mitsubishi' and 'Honolulu' sometimes."

Roscoe said, "But you haven't lost her. And she wasn't selling something that kills people. So you don't know. You can't even pretend to know." He turned to put the cup on the dashboard, keeping his back to Darnell, and Darnell went toward the tree to drag the long mulberry branches. Him and Louis. My pops and Melvin. Brenda and her daddy. I can't see it. Gotta be somethin left, somethin still there.

He bundled the branches tightly while more fell slanted from his father's hand, high in the tree. When he packed the thick stack into the truckbed, Roscoe said, "He'll get out early. Maybe in May or June. I had to call the county to find out. I don't know where he'll go." He walked toward the curb.

Darnell went over the riverbottom on the freeway bridge, seeing a thin, weak column of smoke rise from the wild grapevine covering a bamboo stand. Just cooking smoke—it was cold now, early on Sunday morning, and some homeless guy must have been making breakfast. Another man walked along the bridge, carrying a water jug. Lotta guys tryin to keep warm inside that arundo cane, he thought. He remembered the swaying-round stems, the smell from the willows rising sharp where the sand was damp, his father's big hands on the gun.

The wind had blown all night, was still blowing now. Tumbleweeds tore out of the fields and stacked up against the chain-link freeway fence, sometimes twirling on the asphalt in front of him. He could see almost to LA on the horizon, but the exit sign for Chino was right in front of him now.

Chino—he'd avoided coming here for longer than Louis had been incarcerated. All the brothas doin time here, workin here, he thought. Not me. He swallowed hard at the light, hearing the noise of the jail that one night he'd been there, for the ticket. The cop in Grayglen, stopping him and Victor and Ronnie—he could have found a violation somewhere, given them a ticket. General principles. Probable cause. Who was it, one of Melvin's friends that used to say, laughing, "Yeah, man, Probable Cause my middle name."

Euclid Avenue. Chino. He drove past two Mexican guys with machetes chopping tumbleweeds near a white-fenced dairy farm, swinging smooth, and he ached for the fire station, for the jobs they'd all complained about. Tumbleweeds, clearing fields and chopping brush, digging the roads out. He let his eyes blur for a moment; he hadn't gone yet to pick up the application for paid call.

Shivering, waiting in the line of cars turning into the prison, he looked off into the distance. New housing tracts lined the low hills, moving east of LA. The signs near the avenue directed people to the developments: Collage, Summer Hills, Tango. Arrows pointed toward the red-tile roofs.

The truck moved forward, and he saw the thin-trunked trees surrounding the high fence, breaking for the entrance. All this time, he thought, I never came out here. Didn't want to see it. Carceration time. He drove slowly over the speed bumps, approached the guard shack. How many guys I know doin time? Workin out, gettin them big arms, doin road camp. Soledad—where Danny Smith been since I went to junior high. San Q. Folsom—I passed it in the Lincoln.

He walked toward the glass doors, seeing the new irrigation

trenches dug in the long lawn, the petunias and marigolds in the circular flower beds wet with sprinkled water.

Inside, people were gathered in the big visiting room. Brothas pacin everywhere, Darnell thought, seeing the guards, the prisoners, the visitors. He waited at one of the circular tables, trying not to look around, and a skinny guy with long braids clapped him on the back. "Yo, what up, D.?"

Darnell looked up into Tommy's face. "Not much, man. How you doin?"

"Livin, man, livin medium. Who you come to see?"

"Birdman," Darnell said, using Louis's nickname, the famous one.

"I seen him once or twice," Tommy nodded. "Big place. But he what—six-seven? He tower over most of the dudes when we walkin." Tommy found a face across the room and said, "Later, man. Peace."

Louis sat down in the folding chair, his body long and stiff as a two-by-eight slanted across the metal seat. His feet were boats in the black prison shoes. "You didn't have to come, man. It ain't like we been tight for a while. I don't like nobody comin over here."

"Donnie told me," Darnell said. "But Brenda wanted to tell you hey, and see how you doin."

Louis's face was the same, pale brown, and his hair was short-cropped. He smiled slightly. "She still skinny, after the baby?"

"Yeah."

"Her hair still long?"

"Yeah. But she got bangs now." He waited for Louis to ask about Charolette, but Louis was silent then, folding his arms. Now what? Darnell thought. You don't have a message from his pops. You can't just bust out and ask about what Leon said.

"Been diggin fire roads?" Louis said, nodding at Darnell's callused fingers.

Darnell bit the inside of his cheek. "Nope. Cuttin grass, trimmin trees. Doin some jobs with Pops and your dad, but mostly this." He pulled out one of the new flyers, the last version Nacho had printed: ANTUAN'S LANDSCAPE MAINTENANCE. He'd left off all references to Asian, keeping only the lantern and bridge, and he figured that was enough. "Cold out there now," he said casually.

Louis snorted. "Yeah, how could I forget them freezin windy days on the truck with Pops? And then he expect me to shoot free throws in the driveway all night, so I can keep up my game." He drummed his fingers on the table. "I'm glad Pops don't come around here talkin about I threw away my career. That line was tired first time he said it."

"Man, you left the county, then I was gone, and now we both back." Darnell put his hands over the fake-wood grain, smelling the school aroma of wet palms. "My pops just as hard on me. Your pops think about you. They just don't know how to talk."

Louis shrugged. "All I hear in here is talk. Talk all day." Darnell glanced around at the inmates, laughing, leaning close and serious into visiting faces, black, brown, all their shoulders the same under blue shirts. Louis saw him look at the only white guys, four with brown hair. "Caspers got it serious hard in here."

"What about you?" Darnell asked.

Louis closed his face again. "I got three meals. Ain't no thang. I'm by myself mostly—cool with me. Stay in the library, read about birds. I'm tired of all that palaver."

Darnell knew he was talking about Leon, Vernon, the consultant— the constant talking. The Bronco, the park. Portland. He said, "I seen Rob, man. Went to Portland."

Louis leaned forward. "*You?* What you take?"

"Jeans."

Louis shook his head. "You workin for Leon?"

Darnell rubbed the table. "I did one job. An odd job. What *you* take?"

Louis smiled so slightly that his lips didn't even move his thin cheeks. "I didn't take nothin."

"You pulled trey," Darnell said.

Louis shrugged. "So Leon sent you here, huh? He want to know what happened? Fuck Leon. If you workin for him, make up your own scenario."

Darnell shook his head. "No, man, Leon don't even know I'm here. I ain't seen him for a while. You see my business." He pointed to the flyer. "I go to work. I pick up pecans with my kid. I wanted to bring you one for old times, but I figured that ain't allowed."

Louis flinched. "Yeah." He sat back in his chair and scratched his wrist. "You go down there to the grove?" he said, almost whispering.

"Brenda and I took Charolette," Darnell said, and then he stopped, not wanting to tell Louis about the shade, the crows shrieking in the distance, where they'd been chased by the girls. He leaned closer. "Louis—last time I saw him, Leon was talkin about nubbin big time with some dudes from LA. Some tall, light brotha is supposed to be doin the Wild Wild West, and Leon think it's you, lookin for payback."

Louis half closed his eyes. "Plenty of tall, light brothas in the world. Ax Pops—they all playin ball except me. Lotta brothas play ball in here, too. Not me."

"Come on, man. I'm not askin you about that. I'm askin what happened."

Louis finally leaned forward on the table, too, like he was afraid for anyone to hear him. "This ain't nothin but trey, you know? I just migrate from the yard to the food, wherever they tell me to go. Whole flock of us. Walk in a flock. If I told Leon how I—what happened—he'd go off."

Darnell jerked the coldness from his back so he wouldn't shiver, thinking of what Roscoe had said. "Look. You gon get out soon, right? Leon think you were tryin to move the product to somebody else."

Louis shrugged. "When I get out, I might go up north. Way north. They got more wildlife up there, got forests where I went to school. I didn't have time to check out the trees cause I was always havin to play ball."

"Donnie went back up north," Darnell said. "Where he played ball."

"And you ain't goin back up to the hills," Louis said, smiling, "cause you doin the daddy thang."

"You did it," Darnell said, thinking of Roscoe and Hollie.

Louis shook his head. "No, man, Geanie did it to me. She wasn't even fuckin me—she was fuckin a ballplayer. Everybody else was trippin daily when I got back to town: 'Why you ain't playin ball no more, a brotha your size?'" He paused. "Leon never axed." He smiled slightly. "So she a girl. She look like Brenda?"

Darnell realized who he was talking about. "No, man, Charolette look dead like me, but lighter."

"Oh, man, I feel sorry for the girl. Brenda's beautiful. You ain't."

Darnell whispered, "But she got all my blood cells, she notice the

same things as me." He smiled. "She like trees, man, and birds." He
leaned forward again. "You ever had somebody know every move you
gon make, listen to whatever you say, like you God?" He leaned back
again, embarrassed.

"That's heavy, brothaman," Louis said, mocking. "But that's a lotta
weight, cause you could mess up big time. You could make her do
things she don't want to do, cause you *think* she you, but she really
ain't." He stared at Darnell, then stood up, looking around at the rest
of the heads bobbing close in the big room.

Darnell drove past the cows, thinking that Charolette would be
pointing and naming everything, thinking of basketball and the slapping sounds of Louis practicing free throws into the night while Roscoe
watched. Back when Brenda had lived two doors down from Louis,
when her back was curved, hid in the pyracantha, waiting for him
while Louis stopped looking to watch two crows fight a mockingbird
on a telephone pole.

In Rio Seco, he drove all the way through the city and past the
Ville, up the Sugar Ridge to the flat place, empty now because it
was late afternoon, too early and too windy for serious drinking. He
walked around the powdery-dust lot littered with glass and cigarette
butts and rubbers like shed snakeskins. The wind shuddered in the
brittlebush.

José rarely said more than "It's okay?" He would point at the cut
grass, the gas gauge, the receipt for the dump fee. He spoke quietly
to Juan, usually had Juan interpret for him. His face was almost always
a thin mask; his small slanted eyes, straight-combed hair, and pointed
chin bobbed above the mower handle.

It was hard to tell how old he was. Darnell and Juan could talk
about nearly anything now, still in broken phrases, but José looked
like the kind of guy who didn't talk much in Spanish, either.

Close to Christmas, Juan seemed to watch his brother closely, and
Darnell waited until they'd finished, late one evening, and he was
dropping them off at their place, to ask.

"You go home now?" Juan said, and José got out, standing in the
yard to stare at the lights.

"Yeah," Darnell said. "My brother wants me to pick up two bikes,
for his kids. I'ma hide em at my house." They both watched the

blinking lights travel up the wires strung to the palm trees in the yard across from Juan and José's. This whole block, almost all Mexican, was sparkling with tiny pointed bulbs strung on crosses, bushes, trees, and roofs.

"What's wrong with your brother?" Darnell asked, figuring that since he'd brought up his brother he might as well ask. "He looks, I don't know, like he wants to run away, go back home or somethin."

Juan's face turned color, and his teeth sparkled with the changing lights. "*Navidad*. José is sad from this time for two years. His wife, she is having a baby, and he doesn't know. He work on a farm, far away. I am in college. And he come home from the *posada* in the village, and she die. She have a fever."

José didn't even peer into the truck to see what was taking so long; like always, he stood patiently, dreamily, his face so still only his eyes moved with the rocking Santa on the roof.

"Why you didn't take her to a doctor?" Darnell said, gripping the wheel. He thought of Brenda lying in bed silent, the pains strong. He saw the baby candles in GranaLene's church.

"We need travel for doctor," Juan said, slowly. "We have *curandero*, like, I don't know." He stopped. "For pray."

Like Mrs. Batiste leaning over him, the smoke and prayers and heat. "It didn't work?"

Juan shook his head. "José the oldest. He is twenty-nine. I am only twenty. And he ask me to come away." Juan moved across the seat now, his face down, embarrassed. Then he stopped at the door frame and said quickly, "But José is not sad to work. I don't mean . . . we send the money. He does not change." He turned and said something low in Spanish to José, who nodded and tried to smile at Darnell.

Juan said brightly, "We have the big lady tomorrow, yes? You are come?"

Darnell nodded. "The big property. Yeah." He drove away, saw Juan pause with José in the dirt yard, pointing at the roof Santa.

On the way back to the house, drizzle started to collect on the windshield. Must be a teaser, he thought, cause the clouds aren't even droppin down. But someone had known it would rain, because when he stopped at Pepper Avenue, he saw two figures walking slowly, like they'd been expecting moisture before they started out. Roscoe and Marietta didn't see him; their heads were close, their shoulders touching.

He was in a deep sleep when he felt Charolette's breath in his face. She could climb out of the crib now. "Daddy, what noise?"

"Me poppin your butt you don't go back to sleep," he said.

"What *noise?*" she said again, cocking her head, and he heard the dripping from roofs onto the courtyard.

"Rain," he said. "Somethin you ain't seen." He let her look out the front window, pressing her nose against the glass to see the water fall in a thin veil off the opposite railing. Finally, he got her back to bed, but instead of being pissed because he was awake, he sat in the dark, looking at the light rain, so sparse a thin beam of dry air stayed under the streetlamp.

Brenda said near his neck, "You didn't strangle her, did you? That why she's so quiet?" She put her arms around his shoulders to see. "I forgot how noisy rain is."

Darnell said, "Used to rain hard for five, six days, flood the Hollows."

"It never rains like that now, cause of the ozone or whatever," she said. "Look at the Christmas lights in the street."

He stared at the blurred, Jell-O–bright circles wavering in the water on the asphalt and cement. "No long rain for six years. No torchin trails again."

"You loved that magical torching," she said, but he didn't hear any resentment in her voice, only a grin pressed against his shoulder. Yeah, she think I'm done. She rested her cheek on his back, and he watched the glistening lights flash.

"I went to see Louis," he said. He felt her chest fill with air, lift against him. "He's doin okay. He might get out this summer." Darnell looked toward the corner where Roscoe and Marietta had walked. Brenda stayed still, her wrists under his chin, and he thought, I don't want to tell her about what Louis said. Birdman. Nature Boy—not me. Not yet. I'ma get the application, but I don't want a fight. Not right now.

The moisture only wet up the first two or three inches of dirt, and he slid down the steep bank at Mrs. Shaefer's, his boots scraping in the still-dry earth under the crust. Charolette sat by the koi pond near the house, watching the gold and white fish slash through the water. She had her apple juice in a sipper bottle like Darnell's, and Trent thought this was hilarious.

"She looks so old like that," Trent said.

"She'll be two in a couple months," Darnell said. He watched her move the three plumes of fountain grass Mrs. Shaefer had given her; she swept the edge of the rocks near the fountain. Mrs. Shaefer came out from her sliding glass door to say, "Are those good brooms? Do you need more juice?"

"Mrs. Shaefer get props from me," Darnell said. "She doesn't trip with that 'I'm payin you, so I can't actually converse' attitude."

"Props?" Trent said.

"Man, you're old," Darnell said. "You know, give me my props on that."

Trent frowned, looking down at the hole Juan had dug for a gray-leafed bush. "Like the old Aretha song?"

Now Darnell frowned. His mother used to play Aretha all the time. Give me my propers when you get home.

"Aretha was talking about sex, baby." Trent laughed.

"I'm talkin about respect, man," Darnell said. "Definitely not sex." He looked down at Charolette, who was rubbing her eyes. It was almost noon, and she hadn't slept yet. He went to lay Charolette on her blanket in Mrs. Shaefer's den, just inside the glass door. Mrs. Shaefer said, "I don't have any grandchildren, and this just gives me such a thrill." She bent to listen.

Charolette was grumpy, murmuring, "My pillow, Daddy! Pillow!" He'd forgotten the special flowery pillow Mrs. Batiste had made for her.

"We'll get it when we go home," he said. "Come on—take five. Take a snooze cruise. Take a flash crash." She closed her eyes, holding the stems of fountain grass.

Juan and José were working their way across the top of the bank, digging the deep holes a few feet apart for the black plastic gallon pots. Trent knocked out a ceanothus, holding the small trunk, and put it in one of the holes along the side of the bank, and Darnell picked up the pot nearby. "See, Mrs. Shaefer is cool cause she listens," Trent said. "I put this kind of drought-resistant garden in for one lady in Corona, and she turned on the sprinklers all the time. Killed every plant. If you water ceanothus and flannel bush later, in the summer when they're used to dry heat and no rain, they can't handle it."

Darnell tamped down the dirt around the base of a flannel bush, remembering its pale yellow blooms in the spring on the slopes near Poppet Flats. Where my last fire was, he thought. It wasn't acceptable. He murmured, "All that time I was up at the station, I never thought I'd be makin a damn chaparral slope in some lady's yard."

"Huh?" Trent said. "Hey, your beeper."

Darnell laughed, looked at Trent's pager. "Two brothas with beepers up here—no product in sight." Trent frowned. "We ain't normal, man." He clambered down the slope to use Mrs. Shaefer's phone.

When he went back up to where Juan was pulling the Matilja poppy plants from their pots, he said, "Mrs. Shaefer said those are expensive, so do it soft."

Juan looked at the small plant, its shaggy gray leaves. "Why expensive?"

Darnell knocked them out and smelled the wet dirt. "They're hard to grow. From the *semilla*." He moved away, not wanting to explain it to Juan. The poppies were what Fricke told him about: fire followers. They'd changed over the decades to survive, and the seeds needed intense heat to germinate. Fricke had laughed, saying that people had to build pine-needle blazes around their seeds to try and grow Matiljas at home.

He'd laughed again when people stopped by the station to ask if they could please dig up just one pine seedling to take home. Darnell and his father had taken out countless spindly, brown-needled pines. They hated the smog.

He knuckled down the dirt around the roots silently, feeling the cool wind. When the drizzle started again, he and Juan and José began putting away the tools. "We could leave the plants out," Darnell called to Trent. "Just another teaser."

"Yeah," Trent said. "Won't do much."

Darnell felt the mist on his neck. He went inside to shake Charolette's shoulder. "Come on, babygirl," he said. She turned limp on her side, just hitting deep sleep, and when he picked her up, she fell into one of those new half-conscious too-tired rages. Brenda said they were the beginning of the terrible twos—Charolette was early again. "Come on," he said, and she screamed so loud that Trent and Mrs. Shaefer stared at him. "She's just pissed," he said, heat rising up his back when he carried her kicking and screaming to the car seat.

"My pillow!" she began to scream. "My pillow!"

"Damn, Charolette, how can I get it if you don't get in the car?" he hollered back, and then he lowered his voice. "My monster's in the houuuse," he sang, trying to rap to her. "Charolette's in full effect." He held down her soft knees and forced the belts over her arms. She saw nothing—not his smile, his face, the fountain grass he tried to place in her clenched fists.

When he drove down the twisting Grayglen roads, he said, "There's your rock," at the huge white boulder marking the turn onto the last street out, the stone she loved. But her tantrum had darkened the creases by her nose and between her eyebrows, and her mouth was twisted open shapeless as a rag. He hit Woodbine, racing down toward the city, thinking, Okay, now I'm drivin like I live around here. Trent said to be cool, cause people get mad when the rain cancels golf.

He didn't even see that the red Chevy truck was going first at the stop sign, and he braked the El Camino hard. A white guy with reddish-blond eyebrows leaned out the open window and said, "Damn, nigger!" before he jerked his wheel and sped around the El Camino. Darnell went straight through after he'd gone, Charolette's cries rounder, smaller, like a siren fading down the street. Darnell's eyes, his forehead, rang with anger. Fuck you! Why I gotta be a nigger? Why I can't be an asshole, or blind? Why I can't be pussy-whipped? A new daddy? A jerk?

He swerved around the next turn and got on the freeway. He goin home tonight talkin bout, 'That's why I wanna move—too many niggers out here now." Or "Niggers can't drive." Or "Niggers—he probably had that rap music on so damn loud he . . ."

Loud. Charolette's eyes were closing again, her whole face swollen with spent anger, her cheeks pushing her wet lashes.

He turned on 92 The Beat and kept it low. "See? Luther sings for ladies, and you qualify." He watched the light drizzle on the glass, hearing Victor say the words about a girl. "She don't qualify. She ain't acceptable."

That was what he'd thought over and over about the last fire—the boot stomper loping thin up the hill. He looked over at Charolette's hands, finally falling loose on her leg, and he drove to the county building to get the application.

When the clouds were gone, a freeze settled in for several days, the sky hard and glassy at night. He smelled the fire when he went out to the dumpster with the bag of trash. The smoke was close, and he ran toward the pale roils in the dark sky, hearing the sirens already.

An old two-story house was burning. From the cars crowded into the dirt yard, he could tell it had been converted to apartments. A few Mexican and Vietnamese people stood outside, gesturing and crying, while the fireman trained the hoses into windows and onto roofs. The smell of wet black wood and burned upholstery was chemical and acrid. Darnell stood with the growing crowd. These fires started from space heaters and gas stoves left on, oven doors open, people trying to keep warm. The smoke hung low in the still, freezing air. No wind to move the cold, no breeze to fan the flames. The fire was out quickly, charred wood falling from the attic in chunks.

Darnell had always hated these fires, the way they smelled and burned, the nasty alligator-scaled walls he could see now, blackened thick and mottled into deep cracks. The piles of burned clothes and refuse, people gathered in the yard. No clean woodsmoke or creosote bush, no roar or racing or exhilarating fear. Just melting plastic and smoking paint, wet ash, and the crackle of radios from the hook-and-ladder trucks.

He walked back to the apartment in the ice-tinged air, and before he went up the stairs, he took the application from the glove compartment. Paid call reserve firefighter. He pulled out extra flyers— AnTuan's— and stared at the handful of paper before he clicked the compartment closed.

Sitting at the kitchen table, no sound from the darkened bedroom, he filled in all the lines. When he wrote Fricke's name, he smiled a little and bit the inside of his cheek. I'm still sprung, man, he thought. You knew it. I don't want city battalion, no road camp. I gotta hope they need somebody in the mountains. Even county reserve, like Scott and Perez. Long as it's me.

He parked off one of the fire roads before the station. The chaparral was frosted slightly, but there was no snow this far down the mountain. The pines, with their circular bursts of needles, were bright as thousands of exploded sparklers in the just-risen sun, and the light was hard everywhere.

"I don't even know why I brought you," he said to Charolette's hair after he pulled her from her car seat. She half slept on his chest, her breath under his jaw steaming up her own circle on the glass. "If your mama wasn't sleepin like a hangover, beggin me to take you outta there, you'd be yangin to yourself."

"Time for a serious conflagration up here," he said, pushing her off him and holding her up for a moment. "All this drought, decades of chaparral down there. Plenty of poppies comin soon." She looked at him sleepily. "Did you know some of the burls under there, the chaparral, some of the burls are two hundred fifty years old?" He raised his eyebrows dramatically. "They'll be good to go a week after the flames. No problem."

She reached up to touch the new razored cuts above his ears, like she had yesterday morning. "Come on," he said. "I see you gotta act like a girl just when Fricke might see you."

He'd brought the application just to show Fricke, to hear who might be hiring, but when he pulled into the station's driveway, he saw the door open and the engine gone. They had to be out on a call, Fricke and Corcoran probably still the whole crew. February—they wouldn't get seasonals until maybe April, if the season held off. If anybody got hired at this station at all.

Charolette picked up a few pine cones when he let her walk around, and he slid the application into an envelope to keep it clean before he put it back in the glove compartment. "Time to go down the mountain," he said. "Workday. We need a bear claw for Pop-Pop and a buttermilk bar for Uncle Roscoe."

The men were all sitting in their trucks drinking coffee when he drove up with the box of doughnuts. "Oh, no, babygirl, we gotta share," Darnell said, pointing at Floyd King, Nacho, and Snooter.

They all made a big deal of Charolette, still in her footed sleeper, stamping from lap to lap in the truck cabs, trying to pull dashboard knobs and see what was in the ashtrays. Roscoe gave her a smell of his coffee. "Red Man, this girl stubborn as you," he said to Darnell's father.

Darnell watched Charolette poke at the glass. "Dirty," she said, frowning.

"Least she look a lot better than her grampa," Floyd King said from his cab. "Next one gotta look like Brenda, cause this one look like Darnell spit her out his ownself."

Brenda hated hearing that. He said, "What next one?"

"Oh, your mama keep talkin about some dream she been havin," his father said. Charolette chewed on her glazed doughnut, and when Darnell's mother came out to the driveway for her part of the newspaper, she said, "Why you gon give that baby a sugary breakfast? She don't need y'all bad habits. Bring her in here for a biscuit and egg."

"You still dreamin, huh?" Darnell said.

"I told you I been done dreamed about fish five, six times," she said. "You know what that means." His father snorted and looked at Floyd, who bit his lips to keep from laughing. "Hush," she told them. "Ain't you looked at Brenda's face, Darnell? She full round the jaw, huh?"

Darnell winced. "Mama, I'm lucky if I see the back of Brenda's head now and then. She workin, I'm workin." In the silence, he heard Nacho's lips hissing up some coffee. Darnell said loudly, "Why it gotta be me? Maybe Melvin's having another baby."

His father said, "Melvin don't stay in one place long enough to know," and Darnell turned his head at the anger in the words. Then he said, "And don't even think about my girls. They got sense."

Darnell pictured the boys who came around the driveway trying to talk to Sophia and Paula, unnerved by the linked shoulders and wall of spilling words. Sophia and Paula didn't need boys yet. They told him all the time, "He ain't got nothing for me. He think he so fine." They would turn to Charolette, digging in her widening depression, and say, "He probably don't even know where Cincinnati is, huh, Lette?"

He stared at Charolette now, scrambling from the truck cab, her legs stiff before her. Lette. Like Quelle. Quelle—some girl who was willing to lick his back to get a ride to California. To Rio Seco. Charolette stopped in front of him and held her arms up, her face lifted to his. No. She ain't gon be no nickname. She ain't gon need to do nothin she don't want to. She gon know where Cincinnati is, Honolulu, and anyplace she want to go. Laughin cool like Sophia and Paula. So Floyd King tell her, "Go on with your bad self, girl," when he see her.

His mother's voice broke the quiet. "You ain't gotta look so scared," she said, frowning.

"Damn, man, you okay?" Nacho said, staring at him.

Darnell nodded, lifting Charolette into his arms. His mother tucked the newspaper section into the fold of her robe under her arm and said, "Y'all need to look for a bigger place, even if it's just the three of you. Like you said, you both workin so hard. Charolette need to have a yard to play in, cause she run around here like she just got off a leash. Ain't nowhere to rip and run in that apartment. And you get a house, we can find a washer so Brenda won't drag all that laundry up and down them stairs."

Floyd King called, "Mr. Nard gon be rentin out his brother's house on Pablo pretty soon. About five blocks down. Got two bedrooms, and he want six-fifty a month."

"Yeah, and I can barely pay the rent now," Darnell said. He sipped his coffee, thinking, It ain't been that long I helped pay bills at all.

Charolette went inside with his mother, and Darnell drove to meet Juan and José. At the first tract, he took out the application one more time, fingering the words, and then he wedged it carefully into the envelope again.

He waited a few weeks, to see if she would tell him. On Charolette's second birthday, Brenda's cheeks were gold in the candlelight from the cake, but he couldn't tell if they were wider or not. But he knew that she slept deep as Scott and Perez used to after bottles of Yukon Jack, when even hollering and shoving only filmed their eyes further. And no, he hadn't checked out her jaw, he told his mother. But in the dark he felt the heaviness of her breasts, the curve underneath getting harder. Her nipples had swelled bigger, too, and on Friday he picked up Charolette early and went to Taco Bell's drive-through window. "We gon surprise your mama," he told her. "Cause she waitin to surprise me. We gettin her favorite for lunch. Used to be your favorite. Gave you all that hair."

Man, I always used a jimhat, he thought, sitting on the bench near her office. Great—she havin Hercules Tucker. Victor can laugh uproarious. He saw the women push through the doorway, and he and Charolette went closer to look for Brenda. An older white woman with crinkled eyes behind glasses smiled at him, and Darnell said, "Hi, Mrs. Stovall."

This was the woman named Waltrina. Brenda liked her, and always said she was patient with the computers. "She'll be out in a minute, Dad. She's in the bathroom." She rolled her eyes and said, "I threw up at the moment of conception. Of course, my husband's face didn't help." She laughed and bent near Charolette carefully. "But you have a handsome daddy, huh, darling?"

So all these women probably know, Darnell thought, looking at their faces when they passed, their heavy eyelashes and moving lips. Those smells. They all know. And Brenda don't want to tell me. She probably think I'ma hat up real quick. Book. Jam. Vacate.

He saw her walking with the Oriental girl again. The Asian girl—Connie Lee. One-syllable. He shook his head to clear it. Brenda's face was composed when she saw him and Charolette, but he saw the moisture above her lip when she smiled.

"Hey," he said. "We brought your lunch." He led her to a bench in the shade. "See, we already prepared, so you can get a good spot." Charolette hugged Brenda and laid her cheek against Brenda's neck. Then she saw the bag from Taco Bell again and scrambled down for french fries.

Darnell pulled out the two burritos with red sauce and put them on the slatted wood between him and Brenda. "Here's the appropriate meal, huh? For a woman gets that craving sometimes." He looked under her ducked face, lifted up her small chin. "Must be immaculate conception, cause we ain't even done nothin."

Brenda's eyes glittered with tears, and she pulled in her bottom lip hard, folded her arms. "So go on and holler. Run. Whatever."

"Why should I run?" he said, lifting another french fry out for Charolette, who was instantly surrounded by pigeons when she ran onto the grass. "I know what all the women in the neighborhood say; I hear Mama and them talkin. You want another baby, you ain't gotta ask no man. You just do what you gotta do."

"I didn't do it on purpose."

"That's an original rap," he said, still smiling. "Hey, I ain't mad. I just always wanted to quote that back to you."

She ducked her head. "Everybody says you must want a boy anyway."

"Nope," he said. "They eat too much. That's what Pops always said."

"Come on," she said. "Don't make me cry again."

"I'm serious," he said, grinning. "I don't need a boy. Look at this hard chick over here, wantin to work with me. Every time my mama give her some old dishes and spoons she don't feed her dolly, she start diggin to Honolulu. You shoulda seen her this morning, tryin to rip bark off . . ." He stopped, remembering the silent yard in the station, the puzzle bark she'd pulled. Looking off at the greenish windows, he thought, I damn sure can't show Brenda the application now. I can't go on a three-day call when she's pregnant.

"If it's a girl, you could still name her Darnella," Brenda said, putting her arm around his neck, pulling him close.

"I told you about that," Darnell said, and Charolette ran up to them, slapping his hands off Brenda's wrists.

"*My* mama," she hollered.

When he got home, the phone rang before he could put Charolette down. He held her giggling under his arm and said, "AnTuan's Landscape."

A man said, "This sounds like a really great deal. I live in the Grayglen area, and your prices are pretty reasonable compared to Orange County."

"Yes, sir, we try to keep the prices down." He was out of breath, and he said, "Can you hold on, sir?" He put Charolette down. "When do you want us to start service?"

"Well, as soon as possible," the man said. "Can you come Friday?"

"Yes, Friday is fine." He tried to keep his voice flat. Another one. "We'll come Fridays, and you can send checks to 2897 Picasso Street. Payment is once a month, and please call me if you have any trouble." Darnell spoke slowly, concentrating the way he still had to each time.

"Picasso Street?" the man said. "Isn't that on the Westside?"

"Yes, sir?"

"I thought you guys were Oriental. I bet you want to get out of a minority area like that. Pretty rough in a black neighborhood."

Darnell's face and neck prickled. "Yeah. We're moving soon. Very soon." After he'd hung up, he saw Charolette unfolding the towels Brenda had stacked on the couch. "Daddy talking?" She imitated his clipped voice. "We moving soon?"

"You ain't gotta talk like that," he said roughly. "Leave the towels alone before I get mad." He stared at the laundry, at her round face set hard under the held-still eyebrows. "Oh, you pissed?" he said. "Let's go look at a washing machine for Mama."

"Move, Daddy?" she asked again, since it had bothered him when she said it the first time. When he tried to take the towels away, she said angrily, "Move, Daddy!" and shoved him. He pretended to fall over on his back, and then he caught her on his chest to tickle her, so she couldn't get away.

WILD WILD WEST

"**O**VER THE BRIDGES** and through the hood to Charolette's house we go," Darnell sang, and Charolette clutched the purple hair ties she'd found at the market.

Brenda had told him to buy good coffee. When he pulled into the driveway of the house and parked behind the chalky-dusted Spider, she came out onto the porch.

Dry grass tufts still covered the yard, and he was embarrassed when she said, laughing, "Where's *my* landscape maintenance?" But the owner of the house had been gone for months by the time Mr. Nard showed it to them. Darnell tried to water every day now.

Charolette ran right up on the porch steps. The house was old, dark-blue painted wood, with deep eaves over the porch. The windows were still bare, since Brenda hadn't had time for curtains. Charolette went straight to her own room, with the twin bed.

The windows were the main reason Mrs. Batiste was coming today, but Brenda was nervous because her father had said he might come, too. "He wasn't thrilled that we picked this address," she said, wiping down the kitchen counter. The kitchen was dusty, but bigger than the apartment's.

"Is that right?" he teased her. Then he said, seriously, "Hey, Pablo Street ain't Jackson Park, okay?" He pushed her gently into the living room, where a soot-stained fireplace was empty. "We can have some nice, controlled flames this winter, when you skinny again and the baby's sleepin back there."

She looked around the room at the couch and table, ducked her head. "It's not like the apartment," she said, finally. "I mean, I'd hardly never spent the night away from my parents and you took me to this bare little place and said, 'We gon live here.' Remember?" She watched him.

"Yeah," he said. "I never thought about it like that. Hey, I didn't want to think about it—just wanted to do it. Been a while now." He folded his arms. "You sure you want to live on the Westside? My hood?"

She smiled. "It used to be mine, too."

She'd changed into her flowered sundress and sandals. Charolette brought out the hair ties onto the porch, and when Darnell went to check the oil in the El Camino, he heard the three little girls next door jumping rope. Teneya, Alliane, and Tracey, Charolette had told him. Their braids flew and slapped their shoulders.

"I got places to park my cars," Darnell said to Brenda, who smiled. "I can park my women in separate bedrooms now. Oh, yeah." He sat next to her. "Your old hood. Your pops left long ago. But now you got my moms within walkin distance, you got Sophia and Paula and Hollie. Charolette in girl heaven. Only thing your pops could get mad about is we ain't got no property value—black neighborhood and all like *that*."

"Shut up," she said.

He laughed. "Just playin, baby. I know your heart was always on the Westside, hidin in the bushes, waitin for me to come and get it." She hit him on the shoulder as she watched Charolette stare at the girls.

"Oh Mary Mack-Mack-Mack, all dressed in black-black-black, with silver buttons-buttons-buttons, all down her back-back-back . . ." the girls sang.

"The store up by our house never carried hairdress," Brenda said, watching for the car. "Never had Pickapeppa, and Mama had to come here to get it for my dad."

The New Yorker cruised slowly to the curb, and they both stood up. Brenda's mother got out, looked into Darnell's eyes, and smiled carefully, straight across her lips, over a pie plate.

Darnell grinned and said, "You come to baptize the house?"

"Sweet potato," she said, kissing Brenda's cheek. "Where my baby?" She turned back and said, "Darnell, it's coffee, good coffee, in there, and some other things."

"Just hide that pie, or I won't get a piece," he said. "Brenda into the eat-it-all month, whatever month that is. And Charolette a greedy pig." He went out to the car door, thinking he'd have to lean politely near the window, but Mr. Batiste was getting out.

"Got plants, coffee, measurin tape, a whole damn store in here," he said, but when Darnell opened his mouth, he saw that Mr. Batiste was looking past him. He heard Brenda come out onto the porch, felt Charolette's fingers pushing at the bend of his knees.

"Who that, Daddy?" she said.

Mr. Batiste tightened his lips and said, "Brenda don't look like she starvin," when his wife came to the sidewalk.

"I got y'all some roses," she said, ignoring him.

"They ain't buyin, they rentin," Mr. Batiste said.

"And that's not good enough, right?" Brenda called. She folded her arms, which made her stomach protrude even more.

Darnell saw that her father couldn't look at her for long. Charolette studied Mr. Batiste's face briefly and then turned to poke at the box.

"I'll be back," Mr. Batiste called to his wife, and Darnell thought he would get into the car again, but he started walking down Pablo Street.

"Go with Gramma," Darnell told Charolette, setting the box on the sidewalk, and he caught up at the third house.

Mr. Batiste studied the fences, the yards, the cars, and Darnell stayed even with him. What the hell, he thought. *Cojones.* Say what you want now, cause we been gettin along fine without the man. He thought of Brenda's eyes, how she'd swept the sidewalk this morning until dust swirled in her bangs.

"Lotta Mexicans moved in since you left, huh?" he said. "Everybody gotta be an immigrant sometime."

Mr. Batiste glanced at him. "I drive through here now and then, but I ain't studied the percentages."

Darnell smiled. They passed the truck on the corner with a bumper

sticker that read "COLGADORES—DRYWALLERS" and "YO ♥ MEXI-
CALI." "How you like my guys doin your yard?" he asked.

Mr. Batiste kept his eyes on the house to his left. "One of em left
a few marks on my back fence, from that wire whacker."

Darnell nodded and they crossed Eighteenth Street. Snooter
cruised past with a woman, driving her Honda, and he waved at
Darnell. Behind him was Mr. Moncrief, in his ancient Catalina, the
one all the lowriders kept begging him to sell. He pulled slowly to
the curb and said, "Etienne?" in that Louisiana voice.

Darnell hung back after he'd nodded to Mr. Moncrief. He leaned
on a fence, near the chain-link gate at the corner where he turned
each day. He looked for the greens tree at Victor's sister Sonia's house,
on this street, and at Mrs. Strozier's. Floyd King had always grown
them in pots and given or sold them to people. The plants clambered
up walls and fences and stucco, their stems thickening to trunks with
circling marks where the collard leaves had been plucked off.

The plants liked chain link best. Air circulating, Mr. King said.

"Check out the craftsmanship," Darnell said when Mr. Batiste came
back and kept walking. He pointed to a low block wall set with huge
sunbursts of white iron rays, spiked and arcing.

"You gotta paint iron every year," Mr. Batiste said. "Block walls
all they buildin in them new tracts."

"Yeah," Darnell said. "That's where most of my business is, out
there near Grayglen." They turned down Pablo again.

"Your guys, huh," Mr. Batiste said. He sucked at his cheeks. "Indians own all the motels now. Orientals got the markets."

"Asians," Darnell said.

"Whatever they are, they save their money. And you two got kids
now; you can't save no money," Mr. Batiste said harshly, still not
looking at Darnell's face. "But y'all gotta learn that the hard way. No
college. No plan. You didn't have to get married. That was back in
my time, when people still gave a good goddamn."

"You see em starvin?" Darnell said. "You think your daughter ain't
got the sense to leave if she ain't happy?"

"I ain't hardly here to discuss her lack of sense," Mr. Batiste said.
He leaned up against the New Yorker now, and Darnell stood on the
sidewalk, his arms folded.

"You used to live in Gray Hollow," Darnell said.

"Yeah."

"You don't live there no more." He remembered No More, Louisiana, and stared at the narrow, arched mouth.

"Nope. What you gettin at?"

"I used to live up in the mountains. I don't live up there now."

Mr. Batiste twisted his lips slightly. "I thought you wanted to be a fireman. Big plans."

"I do," Darnell said, digging his thumbs into his ribs. "But I'm kinda busy now." He felt the angry knuckles. "Managing my ducats the best I can and tryin to be a *daddy*. Hard work." He walked into the yard and saw three faces in the screen.

After Brenda had gone to bed, he lay on the couch, staring at the empty fireplace. The evening was warm, but he crumpled up the newspapers they'd used to pack boxes, and he pushed them hard under the old andirons. They burned fast and silent, and he sat in the dark, watching the yellow fire die to faint-breathed spongy red. When he was small he used to imagine that the tight-packed embers were a body disintegrating, the blood fading dark.

The phone rang, and he said automatically, "AnTuan's Landscape."

"Uh, yeah, I'm lookin for Darnell."

"Louis?" Darnell held the phone hard on his ear.

"Yeah." Darnell could hear other voices around Louis. "Man, you know I ain't used this phone one time since I been here?"

"You okay?" Darnell asked.

"Yeah," Louis said. "I just . . . I might get out in a few months. They talkin about early release, you know, cause the flock in here gettin large." Louis paused. "But I might need a place. I mean, I can't just go up north, cause they won't let me out unless I got a place and a job." Before Darnell could speak, he rushed on, his voice much faster than usual. "I know y'all in that one-bedroom, but I could sleep in the El Camino, man. I just don't want to stay nowhere on the Westside, cause I don't feel like hearin the questions."

"Homey, man, me and Brenda moved. We got a house, got two bedrooms," Darnell said, hearing the sparkling sound the ashes made when they shifted. "But we on Pablo Street, man, way down past the Stroziers."

Louis puffed out breath in a tiny laugh. "Shit. You must be doin okay in the yards, D."

"Yeah." Darnell waited. He knew Louis didn't want to stay on the

Westside not just to avoid the raised eyebrows, but to avoid his father.
"When you gettin released?"

"I'm not sure, man." Darnell heard Louis move his mouth away,
then bring it close again. "I'ma call you back, okay? Tell Brenda hey,"
he said, and he hung up.

The fireplace was gray. Darnell slid into the sheets beside Brenda,
who opened her eyes. "Who's calling about a yard so late?" she
murmured.

"Louis," Darnell said, his hands behind his head on the pillow. He
could smell the water drying off the rock-hard ground of the yard.
"He's gettin out pretty soon. He might need a place to stay." He
wondered what she would say—she'd always turned her mouth tender
for Louis, but now he'd done time.

"Here?" she said, still low. "But you never found out what happened. What about Leon and them?"

Darnell watched the pattern of the palm fronds shift across the
ceiling. "I don't know," he said.

He looked for them at Jackson Park a few times when he picked
up Victor and Ronnie. Brother Lobo said, "I see Leon driving, driving, but he doesn't seem to want to linger. He conducts his business
near the alley."

Darnell saw the crowd of men on the porch, saw two women walking
up the alley toward the vacant lot. Leon was supposed to be out of
street level, he thought. He shook his head. I don't even want to
think about it.

He didn't see Leon's Bronco for a few weeks, and Louis didn't call
back. The green that had sprouted like whiskers in the fields and on
the hillsides turned neon bright after the rain, but days passed, and
the lacy filaree and wild oats that were so lush began to bend limp
and silver.

The fire season would be starting. Darnell shaped the branches of
Mrs. Tribeleaux's olive tree with his father; she liked them trimmed
every few weeks into bonsai puffs. Roscoe was helping Marietta Cook
paint all her window sashes blue, like he did every spring, and while
Darnell watched the soft gray leaves scatter, he wondered if Louis
would ever just call Roscoe, tell him he wanted to start from day one,
right now, this minute.

His father sat in the shade to drink some water, and Darnell raked the small pile. "You gon be like them people in Sweden every winter?" his father said abruptly, and Darnell looked up, surprised.

"What?"

His father wiped at his neck with a bandanna. "They get some kinda chemical depression during their winter, cause they don't get enough sunlight. I can't remember the name. But I been seein you for three, four winters now, and you love that cool weather. When you came down from Conservation Corps, when you came down from Forestry, you were always lookin for rain. Now as soon as it turns hot, you get that long face. You start thinkin about what you gon miss up there when a nice dry wind blows through all that brush."

Darnell threw the rake onto the truck and leaned against the door. "Sorry. I'll try to look grateful to have a gig."

His father didn't frown at the disrespectful tone. He drank the last of his water and said, "When you were little, you used to hate the rain, hate bein cooped up all winter. All you boys did. First hot day, y'all were out there runnin around the lots with your shirts off."

They rode silently down the street, and when they reached his father's yard, Darnell opened the door. His father said, "I was just watchin you, tryin to think about how you'd feel doin fire-season clearing. We got all Cacciotti's land to do next couple of weeks. Probably depress you more, but it'll put money in your pocket. Brenda's talkin about a dresser."

Darnell stood with his hand on the door handle. "Yeah. I'll practice smilin, too." He looked away from his father.

When the route was finished for the day and Juan and José had dropped off the truck, he washed it and the El Camino, watching the trickle in the dusty driveway, and then he sprinkled the still-sparse grass.

The sky was black with clouds when he walked back to his father's to pick up Charolette; he was early, and she loved to walk instead of drive. She stopped, holding his hand, to stare into the early dark, and then she bent to study the few drops that fell onto the sidewalk. "Don't worry, Daddy," she said, looking up at him. "Just a polka-dot rain."

It was the last one, only spattering on the cement downtown when they picked up Brenda, her belly rounded slightly now under her

dress. At home, he sat on the steps, but the drops never joined into
a sheen over the asphalt. And by the first week of May the sky was
white with morning heat. The ground was eased dry, the wild oats
tall enough now to bend limp to the ground.

He and José walked alongside a field to the back of a gas station.
The owner had asked him to check on all three stations and give him
a bid for maintenance; then Darnell had to drop José at home and
meet his father so they could start the fire-season clearing.

Darnell and José weeded the neglected banks in front between the
sidewalk and pumps, and then they turned up the rock-hard dirt on
the narrow strip around back, where the planter edged the chain link
and the field. "He wants grass," Darnell told José, who nodded. He
would seed it.

José still didn't talk, didn't even try, and Juan worried aloud to
Darnell that he might get tired of José's silence, take it for indiffer-
ence, and fire him. "Not me," Darnell told Juan. "I ain't into palaver."
When Juan cocked his head in question, Darnell said, "I like José,
okay?"

He did. He had to give the man props. Respect. He didn't feel
like talking. Ever again, it seemed. So he didn't. He listened, he
understood what Darnell said well enough to do his job; he spent his
time thinking. Darnell liked to work with José, in silence, so he could
blur his eyes and see something besides the same lawns and flower
beds.

He drove toward the Westside. Louis had never talked much,
either. Maybe he and Louis could do a lot of the side jobs; Victor
and Ronnie couldn't say he wasn't hiring a brother, and they couldn't
get hot about Darnell helping a brother who'd just done his time.

Darnell parked on his father's street. José and Juan had left in
AnTuan's truck. Looking at his father's yard, Darnell saw Roscoe
sitting at the old wooden cable holder they used as a table. I'm not
sayin anything yet, he thought. But I wouldn't mind workin with
Louis; I wouldn't have to yang like with Victor and Ronnie. Melvin
used to yang, too. Me and Louis more like relatives. Crazy cousins.
Birdman and Nature Boy.

He shook his head and walked across the street. Roscoe saw him
and said, "I thought you were bringing your crew. We gotta get
started. I got enough doughnuts for them, too."

Darnell took a buttermilk bar. "They had to start the route. Anyway,

Juan and José like tortillas or these buns called *bolillos*. They say doughnuts are too sweet."

Roscoe held up his bear claw. "You get *bolillos* from the *panadería*, doughnuts from the *Asian* woman in the minimall, or biscuits from a mother."

Darnell's father came from the sideyard and said, "I'll take the biscuits and homemade jelly. Come on, we need to see if that tractor gon start up."

Roscoe and Darnell drove the tractor slowly and painfully up Pepper Avenue from Treetown, where Mr. Lanier kept it stored. Listening to the iron grating on the pavement, Darnell remembered riding on this old tractor with his father.

When they got to the fields, his father nodded to Darnell. "No fancy government dozer, huh, no nice wide fire roads."

"You can quit remindin me," Darnell said.

His father nodded again. "You up against government dozers right now. Cacciotti gave us the bid cause last year he didn't get around to clearin his property and the city did it. Charged him a leg and half his dick."

Darnell fired up the tractor and started to move the yellow monster he had always been afraid of when he was small, belching smoke and grinding the discs into the dirt. Pink squares of paper were posted on stakes all through the fields, telling owners to clear the trash and brush for fire season. Darnell started the long rows, flattening the tall, spindly stems already beginning to lie down in the sun.

Sweat streamed into his eyes, and he pulled out the bandanna to wipe his face. The heat rose off the crushed grass and empty seed heads in front of him, and gold dust hung heavy in the air. Already ninety out here. Hella drought, he thought. Fricke and them laughing. They gon be busy this year again. I'ma be busy, too. Home boy. But I'll see you next season.

The first field was nearly done when his mother pulled up in the El Camino. Charolette's face popped up, too. He got down off the tractor and chewed on the crispy skin of the fried chicken, giving Charolette strips of breast meat, sips of soda. When she tried to climb onto the tractor, he lifted her onto the seat, and his mother called to him across the fallen stems. "You tryin to make her into a boy, and she wild already."

After they'd gone, he rubbed his fingers on his dusty jeans and tried to fire up the tractor, but it shuddered hard, refused to catch. "Damn!" he shouted after a few more tries. His father and Roscoe had gone to the dump. He walked across the straw to the street.

Jackson Park was the closest; he figured he'd find Victor and Ronnie, but only the old men were around the domino table, and the zombies didn't stir from the far porch. Darnell sat for a long minute on the warm curb, not wanting to walk again. From the avenue, black doors glinted clean and waxed, and he saw Gas's smile flashing in the window behind the music.

He stood up, and then he saw Leon's face beside his brother's. They stopped in front of him, and the singing chanted hard.

"House of Pain," Darnell said, leaning into the window. "Leon like this, too."

Gasanova's face went stony, and he didn't look at his brother. "Yeah, well, Moms just asked me to give him a ride. It jams out the speakers the same for everybody, right?"

Gas got out and walked across the street to the tiny market, and Leon stared ahead at the people half hidden in the shade of the porches. Darnell sat next to him. "Where's the Bronco?"

Leon shook his head. "I didn't want to drive it today. Been rough and shit; I had to let my crib go and get a hotel. Gotta be mobile right now."

"Where's Vernon?"

"He sit up all night in the room, watchin the parkin lot, talkin to his gauge. That's all he care about—he packin a gauge and his nine." Leon folded his arms, his eyes on the porches. "Them LA niggas been hangin over here, talkin yang about product. And some dude got smoked last night in Terracina."

"Terracina?" Darnell smelled the dusty yew branches near his face, heard the shots chopping out.

"I don't go over there," Leon said. "But I heard somebody saw that tall dude over here a coupla times. The enforcer. See, I never knew what was goin on in Louis's head, but he heard all my business. And he fucked up big time for me, so he probably workin with somebody else."

Darnell looked at the wild tobacco, still springing green from the ground near the cinder-block walls; tobacco didn't need water. "Louis just called me, man; he ain't even out yet," Darnell said. He remembered Leon laughing at Louis's upturned face, at his repeating the words over and over: Banded quail? Red hawk. Egrets. Leon had shaken his head when Darnell pedaled toward the smoke. "Louis don't have nothin to do with you now."

Leon shouted, "Damn, he wasn't doin nothin for me back then! Some *ranger* got him! Louis just figured he go and do his time now, get some friends, come out and work for them. Probably the dudes he got busted for." Leon's face lowered back onto his bones, and he slumped in the seat. "He musta called you a while ago. Tommy got out last week, and he told me Louis went to a halfway house when he got his release."

Darnell stared at Gas walking back toward the truck, carrying a soda. Gas kept his face blank. "You remember that night last year when Donnie went off in the Bronco?" Leon said softly. "Everybody's trippin."

"Not me, homey," Darnell said. "I don't have time. I got kids." But Leon didn't even hear the plural; he kept his face level with the dashboard now, closing his eyes like he was sleepy.

Gas said, "You need a ride?"

Darnell sat between them, shoulders sliding against each other, and no one talked into the music.

The tractor still wouldn't start by the next morning, even though Mr. Lanier and Mr. King had spent all afternoon working on it. "Ancient equipment," Darnell's father grumbled. "You gon have to tell Cacciotti to get somebody else. Damn! Two more days of work gone."

Darnell stood looking at the seed heads turning golden in the heat. "I'ma check at the park," he said. "It's Saturday morning—somebody should need money."

The curb was bare again, though, and Darnell got out to ask a guy on the couch under the pepper tree where Victor and Ronnie were. "Man, po-lice gaffled them brothas last night. Talkin about drunk in public. Had the K-9 unit right here, talkin about, 'Watch yo ass, boy, this dog like dark meat.'" The man leaned his head back on the cushion and closed his eyes.

Darnell sat in the cab of AnTuan's truck, feeling the trickle down his backbone, the saliva and clicking paws. Uh-uh, he told himself. No time for trippin.

He drove to Juan and José's, and they stood up from where they'd been sitting in the shade under a tree. Two other men squatted in the dirt near the tree trunk. "Juan," Darnell called. "You know anybody got a tractor?"

"Tractor?" Juan said. "For the farm?"

"Yeah."

Juan said something to José and the other men, and then José gestured to the truck. "Show the job, okay?" Juan said, getting in.

At the fields, Mr. Lanier stood watching the Thompson brothers hook up the tractor to tow it. Juan leaned against the truck and frowned. "Darnell? Is to knock down weeds? Not to pull out?" Darnell nodded, and Juan said, "We do that. Come on."

They stood in the field, the oats thigh high, bending to swing the sharpened machetes in wide swaths, low curves. The ground turned soft-quilted under their feet with the crushed stems broken to straw.

Darnell and his father watched for a minute. "I can't do that," Darnell said.

"I don't want to do that," his father said. "Go on and get that trash from near the fences, and I'll call Cacciotti."

When he brought Charolette, the sweet smell beginning to rise with the cool of early evening, Juan and José were in the third field, their straw cowboy hats bobbing. They're not workin for AnTuan today, Darnell thought. Not with machetes. Charolette pulled him down to squat beside her in the field. "Daddy," she said. "Oatmeal." She touched the burst seed heads, with their fuzzy legs like an insect's.

"Close," he said. "And here's your favorite. Foxtails." She loved those, rescued a few still standing near the fence.

"Tickle tickle baby!" she said, trying to brush his neck like he used to do hers.

That night, he sat on the couch, listening to the helicopter circling near the house. Charolette lay on the floor near his feet, playing with her Barbie, tugging on the skirts and shirts Mrs. Batiste had sewed with tiny snaps and Velcro fasteners. "I can't do this one, Daddy," she said, and he looked up to see Brenda's shadow still in the kitchen, back and forth over the counter, the stove.

He pushed the metal snaps closed over Barbie's pointy breasts, the blue-shadowed eyes staring out from chocolate skin. Charolette peered closely. "She's goin to school," she said. "Like Hollie."

"Okay," he said.

She looked at Barbie's bare feet. "Hollie my cousin," she said. "But she doesn't have daddy."

Darnell rubbed his forehead, still gritty with field dust. "Yeah, she does."

Charolette shook her head slowly, while Brenda stood behind her, a laundry basket bumping her rounded stomach. "Hollie lives with her Pop-Pop," she said.

"But she still has a daddy," Brenda said, softly. "Everybody has a daddy."

Charolette took back the Barbie, frowning. "Not if he don't live there," she said, and walked to her room to get the tiny sharp-heeled shoes Darnell had banned from the living room because they hurt like hell when he stepped on them.

Brenda threw white socks at him, one by one, from the tangle of clothes she'd bleached. She smiled when he held a fistful. "It's like a buncha snakes in here," she said, starting to fold dishtowels and T-shirts.

Darnell straightened the socks into one pile and heard the clattering blades when the helicopter passed over the roof. Drop some Alumagel on all them fields, he thought suddenly, torch the lots and be done quick. He leaned back, feeling the night air on his neck from the screen. I can't even clear private property right. Fire season started, and foxtails and wild oats—that's about as wild as I'ma get this year.

"Is Louis coming or not?" Brenda asked suddenly. Charolette's feet padded down the hallway. Darnell looked at Brenda's hands, stopped in the air holding a small shirt, wrists bent like swan necks.

"I don't know," he said. He didn't want to tell her about what Leon had said, didn't want her even to think about Leon and Vernon, watching, waiting. She said her dreams were full of the babies now, instead of him running, driving, red lights and silver beams circling his neck.

He had to pull foxtails and field oats and the wild tobacco trees from the edges of someone's estate in Grayglen; the seeds blew over the cinder-block wall and sprouted every spring. Now, true summer heat hung in the eucalyptus branches. Darnell added another day to Juan and José's route, finally. His phone rang more often when the sun rose already glaring, when the smog still hid the mountains at dusk. The new transplants to Rio Seco from LA and Orange County didn't want to cut their grass when gray heat thick as syrup coated their lungs with each step.

He drove all over the city, with his father and Roscoe, with Juan and José, with Victor and Ronnie. Talk. Palaver. He was quiet, thinking of all the trees they'd trimmed, fingering the blades of grass clinging to his jeans. Everything manicured. Better be, or we ain't keepin the account. Convenient trees only. Up in Grayglen, on the big estates with oaks and eucalyptus and five acres, there were benches and statues and Jacuzzis and decks. What had Trent called it? Darnell dragged the branches toward the truck. Controlled nature.

When the first riverbottom fires trailed smoke, he didn't drive to the bridge. The cane, that arundo, still green, he thought. Grapevines clingin tight. It won't burn that good yet. Early summer's still holdin wet way down there.

He washed the trucks on the front grass, letting Charolette spray the tires and the windows and Brenda's ankles, resting on the steps.

After Brenda had lain down in the bedroom, near nine o'clock, Charolette kept stalking the living room, saying, "But I'm not sleepy, Daddy." She pulled at her hair, twisted in long spirals and tucked into a stretchy pink headband for sleep. "I'ma comb *your* hair," she said, picking up the brush on the floor.

Darnell said, "I'm tired, *chica*. Let me watch this show, okay? Then you gon have to crash whether you ready or not."

She lifted the brush and then froze. "Daddy! You got a ouchie." She touched the fresh thorn tear on his forearm, the zipper of dried blood.

"It doesn't hurt," he said, watching her eyes well with tears, and he felt a sharp twist in his throat, seeing himself examine his father every night, the rough wrists, the huge palms and thumbs so much bigger than his.

"Look at mine," she said, showing him the lines of her last scrape, the shrunk beaded scab on her leg. Suddenly she bent to kiss his arm, and she fingered the black line on his hand—the stem burn. She put her lips there, too, and then she stood on the couch behind him to examine his ears.

"Ouch!" he said. "Be careful." He tried to keep his eyes on the TV, but she moved his head to the side.

"Is that you, D.?" a deep voice said into the window screen. Darnell jerked his head sharply, Charolette's finger hitting him in the eye, and Louis said, "It's only Birdman."

Charolette eyed his faraway face from the couch once he was inside, standing near the wall, shoulders stiff. She pressed herself into Darnell's back then, and Darnell watched Louis smile. "Is that you?" Louis repeated.

Like they used to ask each other about girls: Oh, man, is that *you?* Yeah, homey, that's me. Darnell nodded. "She's about as me as possible."

Louis sat and waited until Darnell put her to bed; she clung to his chest as he lowered her to the sheets, and she whispered, "He tall like a tree."

"I couldn't hang at the halfway house for too long, man," Louis said. "It was in Pomona, like right near downtown."

Darnell turned the brush over in his hands. "You runnin?"

Louis shook his head. "I told em where I was goin."

Darnell waited. He could hear Charolette's feet in the hallway again; she was probably going to climb into bed next to Brenda.

"I need to make a little money, so I can head up north," Louis said, rubbing his fingertips near his temples. "I can't go back up there with no cash."

"All I got is the side jobs, unless you want to work with Pops and . . . your pops." Darnell watched Louis frown and look out the dark screen. "But if we get a coupla big jobs in a few weeks, you could make enough." He hesitated. "How'd you know where we moved to?"

"I saw Victor at Jackson Park," Louis said, his eyes moving to Darnell.

"You didn't see Leon?"

Louis shook his head. "Just some strawberry girls hangin out."

Darnell said, "You gon have to tell me, man. I can't be nubbin with Leon and Vernon cause they think somethin's up. Last time I saw Leon, he still thought you were out for payback. And he was still ballistic about somethin you messed up."

Louis finally leaned forward, his elbows on his bony knees, like he was afraid for anyone to hear him. "You was just there, man."

"What?" Darnell remembered the Lincoln, the highways, and Vernon shooting out the window. He felt the girl's tongue on his skin.

"By the riverbottom," Louis whispered. "Didn't you go see the fire today?"

Darnell breathed in hard. "No, man, I was workin. I didn't have time."

Louis stared at him. "But you got pecans last year. Past the pecan trees, between the grove and the riverbottom, all them fields?" His eyes were blurred, so close to Darnell's face. "Four blue herons live over there; they like it right there. They steal fish from that county park, where they stock carp and stuff." Darnell nodded. "The fields all covered up with tumbleweeds during winter, and the birds can't get in there. But around spring, the county clean up all the tumbleweeds, in big piles. You know that." Darnell nodded again, seeing the thorns burst from the bushes when he shoveled them, seeing the flames ball and roll.

"The mice been growin all spring, man, and then these blue herons just hang out by the piles, waitin for them."

"Don't no bird eat mice, man," Darnell said.

"Yeah, they do. Herons do. Mice, fish. Herons are big, man, got a big wingspan and long beaks. You ever see them rise up over you you see how big they are." Louis stopped, glancing around as if people were listening.

"What do herons gotta do with Leon?" Darnell said, leaning back.

"You don't never get to be alone with Leon and them. He hates bein alone—he always gotta have his boys with him. Vernon, Mortrice. I wanted to use the Bronco, go over by the river." Louis stopped. "I used to always walk, but then dudes saw me with Leon and they wanted to smoke me, remember? I told you. And I wasn't doin nothin." He took a breath. "Leon let me use the Bronco, but he said bring it back in a few minutes. I got over there and started walkin into the fields to look for the herons. You can't drive, cause it's no roads, just horse trails. I guess somebody seen me, seen the Bronco, cause it was like, two hours later, and the cops busted me. And two rangers. They found some product Leon was gon move."

"Why you didn't tell Leon what happened?" Darnell said, pressing his feet hard into the floor.

"That was big money, D."

"Why you didn't tell the rangers it wasn't yours?" Darnell stopped, shaking his head. "Yeah, I know."

Louis grinned slightly. "Come on, Darnell. Don't you think the rangers was suspicious? Hey—a nigga with no binoculars?"

Darnell heard Brenda's slippers clacking soft into the kitchen, and he waited for her to come out. She clutched her robe around her belly, even though it was hot, and she squinted into the living room. "Brenda," he said.

When she saw Louis, her eyes widened. "You're back?"

"Just for a minute," he said, biting his lips. "Darnell didn't tell me he was doin the daddy thang again."

She lifted her shoulders and pulled the robe tighter, embarrassed. Darnell got up and put his arm around her. "Louis is gon help me out on a coupla jobs," he said, and he ran his fingers up the back of her hair, held her head softly.

"You hungry?" she asked, leaning her head back and breathing out.

Darnell picked up the first broken bottleneck in the lot downtown, and when Victor said, "Brenda gettin big now. Hope you figured out where babies come from this time," he didn't answer. He and Louis worked their way toward the faded brick façade of the next building; he'd called his father for a few days instead of going over there, and Brenda had taken Charolette to his mother's, then driven to work herself.

He and Louis rode in the AnTuan truck. Juan and José were probably standing on the same corner where he'd found them, Darnell thought, like they usually did during the first half of the week when he worked clean-up jobs like this without them. A couple of weeks ago, they'd dug ditches for a plumber.

Victor was waiting near the truck when Darnell and Louis came back toward the sidewalk, bags full. "You see Diante Thomas when you was in?" he asked Louis.

Darnell could see the tongue move inside Louis's jaw, just like Roscoe's did when he didn't want to talk about something. "No," Louis said.

Victor smiled. "You didn't claim no Rio Seco homeys, huh?" he snapped.

"If you in a lousy mood cause it's hot, brothaman, you in for a long summer," Darnell said, hard. "Come on." They moved the skeletal remains of a mattress someone had dumped on the lot, and threw the last of the disposable diapers into the truck with the other trash.

Back at Jackson Park, Louis was slumped down as far as his tall bones would allow, and Darnell said, "We ain't stayin, Victor."

"Yeah," Victor said, serious now. "It's the Wild Wild West out here at night, man. When me and Ronnie came off that weekend in County, brothas was out here tryin to kill each other."

"Who?" Louis said.

"Them fools in the alley," Victor said, nodding toward the crowd of ghost-eyed people.

Darnell leaned out the window, since he didn't see Leon's Bronco, and from the domino table Brother Lobo squinted at him. "Where's your miniature replica?" Lobo said.

"Her mama's gone to get her," Darnell said.

Brother Lobo didn't see Louis in the passenger seat. He told his opponent, "Darnell here has a baby Athena, looking like she sprang from his head fully formed." The guy only glanced briefly at Darnell and then studied his bones. A serious player, Darnell thought, but his arms were so thin that his elbows stuck out like bracelets, and the ankles above his flip-flops were scaled rough.

"Domino," he said, not even grinning at Brother Lobo, and when the men around the table whistled, Louis said, "Come on, D. He's sprung bad, and he gotta be gettin cane from somebody I don't want to see."

He'd slept on the couch for the first few nights. Darnell came out in the middle of the night after Charolette cried for a drink, and Louis was hunched, legs bent, his hand trailing to the floor. Darnell watched him for a few minutes, thinking of how he'd always slept on his back, dreaming of boats and coffins.

The July heat pressed onto them all night where he lay next to Brenda, sheets kicked to the floor. Brenda could sleep only on her side now, and her face was always wreathed with moisture. She was carrying all in front, his mother said, and her back hurt, her feet swelled. She breathed shallowly, her back to him, her elbow curled under her head so that her palm dangled over her eyes. "Look like you don't want to see the sun," he whispered to her when he heard Charolette's bare feet whisper in the hallway.

"Daddy, the yellow sun is here."

"I can't do this," she mumbled into her arm. "I'm so tired."

"I'll cook somethin," he said.

The couch was empty, the sheet folded neatly, and Darnell stood there, feeling Charolette's fingers at the backs of his knees, thinking that Louis never carried anything. He'd changed clothes once, from jeans to sweats, and the two T-shirts Brenda had washed were still on the clothesline.

Charolette had stepped on her stool in the darkness and climbed the counter. Darnell scratched his neck and pulled up the kitchen shades to show her the dawn. "That ain't yellow," he said, pointing to the pale gray disc. "You shoulda given me and him another hour if you wanted yellow."

"I heard your friend, Daddy," she said. "He shut the door. He's walking in the dark."

Brenda came out in a while, and she was worried. "He must be really scared, if he's leaving before the sun comes up."

Darnell shrugged. "He's grown, Brenda. Don't you have enough to worry about?"

But he knew Louis was avoiding Roscoe, figuring they'd be out on the truck early, before the heat swarmed into the branches. Louis remembered all those still-dark summer mornings because Darnell couldn't forget them even now—the coffee steam that the boys frowned up into their foreheads, their fathers' monosyllables, and the deserted streets. Darnell drove to the dump, and when he was finished unloading the truckbed, he stared at the dark green belt of the riverbottom, visible from the hills. Maybe Louis was just wandering around in the grove, looking for birds.

Darnell wasn't in the mood for jokes when Trent strolled into the yard the next morning and said, "This isn't grass, man, it's a collection of weeds you've been cutting short. I see Bermuda, oxalis, and nut grass."

Darnell drank his coffee. "Nobody playin golf on it," he said, short. "Charolette don't care what she stompin on."

Trent sat on the steps. "Uh-oh," he said. "Somebody jam you up about your Mexican guys?"

Darnell stared at him. "No."

Trent shrugged. "I got Juan to help me plant more perennials at Mrs. Shaefer's, and he seems like a good worker. Even if he isn't Asian."

Darnell let himself grin. "I still get nervous," he said. "We got more accounts this summer, all that new sod out there in the tracts. Juan wants to throw more flyers all the time. His English is gettin better, but he still doesn't talk to the clients. They just mail that check."

"Who's this?" Trent asked, glancing past Darnell. "Didn't he play ball?"

Louis walked quickly up the sidewalk and into the yard, his hands in his pockets. "What's up?" he said to Darnell, as if he'd been gone fifteen minutes.

"The sun," Darnell said. Louis looked at Trent, and Darnell nodded. "Trent King."

"You went to county finals, right?" Trent asked Louis. "Didn't they call you Birdman?"

Louis fanned his fingers over his chin and nodded slightly. Darnell said, "So, Trent, you got somebody for us?"

"New guy in Grayglen," Trent said, frowning. "I thought you went to college?"

Louis moved toward the El Camino impatiently. "Takin a break, man."

Darnell started the engine, and Louis fell asleep almost immediately, his knees flung wide under the dashboard, his neck limp. Darnell drove behind the AnTuan truck from Juan and José's, watching their dark heads, low in the back window, not moving when they concentrated on following Trent. Asian. And like he did every time he drove to Grayglen now, he stopped full at the intersections, staring at the other drivers. Nigger. Oriental. Mexican. What you see is what you get. He looked at the construction crews still going strong on custom houses, on the huge new tract going up past Grayglen, almost to the Sandlands. Soon as you guys are done, I'ma be drivin around with Charolette, he thought. Throwin Baggies. Little rocks. Maybe I'll get a dollar sign cut into the back of my head this time.

They followed Trent up through the twisting streets, passing the steep property where the teardown was now a huge frame covered with sheets of plywood, curved bay windows cut out everywhere. Darnell stared past Louis's sleep-shined chin, thinking of Roscoe watching him cut wood in a shower of lemon dust, wondering if he'd thought Darnell would make it. He knew Roscoe had seen Louis somewhere by now.

When they'd parked in a small turnout across the street from the huge house, Louis stepped out, eyes small, and Darnell jumped back from the gutter as a rush of bicycles streamed past. Men flashed shiny bike shorts and sunglasses; the thick-tired mountain bikes were equipped with water bottles.

Trent said, "They have a Saturday bike club. I love to ride, but I don't make it much." They crossed the narrow street quickly, Darnell hoping like he always did in Grayglen that no fool was speeding around the curves. Trent pointed to the edge of the property, where the avocado groves were squared off with chain link and barbed wire. "Guy said people are always stealing avocados to sell," Trent said, pointing, and Darnell saw Juan and José talking, José gesturing to the trees.

When they started digging the irrigation trenches, Trent said casually, "I was only expecting three guys," and Louis straightened with his shovel.

"You don't want to split the money, tell me now," he said softly.

"It's no problem, right, Darnell?" Trent said, and Darnell shook his head, slicing down through the dirt. He hates palaver, man, Darnell thought, but Trent said, "Man, I can't believe you aren't playing. I played jayvee at Fairmount, when I was a freshman, and I kept wishing I'd grow. I used to come to all the games with my dad, before he passed. He was a big fan of yours."

Louis worked his way down the trench silently. Darnell heard Juan talking to José, his voice burbling short syllables like trickling water, and Trent walked away to check the piping he'd laid out near the house.

But when they stopped for a break, in the shade of the gazebo planted in bare, raw ground, Trent said, "So what happened with college? I'da killed for a free ride, man, full scholarship like you got."

Darnell opened his mouth, but Louis said easily, "They didn't have my major up there, you know?" Trent frowned, and Louis narrowed his eyes. "Ornithology, brothaman. Speakin of, D., I got a appointment, I gotta hat up." He put his hand on Darnell's shoulder for a moment. "Meet me at my office later on, okay? I'ma be observin down there, you know, where the herons were last sighted. Later."

He walked quickly around the side of the house, Juan staring at his elbows bent in wide triangles when he put his hands in his pockets. Darnell said to Trent, "Busy man," and moved back to his shovel.

He concentrated on carving the trenches square and exact, the earth shearing off hard behind the blade, but he saw Louis walking through Grayglen, not running because that was suspicious, not loitering because that was worse. Just walking, steady, arms moving, long legs covering the asphalt all the way to the dirt road past Treetown and into the riverbottom.

When they were done for the day, waiting for Trent, Darnell leaned against the truck with Juan. José pointed at the tall hedge and the avocado trees. "What?" Darnell said idly. "José like avocados?"

"No," Juan said, staring at the dark trees that walled them in on the road. "Some men we have see in church, they live there."

"Where?"

"Under the tree." Juan gestured up the hill. "They pick the avocado, the lemon. And do works. They sleep under the tree, one tree, one man, and the *patrón*, he tell him pay." Juan paused.

Darnell looked into the impenetrable grove, at the wrought-iron fence with spike-tipped gates farther down the road. "Pay who?"

José spoke rapidly, and Juan said, "José say one tell him give twenty-five in the week. For one tree."

"Damn," Darnell said. "Don't they have nowhere to stay? Can't they find a place like you?"

Juan shook his head. "They guard the tree, so no steal. Two men, from Oaxaca, by me. They no have money for room."

"They can't stay with you guys?" Darnell asked.

Juan raised his eyebrows. "Everyone cannot stay."

Darnell drove the El Camino down the twisting streets, remembering the smell of the seat under his cheek when he'd slept there, the smell of the ashes in the park when the fire finally died toward daybreak.

The trash barrel was burning faintly when he walked toward the lot. Two older men looked up from the coals, and Darnell passed them to sit next to Victor and Ronnie on the folding chairs near the domino game. Brother Lobo was gone, but three middle-aged men cradled their bones and glanced at the table.

Victor nodded when Darnell stretched out his legs, his boots shaggy with mud shards. "Your pops came by here. Said he see me more than he see you lately."

Darnell said, "You know why." He watched three ghost-mouthed men come out of the vacant house across the lot. Louis can't hide from his pops forever, he thought. Just like I couldn't. He remembered his father's face appearing from the willows at the riverbottom, the hard voice calling him.

Victor said, "Your pops said you gotta do the Thompsons' land. That time a year."

Darnell nodded, leaning his neck on the hard folding seat for a moment and closing his eyes. Every year, they cleared the tumbleweeds and trimmed the trees for the Thompsons, who gave his father towing jobs in return.

More men began to mill around the dusty lot now; the pepper branches over his head hung limp with heat. Darnell heard them talk louder as the beer and soda cans hissed open.

"Man, it's Wild Wild Westside. I heard a shotgun last night over there off Sixth. It was like—boo-yaa, boo-yaa."

"That new brotha? He was strapped, homey."

"Everybody packin. You see Andretta was carryin that little baby Derringer for a coupla days? She gave it to that loc-wild dude. Vernon. He had the rocks—then she had the rocks."

Two of the men at the domino table shouted, "Take that shit elsewhere! I'm tired a hearin it. Go on over there with that." They nodded toward the alley and the plywood-eyed houses.

The heat pressed down harder after four, rose up from the ground and radiated from the car roofs. Darnell wiped his forehead with the can of soda Ronnie had brought him, his back already tight from the digging and now aching from the metal chair. He stared at the church across from the park, at the two women with black *rebozos* pulling open the heavy door. Another woman, smaller, cinnamon face tiny from this distance, came out and paused, staring at the men crowding the lot. Darnell gripped the cool, wet soda can. Could be GranaLene, lightin candles for me now. All the small flames swaying inside when she let the door close and disappeared back into the darkness.

He breathed in the floating dust. He was waiting for Leon, he knew. Brenda would be cooking a big Saturday meal; she liked to make something she didn't have time for during the week. Charolette would be sitting on the counter measuring, flour or cloves or pepper flying back into her face when she insisted on dumping the spoonful too hard into the bowl.

Louis need to get this over with now, he thought. I can't be hidin from everybody with him. Leon, Roscoe, anyone who stared at Louis with those lifted-in-recognition brows and asked about basketball. He knew where Louis was spending his time. That's okay for him, Darnell thought, but I ain't sleepin in the trees anymore.

Ronnie said, "Leon comin around the corner, man. He said he seen your homey Birdman on a street coupla times. He think the brotha sneakin around, like he guilty and shit."

"That's between them," Darnell said, standing up. "I'm out here, right here, just tryin to get paid." He looked at Victor. "I'll pick you guys up tomorrow for the Thompsons. Early."

"Sound like your daddy, boy," Victor said, half grinning. "Not no leisure hours, right?"

"I'm somebody else's daddy, man," Darnell said, shrugging. "And she always hungry."

He walked toward the Bronco, parked far from the lot, near the alley. I'm hungry, too, he thought. I need to get this over with, get home and eat. He saw Vernon's arm hanging from the passenger side, Vernon's face close to a woman who bent into the window. Darnell went to Leon's side.

Leon sat stiff, watching the alley and glancing into the rearview, turning his head slightly to take in Darnell where he stood by the door, hands in his pockets. "Thought you was out the business," Darnell said softly. "Thought the consultant was fixin to move you up."

"If I remember, man, business ain't your interest," Leon said, slanting his face slightly to look at Darnell. "Unless you and Birdman doin somethin besides cuttin grass." He held his mouth tight, but Darnell could see the pearl-sized dark spot where he'd rubbed his tongue at the corner of his lips.

"I wasn't into delivery then, and I ain't changed my mind," Darnell said. "You need to talk to Louis, man, cause all this suspicious shit needs to stop. We suspicious enough as it is." He tried to smile, but Leon didn't get it. Don't let me bring up binoculars, Darnell thought. Vernon bent his head now to see him. "I'ma go get Louis and meet you guys at Taco Bell, okay? Twenty minutes."

Leon frowned. "You tryin to set me up, Darnell, man? You got somethin goin with Birdman?"

Darnell looked at Leon's mink-perfect hairline, at the tongue budding pink by his lips. He couldn't say anything to defuse it; if he said he was just trying to get Louis some cash so he could leave Rio Seco, that would sound worse. Vernon grinned. "You get my man a job at the zoo and shit?" He laughed.

"Come on, Leon," Darnell said. "We ran the streets together for a long time, okay? You could just listen to him. Let's do this, cause I need to get home before Brenda goes ballistic." He paused, stopped moving away from the Bronco. "See? Does that sound like I'm doin extra business? I'm pussy-whupped, remember?"

He saw the flash of a grin from Leon before he turned.

The sun was dull in the thicker band of smog toward the west. Darnell drove onto Pepper Avenue and headed toward Treetown. The olive groves were faded silvery with dust and heat, and the grayish sky made the whole landscape a single blur when he stopped near the Thompsons' to peer at the trees and think about tomorrow. Then he saw the Bronco behind him.

Vernon was gesturing to Leon, he could see in the rearview mirror. Damn! Vernon talked Leon into comin down here, in case Louis is trippin on payback or workin for somebody else. Darnell leaned his elbows on the steering wheel and rubbed his forehead. Maybe Leon had already figured out where Louis was staying; maybe Louis wasn't even in the grove, and he'd meant something else when he said that this morning. Darnell looked down the pitted asphalt toward the riverbottom and started driving again, slow.

He could turn around now, but he knew Leon remembered the pecan grove and all the paths they'd taken when they were kids. Homeys—Leon remembers that, too. He remembers how Louis was back then, how he'd just start walkin and forget everything.

He turned down the riverbottom road, the sand crunching under the tires, and he saw the tumbleweeds rising like a wall near the pecan grove. No fire over here yet, he thought. This place is ready, too. The pecan grove never burned, he realized, staring at the tops of the trees.

He saw a few cars in the clearing, but they were empty. He heard the Bronco roll to a stop at the far edge, staying near the road, and he got out, walking toward Leon. "You best not trip," he said. "This ain't TV, okay? This ain't cowboy shit. Louis just wants to go back up north, like Donnie."

Leon scratched the inside of his elbow, nodding. "All our homeys gone mental," he said, and his voice sounded gentle. "Man, when we started drivin down here, I was laughin, like I could see how skinny and little we was when we used to ride them chopper bikes and get stuck in the sand." He pushed at Darnell's shoulder. "Stall out, man. Let's go."

Vernon was behind them, silent, when they walked toward the trees. Darnell saw the haze hanging thick around the trunks, and the few tufts of grass under his feet crackled dry. He peered into the grove, where the leaf litter and crushed foxtails were still thick.

Louis came from the path that led from the grove to the riverbottom, and when he saw all three of them, he didn't turn or even frown. He nodded and called, "If y'all came to talk, you better do it now."

Leon frowned, and Darnell said, "What you talkin about?"

Louis smiled. "It's almost bedtime." He lifted his face to the sky that showed dimmer now through the leaves. "Don't you remember, Darnell, around quittin time?"

Darnell saw the long legs planted apart, the pale neck thrown back, and he knew Louis meant that the crows would pass over all the yards they'd cut, all the trees they'd trimmed while their fathers watched them and hollered, while Roscoe told Louis to quit wasting time staring at the sky.

"We ain't into birdwatchin," Leon said, quiet. "I heard you was back in town and you didn't even come to tell me what the fuck happened that day."

Louis put his hands in his pockets and leaned against a tree, crossing his feet. "If I told you, you wouldn't believe me."

"I believe you was fixin to move product to somebody else," Vernon said, arms folded, and Darnell looked at Leon.

"Shut up, man," Leon said. "Then why the nigga still cuttin grass?"

Darnell breathed in hard, felt the smog tighten in a pipe down his breastbone. "Yeah, Louis, I'ma have your money for today's job when I cash Trent's check, okay?" He heard the whispering rustle above him and saw the first of the crows circling the grove, and then the flock streamed around the trees, calling and arguing and jostling for place in the sky.

Leon kept his eyes on Louis. "What happened?"

"I came down here to see some birds, and somebody musta thought

I was too tall to wander around." Louis didn't lift his face again. "The rangers came and then they called the cops."

"What the fuck?" Vernon said, mouth open, staring at the sharp feet snatching at branches, at the wings flapping when crows changed their minds and moved again, and the noise was deafening now, the birds screaming at each other and then screaming louder at the men below.

"Ain't nobody usually in here by now," Louis said easily, smiling at Vernon. "If somebody came for pecans or lunch, they gone. Crows are pissed."

Darnell felt the air sway from all the movement, and the shadows shifted crazily near his feet. The hoarse calls went jagged into his ears, and he remembered how scared he'd been the few times Louis showed him the flock all together like this. It was like the movie, like *The Birds*, he'd told Louis, and Louis had said, "Yeah, but you crazier, man, cause fire can kill you for real. That was just a movie. When you took me to that fire, all that cracklin and them trees blowin up, that was scary. The birds are just talkin."

He blinked, his eyes stinging from where he'd been staring at the tree bark near Louis's shoulder, and Leon said, "You lost me five grand, man, and the consultant been usin that shit for a long time, makin me do extra stuff. You owe me."

Louis shook his head. "You know I ain't got money if I'm workin for Darnell," he said, "like a Mexican guy."

"Hey," Darnell said, smiling. "It's worse jobs."

"Oh, you talkin shit now, too?" Vernon said, his voice higher, and Darnell saw the gash lines appear in his cheeks, not because he was smiling but because he had his mouth stretched wide with anger and fear.

"I ain't even speakin to you, man," Darnell said. "Come on, I gotta get home."

Leon bit his lip stubbornly. "I don't know, man." His voice wavered.

Louis said, "It was stupid, man, it's just gone. Cops got it, okay? They did whatever they do with it."

"You lost me money, too, motherfucker," Vernon said, walking away, and then he stopped. "Always sittin up in the car actin like I was a fool. Look at you—hangin out with some goddamn birds. Like you a bag lady and shit. You a crazy motherfucker."

"And you're gangsta-loc-insane, man," Louis said, smiling again. "Like that's better." He shook his head, and Vernon's face went flat and gray around the mouth. Darnell saw his hand reach behind him, and he felt the chemical air all the way in his stomach when he took in breath to leap behind the tree.

But Vernon aimed the small handgun at the branches and said, "Fuckin noise drivin me crazy. They need to shut up. I can't even hear." He fired at the crows in the next tree, and when the shots reverberated in the grove, the screaming rose louder, wings pushing down the sound to whirl it closer to their ears. Vernon dropped his head forward and hunched his shoulder, and then Louis was on him, slamming the gun into the sand.

Darnell and Leon pulled them off each other, and Leon held the gun tight when Vernon backed away, his hair coated with light sand, his eyelids shivering and a piece of thin grass hanging from one brow. "Why you play me like that, Leon?" he shouted. "Why you—"

"Get in the car, man," Leon said. "Birdman, you steady fuckin up. You past insane." He held the gun loose and walked toward the Bronco.

Vernon stood blinking, then staring at Louis. "Two shots to the membrane, nigga. That's what you need." He turned and began to walk away.

Darnell concentrated on holding his shoulders still and tight, not moving his feet, imagining only his veins and arteries working, his capillaries racing in spurts. When the Bronco's taillights had faded to red pinpricks through the tumbleweeds, Louis laughed loud, and Darnell shook his head. "I ain't fixin to call you insane," he told Louis, "but you are crazy." He sat with his back to a pecan tree. "I don't know what you coulda said, though."

The crows' screaming seemed more conversational now, but when Louis stretched his arms, the birds in the closest tree burst into circles of flight for a moment. Louis laughed again. "I coulda told Vernon the crows used to fools shootin at em." He stroked his chin. "If you hit one, about ten more come down for payback and buzz you."

Darnell walked with him away from the grove after his blood had slowed. The cars were still there, and he was surprised when Louis opened the door of the VW. "This one's my hooptie," Louis said. "Two hundred bucks, from some dude in Treetown."

"Why'd you walk all the way home today?" Darnell asked, sitting on the still-hot seat.

"Somebody stole the battery last night," Louis said, dangling his legs out of the driver's seat. He kept his back to Darnell. "You didn't ask what I had to tell you, man."

"I thought I already heard enough for one day, homey."

"I seen two dudes down here yesterday, pokin around, and one of em was bendin down like he was gon start a fire," Louis turned halfway in his seat. "You ain't lookin out for that, for the guys startin all these fires?"

"I'm not into investigation," Darnell said. He watched the outlines of the trees and tumbleweeds fading dark.

"You ain't into firefighting, neither. Never?"

Darnell looked at the blunt toes of his boots, where the mud had turned to powder now. "I'm puttin in my application after the baby comes. Brenda's due in November. I'ma apply in January, but that'll be for summer season." He'd taken out the application and studied it again and again. "Paid call."

"Well, these two guys I saw yesterday, they weren't birdwatchers, okay?" Louis said.

Darnell smiled. "You IDed em, huh?"

Louis nodded. "Yeah." He paused, rubbing his neck. "But it's a lotta guys sleepin down here."

Darnell looked at the other cars. "In there?"

"No, that's some Mexican guys lookin for rabbits, and two Vietnamese dudes catchin crawdads."

"You hungry?" Darnell looked at the hollows in Louis's face, his shoulders wide shelves under the T-shirt.

"Just give me a ride to Taco Bell, okay? I ain't sleepin at your crib."

"Man, I don't care about Leon."

Louis got out of the VW. "I don't either. But I see Brenda over there cleanin, cookin. She works too hard."

Darnell walked beside him to the El Camino. "Oh, so you sayin I don't take care of her?"

"Stall out, Darnell. All I'm sayin is, I just see her and it makes me think of how she used to look, and . . ."

"Okay, okay." Darnell started the car, thinking of how she looked from behind, how that second outline, that other body, seemed to overlap her hips and even her back. "She still looks good to me," he said.

"She looks better to me, cause I don't have her." Louis kept his eyes straight ahead.

Darnell sat for a moment, thinking of school, when all they'd looked at was the body, the full chest or moving booty, when all they'd imagined was the sex. He sometimes touched the softness of extra flesh at the back of her arm at night, when she lay with her back to him. "It ain't like before, man, I mean, what looks good. Her face is wider, like . . . she looks like somebody else sometimes."

"I wasn't lookin at her body before," Louis said, not turning his head. "I was always lookin at her face. Her eyes."

"I got one wild child," Brenda said. "I don't need nobody grown to give me a worrying headache."

"It ain't that late," he said, taking his plate to the table. "I was waitin for this all day." She'd made red snapper fried with onions, peppered rice, and yellow squash cut in circles.

"Charolette had a good time cleaning out the rice," she said, sitting down across from him.

Darnell looked at her hair, shining glossy, tight-pulled from her face, and her fingers nervous near her mouth. "I worked all day with Trent, and I had to help out Louis with somethin."

She cocked her head. "Where is he? Why didn't he come eat?"

"Cause you aren't his wife," Darnell said.

"What's that mean?"

Darnell shrugged. "I forgot Louis used to keep his eye on you, like he was waitin for you to come to your senses and go out with a ballplayer instead of a nature boy. Especially a broke nature boy."

She smiled even with her lips pressed together tight, and then her teeth shone in the kitchen light. "I wanted to be with him some-times—a basketball star, like all the girls used to say. But I couldn't—I mean, I'd look at his chin, way up there, and it wasn't like yours, and his eyebrows, and his hands." She stood up embarrassed, bending her neck, and went to the sink. "So now he's just somebody in the house to worry about. Like I said, I got Charolette, and this one kicking me steady. Louis disappearing. And don't let me start about you." She plucked at his dusty sleeve now, pulling off a burr, and he caught her hand. "No. Uh-uh," she said. "Cause there was another fire tonight, way over by the Sandlands, and I was sure that's where you were. I saw it on the news."

"Not me," Darnell said. "I didn't even see the smoke."

On Picasso Street, while he leaned against the hood and waited for his father, Charolette ran to him. "Gramma Mary nuked me biscuit!" she said, pushing it at him. "Daddy, blow on it!"

"You so bad, blow on it yourself," he said, and she spit rapidly at the steaming biscuit. "Wet it up good."

Darnell's mother stood in the doorway. "Brenda restin?" she said casually, as if he'd just been there last night and not disappeared for days.

"She did too much work in the house yesterday, and now her back hurts," Darnell said. "She wants to sleep twenty-four-seven anyway, every minute she can."

"That's how it is the last three months," his mother said, getting that dreamy look. "You never rest good, and this heat so strong. When you finally fall out, you sleep like somebody drop a rock on your chest. I remember."

"She got all day to rest," Darnell said. "I'm takin Charolette to work."

His father came out, T-shirt fresh-bleached, his chin stubbled with sparse hairs. "You get Victor and Ronnie?" he said.

"Here's my crew," Darnell said, pointing to Charolette in the truckbed.

"You in trouble now," his father said, palming her head. "All her talkin blow the tumbleweeds to the river." He leaned against his truck door, facing Darnell. "Who else you got?"

Darnell knew what he was asking. "I told Louis he could meet us over there. He's still workin now and then."

Darnell's father knuckled at the chin hairs. "People been tellin Roscoe they seen his boy walkin, or they passed by when y'all workin somewhere." Darnell waited. "All Roscoe says is he hope he ain't stayin around here. Doin time never teach you nothin new that's good."

"I'ma get started," Darnell said, swinging Charolette down to the driveway. "Not no leisure hours, right?" His father curved up one side of his mouth.

When Victor and Ronnie got out, Darnell told her again about what she couldn't touch. The cab was her favorite place. She jerked the steering wheel hard, frowning. "Why you dawdlin?" she said, sounding exactly like his father.

He wondered if Louis would show up. Darnell had parked on the dirt lot, under a carob tree, and he leaned inside to ask her, "Where you goin?"

"To Mexico!" she said, as if he were foolish not to know. "And Honolulu."

They forked the tumbleweeds that rolled up the riverbottom each year to pile along the fences. "Long time ago, huh, brothaman?" Victor said, grinning.

Darnell knew what he was thinking. "Fifty years," he said. He watched Charolette in the cab. When she rubbed her eyes, he went to spread her blanket and Barbie on the seat.

"It's too hot," she complained.

"Check this out." He took some of the downed carob and olive branches they'd trimmed to pile them high on the windshield. "Hide in the forest," he said, and she stared at the leaves pressed tightly to the glass. The interior was cooler green, with tiny shaded slants of light and muffled sound.

"You crazy, man," Louis said, standing there when he got out.

"Hey, you do whatever you have to when you want em to crash," Darnell said. "Anything."

Louis joined them to pile the tumbleweeds and branches and trash on the far corner of the property. The Thompsons hated paying dump fees, and nobody cared about burning in Treetown. But when Darnell was about to throw the last load of fallen carob pods and strike a match, Demetrius came out of the house and hurried over to where they stood.

"We can't burn today, man," Demetrius said. "You know they lookin hard for this arsonist, and my mama said don't take no chances."

"Just like last summer," Victor said. "Fire every week, man."

"I'm tellin you, Darnell, I seen those guys," Louis said. "One big Mexican dude and a white dude with blond hair."

Darnell frowned. "You saw Scott and Perez," he said, nodding. "They work the fires, man; they're paid call."

Louis shrugged. "I didn't see no fire engine near em."

Victor pointed. "You bein paged, Daddy." Darnell saw Charolette's head poke out the open window."

He held her, still sleepy, while Demetrius talked to them all near the avenue. "I have to drop her off at home and hit the ATM for some cash," Darnell told them. "I gotta pay you for that other job, too, Louis."

Louis looked up the street. "Ain't that Gasanova?"

Gas was looking for a truck part from Demetrius, and when he came back, the men piled into his truck, Louis hanging out the window. "Speakers in the back, man," Darnell said, laughing. "No room for brothas."

"It ain't far to the park," Victor called. "Hurry up, man, you know my condition."

"He's thirsty," Darnell said to Charolette, strapping her in. She looked straight out the window when he drove, staring fixedly ahead at something, and he said, "What's wrong, babygirl?" He squinted into the glare, where the smog-held sun caught in his eyes.

"It's the sparkly time," she said, pointing to the sides of the road. On the bare sandy shoulder, thousands of glass shards reflected in the hard light.

"You been hangin out with Uncle Roscoe too much," he said.

"Who made those rainbows?" she asked, dreamily.

"Where?"

"Window rainbows." The windshield was dirty, as usual, and Brenda must have turned on the wipers and cleaner. Two perfect arcs, striped by the frayed wipers, shone in the glare.

"Mama did," he said, and she nodded, her mouth slightly open.

Brenda was waiting on the porch, and she held out her arms for Charolette. "I gotta pay the guys," Darnell said. "I'll be back in a few."

The heat rippled off the pavement, wavered the figures of the men standing around the pepper trees and card tables. Darnell parked behind Gas's truck and counted the money again. He glanced up and saw a woman in bike shorts and a pink bra, standing on the corner waiting for a slowed car; her reddish hair stood up stiff and uncombed, like a single dust-threaded flame.

Victor and Ronnie were in the shade, sharing a forty-ounce, and Gas and Louis stood near Brother Lobo, laughing. When Darnell handed Louis his money, Brother Lobo said, "I haven't seen this young man in a long time."

Louis nodded and said, "I was migratin, you know."

"I'm gone," Darnell shouted to them, and Gas walked beside him.

"Yo, Leon," a voice called from the alley. Gas shook his head, his cheek hollow when he sucked his teeth impatiently and ignored the man. "People always sayin we look alike," he said. "Do I look like a fool?" Darnell smiled, and Gas went on: "Man, I'll be due on shift and Moms says, 'Give your brother a ride; he don't want to take his car.' Damn." He grabbed for a swig of Darnell's soda. "He hidin out, says somebody followin him."

"Darnell, man, wait up," Louis hollered from the pepper tree.

"I'm due on home shift," Darnell said to Gas. "Hot as hell at the crib, too. We been livin on the porch."

When they neared the El Camino, Darnell saw a shine of pink, and he heard Louis laughing behind him. "Check you out," Gas said. "Daddy."

Barbie had fallen from the cab, headfirst into the gutter, and Darnell bent low to pick her up by her long hair. He had squatted to brush a leaf from her headband when he heard wheels slipping loose on the corner, an engine accelerating ragged. He balanced himself with his hand on the wheel well, and when the hammering shots sounded, he smashed his cheek against the metal, his eyes burning he clenched them so tight. He heard the beats separately, three, four, regular, each explosion a breath apart, semiautomatic, the time it took the finger to pull the trigger, and when he dropped himself flat in the gutter behind the tire, the doll's foot stiff in his chest, pepper berries crushed to release sharp scent near his face, he heard a bullet chunk into a tree trunk like a high-thrown stone into deep water. The shots, eight, nine, ten, were wet to his ears, and he thought, Cuttin the devil's throat, the chunking image still flickering behind his lids when the last shot sounded, farther away.

The field was so silent that they heard tires loop-screeching all the way on Pepper Avenue before someone started screaming. "Got-damn! This hurts—Got-*damn!*"

Darnell lifted himself from the oil-stained gutter, feeling ferny leaves stuck to his cheek, and he saw Gas lying silent on his stomach, trying to rise, clapping his palm to his ear. And just beyond him,

Louis was curved long on his side, his back fanned wide in the creamy shirt, his shoulder flat. When Darnell bent, the damp explosions still burning in his ears, he saw the blood pooling thick-edged in the dust from under Louis, from the ribs beneath him, the red darkening as if the heat had already hardened it. Darnell pushed Louis's shoulder to find the wound; Louis's head was bent forward, heavy, the blind, paler back of his neck glittering with moisture.

The men were moving everywhere now, shadows falling across Darnell's hands when he felt the throbbing in Louis's neck, and his own chest began to tremble now. Pulling off his shirt, he bunched cloth on the blood at Louis's ribs, looking up to see who was shouting.

Brother Lobo was the one yelling, holding his shoulder when Victor pushed him toward the street, and then Darnell felt hands pulling him up roughly. Mr. Taylor said, "We gotta take him—who knows how long nine-one-one take for down here. Darnell! Come on, now. He ain't gon fit in your truck."

Darnell slid his arms under Louis's rib bones as two other men, strangers from the alley, bent and straightened with him. Louis's back was thick-wet, the chalky-sweet smell of carob dust rising from his hair, and his mouth left a trail of shine on Darnell's bare shoulder when they put him in the long, cavelike backseat of Mr. Taylor's Cadillac.

He felt the blood tightening on his wrists, and Mr. Taylor pushed him again. "I'ma take him! You go and get his daddy, go on, bring him to County."

Darnell backed toward the El Camino. Gas's skull glistened red in a trail through his hair, a line above his temple, and he said to Ronnie, "Don't call Leon, hell, no, you take me to County. I ain't ridin with my goddamn brother."

"I told you where to go," Mr. Taylor shouted, his eyes squinted to slits when he pulled around on the street, and Darnell moved, smelling the residue of burned tires and cordite ahead of him like a trail. The passenger window of the El Camino was shattered, and he stared at the open driver's side, wondering where the bullet was now.

Vernon—it had to be Vernon, he thought, driving, his jaw feeling huge as if metal had gathered above his ears, and he turned the corner to Picasso Street, seeing Roscoe's Apache parked at his father's.

He ran through the sideyard and slammed into the back room,

filled with the wet mixed smell of cold beer and the swamp cooler. His father and Roscoe looked up, and Darnell's forehead felt melted behind his eyes, the sheets of childish water blinding him. "I gotta take you to the hospital, Roscoe," he said, and blinked, Roscoe's face swelling huge when he rose from the table.

That smell, the night he'd been in the hospital lying face down in the swimming chemical air and the fluorescent light, with the razor-cold air on his leg, shivered into his bare chest when he saw Roscoe's back go up the hallway. He turned to face the wall, eyes passing over his father's folded arms, and he clenched shut his eyes, thinking, Don't see that. Breathing in hard, he remembered the smell, clinging to Brenda's hair and neck when she lived here with Charolette for those first days, when Charolette was lavender and spindle-thin as the tubes snaking into her skin. When he brought his palm up to his forehead, though, the tight tracing of blood on his forearm broke; the black-red coating was a mosaic, sealed to his skin, but the edges turned to dust when he laid his fingers over them, and his father said, "God-damn." Roscoe was coming out of the hallway, walking slow, each step away from the door meaning that there was nothing to wait for now.

"Nobody's had to *take* me anywhere for a long time," Roscoe had said, hard, when he stood up, and now he pulled away, alone, in the Apache.

By the El Camino, Darnell's father looked down and saw the glass glinting scattered on the seat, and he shouted, "God*damn* you boys! I drove you and Louis all over in this damn car and . . . y'all killin each other like you think it's a game." He pushed the heel of his palm over his forehead and turned his eyes straight on Darnell, who leaned against the door.

Darnell felt his cold skin prickling in the heat of the parking lot; his neck was rough with dirt when he put his fingers there. "Tell me a Mississippi story, Pops. Oklahoma story. What you think you can do? What you think *I* can do?" he said, keeping his eyes on his father's, staring at the muddied whites almost lost in his father's squint. "Tell me some huntin stories. Open season, Pops." He felt his throat close on the last word, the one that always had to come from far down behind his tongue, and he opened the car door.

His father said nothing all the way back to the Westside, just kept his boots placed carefully on the glass slivers, his eyes on the windshield. When Darnell stopped at his father's driveway, he said, "Roscoe went to Marietta's, huh?"

His father nodded, still in the seat. "What you fixin to tell your wife? You were standin right there." His father turned to look at him.

"I'ma lie," Darnell said. "Lie straight up. You know I can't tell her that—she probably go into labor early again." He saw his father's jaw move.

"Ain't the first time," his father said. "And it probably ain't the last." When Darnell started to speak, his father shook his head. "I wasn't talkin about penny-ante. I'm just talkin about necessity. Go on home."

It wasn't even close to dark yet. He rinsed his eyes with warm water from the hose at the steps, smelling fish from the open window, and he threw back his head and breathed hard. I don't want to go inside and be Pops. Daddy. I can't tell her, not right now, not even nothin about me or where I was—he stopped, closed his eyes, saw the fine dust on the back of Louis's neck, the snail-curled hairs growing long at his nape. Biting his lips until they swelled, hurt, he opened the door, the doll's sharp plastic thighs in his fingers.

Charolette ran to him before Brenda could speak. She grabbed the doll, shouting, "Barbie! You find her, Daddy!"

"Sorry it took so long, but I didn't want to come home without her," he said, looking at Brenda. She glanced up from stirring the rice, but she only nodded. He leaned against the refrigerator, his chest full of water, and he felt Charolette's fingers hot on his elbow.

"You get a ouchie, Daddy?" she said. Brenda looked up, too, and he twisted his arm to see the smears of blood he hadn't noticed above his elbow.

"It's just from a splinter," he said, closing the door to the bathroom, putting his palms on the tile counter. He stared at the bottles of makeup and perfume and shampoo and hairdress—all theirs, all women's things, their smell rising sweet where the sun had heated the counter all afternoon. He washed off the blood, his mouth filling with saliva at the image of the liquid gelling on the dirt, the dust flecking so fast. He checked the clean skin on his arm, clenching his teeth, hearing them talk in the kitchen, and he knew Charolette would examine him closely for wounds. Staring out the window at the El Camino, where he'd parked it far up the driveway, he saw the jagged remnants of glass.

He went down the hallway, through the bedroom, quickly, hearing Charolette still talking in the kitchen to Brenda, and outside by the car, he grabbed a shard of glass from the floorboards. Reaching behind him, he made a quick, thin scratch above his elbow, where she had seen the blood.

He sat on the porch while she applied the Mickey Mouse Band-Aid carefully to the cut. "I fix it up," she said, and Brenda only watched, sitting near the door. How I'ma tell her about Louis? he thought. Not about me—first, just about Louis. He'd thought she would ask about him at dinner, but she sat, leaning against the wall, her eyes closed, her hand resting on that high, hard curve under her breasts.

Charolette began smoothing the plastic strip over his arm again, and he said, "That's enough, babygirl." After Brenda had gone inside to give her a bath, when the sky turned purple, he still sat, hearing the palm fronds rustle and the threading whine of the helicopter.

Just after dark, Leon stood on the porch, his face swollen around the eyes, his tongue working the left corner of his mouth furiously, the skin shined raw.

"You know that was for me," he said. "Darnell, man, you know it was."

Darnell had just gone inside for another can of soda. He stepped out the door, onto the porch. Brenda had come up behind him, and she put her hand on his elbow. "What's wrong?" she whispered.

"Nothin," Darnell said. He felt her soft finger pads press his skin. Charolette was asleep now, and Brenda's hair was damp-curled around her forehead from the shower.

Leon didn't look at her. "My brother won't even speak, man. He don't want nothin to do with me." He moved down the steps, came back up wild. "I can't talk right here, man, come on."

Leon turned, and Darnell said, "I'ma be right back, Brenda; let me go talk to him." He uncurled her fingers gently, whispering. He didn't want Leon to say it, to ask.

"I can't stay out here, I gotta ride," Leon said. "Darnell."

Brenda grabbed his arm and said, "You ain't goin nowhere. No. Uh-uh."

Leon stopped and turned. "Yo, Darnell, man, I gotta talk to somebody. I'm leavin in the mornin."

Darnell moved Brenda's hand gently, whispered, "Brenda, stall out." He called to Leon, "Where's Vernon?"

"I don't know, man," Leon said. "He gone, too."

Darnell's skull vibrated with the humming streetlights, the wires above the yard, the helicopter circling somebody in the distance. He closed his eyes. Gone. Everybody gone. "I'll be right back, Brenda." He moved in a dream toward the Bronco, and she ran after him and jerked him around by his elbows.

"Leon, stop. Cause Darnell ain't goin nowhere." She was shouting, her voice higher than singing. "And I don't want to hear that shit. 'Homey, I got your back. Don't worry.' " She held him hard, imitating him, Leon, all of them. "No. *I* got your back, every time you go out the damn door, I'm watchin your back. Not this time. I ain't playin, Darnell." Her thin fingers were locked around the indentation above his elbow, pressing his muscle against bone, and he saw the streetlamps swimming at the outer edges of her wide, black-lined eyes, she stood so close.

"Come in the house and talk," she said.

"I ain't sittin in no living room," Leon said. "Fuck it. I gotta ride."

Brenda didn't move, Darnell stared at her. Her lips were open, waiting, and she didn't blink. In the porch light, her irises were steady gold. He turned and said, "Hold up, Leon."

Leon hesitated on the grass, and Darnell went to stand close to her. He saw the tiny sharp line cleaving her upper lip. Like a dart. She'd shown it to him last week, told him she'd finally figured out it was from kissing Charolette all the time, absently, lips pursed, her head turning automatically like the nearby fat cheek was a magnet.

He couldn't tell her about the pepper berries under his face in the gutter, the bullets chunking into the trees and vacant house. Louis, the silence, and the blood filmed with dust.

"Brenda," he said, to her forehead. "I'ma take him in the backyard. I ain't goin nowhere, okay? I ain't leavin. Go open Charolette's window and you can see me. I ain't leavin." He turned her shoulders and ran his palms down her arms, and she moved away.

He led Leon through the dark sideyard, the block wall still warm
under his hand. He opened the glove compartment of the Spider and
took out the flat bottle of Jack Daniels, the one he'd bought a long
time ago. After the dog. The gun had been in there, too.

"Get a taste, come on," he said, offering the bottle to Leon. "Sit
down for a minute." He saw Brenda's face smudge pale in the screen,
and then the window was dark again. Leon sat in the low bucket seat,
the doors open, and after he'd had another drink, he slumped down
a little.

"You ain't even askin me," Darnell said.

"I know—Birdman went to County," Leon began, but Darnell cut
him off.

"He's gone." Darnell waited, but Leon's face remained loose and
damp, his eyes on the cinder block. "I didn't see Gasanova over
there."

"He at the crib," Leon said, his voice high. "He got a bandage on
his head—it was like a burn." Darnell saw the red trail in the cut-
short fade at Gas's temple.

"It wasn't a damn burn," Darnell said, and Leon went on, like he
was happy to talk about his brother instead of Louis.

"Gas won't tell me shit—not what the dude was drivin, nothin.
He said he rather walk home from Louisiana than ride with me—
Tamiko told me he said that shit. He told Tamiko pack her stuff, cause
they movin to Vegas." Leon put his forehead in his fingers. "You
should see his truck. It's all fucked up, got bullet holes in the body."

Darnell was silent. He heard the rounds—twelve or thirteen. He
leaned his head back.

"I ain't seen Vernon, okay, so don't even ax me," Leon whispered.
His eyes sagged sleepy, and he rested his head against the seat, too.
"See, you don't know. It was probably somebody jackin for me. Business here all messed up, Vernon been loc wild, and the consultant
said he movin him to Portland, let him go, once he get up there, if
he keep buckin."

"We ain't never gon know who did it," Darnell said, flat, his voice
blurred inside his ears.

Leon said, slurred, "Vernon feel like that money was his, too—
what Birdman fucked up. That was gon be Vernon's first time, his
first big cut."

"That ain't just money," Darnell said, heat ringing his eyes at the shift in Leon's voice. "You know Victor and the brothas at the park gon be lookin at *you*. Ducats ain't a damn thang to them. Vernon, neither."

Leon's legs moved near the stick shift. "I know." He waited. "Vernon one a them LA brothas. Hard as hell. He ain't got no homeys out here in Rio Seco—he like it like that, so he can do what he want." Leon threw back his head. "But I don't know if he did it or not. I ain't lyin. Lotta brothas just do what they want."

"You can't." Darnell wouldn't look at him.

"I know. I'm gone, man. I'm goin to Seattle." Darnell heard a tiny wet click, and he knew Leon's tongue was working pink at the loose corner, but he kept his eyes to the blank, smoggy dark until Leon's shoes crunched grit on the sidewalk.

The silence was thick in the corners, but in Charolette's bedroom he heard a noise, and he saw Brenda kneeling awkwardly beside the sleeping head, holding the tiny limp hand between her fingers, metal flashing. She looked up at him fiercely, warning him away with her eyes, and he saw that she was cutting fingernails.

She came out a few minutes later, holding the tiny clippers. "Every week," she said, holding her side. "They grow so fast, and it's hard to catch her asleep." She began picking up clothes from the floor of their bedroom, and he frowned. Charolette's almost two and a half, he thought, and I ain't never even looked at her fingernails.

When she sat on the bed, waiting, folding a T-shirt, he knew he couldn't tell her in the dark, airless cave of their bedroom, the place where they never did anything but fall exhausted onto the sheets and listen to the night for a few minutes. He said, "Come out here for a minute."

"What?" She drew her brows together. He led her out to the backyard and opened the door to the Spider again. She sat in her old seat, her feet flat on the floor instead of drawn up under her like they used to be, and she rested her hands under her belly.

Darnell leaned over the stickshift. "This is a good place to listen," he said. "Nothin to clean or fold out here. Nobody callin for AnTuan. Only thing to do is talk or bust some slobs." She'd always hated it when the boys said that about kissing.

"Charolette might wake up," she said, moving her back from the seat.

"She'll come to the backdoor if she see it's open," he said. He bent down to lift her feet carefully into his lap, awkward because of her weight, but it was almost like when they used to sit at the city lake. The metal was cooling now that it was late, and the slight breeze moved the curls at her forehead.

"I smell liquor," she said. "Did Leon drink something?" He nodded. Behind her tight-boned cheeks and small forehead were the edges of another face, lingering at the sides of her jaw, even at her temples. "You didn't go," she said, looking through the opaque, filmed windshield.

"I told you I wasn't goin anywhere anymore," he said. "Brenda. Louis got shot. He's gone."

Her head and shoulders jerked involuntarily, hunched, and he knew the cold spasm was twisting through her. He rubbed her knees hard, put his hands on each side of her belly, and it was almost like he couldn't hear the moist-whirring bullets or smell the rust under the wheel well when he said the words. He rushed on. "Nobody knows who did it. Gasanova and Brother Lobo got grazed. Leon just told me Gas is movin to Vegas. Leon's goin to Seattle. Everybody's leavin, except me. I'm right here."

Then he let her turn her moon-pale face up, let her get the question out. "You were there when he got . . . you were there?"

"I was gettin Charolette's Barbie," he said, looking down at her wider knees. He had to. White lie for the good—brotha lie this time. He knew nobody would mention it to her, to a woman—not Victor or Ronnie, no one. They wouldn't even talk about it again at the park—not like the dog, when they all wanted to discuss him and K-9. They hadn't been there, they hadn't seen that. But the noise and dust and shouting were locked behind their molars and belts and kneecaps now.

He said, "Show me your wrinkle, what you said make you look different." She stared at him, and then she kissed the air, the line deepening into her upper lip like a knife had just sliced her skin.

"Did you drink some, too?" she asked. "Did you want to go with Leon?"

"No," he said. "Check my breath. Check my hands." He pushed her feet slowly from his legs and circled her lips with his mouth.

*   *   *

She slept on her side, a pillow propped under her stomach, her arm curled over her ear again. He looked into the bedroom after eleven, seeing her face slack with weight and exhaustion.

He peered into the darkness where Charolette lay with her arms flung behind her like she was diving, her wrists limp and fingers almost touching.

Walking the hallway, the living room, even the porch, he smelled fish and baby shampoo and milk, felt the soft lump of a stuffed porpoise under his foot, brushed a pile of clean towels on the couch. He couldn't breathe.

The truck slid out of the driveway in neutral, and he drove the other way, away from the Westside, from the park and Treetown and the grove. He was halfway through the Sandlands, the fast air rushing through both windows, the August pale hills round and weaving past him, when he pulled over. He couldn't go up the mountain, couldn't sit at the table with the clicking cards and Fricke's denim-pale eyes, because he couldn't say it again. It had felt better to say it the one time, to Brenda. Gone. Louis was gone—everybody was gone. But he wouldn't be able to say the words in the station, because this had nothing to do with chaparral or packing the right gear or six feet deep to keep enough oxygen above a tight-closed mouth.

He stared at the undulating hills, the crisscrossing bands of fire roads and motorcycle trails, the burned mustard weed and grasses. The window was still framed with broken glass, and he reached across to touch the metal frame. Metal had framed the hand holding the gun—metal gun, metal bullets. Small, chickenshit projectiles. No knowledge required—no ID for poison oak so the fumes didn't sear lung tissue, no judging a fire break. No flames rushing over to steal your breath before you even felt the sear of heat—the bullets killed cheap, nasty. All alone. Brothas frozen like puzzle pieces, legs and elbows all bent, necks angling sharp. I ain't goin out like that. I can't. Not me.

He raced back down the highway and went over the bridge to the riverbottom, stopping the El Camino at the sandy road leading to the arundo cane, the stands so vivid in the moonlight, so dark compared to the bleached fields and hills all around. Pops came to get me last time, found me and threw the piece in there, he thought.

He remembered how small the gun had been in his palm, even smaller in his father's. Nine millimeter. He breathed in, trying to remember what caliber bullet was in Donnie's leg. Donnie gone, too. That night I was trippin on the dog, on what I thought was wild dogs in the cane. Pops ain't comin tonight. Just me. He breathed in the shallow-water smell, the old ashes from a cookfire.

Glass still glittered near the curb, where pepper berries had fallen new to cover the ones he'd crushed. Victor rose from the sagged couch, his dark face half shadowed, and Darnell pulled to the curb. "I need a ride, brothaman."

Darnell went carefully down the narrow drive downtown, where Brother Lobo lived. "Lights are off," he said. "Maybe he's crashed."

But Brother Lobo had heard the engine, and he peered through the front window of the tiny garage apartment. "Company," he said. He looked at the bag in Victor's hands. "Victor brings food, and maybe Darnell brings good news. What's my smallest queen doing?" His voice was fast, too oiled.

"All my queens sleepin," Darnell said. "Dreamin. Almost midnight."

"Round midnight," Brother Lobo said, sitting on the couch. "After midnight. In the midnight hour."

"How's your arm?" Darnell asked. Victor sat in a wooden chair, and Brother Lobo lifted his loose short sleeve to show the raw red crease. "You supposed to have that bandaged," Darnell said, wincing.

"It needs fresh air to heal," Brother Lobo said. Then he looked hard at Darnell. "It needs to close up into a scar quickly. A mark." He shook his head. "Darnell. This isn't the kind of tribal mark I need. Scarification . . ." He paused. "It's supposed to be ritual," he whispered. "Show me your marks."

Darnell realized Lobo was pointing to his leg. He sat on the couch and pulled up his work pants, propped his leg over his knee so the very end of the shiny, many-legged scar crawled around his calf. He touched it, the skin tight. Brother Lobo stared and said, "Victor?"

Victor stood up and lifted his shirt, proffering his back. A thin-slanted slash on his shoulder blade, and a perfect grid of squares, small lines that had to be burn scars. "Treetown," he said. "Some brotha I didn't even know." He paused. "And my mama's old man. The heater."

They pulled back their clothes. "There is no ceremony for this," Brother Lobo murmured.

Darnell smelled the harsh perique smoke, remembered when the strings tied around his ankle had finally softened, rotted off. He saw Donnie's face, imagined the bullet flying through his blood, coursing around and around through his heart like a rocket. It got prayers on it—it got bodies on it. He said, "No."

But when he got out of the truck and walked through the dark to the pale cement outlines of the old foundation, he squatted in the dirt and scratched the pebbled concrete with a stick. The voices across the alley were quiet, and no fire burned in the heat that still lingered through the night.

Darnell walked to the wall near the abandoned houses and stripped off a few branches from the wild tobacco bushes, their limber, thin trunks leaning away from the cinder block. He sawed at the wood with his knife, and then sat on his heels in the center of the foundation, setting the branches on fire. They were bending green, not burning but smoking bitter and swirled. He kept his back to the faraway murmurs of the men in the alley, and said to himself, "I got a thousand midnights left to go." He thought of the new baby's feet poking out, pulling back, all the nights Brenda would be awake with the howling, nursing mouth. The short-pounding footsteps of Charolette when she padded to his bedside and said, "Daddy, I had a bad dream. I was crying for you."

On the couch near his grandmother, when he'd finally fallen asleep, he would sometimes wake past midnight. She always said she couldn't sleep in the cold, and the fire would still be a low tongue at the embers, a sparkle. She would be asleep, her eyes closed, head bent to the side, and he would creep over to the fireplace, hearing the dry-seasoned plum wood crackle slightly. From a new glow inside the ember he'd see a single tongue of blue curling up the side.

"Keep you safe," she'd say, without opening her eyes. "Go on back over there."

He rested his wrists on his knees and watched the wild tobacco branches smolder dully, only a faint glow along the stems.

ASHES

In THE MORNINGS, he opened his eyes to white light as soon as he heard birds. He slid his knees from where they were close behind Brenda's, before she could say anything or Charolette could step into the doorway, and he went to his father's.

No one saw Roscoe for five days. Darnell piled dust-heavy branches onto his father's truck, pushed them out at the dump, and sat in gray silence beside his father in the cab of the Chevy on the way down from Arroyo Grande or Grayglen or the landfill, descending back into the thick pall of heat-darkened smog.

That first day after the shooting, Victor and Ronnie got off Floyd King's truck with Snooter, back from a construction cleanup, and they gathered around the sweat-beaded cans on the spool table. Darnell had been surprised when Victor said it, quietly, so only he and Ronnie could hear. "Vernon, that's Leon's boy, right?" Victor said, his lips square. "He a LA nigga, think this is the country and he can hoo-ride on us. I ain't into ballistics. I'll do that nigga with my boots. Wild Wild West."

"You don't even know who it was," Ronnie said. "Man, I heard that fool Leon said somebody probably aimin for his brother thinkin it was him."

Darnell said, "Ain't no need for drama now, okay?"

But Ronnie said, "Some silver Toyota, man. Stolen. They found it today." Darnell couldn't hide his surprise. "Tommy Flair came by and told me."

Victor spat onto the dry grass. "It ain't like the cops too excited. But I'ma kick Leon's ass and his boy's."

"I'm tellin you, it coulda been anybody," Ronnie said. Darnell looked away; he hadn't thought they'd talk about it. "Nine millimeter everybody's favorite. Coulda been for one a those rockheads owe somebody big cash."

Darnell's father stepped out from the sideyard. "Doesn't matter," he said harshly. "You think Roscoe cares about who did it? He lost his son. Somebody else's son did it. Leave it at that, damnit." He passed them all to throw a shovel on the truck.

That night, Darnell stared at the article in the newspaper while he sat in the bathtub, hearing Brenda and her mother in the kitchen. The warm water swayed.

Louis was on page seven. He was a small paragraph. "Westside youth killed in gang confrontation. Police say they have few clues about the drive-by shooting, and it is not clear whether or not the youth was a gang member."

He turned back to the front page, which was dominated by a story about a Japanese student on the summer exchange program at the university; he had run a red light on his moped and failed to stop when police chased him. He was in critical condition after hitting a fire hydrant. Darnell glanced again at the picture of the moped lying on its side in a grassy yard.

"Japanese cops must don't chase people in Osaka," he whispered, closing his eyes. He cupped his palms and dropped water on his head, feeling his eyes swell with heat, trying not to shout. Louis wasn't a banger, he shouted to himself. Why a guy from Osaka a student, and a brotha from the Westside gotta be a youth? He went to college, remember? Y'all forgot to check it out. He ain't a student now, though, right? He ain't page one now.

The day he saw the FOR SALE sign in Roscoe's front yard, he'd gone to get a gas can filled for his father, and he stared at the gleaming letters leaning sideways in the baked-hard lawn.

"He movin in with Marietta Cook," Darnell's father said when Darnell got to the back room. "He stopped for a minute over here."

"He's sellin the house?" Darnell remembered all the nights of faint bouncing thumps from the driveway, the purple figs dropping from the tree where Louis had always watched mockingbirds and Roscoe complained about their midnight singing.

"Why should he stay there?" Darnell's father said angrily. "Ain't no reason to look at all that now." Darnell knew his father was seeing the same tree, the trophies in the front room where no one ever sat. "Hollie like it over there at Marietta's. She hardly know she had a daddy."

"He didn't know it, neither," Darnell said slowly. "He always said Geanie was lyin about the baby bein his."

"Hollie been had Roscoe," his father said. "That ain't changed."

"Pops," Darnell said, "been five days, and I ain't heard nothin about . . . what's Roscoe doin about a service?" He'd been waiting, between the roar of the chain saw and the scraping shovels, to ask, but his father only shook his head. "I'ma go over to Marietta Cook's," Darnell said, uncertainly, and his father touched a wavery stain on the table.

"I think he'll be back tonight," he said. Then he looked up at Darnell, and Darnell saw the air rise in his chest. "You come back, too."

The Apache was parked in the street, the huge, blunt hood like a sleeping dinosaur. The light was yellow from the back room. His father and Roscoe sat with only the squat glasses near their knuckles— no dominoes, no cards, no pliers or receipts or drawings of someone's property. The swamp cooler clattered soft, damp.

"I don't want to know who did it, Darnell. Don't want to know how it happened," Roscoe said, smearing a moist ring on the table. He glanced up at Darnell, his eyes rust-rimmed.

Darnell stayed standing. "He was stayin in the pecan grove sometimes and this dude got in a fight with him down there," he said. "I shouldn't . . ."

"I said don't," Roscoe said, and Darnell's father drummed his fingers soft on the table edge.

"I owe him some money," Darnell said, the words sounding foolish. "I still owe you money." He stopped. "I wanted to help pay for the service."

"No service," Roscoe said. "Sit down, Darnell."

Darnell couldn't look at him. He raked his fingers through the hair at his temples, staring at the scarred wood, the ancient cigar burn like a pitted rose.

"I'm not from Louisiana, where the headstone's so sacred. I'm from here, remember?" Roscoe stopped. "Palm Springs. They always had trouble digging graves in the desert. I never went to see my wife when she was buried in LA." Roscoe stopped, and Darnell could only look at his father's fingers, web-threaded with oil. "Marietta, she has some saying about the spirit leaving the body," Roscoe said, hoarse now. "Where she's from, they think it happens at sunrise." He stared out the black doorway. "I took Louis to the Neptune Society. Nobody needed to see him and make a big deal." Darnell stared at Roscoe now, at the lips pulled in hard between sentences. "Nobody figured him out before, least of all me, and no sense in strangers standing around a goddamn hole talking about what we didn't know."

"Roscoe," Darnell's father said softly, but Roscoe went on.

"My child. No mother to ask. No wife. Hollie's mine, too. Officially." Darnell heard the words, each small and dull as grains of dry rice in Roscoe's teeth, not the poemlike lines he usually spun around them. "Official papers—you don't want to fill out papers on a child. It's—wrong. Wrongest thing I've ever written."

Darnell felt the clammy wet gathering in his hair, and he stared at the petaled burn scar, at the thin line on his hand. He dropped his hand under the table and shook; burning, in a cement square? An oven? "Brenda gon be worried," he mumbled, swaying.

Roscoe stood when he did, and suddenly he wrapped his arms around Darnell, fists knuckled to his back. "Don't," he said.

"What does that mean?" she whispered, close to him on the couch.

He'd said the name. "It means he got cremated," he said slowly, and he heard her hiss in breath. He leaned back on the couch automatically, and she put her head on his chest, head shaking with her sobs, her taut belly hard against his ribs and side. He watched the revolving lights from a passing car. Bones—were pieces of bone left?

What was left? It wasn't like a firestorm. He flinched and Brenda pushed her cheek from his damp shirt.

"I know you saw it," she whispered, her eyes so close to his face he could feel her lashes move. "I looked in the car for your shirt. And I found broken glass. I know you were near, Darnell." But her voice wasn't accusing; it was asking.

"I didn't see anything," he said, staring at the wall.

"What does Roscoe call it?" his father asked quietly, sipping his coffee, checking the glare of just-risen sun.

"What?" Darnell said, his throat dull with heat already, and he saw Juan and José watching him carefully from AnTuan's truck.

His father drank again and paused. "Silver morning. He's been callin it that for years," he murmured. "We're waitin for silver morning, for the first one, for a break."

Darnell looked at the sharp outline of the mountains, no mist or clouds to soften the dawn, and he remembered sleeping twisted-hot on a mattress in the backyard with Melvin. Every fall, when long days of heat hit a hundred degrees, his father would move their beds outside, and Louis, Gas, Leon, Snooter, all of them would sneak over. And sometime long after midnight, moisture would cloud the sky, not enough to gather in the grass or bead on the clothesline pole near his face, but enough to dim the sun.

But the fall sun refused to soften or change color, and when Darnell bent his back to work, he could smell only garbage settling, desiccating, in the lots and lawn clippings shriveled to threads in the cookie-cutter yards. Juan and José trotted behind the mowers, twisted under the burlap bags of refuse, watched him carefully. Charolette splayed out her fingers, her palms reaching for him, crying, "I want come to *work*, Daddy," but all he could see was her bones, her shoulder blades shifting under her back skin like wings when she swung her arms, her chin jutting out like a bottle cap when she was angry at him getting into the truck alone. Brenda stood behind her, and he saw her swollen, straight ankles and the distended, falling belly of more tiny, toothpick finger bones and amphibian feet.

He reached for the top of the spear-leafed oleander hedges at the woman's house. His father had gone off somewhere; Roscoe had only worked a few days in weeks, and the sign in his yard had grown smeared with dirt, the screens shrouded with swirled dust. No chaparral smell rising in the sun, he thought, no oily-bark creosote or bitter chamise. Greenhouse effect? Who had said that? Fricke—he was just tryin to change the subject to the drought back then, cause I wanted to talk about torchin trails. Not hardly acceptable now.

His father's client, the older woman with spiderweb hair, brought him some iced tea, and he drank it while she stood there marveling at the heat. "I remember when we first came from Massachusetts, my husband and I, and we couldn't believe that this was what you southern Californians called fall!"

Sparrows jumped off the hose trickles while he was standing near a flower bed. Flies and sweat bees and even wasps drank from the sheen on Juan and José's arms, landed on the back of Darnell's neck to probe for moisture. When they all bent in one yard to pull out the knife-blade palm fronds springing from the crusted ground, Juan said, "We are past the season of harvest. It is not the harvest here. It is only hot, every week." He spoke timidly, not looking at Darnell. "The client, two or three, they want the drip system to be more on, for the dry, but I don't know how. I say, 'Call my boss.' "

Darnell shook his head. "Yeah, and I gotta say, 'Call the guy that installed the system.' Like Trent. I don't know about automatic timers and drips."

That night, they lingered on Darnell's porch for a moment, and Darnell gave Charolette the last metallic green-bellied fig beetles in a jar, because he felt bad about the empty car seat beside him. She turned the round jar, marveling at the spiky legs, and José said something to Juan. Juan nodded. "José say it is the angry season."

"I heard that," Darnell said. "The season of the hot and pissed go on a long time in Rio Seco, man. It's not even close to the end."

The temperature never went below ninety during the day, and gray dusted the sky. People called it earthquake weather, but the ground didn't move—it just lay still, hardening, pushing up tree roots, refusing hose trickles and shovels, burning Charolette's feet. Darnell worked in a cloud of moving grit, and only the sliding drops of sweat carried the dust from his forehead, his neck. He stayed away from Jackson Park, working alone on the gas stations, feeling the black heat rise on the asphalt all around him until he imagined that he looked like one of the zombies from the alley, his eyes sunk gray into his skull, his palms permanently gray. Zombies, he thought, blinded by the whirring wires of the edger. And everybody else gone.

"A very angry season," Juan said again, and lawns were thatched high, the blades and roots pushed out of brick-hard earth. People called about wilted plants, burned leaves, dead patches in the grass. Juan hit a PVC sprinkler head one Friday and didn't notice; by Wednesday, the lawn had a huge brown spot and the owner came home from work early to jam up Juan. He had wanted to tell the man his eyes were full of salt, Juan told Darnell. He couldn't identify the house; he was wavering with nervousness on Darnell's porch. "I say to him my English not good."

The guy called Darnell. "I want *you* over here to replace the sprinkler head today. Please."

Darnell said to himself, "I hate irrigation." He drove to Grayglen, his head sifting chalk the way it had been for all these weeks, and saw the broken sprinkler head near a landscaper's boulder. He got out of the El Camino and squatted by the spreading dead circle, thinking that this looked like one of Trent's yards, with the river-rock edgings. A shadow moved behind the etched-glass panes of the front door, and he said, "Damn!" under his breath.

"Can I help you?" the man said over him, voice guarded.

Darnell sighed. "Yeah, you called AnTuan's . . . ."

"Oh," the man said, brightening. "I didn't recognize you, Trent. Hey, their Oriental kid really took out this sprinkler head. I'm glad you could come out, cause the dead grass looks like shit."

Darnell stayed bent to the pipe. "I'm not Trent King," he said.

"I've seen you around, doing landscape construction," the guy started, flustered. Darnell saw his face fill with pink like rising water. "I guess I thought you . . ."

"I own AnTuan's," Darnell said, giving up on the pipe, standing up, and the man's cheeks faded back to beige.

"I must have misunderstood," he said, a little harder. "I thought the company was owned by Asians."

"No," Darnell said. Okay—here we go, he thought. "It's me."

The man flicked his thumbs against his index fingers nervously, and Darnell knew he was flashing the flyer in his memory. "You ever hear of truth in advertising?"

Always respect the client, Darnell thought, that's what Pops said a thousand times. To me, to Louis. Don't touch nothin—don't say nothin unless they ask you first. He felt saliva rolling behind his molars. "Hey," he said, keeping his voice light. "Asia's a lot bigger than people think. Mongolia—that's Asia. Alaska is Asian."

The man gestured at the spreading brown. "Well, we might have to change services if the lawn's going to look like this."

"I didn't install your irrigation system, but I'll call Trent King for you," Darnell said, raising his brows, and the man's eyes flinched when he said the name. He went back up the lawn, and Darnell got into the El Camino. "He probably think Italians make his pizza instead of Mexicans. He probably got a Latvian domestic. Damn, when he hire somebody else for his grass, I hope he stay home from LA now and then to check." He took out the route schedule, surprised that his chest was still cool and empty, and drew a line through the address.

"Fuck you, Jap!" the voice in the phone snarled. "I'm tired of your goddamn flyers! If I see you drop another one, I'm gonna shoot your yellow Jap ass!"

Tuan ain't Japanese, you ignorant bastard, Darnell thought, hearing the dial tone. He put the receiver back. But they all look alike, huh? Chinks, Japs, Nips. Wetbacks, Beaners, Mescans. But Juan look like a Jap, huh? And me—I look like a nigga. Most def. Talk like one, too.

Darnell went into Charolette's room, where she lay on the bed napping, her hand still clutching a few of the flyers they'd thrown onto lawns early this morning. She had the last of them; he and Juan had saturated the new tracts last week, because they still wanted to work up to five days, and not many half-sheets were left. Charolette had played with the small rocks for hours, and she'd ridden with him in the dark today, chattering and handing him Baggies when he drove to a few houses just for her.

Darnell slid a flyer from her hand to look at the lantern Nacho had drawn a long time ago. A brotha drew this, he thought. He shook his head. Damn—for the black AnTuans, I guess I should change it to—to what? A lantern and a bridge and a bonsai are on there now. His head throbbed in the heat, and he saw the pecan grove. He bit the inside of his cheek, turning to the door. Wouldn't nobody recognize that. Or a greens tree. Yeah, I could see it.

He heard Brenda and her mother in the living room, but he went out the kitchen door to the driveway, reaching into the truck to check the glove compartment for stray flyers. A bird, he thought suddenly.

Yeah. A mockingbird. I don't care if it don't have nothin to do with yards. A mockingbird for one brotha who's gone. Pine tree for me. Nature Boy. Birdman.

He glanced at the envelope with his application for fire season, and closed the glove compartment without looking at it or the article about Louis. He thought of the spit-out word a few minutes ago. Jap. Articles had filled the newspaper since the Japanese student on the moped had remained on life support, and when the paper had printed a plea to raise money for his family to visit from Japan, mentioning that the Japanese were critical of the police chase, angry letters had poured in. "Take him back to Japan and pay for his tubes there. He wasn't obeying American law, and I don't want my tax dollars spent to keep a criminal alive." "I'm tired of the media bashing our police. They were doing their job."

Inside, he went to the living room, where Mrs. Batiste sat with Brenda, who lay on the couch. She'd felt early contractions in the last week, and the doctor told her to take it easy, stay home from work, keep her feet elevated. He touched her shoulder, shook his head at the mound of stomach so high it was almost level with her face, and she grinned. "You tired that little girl out," she said. "She never naps that long for me."

"I can do that," he said. "I'm good."

Mrs. Batiste was crocheting a baby blanket, and he had already laughed at the safe colors: yellow, pale green, lavender. "Pretty hot for afghans," he said again, the way he had every day when she came to cook, clean, wash, and braid Charolette's hair.

"Get cool before you know it," she said, as always, and he stared out the front window, thinking that this is what you did when you got a family. You said the same things over and over. He'd watched all the ceremonies, the folding of new baby clothes and washed old ones, the padding of the crib, the tea Brenda drank, the way Charolette sat on the counter with Mrs. Batiste rolling the dough, the baby fingers pushing the floury-edged glass for each biscuit. Had he done that? No—he'd been outside with his father and Melvin, working on chain-saw motors and turning lug nuts for practice. His sisters had gathered flour and lemon rind under their fingernails.

"Gettin late," he said, like always.

Mrs. Batiste shrugged. "Etienne a grown man. He ain't miss me that much." She went home in time to make his dinner each night. They heard Charolette's bare toes swishing on the floor, and her first words were "Where's Daddy?"

"She don't need to be goin far from her mama now," Mrs. Batiste said. "It's too hot."

But he smiled, and she ran to hold his legs. "Can we throw rocks?" she said. "Mama, you tired, huh?" She knew that was the best excuse for leaving the house.

"Give me a kiss," Brenda said.

The flames were only racing edges up the bank of the freeway, gapped as lace on the edge of his mother's curtains, and he slowed at the off ramp. He'd taken her with him to Corona to buy a used edger. "Check out the fire, Charolette," he said, and she stretched her neck like a turtle to see over the dashboard.

The fire was quick-burning, just started, probably from a thrown cigarette, and the flat grass flames skipped like string. "Be careful, Daddy," she said when he got out and stood on the freeway shoulder to look down at the well of field in the cloverleaf, at the cars circling around without slowing. "Daddy, when you cook on a fire you get a ouchie."

"This ain't the stove," he said. "This is different." He heard the sirens, and the fire pulsed thin over the drain at the bottom of the field. Charolette watched intently from his arms when the trucks fed out hose that the men pulled toward the scattering of orange. When the blackened ground was patchy gray and damp, she said. "I'm thirsty, Daddy."

He started the engine, saying, "Your mama always used to want a milkshake after I took her to a fire. She was bored."

But that wasn't what Brenda said when they got home and Charolette said casually, "Daddy and me seen a fire."

Brenda shot him a glance from the kitchen chair, where she was looking at the checkbook. "Where? You took her to Jackson Park?"

"Gettin pretty hot to break out the trash barrel," Darnell said, ready to stall her out. "Nope, we saw a brushfire."

Charolette said, "It was pretty. It was dancing on the ground, huh, Daddy?"

Brenda fanned her fingers through the hair above her ears, and her eyes glared wide. "I don't know what the hell you're thinking, taking her to a fire. What if the wind changes and you get surrounded?"

Darnell said, "Give me a break, Brenda. I fought *fires* up in the range, not boot stompers like that."

"So you God now, huh? You know everything a fire gon do, even when you got your daughter in danger?" She stood up and slammed her plate into the sink, and Charolette started to cry.

"Brenda, I survived fuckin Seven Canyons. Don't tell me shit about a fire," he yelled, watching Charolette's lips begin to stretch wider.

"Well, you won't survive one fuckin Brenda if you do that again," she screamed.

"She's my kid, too, that's what you always tellin me," he shouted. "I can teach her somethin—she smart, she ain't just into dolls and hair like you and everybody else think she should be."

Brenda took a deep breath, her too-wide face shifting, and said, "This isn't about her, so don't even try that line. After Louis, and Donnie, your leg all torn up—you think I'm playing, huh? You think this is a game." She was shouting again, and Charolette's screams were high-pitched. When he threw the milkshake into the sink, her cries went clotted in her throat; Brenda swung her up awkwardly onto her thigh, and Darnell slammed out the door.

He drove past the park automatically, but the shadows crowding around the tree and domino table, the crouched figures in the alley, were too many for him, and all he could think of was the word. Gone. Zombies. Gone—Donnie, Gas, Leon. Louis. He drove past Marietta Cook's house and saw the Apache, but he was afraid to knock on the front door. His chest ached. In the mornings, still too yellow and hot, when his father sat at the spool table in an early sliver of shade, no one rearranged words for a poem about oranges or *bolillos* or crows strutting along the gutter.

But as soon as he was in the Sandlands, keeping AnTuan's truck even with the big semitrailers on their way to Arizona and New Mexico and farther, their trailers tight as boxcars in the slow lane, he felt calm. Drivin, just like Leon wanted to do that night, just like we all do. Drive all the way to Portland, see if the girl named Quelle still hangin out at Rob's crib. That's when I was doin something wrong. Yeah. She take me out with that tongue right now, wouldn't say nothin. Just California. Take me back to Cali, baby.

October—y'all ain't goin home for a while, he thought, winding up the highway to the station without even seeing the curves. They were still imprinted, habit, the wheel under his fingers turning without thought. Gone—Scott and Perez and Corcoran. All those hours, days, weeks he'd spent with the square-held lips and clicking cards and screaming radio were faded. He watched the first, low slopes. All summer, the sun had straightened and stiffened the grasses, but by now, late October, the hillsides had passed gold and were tinged rusty-brown. Only the new tumbleweeds were cool blue-green puffs, and they held fast like lichens when the wind tore at the ground. Seven years of drought? Uh-uh. You guys still got a big one to look forward to up here, he thought, pulling into the gravel lot.

He stood by the truck, breathing the hot resin in the air, looking at the closed garage door where the engine was resting or gone. Fricke's face appeared in the window, and Darnell thought, he's gon say, What, your woman let you go on a casual trip up to the hill, huh? Kept on a leash like you—awhooh.

The Steller jay screamed from the branches when he moved, but Fricke, coming out the doorway, grinning enough so that Darnell could see teeth under the mustache, said, "Came up here to congratulate me for my well-worded quotes, huh?"

Corcoran came behind him, hollering, "So, Tucker, how come you didn't bust Scott and Perez? You never saw em all that time down there in Rio Seco, all those fires?"

"What are you talkin about?" Darnell said, frowning. "I saw em a coupla times, workin paid call jobs."

Fricke grinned again. "They had plenty of work. You didn't see the newspaper?"

Darnell looked at his sunburned face, at the blond hairs glinting on his wrists where his arms were folded. "I ain't been keepin up with the paper every day. The news ain't always news to me."

Fricke opened his mouth and ran a finger down his mustache, nodding. "Been busy, huh?"

Darnell nodded, and Corcoran brought him the newspaper before he could say anything. Scott and Perez stared at him from the county page, Scott with his buzz-cut hair and narrow nose, Perez with his Fred Flintstone jaw and caterpillar brows. "Louis said he saw these guys," Darnell murmured. "He IDed it right."

"That a friend of yours?" Fricke said. "He called the tip in?"

Darnell's chest felt stained with heat. He shook his head, hearing the single jay's repeating shriek, making his eyes see the wings, the cocked head watching him. No bullet stories; I'm not tellin Fricke, he thought. It was just a drive-by, buncha home boys standin around. Gang-related. Fricke read it in the paper—just like this. He know what he need to know. No clues.

He bent his head to the article again to avoid the sky-pale eyes. The fire investigator was quoted: "These two men knew what they were doing. They set the blazes in the riverbottom and vacant lots very naturally, and they didn't use accelerant because they knew we'd be looking for that." He read Fricke's quotes, and Fricke's dry cowboy voice came in when he read along. " 'We didn't have any problems with them up here,' " Fricke said, grinning. " 'We had plenty of fires that year. Seven Canyons kept us all busy.' "

"You see Fricke's famous now," Corcoran said, leaning against the doorway. "Big shit."

Darnell handed the paper back to Fricke, who said, "Perez told the reporter he needed the ten dollars an hour. Something about you Rio Seco home boys—maybe it's the toxics and heavy metal in the river."

"They don't live with me," Darnell said. "And I don't set fires."

"They didn't do it for pyro love, man, they did it for money," Corcoran said.

"You know a thrill was involved," Darnell said. "Get a bottle of Jack, check the riverbottom fuel. Everybody blames the homeless guys."

Fricke shook his head. "Homeless. What an urban media term. In Montana, they're still bums."

Darnell saw the needle-shifting light through the pine branches. Jackson Park—sleeping in the car, in the cane stand. Louis—dozing in the pecan grove. "Maybe they're just peripatetic," he murmured.

Fricke stroked his mustache exaggeratedly. "Whoa—been taking college classes?"

"A client," Darnell said. Fricke and Corcoran waited, but Darnell didn't mention the truck, the name. "I'm doin landscape mainte- nance. Got two guys workin for me. I work for the guys drivin their Beemers to work in LA. Just like you do. Sometimes."

"They're multiplying out here like cancer," Fricke said. "Canyon Estates. Wildridge Ranch."

"You guys should be gettin a big job out here pretty soon, all this heat and no humidity." Darnell watched Corcoran smile and walk toward the door; he remembered all the mornings, waking up to smell the resin in the wind, the sage-sharp dirt flying. He handed Fricke the envelope he'd been holding all this time. "I'ma turn the application in for next season. Paid call. You put in a few good words for me?"

"My words don't mean much when the legislature cuts the funds," Fricke started, but he scanned the papers, avoiding Darnell's eyes. "I heard they might need a few paid-call reserves out in San Bernardino soon." When he handed the papers back, he slanted his head thoughtfully to one side. "Remember your stunt in Seven Canyons?"

Darnell nodded. He touched the stem scar near his knuckles; Charolette still kept trying to put Band-Aids on it.

"We used to talk up here, right, about some guys having liquor in their veins," Fricke said. "Remember? And some guys have travel. Some guys have smoke." He scratched his neck.

"Yeah, well, I drained a couple of my veins, okay?" He saw that Fricke didn't get it. "My kid's got some a my blood. Maybe I gave her some smoke." He thought of Charolette's wariness near the flames. Fricke's lips were curling, and Darnell said, "I ain't lyin, I still got it, but maybe not like before. Maybe not like dyin."

He went farther up the mountain, not down, and he spun into the scenic turnout to look at the blank, black chamise covering the slope below. One match. Some *ready* wood. Not a boot stomper. He reached into the glove compartment, touching a few of the white rocks, and pulled out the matchbook. He lit one, and the windows reflected him back, wavering. What up, homey? He watched his fingers hold the lengthening flame, felt the heat closer to his fingertips. My ID. You gon ID me, sittin here, when you pass? The flame burned him, and he sucked the thumb and forefinger, then lit another match. He saw the cover this time when he pulled it across. Zamora's. He'd treated Juan and José for lunch last month, told them it was his favorite. Mr. Zamora had given him a stack of tortillas for Brenda.

Darnell let the match burn until the fire touched his fingers again, and he held it until the pain seared down the knuckle and bone. He leaned back against the seat, sucking on the throbbing skin, but his spit was too hot. He started the truck and drove to the spring a mile up the highway, and he let the water trickle icy over his hand. Then he sat, hearing the rustle of animals and leaves and wind, until a camper passed slow, laboring up the grade, and moon faces stared at him. He nodded to the moving windows. "What up?" he said to the black air and asphalt trailing them.

She sat on the porch awkwardly, legs wide under her belly. He dropped the keys on the cement and sat down one step lower, so that her voice brushed across his temple.

"When we were sitting in the car that night, after you told me about Louis? I kept looking at the Spider, and I remembered how I used to act mad when you were always fixing it in your dad's driveway. But I'd be sitting in there while you worked on it, remember? You'd have me test the brakes or the signals, and I'd be thinking that at least I knew where you were. You couldn't get in trouble."

"Nobody to get in trouble with now," he said, staring at the sidewalk, the deeply chipped curb.

When he finally came inside, Charolette was stumbling toward him, blinking, carrying her brush. He could tell she'd been crying; the skin around her eyes was still swollen reddish. "You supposed to be asleep," he said, but Brenda came behind her, shaking her head.

"She's been waiting for you for hours," Brenda whispered. "She thinks you're gone."

He sat down heavily on the couch. Lately, she kept wanting to brush his hair, to finger the razored lines. "I'm not in the mood, *chica*, my hair already hurts from too much thinkin."

But she stood on the pillow behind him, stamping a moment for balance, saying, "Turn around, baby. You got pretty hair." She pushed the soft-bristled brush roughly down the back of his head. "Be still— you gon look real pretty when I'm finish," she said. She applied the brush carefully to his temple, his nape. She put her palm right on top of his head to steady it, and the hot air from the screen door rushed in. Her belly pressed warm against his back, her knees digging under his armpits. He remembered all the times he'd watched women do hair in his mother's living room, the faces under hands dreamy-still, slack with sleepy thoughts. His mother, GranaLene. His sisters, Brenda. The brush tingled his scalp, and she pulled on his ear, her voice not sleepy at all now. "Be still," she commanded. "I'm not finish."

*   *   *

When the wind came, the sky turned blue-gold again, the smog swirled away and trash blew from the dirt to cling to chain link and wrought iron. It took two days for the gusts to pick up grit and fling it into ears and windows, to loosen the dry-heaved roots of eucalyptus, to cut power and telephone lines here and there. Juan and José squinted into the dust that rose even from soft new sod, and Darnell worked silently, hearing people argue, chasing leaves and branches that flew away from the chain saws while his father shouted and finally had to come down from the tree. The wind dried people's eyes, coated their teeth, sucked up the damp from drip systems, splintered pepper trunks. The streets were laced with fallen palm fronds.

The sun had been hundred-degree hot for seven days, glaring onto boot-tamped dirt and broken-fine stems and ground glass. The old women on Picasso frowned at the too-yellow mornings, dragging hoses and waving weakly at sunrise when he and his father passed on their way to a downed eucalyptus. Roscoe hadn't worked for weeks; he'd been driving around the desert, even the mountains, he told Darnell's father, and he'd been to the Salton Sea, fishing with Marietta Cook, thinking.

The wind was steady, making its way through hair, even protective-tight curls, to layer itch around the forehead. Darnell woke on the eighth day with a wind headache, from the dry air riding under the scalp to pull taut the damp covering around his brain, and he rubbed the sand at his lashes, looking at the bronze-warm windows.

Charolette whined to come with him after Mrs. Shaefer called. "I'll bet your daughter misses the koi pond," Mrs. Shaefer said. "I've got a gift for her. And I've got a friend who'd like you to give an estimate on maintenance for her property up here in Grayglen."

"It's too hot, babygirl," Brenda said absently when Charolette tripped, "*Cam*Icome witchu Daddy?" four times off her tongue.

That made Charolette angrier. "I'm not the baby girl, I'm the *big* girl," she said. "*That* gonna be the babygirl." She jabbed her finger at Brenda's belly.

"I don't know if I can hang with three women," Darnell said.

"It's hot," Brenda murmured again, her eyes closed.

"It's too hot in here," Charolette said, and Darnell shrugged when she clutched the outer seam of his jeans. She never let go of his knee, his sleeve, his baby finger, it seemed. In a moment, she was on the floor, trying to force her feet into her stained pink canvas sneakers, the ones she called her work shoes. "The *tongue*, Daddy, it's stuck."

She brought the tea-party set his mother had given her for Christmas, along with the new Barbie his sisters had bought her last week. In the truck, Darnell looked at the doll's Hershey skin and long hair, her chest pointy as two pyramids. "So what's this home chick's name?" he asked.

Charolette frowned at him like he had no sense. "*Bar*bie, Daddy."

He drove blindly up the avenue to Grayglen, remembering the ginger-colored Barbie in the gutter, feeling her sharp ledge of toes in his breastbone. Louis lying curve-backed in the dust.

He blinked hard when they began to wind up the narrow streets toward the address Mrs. Shaefer had given him on the phone. Darnell parked at the turnout in the street; the woman was on vacation, but he didn't want to take a chance on getting too close to the house for security. Security. He stared ahead at the tiny sign planted in the flower bed, and that only made him think of Donnie, of the metal lodged in his blood, liquid racing around it like a stream around a stone. Or white tissue growing around it like a pearl?

"Stay here," he told Charolette, fanning his fingers over his forehead and pushing hard. She smiled; she loved the white truck, always clean because Juan washed it almost every day. She loved to trace the fancy lettering on the doors, to say "AnTuan's," to snap open the glove compartment.

When he was finished walking the yard, he sat on the curb to rest. The property next door was silent, too, and someone was watering far up the sloping street, just a trickling hose. The overflow ran slowly down the gutter. Still no rain, he thought. Nothin to wash all this stuff out. Charolette bent to watch the water finger through pine needles, pepper berries, tiny sand dunes. The gutter was bone dry, and the rivulet crept along like all the fine dust was catching on its belly, to slow it coming toward her sneakers, pushing through leaves and falling into cracks by the curb.

"It's a river, Daddy," she said, putting down the jar with filaree seeds she'd found. "A honey river. Go, river, hurry!" She jumped up and squatted by the water, rushed with the stream when it finally burst free of a pine-needle jam, and crouched to help it along like a TV golfer urging his ball to roll the right way.

Darnell watched the water turn bronze when it ran under the shadow made by his legs. "Daddy, it's leaving! Come on!"

"You go—I'ma sit here," he said. Pepper berries and sparkles of silt were magnified in the tiny pool left behind. A lake—she hadn't seen a real lake yet. He could take her to the mountains and show her one near the station. He'd always hung out there when he could. He watched her bend to touch the water and then jump up to follow it, oblivious of everything else. When he was small, he'd followed a gutter creek like this, in dusted hot concrete on Picasso one day, and then the meandering water had turned the corner to head down Pepper Avenue. He'd kept going, following the turns until the deep shade overhead made him look up and realize how far from home he'd come. He was all the way to Treetown, where the gutters turned to gullies and the water slipped down into the ditch carved off the asphalt.

His father had yelled at him. "You only six! Who you fancy yourself to be, runnin off like that? What the hell you thinkin? Oh—you was in dreamland again, huh? You *wasn't* thinkin!"

I still ain't always thinkin. Wasn't payin attention with Louis, with security, with the girl named Quelle. Pay attention, man. "Charolette," he called, and her face swung up from the water. "Come on back, it could be a car comin."

"The river's down here," she called, and he stood up.

"Come on!" He heard tires, and he was standing beside her when the minivan chugged slowly up the hill. The two boys' faces pressed against the glass to see Charolette, who knelt by the trickle.

"Let's go," he said.

Mrs. Shaefer's house was cool and mauve. She heard the truck come down the drive, because she had opened the front door, flanked by pumpkins. "My fishies missed you," she told Charolette. "I don't have any grandkids to play with them." She gave Charolette a papier-mâché goldfish, light as palm bark when Darnell held it.

By eleven, it was 92 degrees and the wind was gusting hard. The pond water was murky at the edges, but the fish darted and Charolette bent close. Mrs. Shaefer had shown Darnell the bank, the patches of flannel bush and ceanothus solid like the mountains. The helicopter went over, circled back again, and Darnell looked up. The blade-whirring halo hovered, then sped somewhere else. The lady standin right here, Darnell thought, so I can't be burglin the house, okay?

Mrs. Shaefer knelt next to Charolette, telling her about the fish food, and Darnell drank the juice she'd brought him. No competition—this is the best client I've had, he thought. The helicopter zoomed over again, circling somewhere close, and Darnell said, "I guess we better get back home, *chica*. Your mama said it's too hot to keep you out long."

Mrs. Shaefer walked them out to the white truck. "I look forward to Juan every week," she said. "I love the way he trims the rosemary and the weeping willow."

Darnell heard the blades clattering, and he smiled. "Thanks for the fish," he said, putting Charolette into her car seat.

"Thank you, Gramma Tend," Charolette said.

Mrs. Shaefer leaned close to Darnell. "I told her I could be her Pretend Gramma, for visiting sometimes," she whispered.

He drove slowly from the yard, letting Charolette wave, but on the street he felt fear spread across his back. The helicopter flew in a regular circle now, and Darnell drove up to the stop sign.

The first puff of smoke he saw was a delicate balloon, collapsing and curling back around itself like a jellyfish, rising slow. The fear spread under his armpits and around to his chest, a warm prickle he breathed in quickly, familiar, tingling. Charolette was absorbed in the small picture book about fish Mrs. Shaefer had given her, and he thought, I'ma just see if anybody else know about the smoke. Maybe I could help out with a shovel.

But he knew now the helicopter had been eyeing it. He drove up past the avocado groves near Mrs. Shaefer's, but the street narrowed here and he couldn't see anything but the still, sullen leaves. If I go up to the water tower at the top, I can see the other side of this hill. I think this is the street. The warmth was different from the heat pressing in outside, blowing in the window. He felt the relaxing of his muscles, like Scott used to say about whiskey. Like when he was on the line. Itching. Yeah. The itch. Who told me about the itch? He drove, turned, and then saw the concrete water tower, squat and circular, with graffiti all around the base. He drove up to the chain-link fence.

The mass of flames was rising in a eucalyptus grove, and the wind wouldn't let the long streamers of fire rise up for a few minutes; it blew the blaze across a small road and over to a gray-wood grove of dead orange trees that someone was trying to sell. Another teardown, Darnell thought. The flames caught in the gnarled branches for a moment, and then the wind blew the fireball in a wall across the rows. Better get down there and start a line, over by that dirt road in the grove. He put the truck in gear.

Who the hell threw a match in some eucalyptus? Nothin else could have started a fire up here—sure as hell no train tracks in Grayglen. And as the helicopter lingered over him, puzzling at the truck, the fire shook and roared into a hedge and a house. He saw the windows glow and explode, the white stucco walls disappear under orange, and the red-tile roof melt lighter. Charolette smelled the ashes now, heard the helicopter close, and she said, "Daddy, a bad man run away?"

"No," he said, moving the truck. Sometimes the helicopter circled for a long time near their house, and over the loudspeaker she'd heard the police tell a suspect to stop running, telling residents to stay in their houses.

"A fire," she said, nervous, leaning toward the dashboard to see out the windshield. He turned the truck around in the sandy dead end and heard the sirens pulling ribbons of sound up the hills.

This was a county road, he remembered from when Trent had brought him up here to see part of Grayglen overall. He could smell the wind carrying traces of smoke into the car. It was blowing west off the hills. We going west—back to the Westside.

They were higher up than usual; he hadn't worked any jobs over this far, where the houses were still older, original Rio Seco money, his father had always said. A few scattered tree-trimming jobs, but most of the teardowns and new tracts were just below. He wound around the street back to the main avenue, and fire trucks raced by, Charolette pointing at the men in yellow holding on to the back. "They gon fall off, Daddy!" she yelled, and he looked at her panicked face. The smoke, wind, the sirens, and the truck spinning around on the curving streets—he'd been casual, thinking of Seven Canyons and Fricke, wondering if they'd call a crew from the mountains for a city fire like this one. Was CDF closest? And Charolette was crying now, looking up the road where the yellow coats had disappeared. Several Mexican men on ten-speeds flashed around the curve and sped downhill.

"We're goin home, babygirl," he said. "It's okay." He drove over the crackle of fallen eucalyptus branches in the gutter and followed a van and a Bronco. He remembered doing the teardown, trying to think of which street it was on. Damn, we had trouble gettin a little dozer up here for that job—how they gonna get the fire rigs up these roads? That bridge over the gully is too narrow for fire trucks. He shook his head, Charolette craning her neck to see landmarks like she always did. "Daddy! My honey river!" she yelled, and he couldn't tell by now if her voice was loud from fear or excitement.

"Yup," he said, glancing at the curb where she'd watched the water. The long cement drive where he'd faced the Doberman's heated breath and curled tongue, the ridged gums. Why we stoppin here? The driver of the Bronco leaned out his open window, and so did Darnell, but he couldn't see anything around the curve.

"That's where we said goodbye to my honey river," Charolette said, looking for the exact spot, next to a white boulder with an address painted on it. "My big rock is bigger than that," she said.

Darnell felt the wind scouring the wetness under his arm. The moving air was taking on that edge of sound, that absent roar, that he remembered, and he knew the fire was turning to a storm, making its own wind, its own weather. "Shit!" he yelled out the window. "What the hell is goin on?"

Charolette started screaming, and he said, "Stay here!"

"No, Daddy! Nooo! Don't go!" she said, but he screamed, "Stay here! I'll be right back!" He got out and ran behind the Bronco driver to the curve, where he saw the van and two small cars waiting behind a moving van that had turned too sharp trying to get out of someone's tiny driveway. The cab was at odd angles to the trailer, and three men stood hollering at each other near the open door. "It's full of my goddamn house!" one guy yelled, and the Bronco driver, his heavy beard hiding his mouth, shouted, "There's a fucking fire coming!"

"I know that!" the guy yelled, and a young guy in a baseball cap and brown uniform said, "Fuck it, somebody give me a ride." He jumped into a car, and Darnell ran back to Charolette.

She was purple near her temples, around her mouth, screaming, her hands held stiff out in front of her for him to pick her up. "We're goin!" he shouted, and he saw the van had backed up into someone's hedge, the doors open, driver gone. The Bronco wheels ran up the side of the bank when the driver tried to go around the cab blocking the street, and Darnell dug into the hard dirt, skidding down the other side. "Shit!" Darnell said, feeling his left tires go up. This ain't no four-wheel drive. He tried not to jam the gas, felt the tread skim for a moment, and he kept his foot steady, the tread catching again. Charolette's screams were regular waves of sound, and sirens floated everywhere. The truck slid down the other side with a jerk and he hit his head on the window frame.

He raced down the wall of hedges and trees and came to the open field at the corner of the next street; the Bronco was long gone, and when he looked up the street to see if anyone was racing fast enough to hit him, he saw embers flying, shooting from a ranch-style house above, landing in the field. Fricke called it spotting—the fire was hitting houses with enough force to blow shakes off the roofs and burning debris from the windows, sending baby torches raining and arcing everywhere to start the next blazes. And the wall of flame was shaking the trees up the street, breathing into his window. Down-hill—now it was stronger than nature, creating its own balance. A shingle shot past him when he stepped on the gas; it landed in the branches of the eucalyptus that sheltered the next house, and the dangling leaves exploded into flame.

No ax, no shelter, no guys' shouts to surround him. He had to touch her, try to calm her while he drove, and she was rigid, fingers splayed in the air. He saw sparks curling above him when they raced down the grove, and he ducked instinctively. No canyon to hide in, no rocks. Just metal cab, Charolette's skin, black clouds of smoke billowing from the grove across the road, and in the rearview mirror he saw her boulder, the white boulder that marked the wide avenue, disappear behind the flames when the truck raced onto Woodbine and into the gapped line of speeding cars. He ran the corner stop sign by going around the shoulder, and headed the back route toward Terracina, where no one was going. He held Charolette's stiff fingers, but she wouldn't bend them to his, and he turned around to see the veins of flame advancing across the block walls into the newest tract, a huge plume of black smoke darkening the western sky and the hills.

He wanted to stop when they reached the flats of Terracina, but he waited until he found a McDonald's at the far eastern edge, and she was quiet, stunned, in the walled parking lot. He unbuckled her and pulled her onto his lap, and her hands dug into his ribs, her braids under his chin. "It's okay, it's okay, it's okay," he said, like Brenda, repeating himself and not getting tired.

EL DIA DE LOS MUERTOS

A SHES AND BURNT VEGETATION had sifted all the way onto the Westside from the smoke that raced over the sky from Grayglen. The fire was so explosive that whole eucalyptus leaves littered Darnell's yard, their gray merely blasted to brown, their oil leaving a scorched-popcorn smell on his hands when he gathered them. And long ribbons of bamboo, charred, but the faint grooved striations still intact, caught in his rake.

Charolette held out her sugar-sticky fingers to him, and he took the last bite of cinnamon toast, handed her the paper napkin after he'd wet it between his lips. He saw the sparkle of sugar grains on her cheeks, heard Brenda's heavy steps in the house.

He had lied again, lied straight out. Necessity. Charolette's face had shone copper-clear, new, after they'd eaten cheeseburgers, drunk milkshakes, played in McDonald's children's room and on the slide. She'd slept for a long time at his mother's, while he pretended to work on the chain saw and washed the truck. "Juan and José still don't feel good," he'd told his father, who wondered why he was hosing down the windshield. He watched the waves of water push black cinders from the ridged truckbed, the papery shreds of burned leaf and bark. He tried to breathe slow when he took a rag to the faint brown stain near the front fender, where the flames had roared close, blown onto the paint, where they had started to melt the tires and make rubber smoke, thick and black.

He had pulled out a eucalyptus leaf from the wheel well, the spear tip curled black, when Brenda came out, her feet soft and swollen as sponges. "Where you going?" she asked.

"Lawnmower repair shop." Darnell dropped the leaf, but he ran his fingers under his nose to smell the oil.

"She shouldn't go with you," Brenda said, nodding at Charolette, who rubbed her face with the napkin. "I didn't do her hair yet."

"Daddy," Charolette said suddenly, staring at his chest. "You better don't leave your shirt in the truck if you want Mama to wash it. Last time you was naked on your skin, you got a ouchie."

He stopped, leaning the rake against the side of the house, remembering the dried blood he'd chipped from his forearm, and then he dragged the trash can to the backyard, smelling the acrid ashes piled on the cinder-block wall. Pressing his palms against the powdery flakes on the Spider's hood, he felt the jagged twist inside his ribs, like a leap of metal, when he saw Louis's blood, mixed with his, dried black over his skin. He smeared the ashes on the hood—ashes, Louis's skin and bones charred to powdery fragments. He brought the hands to his face to breathe the wood in these curled flakes, but then he remembered that houses had burned in Grayglen, houses and cars and people.

When he came back, keys in his hand, Charolette said again, "Daddy!" but Brenda cut her off sharply.

"Quit nagging your daddy," she said. "You want him to run away?"

Darnell looked at her, surprised, but Brenda moved her knees carefully where she sat on the porch. "What if this one is a girl, and you have three women nagging you?" she said softly, looking past him to the palm tree at the edge of the yard. Darnell didn't answer. He saw Charolette's lowering brows, her poked-out lip, and when he got into the truck, he heard Brenda say, "Or maybe it's a son."

The baby pine cone Charolette had found yesterday, the one that had slid wildly back and forth on the dashboard, was in her car seat, and he heard the last word again. A son? He'd asked Roscoe, What would you keep? He held the tight-sheaved cone, felt its weight, and after he left the repair shop, he drove up Pepper Avenue, watching the thick, swirling pall that still darkened the sky to the east. Can't drive up there even if I wanted to, he thought. Nobody's allowed past Hampton Avenue, and ain't nothin to see now.

But he turned on the road he and Charolette had fled down yesterday, the seldom-used route, and found that someone had taken down a barrier. He made it to the edge of the still-smoking tract that had lost the last street to the flames, and from there he could stand outside the truck and look up the steep, nude slope at what was left.

Like a cemetery, he thought, his breath shallow. Like GranaLene's old cement outline, only gray-squared foundations in uneven rows like neglected gravesites. Two cars were blank-eyed on the street, and tall evergreen cypress spears were the only things standing near the heaps of smoldering rubble. Chimneys were short and lonely as headstones, and he squatted, his nostrils stinging, watching the ground still breathing, still smoking, alive.

Like zombies, he thought, eyes blurred, covered with ash and barely panting, like the souls his grandmother said breathed under the earth, trapped, roaming at night; like the haunts in the alleys breathing white smoke. Ghosts. Louis gone. Donnie and Leon and Gas—all floating. He stared at the ground, wishing for red embers, not ash, remembering the shooting flames arched across the asphalt and the taste of clean heat in his throat. I need flames, not ashes, he thought, not just the skeletons that get left. I had Charolette in the truck and didn't even know—I need to be back up there in the hills, just me. He bit the inside of his lip until he tasted salt.

He drove toward the Westside, trying to think of how to tell Brenda, and Victor shouted him to a stop near the market. "Brothaman! We need a ride to Picasso!"

Darnell looked at Victor's braids, fading blurry and wide from his forehead, and he nodded. When he'd slid across the seat, Victor complained to Ronnie, "Man, why you always get shotgun? I'm tired a sittin bitch."

Darnell pulled back onto the street, taking shallow breaths with his lungs full of grainy smoke, his shoulders mashed to window and skin. "Victor, I'm tired a hearin 'bitch.' Stall out, around me, okay? Bitches, hos, skeezers, hoochies." He paused, seeing the unborn baby's foot trace itself down Brenda's skin, a blind nub moving quickly. "My house fulla sistas, okay?" Darnell forced a breath farther down.

"So you a damn fool," Victor said. But he grinned slightly. "Man, I gots to give you a few props. Take a brave fool to live in a house fulla . . . females."

Ronnie laughed. "Man, call Esther a bitch while she braidin your hair and she liable to do it so tight you look Chinese." He gestured with his chin then. "There's your pops, Darnell. And Mr. Wiley."

He left them at Esther's and walked into his father's driveway. His father sat with a pair of clippers on the spool table; his fingers tested the new-sharpened blade, still etched silver from the grinding stone.

Darnell raised his eyes to Roscoe, who leaned against the tailgate of the Apache, slumped comfortable like he used to be, but his forehead carved with a triangle of lines above his brows, like he'd been squinting for days. "I went by your place, and Brenda told me you went to Harper's shop, so I knew you'd stop by here to complain about how much he's charging to fix the carburetor." Roscoe didn't smile, but he pulled one side of his mouth hard.

Darnell licked his lip. "Charolette see you?" he asked. "She been missin you."

"She told me you saw a fire," Roscoe said. Darnell saw his father's eyes narrow, fix on his face.

"Everybody saw it," Darnell said. Necessity. All kinda necessity.

"I saw it from Marietta's," Roscoe said. "All those ashes floating down, big as cornflakes." He stopped, lifted his face slightly. "I watched for the crows. They hit that smoke and got so confused that the whole flock broke up."

"Saw whole sticks and pieces a bark flyin in the air," Darnell's father said. "Musta been explodin trees all over. I was in Arroyo Grande."

"He's been in a bronze box, all this time," Roscoe said, his eyes above the roofline. "At Marietta's. Damn—I'm scared as hell, but I'm gonna have to do it. I figured it out yesterday, when I saw all that in the air." He looked at Darnell's father now, then at Darnell. "I've never flown before. But I was thinking about going up in one of those small planes, letting the boy fly." Before they could say anything, he turned on his hip, jarring against the tailgate, and got into the Apache.

When the engine had faded around the corner, Darnell's father worked the clippers and put them in their leather sheath. "You have the symptoms yesterday? You get the shakes, wantin to pull a hose?" he finally said.

Darnell leaned against the warm wooden gates full of branches, a leaf brushing his neck. "Yeah," he said. "I got em. I'm applyin for paid call reserve, so they can give me a coupla jobs a month. Make some extra cash."

"They musta called in the whole damn state yesterday," his father said. "Gave a lotta guys work. Still ain't out all the way."

"No," Darnell said, imagining the still-throbbing embers, the red veins coming to life. "Contained."

"Roscoe's got his truck back in shape to work," his father said, studying a wrench. "Said he's had trouble with the gas line." He looked up. "I appreciate you helpin out. Seem like the three of us could keep up a good schedule, if Juan and José do all right on their own."

"Cool with me," Darnell said, swallowing, pushing off from the truckbed. "I gotta get home."

"Hey," his father said, clenching his fists on the splintery tabletop. "I thought—seem like a couple times this year, I thought I'd have to figure out how to say goodbye to you. Like Roscoe. I don't want to do that. Like he said, it ain't natural."

Darnell's throat was full, and he said as casually as he could, "Hey, I'm the nature boy, right? Nothin but natural. See you tomorrow, Dad."

He saw his father run long fingers up the hair at his temples, and only the wide, swollen knuckles showed in the curls, like stones.

They were in the baby pool, under the elm tree. He'd bought it at Kmart, and Charolette had begged him for a Big Wheel, too, but he'd told her to wait until Christmas. The hose trailed into the pink plastic, and Charolette was splashing naked, Brenda sitting on the low beach chair, soaking her ankles. He went down the driveway and inside, to the kitchen.

"Let me be whore of the day," he murmured absently, looking at the dishes in the sink. He rinsed the plates. Whore of the day. Can't be sayin that now. Ho—can't you say it right, man? Two years ago? Ho, ho, ho. Almost time for Christmas. Brenda told Charolette that Santa Claus might bring her the Big Wheel. Pops always did the Santa thang—ate all the cookies Mama put out for him, drank the milk.

He breathed the ashes that had drifted powdery onto the window screens, sifting through to the sill. He scoured out the spaghetti pot. Whore of the day, when it was fire season. Ho. Strawberries. Andretta—somebody said knock the rest of her teeth out so she can do it better. Collarbones like broom handles on all the zombies. Two women at my crib. Maybe three, if this one's a girl.

I acted like a zombie yesterday. And she was with me. I'ma show Brenda the papers tonight, tell her I'm going for next season. I don't want to go for long—just if they call me. For a couple days, maybe, if there's a Seven Canyons. And then I'll be home. He looked down into the sink. This is where Charolette took a bath when she was a baby—in the sink. He saw how scared he'd been to hold her sliding butt in the water, how scared he'd been of the crease where he'd had to clean when he changed her. No bitches in my house. Man, you need to stop trippin like this. Just tell her.

He dried his hands by wiping the water across his neck, up his arms, and he went out to the driveway to clean the truck again, running the rag over the painted letters, the hood, the smoke-licked wheel well.

Brenda leaned against the door with her hand resting on her belly, on the baby. "You afraid Juan and José'll be mad if you don't keep their truck clean as they do?" She smiled.

"Maybe," he said. The sky was turning lavender between the branches, dark as eggplant toward Grayglen. This was the time he'd lied to her yesterday, right about bath time. "We saw a fire," Charolette had told Brenda, taking off her shoes. "It was big."

He went inside now and turned on the news. The fire was still smoldering in areas higher than he'd seen today, and the cameras panned over the houses reduced to charred tangles between driveway tongues and cloudy pool eyes.

Brenda had frowned last night when Charolette pointed to the flames on television and said, "See?"

"You could see it for miles," Darnell had said casually, and Brenda studied him.

"Yeah, I know," she said. The screen showed aerial shots of whole streets aflame, and she narrowed her eyes.

The same footage played now, and a quick-dripping Charolette came out of the bathroom, Brenda behind her. "You still watching that?" Brenda said. "You didn't get enough yesterday?"

"Enough TV?" He held the papers rolled loose in his fingers.

She shrugged. "Enough whatever."

He handed her the application and said, "I think I'ma take this to the county. For next year."

She was silent, reading, and Charolette struggled to pull up her panties over her damp legs. Brenda handed it back to him and said, "So you can't just watch it on TV. You still wishing you were a hero."

He kept his eyes from the bright mass of flames on the screen. "Hey, don't make me all that," he said, trying to grin right. "When I was up in the mountains, I had *stamina*, baby. Now you women got me workin myself to death. I just have the energy for a few calls now and then, and that's probably all I'd get. Especially since Scott and Perez got busted."

She didn't laugh. She got up and went into the bedroom, and before he could get up, Charolette came at him with the brush.

"Oh, no," he said, and he grabbed her, set her down fast, and clumsily twisted her hair into a puff that he fastened with a pink-sparkled tie. Then she whirled from his hands and went behind him, saying, "Be still now." She rubbed the bristles over his scalp, pressing her wet knees against his T-shirt. The skin on his forehead, then his neck, felt melted-warm, but he stood up.

Brenda was bent over the sink, her sides showing plump as bread loaves around her back. She scrubbed the grime from the soap dish, then took an old toothbrush to the grout around the tile. He looked at his oil-blackened knuckles and put his hand on her shoulder, but she didn't turn.

This whole lie part of my life, this way I'm addin up secrets—I can't do this, he thought. "Look," he said, "I come home every night. I give you my money. I'm a good boy. When I go on call, if I'm gone three days on a fire, you can't trip out. If I don't call you then, it's cause I'm workin. But can't nothin happen to me up there worse than down here, Brenda."

She swung around and leaned against the rim of the sink, slanted on one arm, and he saw two small tucks under her bottom lip where she'd held it hard. He imagined her seeing the flying embers yesterday, the shingles arcing across the street, the tears joined by saliva at Charolette's chin, and he pulled her forward against him as well as he could with the baby between them, so he wouldn't have to look into her eyes.

Hell, he thought, if I get hurt up there, if I get caught in a canyon, at least the government's gon call her. If I get smoked down here in the Wild Wild West, I ain't nobody. He remembered that long night in Jackson Park, when he'd thought about the gun, the insurance, and he blinked. If somethin happen while I'm on call, the government owe her and Charolette some dinero.

But he couldn't tell her that, couldn't say it out loud. He said, "It's extra money, Brenda. And I won't be around to mess up the sink or make dirty laundry a few days a month."

"Like I'm worried about that," she said, pushing away from him to stare at his face.

He stared back, into her gold eyes, flecks of dark like silt near her pupils, and then he grinned. "You holdin that old toothbrush like a lethal weapon. You must want me out your way. Or you gettin that energy burst right before the baby comes. Either way, I won't do nothin to make you mad."

"Now you know that's a lie," she said, and her mouth quivered upward. "But you're hopeless. I can't fix that."

"Nope," he said, lacing his fingers behind her neck.

"Silver mornings used to balance my skin," Roscoe said quietly.

Darnell sat by the spool table, and when he sipped the coffee, he finally felt it. Hot coffee inside hot skin made you run sweat and work loose. But the heat that radiated out to touch chilled arms and necks was what used to make Roscoe smile and raise his steaming cup to the mist. Darnell remembered his confusion during those late fall mornings when Roscoe would call them that, silver, when he'd name the days by color over his coffee cup.

At the fire station, with Fricke, was where Darnell had finally learned to drink coffee. Mrs. Batiste had always offered it to him in high school, when he came to pick up Brenda, but the mud-rich liquid she held had always scared him, reminded him of Mr. Batiste's uninterested gaze and the certainty that Darnell would disappear eventually if he refused to look at him.

And he and Melvin used to hate milk in the mornings, wanting root beer in old coffee cups so they could swirl something brown, trying to be grown. His mother would laugh and push them out the door to the driveway, where the men talked, warmed their hands, laced their boots, where later Louis and Darnell and Nacho folded their arms and glared at the foggy-morning work.

Charolette ate her buttermilk bar, sitting in her pink plastic chair near his leg. Darnell's father said, "Old ladies gon be lightin fires today, wantin some wood, and still got ashes all over their yards from Grayglen."

"Maybe them little pieces of Grayglen that fell down here make our property values go up," Floyd King said, and Nacho crossed the tired, drought-matted lawn, raising powder with his boots.

"Charolette, you workin with your daddy today?" Roscoe asked her, his voice thick, and she shook her head.

"Halloween," she said proudly. "It's a holiday."

Darnell's father raised his eyebrows. "Halloween? On a Wednesday? Your lazy daddy gon call that a holiday? Boy don't *never* want to work."

"We gotta go around and look at all the decorations," Darnell said. "It is a holiday—ask Juan and José. They're takin off for Day of the Dead."

"Some Mexican guys up there died in the fire," Roscoe said, staring toward Grayglen. "Does Juan know the guys who started it?"

Darnell shook his head. Maybe it was the three guys on the bikes, he kept thinking. But who could ever tell? Some workers had been sleeping in the eucalyptus grove, maybe guys who didn't want to pay someone to sleep under an avocado tree, maybe guys who'd just gotten to Rio Seco that night and heard there was work in Grayglen. The arson investigators had found a cooking fire that was probably the first small embers.

"Day of the Dead," Roscoe said. "All the souls flying around?"

"Juan's gon show me tonight," Darnell said. He looked at his father. "Like GranaLene's day. La Toussaint. All Saints."

"Lotta souls hoverin around here," his father said. He worked his lips. "Been a long summer. And they say what—five or six people died in their houses?"

Darnell nodded, thinking of the swaths of hillside looking like graveyards. Countless houses gone—the teardown they'd done, new houses and old mansions. Cars melted to heaps. And the fire had skipped, random and powerful, like all storms. He'd seen Mrs. Shaefer's house on TV, untouched, and another home still had pumpkins on the porch. The wind had blown the firestorm all the way across streets and block walls to the end of Trent's tract, burning the last five houses on his cul-de-sac.

Trent's house was rubble. He'd called Darnell to say, "Man, I lost it all. Everything."

"What you plannin?" Darnell had asked.

Trent paused. "I don't know. Get some land, maybe plan a custombuilt somewhere. New garden."

Darnell stood up and said to his father, "We gotta go." He took Charolette's hand. "You notice how the Mexican yards look? They serious into Halloween."

Many of the houses were festooned with spiderwebs, trees hung with sheet ghosts, and a few had real dummies hanging, and headstones pitted gray, and half-propped coffins with dry-ice smoke wafting out gently. "You scared?" he asked Charolette, and she shook her head, staring. "That's right—you don't know what none a this is." He blinked hard, thought of the row of headstones her grandmother would whitewash, the ones his grandmother used to decorate. He walked faster.

Juan saw them coming down the street, and he waved. Charolette waved back. Darnell nodded, still breathing hard, trying to keep his eyes clear. "Come in," Juan said. "His wife's grave is not here. So he make this."

José sat near a shrine by his mattress in the garage, and he nodded at Darnell and Charolette. There was a picture of his wife, her almond eyes, her hair in a wide bun. Marigolds, candles, crosses, and sparkling candies were arranged around her, and the candle flickered to make the sweets shine. "Here," José said, giving one to Charolette.

It was a skeleton, his bones white sugar. "*La calaca*," Jose said, when she peered down at the ribs, the skull. "Eat." He mimed, bringing his hand to his mouth, and Darnell felt a chill in his own ribs.

But Charolette had only seen the skeletons made of paper, dangling from people's porches and guarding their windows, and she didn't know they were scary. She said they looked funny. She licked the glittering hipbone of the skeleton and said, *"La calaca."*

"The candle burn for three days," Juan said. "So *los muertos* can see to visit, and eat and drink. If a man, you give mescal and tequila and cigarettes." José's wife's altar held bread baked in special shapes, and the candies.

"The dead people come to visit?" Darnell asked.

Juan nodded. "The inside," he said, touching his chest.

José held out a skull to Darnell, and he licked it, the grainy sweet rough on his tongue. When I take Charolette out tonight trick-or-treatin, maybe Louis and Antoine and GranaLene might come. He licked the skull again. But what about all the ones that aren't dead— just gone? Floatin. Like Leon and Donnie and Gas, Melvin, all the zombies? He watched Charolette cradle the skeleton in her palm and stare at the picture of the young woman.

José spoke in rapid Spanish to Juan, and Juan said, "You have no *zócalo*, like Mexico, no place to meet."

"Like a mall?" Darnell asked.

Juan hesitated. "Like a park. A plaza, that's it. So the kids walk around the street and trickitreat. They have trickitreat in Mexico now, too." José said something else. Juan smiled. "He says when you walk tonight, his baby walk, too. He no have picture, but he know what she look." José smiled and nodded at Charolette.

"You don't need to take her out in the streets, it's too dangerous," Brenda said. "The paper said there could be poison in the candy, and I heard people saying some gang might even be shooting." She folded her arms high in the crease between her breasts and belly. "I can't walk, cause my feet are too swollen."

Charolette was trying on her costume. Her two grandmothers had taken a long piece of lace, sewed pearls and sequins and ruffles on it to make a princess dress. She glowed white, twirling on the porch.

Brenda said, "Waltrina said her grandkids only go to a party in the mall now, cause it's safer." Darnell rolled his eyes. "And I thought you were only gonna take her to your mom's and Marietta Cook's."

"We're gon walk over there and meet Hollie." Darnell spun Charolette around by her braids and said, "She's magic." He looked at Brenda. "She's mine, okay? I got her back. Nothin's gon happen to her when she's with me."

After dinner, she gave in. "Okay, let me put on her makeup and do her hair," Brenda said, and they disappeared into the bathroom.

"I better get used to this makeup stuff," Darnell said to himself, sitting on the steps to read the paper. Another article called the fire an "urban interface" blaze and then discussed the drought, development, and future fires. He put the paper down and stood on the sidewalk. The night was cool. The day had stayed mild gray, as if all the ashes had risen up to the sun and said, "Give it a rest."

He heard them coming. A group of kids paraded down the sidewalk already.

Clinton swung his stuffed-sock blackjack and said, "Homey don't play dat!" Lamont wore his junior-tackle football uniform, with black slashes under his eyes. And another boy with them opened his overcoat to show Darnell a black plastic Uzi. "What the hell are you?" Darnell said. The boy grinned and pulled out two plastic bags: one held flour, the other grass clippings. "You better take your little ass home with that shit," Darnell said, hard. "That ain't funny."

"You gon give us some candy or what?" the boy said, hard-voiced.

"That's my uncle," Lamont said. "Don't try and front on him."

Darnell gave each of his nephews three of the miniature chocolate bars he'd bought, and the other kid stomped off. He took the bowl to the porch, eating a baby Milky Way. Brenda had said they were too expensive, but he remembered how happy he and Louis and the others had been when they saw chocolate bars.

"You know it's too cold to be out long, cause she has a runny nose," Brenda announced behind him, and he turned.

Charolette wore a glittery tiara on her braided hair, and she had on pink lipstick and sparkly eyeshadow. She grinned and held up her princess wand and her plastic pumpkin. "Let's *go*, Daddy."

The sky was fading behind the trees, and he held Charolette's hand clenched around her wand. "I thought you were a tomboy," he said.

She looked puzzled. "I'm a queen."

"You kinda young for a queen," he told her. "Queens are married, like your mama." He smiled. "Yeah. Mama's a queen, okay? You can be a princess."

"I'm a princess." She turned up her face. "We goin to see Hollie and Gramma Mary and Pop-Pop and Unca Roscoe . . ."

"Yeah, all of em. But you better go next door and get you some candy." He walked her up the steps, and the three girls answered.

"Trick or treat," Charolette said shyly, and they dropped bubble gum into her pumpkin.

The next house was dark, but the one after it, and all the rest, had jack-o-lanterns with wide grins and glowing eyes. Darnell hadn't seen many decorations in the new tracts when he'd worked all month, he realized. He looked down the street at the graves surrounded by wispy cotton, the sheet ghosts in the trees, and *calacas* everywhere, loose-jointed, smiling, wearing black suits and top hats. He held Charolette back while two big groups of kids raced up the next driveway, and a breeze flickered all the tiny flames in the pumpkins. Charolette frowned and said, "Fires in the pumpkins can't burn us, huh, Daddy?"

"No," he said. "They're just candles."

She looked up at the trees lining the street. "The wind is soughing."

"What?" He laughed.

"Uncle Roscoe told me and Hollie. The wind is soughing in the leaves."

"Like blowin?" he said. "We gon walk over there and see Hollie and ask Uncle Roscoe. I never heard that word, and I spent a long time around trees."

She drew her chin back and said, "You don't know everything, Daddy."

"Yeah?"

She rolled her eyes. "You don't know how to sew pearls."

"Nope," he said. "You ready?" The kids swarmed past. Then Charolette shook off his hand.

"I can do it *myself*," she said, marching up to the door. He waited. The soft wind came through again. Soughing? Palm trees sounded sparkly. All those Halloweens with Donnie and Nacho and Leon and Louis, running the streets, roaming all the way to Treetown, where the Thompson brothers fought them for their candy-filled pillowcases. The palm fronds always sounded sparkly. And the pepper branches moved silently, waving. He saw Charolette turn, her pearls gleaming and crown falling crooked, and she came down the porch steps holding out her hand for him.